Praise for William Nicholson

'Unexpectedly startling . . . thought-provoking' *Spectator*

'Sympathetic and skilful . . . Nicholson writes well about female sexuality, seen here to be every bit as powerful as its male equivalent' *Observer*

'Nicholson's great strength lies in his ability to make the reader understand and care about his characters . . . He is particularly concerned with morality and love, subjects that have inspired all great novelists. It is a joy to find a contemporary writer passionately engaged with both' Elizabeth Jane Howard

'A subtle and addictive writer who deserves to be a household name . . . with his remarkable eye for detail and for the weaknesses of human nature' *Observer*

'So incredibly accurate and true. Utterly captures the sense of quiet desperation of ordinary lives, the huge emotional vulnerability of having children and the ways in which life turns on a sixpence' Kate Mosse

'A slice of English countryside viewed in the manner of both Anthony and Joanna Trollope; substantial, richly detailed and acutely observed' *The Times*

'He writes about doubt, love, equivocation, treachery, loyalty and joy, but he does so with such empathy and shifts one's perspectives with such unobtrusive skill that he widens one's sense of what it means to be human' Jenni Russell

William Nicholson grew up in Sussex and was educated at Downside School and Christ's College, Cambridge. His plays for television include *Shadowlands* and *Life Story*, both of which won the BAFTA Best Television Drama award of their year. His first play, an adaptation of *Shadowlands* for stage, was the *Evening Standard*'s Best Play of 1990. He was co-writer on the film *Gladiator*, and his film writing credits include *Elizabeth: The Golden Age*, *Les Misérables* and *Mandela: Long Walk to Freedom*. He is married with three children and lives in Sussex. Visit his website at www.williamnicholson.co.uk

Also by William Nicholson

The Secret Intensity of Everyday Life
The Golden Hour
All the Hopeful Lovers
Motherland
Reckless
The Lovers of Amherst

Adventures in Modern Marriage

William Nicholson

Quercus

First published in Great Britain in 2017 by Quercus
This paperback edition published in 2017 by

Quercus Editions Ltd
Carmelite House
50 Victoria Embankment
London EC4Y 0DZ

An Hachette UK company

A CIP catalogue record for this book is available
from the British Library

PB ISBN 978 1 78429 854 8
EBOOK ISBN 978 1 78429 855 5

10 9 8 7 6 5 4 3 2 1

Typeset by CC Book Production

Printed and bound in Great Britain by Clays Ltd, St Ives plc

DESDEMONA: Dost thou in conscience think – tell me,
  Emilia –
That there be women do abuse their husbands
In such gross kind?

EMILIA: There be some such, no question.

DESDEMONA: Wouldst thou do such a deed for all the
  world?

EMILIA: Why, would not you?

DESDEMONA: No, by this heavenly light!

EMILIA: Nor I neither, by this heavenly light;
I might do't as well i'the dark.
. . . Let husbands know
Their wives have sense like them: they see and smell
And have their palates both for sweet and sour,
As husbands have. What is it that they do
When they change us for others? Is it sport?
I think it is: and doth affection breed it?
I think it doth: is't frailty that thus errs?
It is so too: and have not we affections,
Desires for sport, and frailty, as men have?

William Shakespeare, *Othello*, Act IV, Scene iii

Wednesday, 6 May 2015

1

Today, thinks Henry Broad, later today, this day that has now begun, the red digits of the radio alarm clock by the bed reading 12:44, we must put aside time for sex. Late afternoon, perhaps, with the curtains drawn against the glare of day, in the kindly half-light. Laura, so unapproachable by day, her slight figure armoured in tight-fitting trousers and high-necked tops, will let the barriers fall one by one until at last, turning towards me, she takes the few steps to join me, permitting me to see, as a promise of the joy to come, her beautiful, familiar body. Strange to think, he thinks, lying wakeful beside his sleeping wife, that I see her fully naked only at such times, after thirty years of marriage. Of course, dressing and undressing, in and out of the shower, there are glimpses, but always the body turning away, folded, preoccupied. This crossing of the room before we make love, this is her gift to me, because I've told her, I love to watch you come to me naked. But even though it's already May the bedroom is cold, and she remains naked before me only for a few moments.

3

There have been times when he's said to her, No, wait. He stands before her, takes her in his arms, delaying the moment. He kisses her and says, Let's go slowly, and she laughs because always he becomes impatient.

You never go slowly, she says.

In the early days of their marriage they always slept naked. Now he wears a T-shirt and boxers, and Laura is buttoned up in soft red check pyjamas.

And soon I will be sixty years old.

How many times have we made love, Laura and I? It was more often in the beginning, of course. Every night, almost. Now every ten days, every two weeks maybe. He tries to remember the last time. It was before Carrie came home, on a Thursday or a Friday, it must be over two weeks ago now. Curious how the desire quietly builds, day by day, you don't even notice it at my age, and then quite suddenly it's all you can think about. Not the same for Laura. She doesn't think about it at all until I suggest it, and even then she often forgets. Then the time comes, and she's standing before me naked, and I'm shivering. After all these years.

What's happening today? Last day of the election campaign, all to play for, every vote counts, God knows don't we all know it. Oh yes, and Michael Marcus is coming to lunch.

He listens to Laura's breathing in sleep. When she gets into bed at night, always after him because she takes so much longer in the bathroom, she lifts up the duvet, letting in cold air, but he's learned to hold on to his side. Then she's in bed and her hand reaches for his, and for a few moments they lie there, hand in hand. By day she loves to wear rings, bold modernist silver, a brick of amber, a bar of carnelian, rings that guard and command respect; but when night falls the rings come off, one by one, to be placed on the fingers of the ceramic hand on her dressing-table, and her real hand lies soft and unprotected in his.

A few moments, and their hands part. As he slips into sleep she murmurs, 'Night,' and he says, 'Night.' Often she reads, her book illuminated by a tiny long-necked lamp by the bed, and he goes to sleep to the sound of her fingers turning the pages.

And then he wakes. Usually around two in the morning; tonight it's not even one. Always as he wakes there's a momentary tremor, as if something has entered the room and disturbed him, something that even as he emerges from sleep is slipping away. Often there are noises in the night, the wind rattling the ancient, poorly fitting doors, the steel radiators contracting after the central heating turns itself off, the dishwasher set to run later than usual, shuddering towards the end of its cycle. This night he has not been woken by sounds, but by a presence. It's something he knows and has forgotten, something on the periphery of his mental vision, something he does not want to know. People think the night is filled with imaginary terrors, and waking returns us to the consoling commonplaces of the real world. 'Ah! It was only a dream.' But Henry sleeps peacefully, and wakes into fear, and does not know why.

The trick is not to interrogate the fear, not to waken the rational mind, not to open the box of anxieties anaesthetized each night by sleep. But already it's too late. Betrayed by his needy body he lies beneath the duvet thinking about sex, and when to broach the subject with Laura, and so the day ahead begins to unfold, with all its concerns.

How annoying that Michael Marcus should be coming to

lunch, coming all the way down to Sussex for lunch, at his own request. What can he want?

The room round him is dark but not lightless. Bigger in the dark, almost infinitely big, the walls lost in the night. *And we are here, as on a darkling plain, Swept with confused alarms of struggle and flight.* The junk of memory floats to the surface, Matthew Arnold from some long-ago lesson in school. *The sea is calm tonight.* The wine-dark sea. On to Homer now, one of his many pairings repeated so often they snag in the brain. *Aegis-bearing Zeus. Ox-eyed Athene. Then night came down on his eyes.* Death, that last one, usually by spear-thrust, with each defensive layer through which the bronze point penetrates lovingly listed: ox-hide, felt padding, armour, flesh. Reading the *Iliad*, as he is at present, induces in him a kind of hypnotized passivity. So many violent mortal passions, so much heroic self-sacrifice, all rendered futile by the bickering of the gods. Why am I reading Homer? Because that's what you do at my age, you tell yourself, I've no time now for the second-rate. So many classics missed in my youth. These are the works that framed the mental horizons of educated people for centuries. But what a cheat the *Iliad* is turning out to be! Almost at the end, Hector is dead, but Troy hasn't fallen, and there's no wooden horse. The most famous part of the Trojan War, and Homer never even gets to it. Instead the Greeks are running races, playing games.

I must talk to Carrie.

He lies in the dark, not looking at the marching red numerals, listening to his wife's soft breath.

Carrie's been home a week and more and I've hardly seen her. You'd think it would get easier when they're grown-up, but he feels oddly shy in her presence. A sort of courtesy. You can't come right out and say, You're unhappy, what is it that makes you unhappy? Is it my fault? She always was a prickly child, fiercely proud, brave, magnificent. Coming down the flank of Caburn, running into my arms, she fell and scraped the skin off her knees. Hot eyes staring at me, blood streaming down her shins, and not a sound. Oh Carrie, my darling daughter.

Past one in the morning. There are tricks to aid sleep, though no guarantee they'll work. Breathe slowly, hold the out-breath for a count of five, then slowly in again. Out, and hold. Create a picture in the mind, a place of peace. The view from the flank of High and Over, as you climb the hill out of Litlington, and there below you lies the river winding to the sea. On a dull day the grey sea merges into the grey sky, and with the wind on your face you front infinity.

I should do that walk again, it's been too long. Maybe after Michael Marcus has been and gone, he surely won't stay long. Why can't he say whatever he wants in an email, or over the phone? Perhaps Laura would come on the walk too. Once long ago they made love on the Downs, under cover of a copse of trees, not comfortable but never forgotten. Both remained almost fully clothed. It didn't take long, the idea more exciting than the act, but it lingers still in his memory. Today, he promises himself, after Michael Marcus has gone, we'll draw the curtains and lie in each other's arms, as we have now done for thirty years.

Oh, but Carrie will be in her room.

Still he does not sleep. Is this part of the ageing process, this waking in the small hours of the night? I have no sensation of ageing. I'm the same man I was when I got married. It's the world round me that has grown weary. The years pass, and the longing does not abate, but the days grow shorter. The gods play their tricks; they deny poor mortals their little triumphs. Why must Homer mess so with his Trojans and Greeks? Why allow them no control over their fate? But perhaps this is to misunderstand the nature of the gods. What if the gods are not agents after all, but explanations? So Hector storms the wall built to protect the hollow ships, and later the Achaeans turn the tide of battle, and the poet, recounting the tale for his fireside listeners, concludes that Zeus rode at Hector's back, and Poseidon rallied Agamemnon's spearmen. In such a way we suffer the accidents of life and make up stories to give them meaning. In Homer's time it was the immortals on Olympus. Today, what? The working out of childhood trauma. The invisible hand of the free market. Each age to its own excuse for things fucking up.

Perhaps Carrie would join me on the walk. She's grown up here under the Sussex Downs, she must have some feeling for it. But she rarely goes on walks. Her French exchange partner, all those years ago, Dominique, she was so uncomprehending it made them laugh. 'Why do you make this walk? You have a car.' Her fourteen-year-old worldliness delighted Carrie. Offered a trip to the National Gallery she responded, 'I 'ate art.' Carrie took up the refrain and made it her own. 'I 'ate art.' What Dominique wanted was to be taken to 'Arrods. Her contempt for culture astonished them all. Are you allowed to hate art?

Why do I wake in the night?

When the children were babies they woke in the night, and for months both he and Laura assumed this was the nature of

8

the infant sleep pattern. Then a doctor friend told them this was not so, that babies were meant to sleep through the night. There was an expert, an American called Ferber. Ferber was a revelation. You, he told them, you, the loving parents, are denying your babies the sleep they need. When the baby's sleep becomes shallow, following its natural cycle, and the baby, almost waking, cries out, you hurry to the cot side and thoroughly wake the child. Your soothing words, your loving cuddles, rob your baby of the moment when he can slip back into deep sleep. Let the child cry a little. Sleep will return. And so it did.

Now it's my turn. I wake when my sleep becomes shallow. I don't cry, but I do hurry to my bedside, I do fuss over my wakefulness. Better to harden my heart and stand outside the bedroom door until the whimpering ceases.

2

Once upon a time there was a princess who lived in a castle. Her name was Carrie, and she had everything the heart could desire. She had a room all to herself with a comfortable bed. She was never hungry or cold. She had a wardrobe filled with pretty clothes. She was young and healthy and interesting-looking. And yet she was not happy. Her mother and father, who loved her very much, knew she was not happy, and this made them unhappy in their turn. But no one talked about the princess's unhappiness in the castle because they didn't want to make the princess even more unhappy.

Not far from the castle there was a bog, and in the middle of the bog lived a frog. When the frog heard about the unhappy princess he came hop-hop-hopping to the castle gates.

'I know how to make the princess happy,' said the frog. 'But you must pay my price.'

'What is your price?' said the king.

'You must give me your daughter in marriage.'

The king conferred with the queen and they agreed to give

the frog their daughter in marriage if he succeeded in making her happy again. The frog then climbed the castle stairs to the princess's room.

'Get the fuck off that bed, you spoiled cunt,' said the frog.

The princess got off the bed and began to sing a song in a pure and interesting voice. It was a song she had written herself, a sad but truthful song.

When she finished singing the frog said, 'Are you happy now?'

'No,' said the princess.

'Fucking loser,' said the frog, and went hop-hop-hopping back to his bog.

The princess wept bitter tears.

'Who will marry me now?' she said.

The world is made for happy people. Unhappiness is contagious, and must be quarantined.

Carrie sits in bed in the middle of the night with her laptop open on her knees, its glow illuminating her face in the night-dark bedroom. As pictures enter her head she taps them onto the screen, chains of sentences that are her waking dreams. She likes the night time best, when edges are blurred and nothing has to lead anywhere. Daytime is cruel with purpose. The night is inattentive and kind.

That word, *quarantine*. How can one word come to bear such a complex meaning?

A state, period or place of isolation in which people or animals that have arrived from elsewhere, or been exposed to infectious or contagious disease, are placed.

Arrived from elsewhere!

A word based on the Italian for forty, *quaranta*. Jesus fasted in the desert for forty days and nights, so 'forty' becomes 'isolation'.

You arrive from elsewhere, they treat you like you've got the plague, they isolate you. They, the people of the daylight.

So a new song forms in her mind.

> *Now love is dead*
> *Hey, go ahead*
> *Quarantine me*
>
> *I come from elsewhere*
> *Cheap hotels where*
> *I belong*
>
> *Cry unclean me*
> *Search me, screen me*
> *Forty days and forty nights*
> *Bring on the dimming of the lights*
> *You're right, I'm wrong*
> *So here's my song —*
>
> *Quarantine me*
> *In the dead room*
> *In my bedroom*
> *I don't care*
>
> *You've not seen me*
> *Never been me*
> *I'm not there*

I'm flying with the angel queen
Dancing in the air
Yeah –
I'm in
Quarantine . . .

You sit on a stool on what passes for a stage in the back room of some poxy pub, and you tune your guitar and look round the room and no one's looking back. You start to sing and they go on talking, drinking, laughing. So you sing for yourself.

3

In this same endless night, Laura Broad is dreaming that she's coming out of a restaurant after dinner with a group of friends, and they all disperse, kissing and laughing. As she walks down the road to her car she realizes she can't remember where she parked it. There are cars on both sides of the road, drawn up beside terraced houses in a long, lamp-lit street. She walks down the deserted pavement, looking for her car, but what does it look like? What make is it? What colour? She has no idea. Did she even park in this street? There are other similar streets running away into the distance at every corner. Numberless cars standing silent in the night. Then she remembers she left her handbag on the passenger seat. That's how she'll know her own car. But what if it's been stolen? How stupid to leave a handbag in full view! She should have pushed it into the foot well. It contains everything, her bank cards, her passport, her keys. Her car keys! She starts to run, looking into every car she passes, panicked by the thought that the car has been stolen. She's appalled by her own folly, and also a little frightened. She no longer knows where she is, there's no one about, there are no lights in the windows of the houses. The street ahead is so long it seems endless. She runs faster, now pumping her arms, running like an athlete. A hand touches her shoulder. Turning, startled, she stumbles and falls—

Henry lies asleep beside her. Past three in the morning. The dream fades, leaving her skin flushed, as if she really has been running.

How could I do something so stupid?

No, only a dream.

She slips quietly out of bed to go to the loo. Through the uncurtained window of the unlit bathroom she sees the line of the Downs, darker than the night sky, and a faint reflecting gleam in the ribbon of water that is Glynde Reach. The night is never entirely dark. When was the full moon? Sunday, was it, or Monday? She pees inattentively, not wanting to wake too fully, and returns to a bed still warm from the pressure of her body. Henry is making noises in his sleep, less than snoring, more than breathing.

Too much dairy makes you snore, they say.

Today's the day I'm going to start my new diet. That means I have to tell Henry, and he won't like it at all. No point thinking about that now. Except of course the minute you tell yourself not to think about something, you've started thinking about it. The trick is to pack up the unwanted thought and put it away, like a skirt that's still perfectly wearable but you know you're never going to wear it again. Like leftover pasta, conscientiously scooped into a plastic bowl and covered with cling-film and pushed to the back of the fridge.

There. In the bottom of the drawer. At the back of the fridge. Out of sight, but available when wanted.

Calling it a diet is clever, isn't it? You diet to lose weight, everyone does it, a diet has no moral overtones. It's only when you say you've decided not to eat meat any more that it makes other people angry. They think you're telling them not to eat meat too, though you're not.

Except you are.

'It's only a diet. You won't even notice.'

Henry will hate it. At least Carrie will understand.

Lying beneath the warm duvet, willing herself into sleep, Laura feels the ache in her chest that always comes these days when she thinks of Carrie. She deflects her mind to other concerns. Isn't someone supposed to be coming to lunch? Nothing to eat in the house as usual. Maybe Carrie could be persuaded to make a trip to Waitrose. Is it wrong to expect her to help? She's twenty-four years old, she's living here free. But ask her to do anything and all you get is a sullen look, as if you're making unacceptable demands. It's not as if she's actually got anything else to do. But say that to her and she says, 'How do you know? You don't know what I do.'

Laura rolls onto her side, now feeling restless and irritable. How is it she's doing exactly what she wanted to avoid? If she starts arguing with Carrie in her head she'll never get back to sleep. Henry says Carrie's going through a bad time and best to leave her alone, but what is this bad time? It's as if Carrie's lost all her motivation. She's supposed to be a singer but she's stopped doing gigs, she says no one pays any more, and no one listens anyway.

Laura remembers the time they went to hear her sing in a pub in Ladbroke Grove. She sang so beautifully, they were so proud of her. Afterwards they all ate in an Indian restaurant and she asked Carrie if she really was as sad as her songs, and Carrie said, 'Don't worry, Mum, I put all the misery into my songs. The rest of my life I'm happy as the day is long.'

Later, after Carrie had gone wobbling off on her bicycle, her guitar over her back, Henry had said, 'The day is long, but then comes the night.'

Is it wrong to want your child to be happy? It hurts to see her unhappy, and she sees the hurt in my eyes and she hates me for it. 'Don't pressure me, Mum! I'm fine! Don't look at me like that!' But how else am I to look at her? She's not fine. She's come home to hide. Is it helping her, giving her somewhere to hide? Maybe what she needs is pressure. If she had to earn money to eat she'd be out there doing something, somewhere.

I can't bear it that she never comes out of her room.

Sweetheart, darling, my baby girl, whatever it is that's hurting you, tell me. Make me understand. I don't want to turn into a nagging mother. I don't want to mind so much that you never help round the house. I want to believe you when you say you're tired, but how can you be tired when you do nothing all day? I don't mean to make you feel guilty, I just can't help it. Life's not easy for any of us, you know. Sleep now out of reach, Laura reconciles herself to lying wakeful until dawn. The dawn of the day that is to be Day One.

Maybe I could just do it and say nothing, and wait for Henry to notice. It could take days. But Henry will take it personally. He just will.

Moonlight pushing at the curtains. No night lasts for ever. Except the night you die, that never ends, but mercifully you know nothing about it. Imagine lying unable to sleep for ever.

4

The same waning moon sails out from behind clouds, washes the town of Lewes in its incurious light, and then is veiled again. On the western fringe of the town, in a house with dormer windows, a bed is breathing. Every few seconds it draws air into the mattress, causing small ripples in its surface to change the pressure points. The mechanism coughs and rumbles in the night. Beneath the pillow the green light of the syringe driver winks as it eases into a withered vein another drop of oxycodone. The bed has been erected in the room that was once called the study. It stands like an island fortress between the writing desk and the fireplace. The lamp in the front-door porch has been left on, and shines through the study window where the curtains have not been fully drawn, casting a bar of light over the polished wood floor, and the yellow cellular blanket on the bed, and the mottled skin of the arm that lies on the blanket. Across the hall, on a fold-out bed made up in the sitting room, the night carer lies fitfully sleeping. The grandfather clock in the hall strikes the three-quarter hour, ding-ding-ding. Soon it will be four in the morning.

Aster Dickinson, eighty-six years old, is maybe, or maybe not, on the point of death.

Her eyes open. She gazes at the ceiling. Her mind slowly wakes. Thoughts form like the moonlit clouds and sail silently towards her.

She's unsure where she is. She thinks she might be in her mother's bedroom. If so, she must be ill. She feels for the silk eiderdown with which her mother's bed was always covered, and listens for the sounds of the other children on the veranda outside. She knows her mother's bedroom without looking: the dressing-table with its three mirrors, its array of cut-glass bottles with silver stoppers; the round cane-topped table with barley-sugar legs; the jug of lemonade covered with a square of muslin, its corners weighted with beads. The blinds must be drawn, there's so little light. To raise the blinds you pull on the little wooden acorns at the ends of the cords; pulling down makes them go up.

She moves her arms so that she can begin the business of sitting up, but her limbs have become heavy. If she's not well she'll need help to get about. Who helps her?

She thinks she can hear her mother in the passage outside, calling her name. 'Ast-*er*! Ast-*er*!' In a moment she'll come in and find her in bed. 'What, not up yet, lazybones? Chop-chop! Rise and shine!'

We're to have a picnic by the river. She remembers now. There's to be Gentleman's Relish, cheese straws, lardy cake. A camping stove to make tea. The special picnic smell of methylated spirits.

But why must everyone walk so fast? Wait for me! I tied up my shoelaces wrong and I have to re-tie them. I'm not dawdling. Daddy laughs and says, 'Aster looks like a monkey!' and I burst into tears. But surely that's wrong: Daddy would never say such a thing.

She becomes aware of a stiffness in her back. She's been lying in bed too long. The morning is the best time of the day. Only it's not morning yet, it's night. And she's not seven years old in her mother's bedroom in the big house in Parktown, Johannesburg. She's in the house Rex bought, in Sussex. He paid over the odds, of course. People always took advantage of Rex. £4,500! Plain robbery! But she'd got the carpets for a good price.

Help me to get up, please. Move the kitchen carver chair into the back doorway and I'll sit there for a little while. It looks east, I shall be able to see the sun rise beyond the elms. Please hold my hand. I expect you think I'm making a lot of fuss about nothing, but I can't quite manage on my own.

Are you going already, Elizabeth? Always so busy, no time for your mother these days. Go, then. Go, go. Victor can help me when he comes to cut the grass. Close the door quietly as you leave, I hate hearing a door slam. Go, go. Don't worry about me. I've lived on my own long enough.

I shall wrap the bedcover round me and sit on the chair by the back door. Perry will jump onto my lap and curl up there so I can feel his warmth. Together we'll watch the sun rise.

5

A mile upriver, in the hamlet of Hamsey, Liz Dickinson wakes before the alarm goes off, not wanting to disturb Alan. She fumbles for the phone by her bed, lights up its screen. No message in the night. So her mother hasn't died yet.

Every evening the community nurse says, 'It could be tonight, but who knows?' Every morning there her mother lies, still alive. Liz's pity is exhausted, she asks now only for relief. Her mother's protracted dying has put her own life on pause for weeks now. All those long days sitting with her, before she fell silent, enduring her spite, failing to meet her ceaseless demands.

'Sit me up. Move my pillow. Get me a cup of tea. Where's my book? Put the phone nearer. Put my hearing aids in. Sit where I can see you. Move me to my chair.'

All the long days attempting to divert her mother's anger at her carers.

'I don't want them. They abuse me. Send them away. I hate them all. They hit me. They want to steal my house. Don't tell

22

me it's not true. I'm lying, am I? Or am I off my head? Do you have any idea what it feels like to have your own daughter not believe a word you say?'

Karen, the night carer, raised in Zimbabwe, last of three generations of white farmers, driven off the land by Mugabe's veterans; she's had a hard life, but it takes my mother to reduce her to tears.

'I don't hit her, I swear to you.'

'Of course you don't, Karen. She doesn't know what she's saying.'

Then two days ago she slipped into what seemed to be a deeper sleep, and a new kind of waiting began. But is she really asleep? Sometimes Liz thinks she's playing a game with them all, playing possum. One morning she'll sit up unaided and say, 'Boo!' Maybe she won't die at all.

Karen tells her that often in the small hours of the night her mother comes back to life, like a zombie. She moves her arms and cries out, but not in words anyone can understand. The palliative-care nurse who controls the sedative dose visits in the daytime when she's fast asleep. 'She seems to be comfortable. There's no need to increase the dose.' But at night the zombie returns.

There's nothing left in her. Half her insides exploded three weeks ago. She can't swallow. She should be dead. But she goes on living, driven by anger and a lifelong demand for attention.

For pity's sake, Mummy, why can't you go gracefully?

'Look,' says the nurse. 'Her hands are puffy. That's fluid retention.'

'What does that mean?' says Liz.

'She could go any day.'

But she doesn't go. Liz's horror is that she'll never go. This half-life will last until she, too, is old and frail. And the cost of it – my God! The expense!

These are monstrous thoughts. How has it come to this? But Liz is long past the stage of guilt and self-blame. Not long ago, a month or so, something in her snapped. Her mother had begun again on the litany of complaints against her carers, and her demand that they be removed, and Liz suddenly abandoned her wearily repeated explanations.

'They're not going, Mummy, and that's that.'

Her mother gazed up at her from the bed, her face sunken, her bare arms corded, her hair so thin you could see the scalp, her little eyes that she called *my button eyes* fixed upon her.

'I hate you,' she said. 'I want to kill you.'

Liz answered, unmoved, 'Well, you can't.'

Nowhere to go after that.

Mrs Huxtable, a good lady of the village, visiting the elderly out of pure kindness, said to Liz, 'Try to find a moment to be reconciled to your mother before she goes. Tell her you love her. You'll be glad of it later.' Liz only nodded in reply. What can you say? People think the approach of death brings with it a loving serenity. Instead it brings pain, helplessness, fear.

They haven't put her on a drip because she's supposed to be nearing the end. If she goes on not dying maybe they'll decide to rehydrate her. Then what? She becomes a living corpse. No food for three days, but still she breathes on, steady as a steam engine. Never smoked, never drank, her heart and lungs undamaged: the engine could run for ever.

This is why Liz dreads going round to sit by her bed. She

can hardly bring herself to look at her in case those eyes open and she hears that demanding voice again.

'Pull me up!'

In the bathroom, cleaning her teeth, she stares without flinching at her reflection in the mirror. She notes the lines round her mouth, the shadows under her eyes. Forty-seven years old, you can't expect the bloom of youth. And yet her eyes haven't changed, nor the twitch in her lips that Guy used to call her fuck-me smile. She still moves in the confident way of a woman who enjoys her own body.

I may not be beautiful, but I'll do.

She pads down to the kitchen, barefoot, in her pyjamas, to put on the kettle for a cup of tea. The house is quiet. Alan will be up soon, and then Cas, forever late for school.

She texts Karen.

How was the night?

You never know. It might all be over.

As the kettle boils and she makes her cup of tea she remembers how, when she was a child, she used to take her mother a cup of tea in bed. Her mother was always so grateful. This little ritual made Liz feel proud and caring and grown-up. But when she stopped doing it her mother gave her reproachful little smiles and said, 'I do miss my morning tea.'

The last ten years have exhausted me, that's the truth. I can't carry the burden of her unhappiness any more. I have been everything to her, but she has not been everything to me. So much sadness in that, for both of us.

She drinks her tea and gazes out of the kitchen window as the light of the rising sun falls slantwise across the tops of the

Downs. From upstairs come the sounds of Alan rising, the rush of water as the lavatory flushes, the chatter of the radio.

She goes to her work room and checks her emails on her desktop. Life turns out to be going on. She fields several Twitter alerts of no interest, and two work requests, both from friends. Paula Goodman is one of the few journalists left standing on the *Daily Express*:

Poll on sexiness of party leaders, rate Cameron/Clegg/Miliband/ Farage as (a) potential husbands (b) potential lovers, need supporting quotes, ordinary women in your region, copy by 6 p.m. latest.

Chrissie Charteris runs the features pages for *Stella*, the *Sunday Telegraph*'s women's magazine. She's on the hunt for 1,200 words to plug a gap:

Anything about women and sex that feels new.

What is there new to say about women and sex?

She taps out a quick reply to Paula: *Tight for time today. Try to get you something.*

No good doing the usual ring-round of her friends, they'd sooner die than appear in the *Daily Express*. But she could spend an hour in the Churchill Square shopping centre in Brighton, buttonholing strangers. As for Chrissie's request, that'll take more time, but it'll pay a lot better.

Alan comes down, already dressed. Despite being washed, shaved and wearing clean clothes, he manages as always to look unkempt, an incomplete sketch of himself. His hair resists grooming, and his shirts even when new-ironed crumple as they encounter his bony frame.

'Any news?'

'I'm waiting for Karen to call.'

On cue, Karen calls.

'We're still here,' she says. 'We're breathing evenly. The pad's bone dry.'

'She had her night injection?'

'Enough to knock out a horse.'

Karen's soft South African vowels give Liz comfort. The carers are on her side.

'I'll come round soon. Bridget should be there by nine, and you can get some sleep.'

To Alan she says, 'No change.'

'You know I'm in London today?'

'Damn! I'd forgotten. Can you still take Cas to school?'

'Of course.'

She should go and get dressed but she can't move. Early morning and already she feels worn out.

Alan puts his arms round her.

'Not fair,' he says.

She leans against him, grateful that he understands.

'I have to rate the sexiness of the party leaders,' she says.

'Wasn't Clegg supposed to have had a lot of lovers?'

'About thirty, he said.'

'Let's hope they all vote for him.'

6

Henry Broad sits at the kitchen table with his mug of tea before him, spreading butter on a slice of toast, reading the morning papers, half attending to Laura's movements as she prepares her own breakfast. Laura has a meeting today, and is dressed in what Henry calls her headmistress look, neat navy dress and black high heels. Her heels click on the kitchen floor tiles as she moves about. He wants to raise the matter of sex but thinks maybe he should wait until they've had their breakfast.

The Times is leading on the fear that Miliband will 'con his way into Number 10' by forming a coalition with the SNP. The polls are still showing the two parties running neck and neck.

'Labour might actually make it,' Henry says. 'The Tories aren't going to be able to command the confidence of the House.'

The key terms trip off his tongue, mastered in the last few weeks: *command the confidence of the House, Fixed Term Parliament Act, confidence and supply*. In the Broad household, Henry is the one who has taken ownership of the election, and feels personally invested in its outcome. He supports the Labour Party because when he was young that was how people like him voted. It was a simple badge of moral decency.

The *Guardian*, his preferred newspaper, declares: *It's a hung Parliament. So what happens on Friday?*

'It's going to go on into June,' Henry tells Laura. 'The Queen's Speech isn't until the end of May, and it's bound to be defeated, which means Cameron resigns and Miliband has a go. The Tory press will howl like stuck pigs, but if there's a left-of-centre majority across all parties, that's true democracy in action.'

Laura isn't listening. She's making porridge with special oats, and brewing coffee with the Nespresso machine she bought for herself, known as George because it's advertised by George Clooney, and wondering whether to tell Henry about her new diet now. Get it over with.

She steams milk in the little steamer that comes with the machine, making herself a strong cappuccino. Her mind turns to all she must do today. She has a sales catalogue to complete, on early twentieth-century rare books, including a Shakespeare & Co. first edition of *Ulysses* that has a reserve price of £25,000. And the Vickery library may be coming her way. And, dear God, the emails! They breed overnight like flying ants.

She stands by the Aga, the morning light falling in a glow down her right side, and sees Henry looking at her. Henry is thinking, Later this afternoon, dear wife, will you make love with me later this afternoon? Laura is thinking, The quantity of butter he puts on his toast!

'Must you gobble up all the butter, Henry?'

'Yes,' he says.

Laura pours her porridge into a bowl, sets the pan to soak, and brings the bowl and her cappuccino to the table. They have their accustomed places, she at the Aga end, he at the door end. The porridge is hot: she blows on it in the spoon, pursing her lips.

Tell him now, she thinks.

About five o'clock, thinks Henry, when Michael Marcus has gone. We could climb the stairs hand in hand, and draw the curtains against the afternoon sun. If the day doesn't warm up I could turn on the electric blanket half an hour or so before we lie down. That way we might not need to cover ourselves.

'You've got someone coming to lunch,' she says.

'God knows why,' says Henry. 'I'm in town all day Friday, going through the schedules.'

'Is there anything he doesn't eat?'

'I've no idea. If there is, he should have warned us.'

'So long as he eats cheese.'

Tell him. There'll never be a better opportunity.

'You know I've been thinking about what we eat?' she says.

'No,' he says, inattentive.

'About our diet in general. My diet, I should say.'

'Is this about butter?'

'No,' she says. 'It's about meat. I'm thinking of stopping eating meat.'

He looks up from his newspaper. His gaze is incredulous.

'But you're not a vegetarian,' he says.

'Well, that's just it. I think I may become one.'

'A vegetarian?' Stretching out the word as if it's something shameful. 'You can't be.'

'I think it's what I'd like.'

She's keeping her voice calm in the face of his rising tone.

'Why?' he says.

'I just think that maybe it's the right thing to do.'

'Why?'

She has all her arguments rehearsed. How one-third of the world's grain goes to feed livestock. How one-sixth of the world's population survives on starvation rations. How meat-eaters are far more likely to get heart disease. How meat production generates greenhouse gas emissions. But now that the moment has come she realizes simply by looking at the dismay on Henry's face that no argument will touch him. When she says, 'I'm thinking of stopping eating meat,' he hears her say, 'I no longer approve of you as you are.'

Best to take it slowly.

'I've been thinking about it on and off for a long time,' she says. 'It's only for me. You can go on as usual.'

'I go on eating meat and you don't?'

'Yes.'

'How's that going to work?'

'We'll find a way,' she says. 'Lots of people are in the same position. A bit of give and take and we'll be fine.'

'Give and take?'

She can see he's starting to get belligerent, as he always does when he feels threatened. Move on to other matters.

'Remind me who's coming to lunch.'

'Michael Marcus.'

'I may have to ask Carrie to go into Lewes for me. We need bread, and salad. I'd like to encourage her to get out a bit.'

'Waitrose doesn't count as getting out.'

He always ducks when they start talking about Carrie. He's no good at handling emotional tension. He wants to be told everyone's happy.

But right now Henry wants something else. He's unable to focus on Carrie, or even the new shock of vegetarianism, because his mind is elsewhere.

'I was thinking we might go for a walk,' he says. 'After Michael's gone. And then—'

'I don't have the time to go on a walk, Henry.'

'Of course you do. Time is exactly what we do have. We're at the stage of our lives when the pressures ease, and we can think about ourselves.'

'Speak for yourself. I have to finish my catalogue.'

'The Hindus call it the third stage of life. The forest dweller. You retire from worldly attachments and lead a life of contemplation in the forest. With your wife.'

'Well, your wife doesn't want to come.'

Aren't Hindus vegetarian? He doesn't seem to be aware of the connection.

Sunlight on the steam rising from her porridge. The things he comes up with. They went into the woods once and made love. Does that count as forest dwelling?

'Michael will be gone by half three,' Henry says. 'We go out on the Downs for an hour or so. And then, when we're back—'

Carrie appears, looking mostly still asleep, wearing the spaghetti top and shorts she uses for pyjamas.

'You're up early, darling.'

'I'm not up.'

She shuffles to the electric kettle and turns it on.

'Got any plans for today, Carrie?'

Laura knows her tone is too bright, too pretend-casual. Why can't I just say, Please don't spend another day in your bedroom?

'I don't do plans,' says Carrie.

'I was thinking,' says Henry, 'we could go up the Downs after lunch. I was thinking of doing the High and Over walk. We haven't done it for ages. You could come with us.'

Carrie shakes her head. She pours boiling water into a mug.

'I'm not up yet,' she says.

She pads back out into the hall, mug in hand, and up the stairs.

'You know she never goes for walks,' Laura says to Henry.

'She does sometimes.'

'Maybe we're too soft on her.'

Laura has a cousin who's an alcoholic. The alcoholic's sister sent an email round the family saying please don't give him money. He has to *not be helped*. He has to *hit bottom*. That's the only way he can be made to face the reality that he has a serious problem.

Has Carrie got a serious problem?

'She's all right,' says Henry. 'She's just going through a bad time.'

'So we should be helping her.'

'She has to ask, Laura. We can't force her.'

'Don't you think she might need, I don't know, a push?'

'She needs unconditional love. That's all anyone ever needs.'

Laura shrugs and goes on drinking her cappuccino. She distrusts Henry's motives. It's all well and good offering unconditional love, but it gets you off the hook of dealing with the problem. Anyone can do nicey-nicey.

Henry understands Laura's silence. He knows he's always been hopeless at telling the children off. Laura's the one who calls them downstairs and points at the dirty dishes in the sink and says, 'Who do you think's going to clear this up?' He claims there's method in his passivity. 'In the end they learn from what we do, not from what we say.' But it's Laura who braves the tantrums and the tears.

'Whatever her problems are,' he says, 'we can't solve them for her. She has to get there in her own way.'

'I don't know, Henry. I just worry about her. Maybe you could talk to her? I never seem to get it right.'

This is an appeal to his vanity, but for all that, it works. Henry likes to think of himself as someone people can talk to, someone who is *good with people*. 'It's very simple,' he likes to say. 'All you have to do is listen.' The truth is it's only simple when you don't really care about the other person. Once you become emotionally involved, and your own peace of mind is in jeopardy, it's not simple at all.

'I'll try,' he says.

'I have to be in Rodmell by ten,' she says. 'The Vickery family council.'

'When will you be back?'

'Twelve at the latest. I'll stop at the supermarket on the way. It won't take me five minutes.'

'So maybe at the end of the afternoon, around five o'clock?'

He doesn't need to say any more. It always amazes him that she picks up at once when he's asking for sex. How does she know? Is there something in his tone of voice? If she were to ask him a similarly non-specific question he'd think she was

34

wanting him to do something he'd been failing to do, put up a picture hook, dig the leeks. But it's always he who asks, and she who understands.

'Oh, God, Henry, I don't know. What about Carrie?'

Of course, Carrie. Carrie will be in her bedroom across the landing.

'We could be very quiet.'

Laura looks at Henry's face, so exactly like a dog who's brought back a stick and laid it at her feet and waits for it to be thrown again. His brow furrowed, mutely imploring. He still wants her, after all these years. She loves him for that. She wants him too, in theory at least, but it's odd how her desire doesn't really awaken until they're in the moment, in bed together. Up to then her mind's on other things. Henry once told her that when he starts thinking about sex it pushes out all other thoughts until after they've made love. 'What, *all* other thoughts? How about feeling hungry? Or the general election?'

'All of them.'

She tries to imagine what this must be like and fails. You can't just think about sex and nothing else. 'I can,' says Henry.

'We'll see,' she says.

'If we don't have time this afternoon, there's always tonight.'

'We'll see,' she says again.

But this isn't good enough for Henry. He needs to know for sure that she's agreed to have sex before the day is over. It's like an athlete preparing for a race. You have to pace yourself. You have to condition your mind. It's all about peaking at the right moment.

'Five o'clock, or if that doesn't work out, bedtime. Promise.'

'Promise,' says Laura.

He doesn't say anything more about her wanting to be a vegetarian. Does that mean he's accepted it?

7

Liz Dickinson enters her mother's house through the back door into the kitchen. This is the room that is least changed, apart from her own bedroom upstairs. Here, before she became bed-ridden, her mother was always to be found, sitting in the worn red armchair, a mug of tea undrunk tilted in her lap, her eyes closed. As Liz came in she would open her eyes and the lines on her face would relax. 'Oh, Elizabeth!' So much contained in the familiar greeting: joy that she'd come at last, reproach that she hadn't come earlier, relief that she can release the pent-up stream of her ill-treatment at the hands of life. 'Oh, Elizabeth!'

But now the chair is empty, the table clear, the floor swept. This house is the locus of too much emotion. Liz was a lonely child here, but it was also her place of safety. Now the house is dying alongside her mother.

She goes through the hall to the study. Karen is sitting in one of the displaced armchairs, dozing. She jerks awake as Liz comes in.

'You go and lie down,' says Liz. 'Get some proper sleep.'

'I wouldn't mind,' says Karen, rising, yawning.

She's a comfortably built woman, about Liz's own age, with deeply tanned skin and brown hair wound up into a loose bun. She costs £77 for each twenty-four-hour period, though of course she's only on duty for part of that time. It's a modest enough return for what she's endured, and Liz feels grateful and guilty. She also worries about the drain on their finances. There's Bridget to pay too. Alan says, 'We can cope.' But for how long? So many people live past a hundred these days, and her mother is only eighty-six. Do the sums. If this care regime goes on for a full year that's £56,000. If she lives for another eighteen years, that's more than a million.

Karen pads off into the sitting room, which has become her bedroom, so that even when sleeping she's within earshot of the dying woman. Because Liz has come she allows herself to close the door.

Alone in the room with the hospital bed, Liz draws an upright chair to the bedside and settles down beside her mother. She has barely glanced at her, beyond one quick look to establish that she's breathing evenly. Liz can't bring herself to gaze on that lined face, so bitter even in repose. It's not the dying she fears so much as the stillness and silence. Always before, all her life, her encounters with her mother have been active, even assaultive. She has braced herself for them in the way that you brace yourself when opening a door to go out into bad weather, head down, teeth gritted, hat pulled low. Her mother's beady gaze stings her face like wind-driven rain. When she speaks, both the tone of her voice and the words she says, Liz feels herself duck and dive as if she's under gunfire. How can such a small, frail, friendless old woman be so formidable? Liz knows she is no longer in her power as she once was. And yet every meeting with her mother exhausts her. There's an energy there, a fierce and active will, that she has known all her life she must hold at bay. Somehow she's always understood, even as a little girl, that her mother, unhappy in her own life, has sought to feed on hers, to live again through her, and this time not to loose her hold on the love that is her right. And, of course, Liz has failed her. She has replicated her mother's story: abandoned by her lover, she has raised a daughter without a father. And then came the final betrayal: the finding of happiness, a happiness that does not include her mother, a happiness that is stolen from her and leaves her the poorer. Such a complicated web of needs and resentments, played out in nods and grimaces, sighs and silences, shooting glances and rolled eyes.

And now, nothing.

Old Mrs Dickinson lies on the hissing bed, her eyes closed and gummy, her mouth a little open, breathing with a sound like a low, regular groan. She has pronounced whiskers on her chin, they catch the morning light. Her lips are folded inwards, she no longer has her false teeth. The lips shine, moistened with salve. The wrinkles round her mouth are deep, formed by all those years of pulling her mouth wide and down, in a habitual expression that said, You think you can destroy me but you can't. There's a kind of nobility there, thinks Liz, at last allowing her gaze to linger. If only I wasn't her daughter, if only I wasn't so afraid of her, I'd find it in me to admire that indomitable spirit. Aster the star, the late only child of remote parents, left to run wild in an African garden. A story told so often it seems part of Liz's own life: the golden days, the return to drab England, the slow slide into genteel poverty. Then the shuffling into adulthood of a proud, hurt young woman who lacked the skills to attract a mate, who felt herself to be undesirable, or at least undesired. The unlooked-for falling in love at the age of thirty-six with an older man, a gentle doctor who had been suitable in every way, until he departed. After that the blinds came down. With him went Aster's last hope of respectable contentment, and she was left with her anger and her child.

Liz has been in contact with her father, to let him know of her mother's decline. Rex Dickinson is in his late nineties now, in no condition to travel, even though Maidenhead, where he lives with his second wife, *the doormat*, is no great distance.

'I'm sorry to hear that,' he says over the phone, his voice slow and thoughtful as always. 'I always assumed I'd be the first to go.'

So did Aster.

'I'll stop missing him after he's dead,' she often told Liz. 'It's knowing he's alive and with the doormat that I can't bear.'

And this forty years after he'd left. The betrayal was so fundamental, it was the rock on which their existence rested, Liz and her mother's; like the German nation after the First World War, sustained by a shared belief in the 'stab in the back', so mother and daughter scratched away at the primal wound, as if its bleeding was necessary for their sustenance.

'He was such a coward,' said Aster. 'He just slunk away.'

It might have happened yesterday, it was so fresh in her mind.

'He didn't care about you,' said Aster. 'He left you like you were an unwanted parcel.'

Little Elizabeth, barely two years old, the unwanted parcel. That was never to be forgotten. But of her father, the slinking-away coward, she has no childhood memories. His parting gift to her was guilt.

'It was too much for him, a wife and a baby. He didn't understand I had to look after you. He wanted me for himself.'

This was her mother's story, and for years Liz believed it. Her arrival had driven her father away. But it was all a self-serving lie. When at last she had grown old enough to think for herself she had sought him out, the coward and his doormat. She found a kind, shy, ageing man, living in modest circum-stances with a decent, devoted wife. He was deeply moved to meet her, but he had nothing to say to her. They shared nothing except Aster, and he was scrupulously careful to speak of her only with respect. He blamed the failure of the marriage on his own immaturity, though he had been well past forty when they met. By then Liz had begun to guess at what had driven him away, because it was driving her away too. But of course for her there was to be no escape.

Does it have to be this way? Other marriages fail, and life goes on. If Alan were to leave me I'd build a new life of some sort. I wouldn't cling to Alice and Cas and make them believe all the world was against us, would I?

She's watching her mother now, seeing the way her hand, lying on the blanket, makes little movements from time to time. The fingers contract, clutching for something. Is she dreaming? What goes on in a brain so starved of nourishment, so deeply sedated? The wrist bones stick out on the shrivelled arm. The arms that held me.

Liz feels a sudden sharp contraction in her chest. It catches her by surprise. It's purely physical; there are no accompanying emotions. But she thinks it might be grief.

The old lady knows there's someone else in the room. But who? She can't quite see, it's so dark.

'Is that you, Mummy?'

'I don't know what to do with you, Aster. Whatever I do, you look a fright.'

Mummy tugging at the shoulders of my camel-hair coat, trying to make it neat around my chest.

'You're such an odd shape. I don't understand it.'

The nursery floor is up a little staircase at the end of the telephone passage, past the nursery bathroom on the half-landing. At the top of the staircase is another passage, with the night nursery on one side and the day nursery on the other. The day nursery is the biggest room in the world. At its far end it has a stoep, and from it you can see all the way over the kopje garden to the orchard, and the endless veld beyond.

When you come down the little stairs you reach the big stairs. At the foot of the big stairs, above the umbrella stand, there's a mirror. As you come down, step by step, you see yourself reflected in it, but you don't look. You look over the side of the shiny black banisters, down towards the dining-room door. Of course! It's my birthday! The birthday tea will be laid out on the dining-table. The candles will be lit in the chandelier. There'll be a cut-glass bowl filled with the heads of roses. There'll be tiny meringues and fairy-cakes with wings, and brandy snaps with cream, and best of all, triangles of bread and butter sprinkled with hundreds and thousands. Only I don't see the birthday cake. There has to be a birthday cake with my name in pink icing, with silver balls between the letters, and sugar roses with candles.

I don't understand why it has to be so dark.

My father looks at me, smiling. He's in his linen coat with the baggy pockets, wearing his old Panama hat, and the dogs sit in a circle round him, Lion and Tiger and Jock. Lion died.

Daddy died too.

I don't understand why it is but everything I have ever loved has always left me. I try not to do things the wrong way, but I don't have the knack of it. Mummy says I'm a clumsy child. I know it's my fault but I don't know what it is I'm doing wrong.

Who's there? Is that you, Elizabeth? Where have you been? I've been calling and calling. I don't want these carers any more. You have no idea how they treat me. They maul me and beat me. Why do they hate me so? What have I ever done to them? Send them away, I don't need them, I can look after myself. If you could manage to pop in once a day, just to help me with the things I find difficult these days. I can't get my shoes on, it's the bending down that's hard. Perhaps you could find my shoes for me now, I think they're by the back door. I'll take Perry out for a little walk. He'll start yapping as soon as I pick up his lead. It does get on my nerves, the way he yaps, but I always forgive him. Perry is my friend. I suppose that sounds silly, he's only a dog, but that's how I feel. He never criticizes me, which you do, Elizabeth, you know you do. I don't know why. If you only knew how small and foolish I feel inside you'd never snap at me. Really, you must be kind to me. I have no one else.

Sit where I can see you. I can't see you. Why doesn't the doctor come? I don't feel right at all, I'm so tired all the time, there should be something he can give me. Iron tablets, perhaps. I keep telling you my body isn't right, I shouldn't be so weak. You'll not believe me, but I can hardly stand on my own legs any more. It's not as if I'm so very old. Rex is twelve years older than I am, he'll be dying soon. How odd to think that if he dies he'll go to Heaven, and then I'll die and go to Heaven, and then we'll meet. What will we say to each other?

Don't laugh at me. I know my coat doesn't fit properly, it's because I'm such an odd shape. I never was a beauty. Daddy calls me Funnyface, and sometimes Monkey. It's his way of telling me he loves me. Rex never had any names for me.

Pull me up, will you, darling? And open the curtains, it's so dark, I can't see a thing. It must be morning by now. I wake in the night, you know. I come down and make myself a cup of tea, but I'm so clumsy I spill the water from the kettle. It gets so cold at night.

Why do they call them carers? I don't want to be cared for, and they certainly don't care. What do they do all day? I hear the sound of the television, but I don't know what programme they're watching. They always sit where I can't see them. I've told Elizabeth to send them away. She always had a stubborn streak, she never answered back, but she did as she pleased. 'One day,' I told her, 'you'll walk out on me, just like your father did.' Not a single word, no explanation. I still don't know why.

Animals don't leave. Animals die. When I die I want to go to Animal Heaven, with Lion and Tiger and Perry. Daddy always said Lion knew it was me coming even before he saw me, and made his whiffling sound. Mummy said Lion had to go away, he was sick, and I said, Will he die? I said, Let him die here, in his basket. But Mummy said he had to go away.

Open the curtains, please. It must be morning by now.

The back door opens and closes. Liz hears the sequence of deep sighs that Bridget always emits while taking off her coat and boots. Then the sound of the kettle being filled and put on to boil. Then her ample form in the doorway.

'Any funny business in the night?'

'Yes,' says Liz.

'That poor Karen.'

Bridget goes over to the bedside and gazes down at the sleeping woman.

'She's a wonder, your mum,' she says. 'They should bottle her for science.'

'I wish they would.'

Bridget peers at the syringe driver behind the pillow.

'Kim from the hospice told me yesterday she had one old lady lasted two years like this. Imagine sleeping for two years!'

'Don't,' says Liz.

'Tell you the honest truth,' says Bridget, 'I'll miss her when she goes. I know I will. It won't be the same. I won't know what to do with myself.'

She hears the kettle boiling in the kitchen.

'Cup of tea?'

'No,' says Liz. 'I've work to do.' She gets up from the chair by the bed. 'I'll try to be back for when the nurse comes this afternoon. But I've got my phone on all the time.'

She looks down at her mother in the great bed, sleeping, dying, refusing to die.

I have to go now, Mummy. I can't sit here for ever. But I'll be back.

8

Alan Strachan takes the tube from Victoria to Oxford Street, heading for a meeting at a production company where he's due to pitch an idea for a film. His mind is full of his story as he travels, rehearsing the manner in which he'll unfold the plot, trying to anticipate how his listeners will react. Stuart will be thinking, Are there any parts that will attract A-list actors? Jean-Claude will be thinking, What other pre-existing movie is this like? Neither of them will go for his ending, but it's the ending that Alan loves most of all.

Pitching has a bad reputation, but Alan far prefers it to the alternative, the treatment. Write them a treatment and you put yourself at their mercy, like a patient on an operating table. They come at your poor story with their scalpels and their needles and they perform cosmetic surgery on it until it's unrecognizable. But sit them in a room and tell them your story out loud and they show some respect. Instinctively they understand that it's yours. It's coming out of you in the form of breath and vibrations, facial expressions and bodily contortions. Pitching is performance. Like all performance, you adjust what you do to the response of your audience. It's dynamic, flexible, intuitive. In a sense, when you pitch you don't so much sell your story as sell yourself.

It's a form of flirting, Alan thinks, coming out of Oxford Circus tube into the bustle of Oxford Street. My aim is to make them fall a little in love with me.

As he makes his way past the restaurants and food bars of Argyll Street, he finds himself noticing the number of people either staring at or talking into their phones as they go by. They move a little more slowly than him, their minds elsewhere. It feels as if he's passing down a street of ghosts.

Or am I the ghost? They don't see me. Their eyes are open, but they don't see.

Past Liberty's, into Carnaby Street, he makes his ghostly way unseen. This idea that people are physically in one place and mentally in another feels fruitful to him. What if we could park our bodies and take mind trips elsewhere? The body could remain faithful, the mind could have affairs. Maybe it does already.

The woman coming towards him looks familiar. She has short dark hair and she's talking on her phone, moving her free hand about as she speaks. Not young, not old, but beautiful.

She sees him staring at her, and ends her call. She stares back. Wide black eyes, high cheekbones, lips parted—

Time and space come to a stop and he's eighteen again.

'Annie?'

Her face breaks into an enchanting smile.

'Alan?'

Her hair's shorter, she's more smartly dressed, but otherwise she's the same as she ever was.

'Annie Munro,' he says.

'How long is it?' she says. 'No, don't tell me, I don't want to know.'

He feels his cheeks beginning to burn. This is ridiculous. Over twenty years and he's barely given her a thought, and now she appears before him and he's actually blushing.

His first impulse is to reach out, not to embrace her but to detain her.

'Look,' he says, 'I've got a meeting, but I'm early.' This is not true. 'Have you got five minutes for a coffee?'

'Why not?' she says.

They go to Patisserie Valerie on the corner. They order cappuccinos. Alan realizes he's in a state of some confusion. What exactly is it that he expects of her? Nothing at all, he's living with someone else, as is she, there's the wedding ring on the finger of the hand she holds out before her, tracing laughing shapes in the air.

'Do you still see any of the old crowd?'

Alan tries to remember the names of the people they knew back then. Mick? Laurie?

'No,' he says. 'I seem to have lost touch with everyone.'

'You look just the same, Alan. I'd know you anywhere.'

'Don't I at least look older and wiser?'

'That too,' she says. And she smiles and pushes her hand across her brow the way she used to, even though there's no longer a curtain of hair to draw back. 'I hope I'm a bit wiser.'

'You were always much more grown-up than me,' says Alan.

The one with the power is always the grown-up. Annie had

the power in those days because he knew he was losing her and he couldn't bear to lose her. Life without her was unthinkable. It was more than love, it was survival itself, without her he had no existence. Desperate days! And desperation, of course, drives out love.

The part he remembers most clearly about their break-up is going to her bathroom and picking up his toothbrush and razor. He didn't have a bag so he put them in his jacket pocket. Having a set of wash things at her place had been the outward sign of their union. The sacrament of the toothbrush. Taking them away was a kind of dying.

Here in Patisserie Valerie they bridge the years with politeness and photographs. She shows him her daughter. Her name is Ellie, she's eighteen now, and she looks so like the Annie he once knew that it frightens him.

'She's lovely,' he says.

'And this is Mitch. Mitchell, I should say.'

Her husband: a big handsome serious-faced man, more or less bald. Alan feels at his own thicket of hair, just beginning to be tinged with grey.

'And this is Pretzel.'

Pretzel is a dog of indeterminate breed.

'Pretzel?'

'Yes, I know. Stupid name, stupid dog. He's very old and half blind.'

Alan reciprocates, showing his little stock of phone pictures, his evidence that he, too, has had a life.

'This is me and Liz. This is Alice, my stepdaughter. And this is Caspar. My son.'

'So Liz was married before?'

'She was a single mum. We're not actually married, but as good as.'

'She looks so nice.'

'And this is Alice with her boyfriend, Jack.'

'Ellie's just got a boyfriend,' says Annie. 'Mitch is terrifically wound up about it. He thinks he'll mess her about.'

'It happens,' says Alan.

'So where do you live?'

'Sussex. Near Lewes. Where are you?'

'Notting Hill. Well, Westbourne Grove.'

He wants to know so much, but all of it things he can't ask. Are you happy? Do you love your husband? Is your life with him better than it would have been with me?

'I can't believe you just walked back into my life,' he says.

'And there I was thinking you'd walked into mine.'

They share a smile. In that smile he thinks he sees an un-spoken collusion. But maybe she's just being friendly.

'Have you got a married name?' he says.

'Hamer.'

Her eyes never leaving his. That enchanting smile.

'So what do you do?' he says.

At once he regrets it. What if she does nothing? She has the groomed look of a kept woman.

'Commercial art,' she says. 'I source works of art for corpo-rations.' Alan's lack of comprehension shows on his face. 'Don't worry about it. What about you?'

'I'm a screenwriter,' he says.

'Alan, that's wonderful!'

He was always going to be a writer when they knew each

other all those years ago. The surprise is that he's managed it, after a fashion. This reminds him that he was supposed to be at a pitch meeting ten minutes ago. He must go. But not before he's made sure that he'll see her again.

'Give me your phone,' he says.

He taps his name and number into it.

'Call me some time. Now I have to run.'

He's late for his meeting, but he's still asked to wait in Reception. Sitting on the deep leather couch, he thumbs the pages of *Variety*. This is for the purposes of cover, so that he can appear idle and unconcerned. In fact, all he can think about is Annie.

Her re-entry into his life has had more impact than he at first realized. The picture of her daughter has merged with the memory of the girl he knew all those years ago, and now it's as if the forty-four-year-old woman he met in the street is eighteen again, and the boy who lives inside him still is dazzled again, as he was all those years ago.

He has no idea what this means, or how it relates to his love for Liz. He doesn't ask. It exists in a different part of his life; the one has nothing to do with the other. He doesn't love Liz any the less because Annie has come back into his life. His Liz-self remains as loving and loyal as ever. But his Annie-self, so long dormant, seems to have unfinished business.

None of this presents itself to him as an excuse. There is no excuse. There's only the reality of his feelings. Or, to be more accurate, his desires.

Of course. How simple it all turns out to be.

I want to make love with Annie. I want to hold her naked in my arms and—

'They're ready for you now,' says the receptionist. 'Third floor.'

The meeting is in a room almost entirely filled with a big table. Jean-Claude, the script associate, bounds up as he enters, compensating in the vigour of his welcome for the fact that the team is still not all present.

'Alan! Great to see you! Stuart'll be here any minute!'

Stuart duly arrives, honouring the code that ordains the last person into the room is the most important. He is preceded by a pretty young woman called either Stacy or Stella, who carries a mug of black coffee that she places on the table before her boss.

'Alan,' says Stuart. 'Good of you to come.'

Stuart is small and ageless. Rumour has it he's over fifty, but he dresses and acts like a teenager. Alan knows him well, and neither believes nor trusts him, but he likes him. He looks on with a smile as Stuart spoons sugar into his black coffee.

'Still on the hard stuff, Stuart,' he says.

'My rocket fuel.' Stuart raises his mug and takes a long sip. 'Over to you, Shakespeare. The floor is yours.'

Stacy or Stella has her pencil poised to take notes. Alan parts his hands in the air before him, like a conjuror readying his trick. Now for the pitch.

'We're in a spacecraft,' he says. 'We're on a mission to an unknown planet. Our main characters are a crew of four.'

'Wise old guy, cool young guy, hot chick, and an ethnic.'

This is Stuart's wry contribution. It's also an annoyingly accurate guess.

'Plus a comic robot,' says Jean-Claude.

'No robot,' says Alan. Keeping his face deadpan, he teases them. 'All four leads are over fifty. They're paedophiles, and they signed up for the mission to have sex with alien children.'

'Kiddy porn I can live with,' says Stuart, not missing a beat. 'But over fifty? That's sick.'

Everyone grins. So it goes. The creators of mass entertainment offer their cynicism as a sacrifice to the gods of success.

Alan proceeds with the pitch.

'They've come to this planet because earlier missions have failed. Worse than failed – they've vanished. Why? The spacecraft lands. The crew step out onto the unknown planet. And there, waiting for them, are the aliens. And they're beautiful. I mean, truly, seriously gorgeous.'

'Are they all female?' says Stuart.

'No. Male and female. And they're gentle, and funny, and a little scatty. In fact, they're all over the place. Absent-minded. They don't even seem to have names, so the crew give them nicknames. Blondie, Smiler, Honeybun, that sort of thing. One of them, a beautiful young woman, becomes our hero's special friend. And then – they start dying.'

'The aliens?'

'It's like they're picking up some kind of infection from our heroes.'

Stella or Stacy says, 'Like Columbus brought back syphilis from the Americas to Europe.'

They all stare at her.

'Did he?' says Stuart.

'It's true,' says Jean-Claude. 'The pox is American.'

'So the aliens are dying,' says Stuart. 'The poor gorgeous things.'

Alan continues.

'It's a nightmare. The aliens start to fear our heroes. A leader emerges who tells his people the only way to save their race is to kill the invaders. The friend-alien pleads for them to be spared, but aliens are dying every day. So the decision is taken. Kill the invaders, burn their bodies, eliminate the infection. So now our heroes are on the run. One by one they're hunted down and killed.'

Stuart says, 'Our heroes are killed? Our name cast, and you're killing them off in Act Two?'

'Very *Game of Thrones*,' says Jean-Claude.

Stuart shrugs, unconvinced.

'So now,' says Alan, 'only our hero is left. He has to convince the aliens he's not infectious. But what is it that's been killing them? He's been trying to puzzle it out all along. He's been so careful – gloves, masks. So now he's alone with his alien friend who's protecting him, and the friend gets sick. How? What did he do?'

'The friend,' says Stuart. 'This is a gorgeous female?'

'Yes,' says Alan.

'Thank Christ for that at least. So what did he do?'

'He named her,' says Alan.

This is the punchline. The twist. As he feared, it doesn't go down well.

Stella or Stacy says, 'Did you say he named her?'

'Yes,' says Alan. 'What our heroes never understood is that these aliens are the ultimate free beings. Not just free to do as they please, free to *be* whom they please. Lock them into one single identity, call them by the same name too many times, and they suffocate. Like a wild animal in captivity. They die of psychic suffocation.'

A silence follows. They're all gazing at Alan.

'Wow!' says Jean-Claude. 'That is so cool!'

'Clever,' says Stuart. But his tone of voice says: too clever. 'So how does it end?'

'Our hero learns what he's doing wrong, but he can't stop himself. He goes on projecting the same identity onto his alien friend. And she dies. After that he knows he's the disease. We all are, with our demand that everyone fits a stereotype. He knows that if he's left to run free he'll kill this whole beautiful race. So he comes out of hiding, and he takes a vow of silence. He never speaks again. He lets them capture him. And it ends with his sacrificial death.'

Another silence.

'So not a comedy, then?' says Stuart.

'Dark,' says Jean-Claude, enraptured.

'Dark,' says Stuart, meaning: too dark.

He rises.

'Give me a couple of pages, Alan. Something I can run by the money. I'm in LA for the weekend. You have a title?'

'*The Human Disease.*'

Stella or Stacy writes this down. Stuart pulls a face.

'Heard it before,' he says.

'*The Human Stain,*' says Jean-Claude. 'Anthony Hopkins and Nicole Kidman.'

'Novel by Philip Roth,' says Alan.

'We can do better,' says Stuart. 'Movies that start with *The* always feel like hard work. Get straight to it. *Star Wars. Titanic. Avatar.*'

'*The Lord of the Rings,*' says Jean-Claude. '*The Lion King.*'

Stuart stares at him.

'Just saying.'

'Oh, and give your hero more to do, Alan. Sounds to me like his big move at the end is to do nothing. A man who does nothing is not a hero.'

He glances at Stella or Stacy to confirm that she's writing it down.

'Gotta fly,' he says.

Last in, first out: the prerogative of the chief.

9

'My grandmother knew Virginia Woolf, and my mother met her when she was a little girl. But I, of course – well, I'm old, but not that old!'

Christopher Vickery laughs, and his eyes twinkle. Laura Broad guesses at his age, over seventy, certainly. Through the French windows she can see a large, well-kept garden, and beyond its shrubbery, the water meadows of the Ouse valley.

'Anyway, here we are. The whole catastrophe.' Two daughters, a son, all middle-aged. 'They have to have their say.'

'Have you come to a decision?' says Laura.

The younger generation of Vickerys exchange glances. The daughters are sitting side by side on the library sofa. Charles, the son, is facing them, pressing the tips of his fingers together, his balding brow judiciously furrowed.

'Dad's the one who has to decide,' he says.

'But I want to know your wishes too,' says Christopher Vickery. 'You must all be treated fairly.'

He speaks with the smiling self-assurance of a high-court judge, which until his recent retirement is exactly what he was. Now he presides by the empty fireplace, a tall, stooping figure in a brown suit, a mischievous gleam in his eyes. Of course, thinks Laura. He's playing Lear. He wants some fun out of his bequest.

'You said you don't want to sell,' says Charles.

'I didn't say that, Charles. I merely laid out the options as Laura here has presented them to me. The library is part of your inheritance.'

The book-lined room shimmers with tension. There's money at stake, a division of the spoils. The inheritance in question is arrayed on the shelves all round them, but no one regards the actual books.

'I don't mind admitting,' says Joanna, the elder of the two daughters, the one with severe hair, 'a little extra would be very welcome right now. A lifesaver, in fact.'

'Surely the library isn't that valuable,' says Henrietta, the other daughter.

'Laura?' Christopher prompts her.

'It is, actually,' says Laura. 'There's a large number of Hogarth Press first editions, including four Virginia Woolf novels signed by the author. There are fourteen autograph letters. If you go to auction, I would recommend a reserve price of five hundred thousand.'

'Or Dad can give the lot to Sussex University,' says Charles, 'in which case the reserve price is nil.'

Laura says nothing to this. Her commission is four per cent of the sale price, which on a gift would amount to zero.

'Sussex would keep the collection together,' says Christopher. 'The Vickery Library. That's a value of a kind, isn't it?'

'If that's what you want, Dad,' says Charles, refusing to be drawn.

'I just want to know your wishes, the three of you. If you really need your share, now, before I die, then of course I'll ask Laura to put the library on the market and seek the highest price.'

'Well, I wouldn't say no to two hundred thousand pounds,' says Henrietta.

'More like a hundred thousand after tax and commission,' says Charles.

'So what would you do if you were me, Charles?' The old man pretends to defer to his worldly son. 'You've always been so practical.'

'If I were you, Dad, I'd sell up and keep the loot for myself.'

'What do I need that I haven't got? What do you need, any of you, that you haven't got?'

'I'm not begging for hand-outs,' says Joanna, 'but I'm not ashamed to admit I could do with it. If you're doling out your inheritance I'll take my fair share. I have a whole lot more need of it than Charles. And Henrietta has only herself to think of.'

Henrietta jumps as if she's been stung.

'If you can't afford children, you shouldn't have them,' she says. 'I don't see why you should be rewarded for living beyond your means.'

'We all have needs,' says Charles. 'I need twelve thousand a month for Alex to go on running a house that's far too big for her, because she says that's what she needs.'

'This is getting embarrassing.' Henrietta turns to Laura with a smile. 'I'm so sorry, Laura. What must you think of us?'

'It's never easy making this sort of decision,' says Laura. 'There's often a lot of emotion bound up in books.'

'None of us cares tuppence for the books,' says Charles. 'Not even Dad. He's never read any of them, have you, Dad?'

'Of course I have.' But he says it smiling, as if to imply that his words are not to be taken at face value. 'Virginia Woolf feels like one of the family.'

'The family!' Henrietta gives another sardonic laugh. 'She never had children.'

'So now Virginia Woolf is your role model, is she, Henrietta?' Joanna rises as she speaks, reaching for a jacket draped over the arm of the sofa. 'That ended well, didn't it?' And, turning to her father, 'You do as you please, Dad. I shall go home, and get ready to do my democratic duty tomorrow.'

'There's no point in voting in Chichester,' says Henrietta. 'It's as blue as a baboon's bum.'

'That's what you think,' says Joanna.

'Please don't tell me you're voting UKIP.'

'I've no intention of telling anyone anything.'

'It's all a disaster,' says Charles. 'Cameron's blown it. We're heading for a minority Labour government propped up by the Marxist SNP. This country gets more like Italy every day.'

'Perhaps I should offer the library to Sussex,' says Christopher. 'I like the idea of a living memorial. The Vickery Bequest. It honours the whole family, do you see?'

'Yes, Dad,' says Henrietta. 'The perfect family.'

'Well, I'm off,' says Joanna, looking for signs that her brother and sister are leaving too. 'We're done, aren't we?'

'I haven't quite decided, of course,' says Christopher, meditatively. 'But if I leave here, the library will have to go.'

His three children stare at him in shock.

'You're selling the house?' says Charles.

'It's far too big for me, don't you think? And if Labour takes over, as Charles assures me they will, there'll be the mansion tax to pay.'

'You can't assume that,' says Charles, hurriedly. 'They'll never make a mansion tax work.'

'Even so, selling the house would release some capital, I suppose.'

'For what, Dad?'

'Oh, I don't know. Now I'm retired I feel a new lease of life. Maybe I should marry again. What do you think?'

'I think you should have a whole new family, Dad,' says Henrietta.

Joanna sits down again.

'This is family business,' says Laura. 'I'll leave you to it.'

Christopher sees her to the door.

'I'll let you know what I decide,' he says.

He takes her hand. As he holds it he looks directly into her eyes and smiles.

'Thank you for your patience, Laura.'

Driving from Rodmell to Waitrose in Lewes, Laura reflects on the little domestic drama that has just been played out before her. It seems that for some reason the old judge wanted her there, but why? An audience for his display of power, perhaps. His own children have no real affection for him, that much seems clear. What must it be like to grow old knowing your children are waiting for you to die?

She thinks of Jack and Carrie. It seems impossible to her that they could ever be like that. They'll always love and need her. But, of course, that's not the fear. At some point in the coming years it's she who will love and need them, more than they will want. Henry, his arteries overloaded with butter, will die, and she'll be alone. Jack and Carrie will quarrel with each other over who visits and for how long. Her need will grow into dependency.

She winces as these thoughts pass through her mind. She's driving between fields where sheep are grazing, each one with an attendant lamb. One lamb clambers to its feet and prances over the lush grass, just for the joy of it. Is that why I want to stop eating meat? Because I'm sentimental about the lambs? But Laura knows she's as capable as anyone else of thinking two opposing thoughts at once, smiling at the lambs in the spring-time fields even as she looks forward to the taste of lamb on a plate. You allow yourself to think whatever suits your needs at the time.

Now she's driving down a Sussex road dotted with blue signs featuring the Tory candidate, Maria Caulfield, a young woman with long, blondish hair and a smiling face. For all her smiles she has no chance of taking the seat: this is LibDem territory. After tomorrow, following the few weeks in which everyone in and around Lewes has become familiar with her face, she'll return to obscurity. The years will go by. She'll cut her hair shorter. Her children will leave home. She'll join a book group. The long days and nights of unnecessary existence will begin.

I suppose my needs have changed, Laura thinks. I'm becoming a different person. You think when you pass the age of fifty that you've become whoever it is you're to be, and that the time of transformations is over. But it's not so.

My diet is an act of self-reinvention.

10

Liz Dickinson stations herself in the Lower Mall between Debenhams, Mothercare and Clinton Cards. If that doesn't work out she can always go upstairs to the younger cluster of Urban Outfitters, Pineapple, H&M. But her assumption is she'll get more response from women in their forties and over.

'Excuse me, do you have a moment? I'm doing an opinion survey.'

A mother and daughter, she guesses, the daughter pushing a buggy with a sleeping infant, coming out of Mothercare.

'Oh, yes?'

'It's about the party leaders. David Cameron. Ed Miliband. Nick Clegg. Nigel Farage. Which one would you go for as a husband?'

She holds up her phone, using it as a sound recorder.

'I've already got a husband,' says the younger woman.

'Oh, come on, Mandy,' says her mother. 'You can do better than him.'

'But I'd rather him than that Ed Miliband. He's creepy.'

'What about the others?' says Liz.

Mandy puts her head on one side, as if the offer is real and must be given serious consideration.

'I like that Nick Clegg. He'd be all right.'

'Not David Cameron?'

'Well, he's shiny, isn't he?'

'How about not as a husband, but as a lover?'

The two women laugh.

'I'd take any of 'em,' says the mother. 'No, not Nigel. I'm not that desperate.'

Some of the other shoppers have stopped to listen. One of them, a well-preserved sixty-year-old, offers her opinion.

'Take Cameron,' she says. 'I guarantee you he's a spanker.'

'I don't want to be spanked!'

'You haven't lived, love.'

The crowd is growing.

'I'll tell you who's sexy,' says a youngish woman in a stripy top and leggings. 'Ed's sexy. Those eyes.'

'Gives me the creeps,' says Mandy.

'Use your imagination! Imagine him fixing you with those eyes and saying, Hell, yes, I want you!'

A wave of laughter rises from the crowd.

'How about Nick Clegg as a lover?' says Liz.

'He'd wear striped pyjamas.'

'He's a sweetheart.'

'He's a bloody liar!'

'I'd give him a cuddle any night.'

The voices overlap. It's all getting out of hand.

'Slow down,' says Liz, keeping her phone high. 'Who's willing to go on the record?'

'You send 'em round to my place, love. I may not look much, these days, but I know how to give a fella a good time.'

'Can I use your name?'

'I'm Ginger, on account of me hair, though I'm blonde today. But I'm ginger in other places.'

'And you're going for Nick Clegg.'

'Oh, I'm not choosy. So long as he's got a pulse.'

'That Cameron's a smooth one. I like 'em posh. You can send him round.'

'Bet he's got a tiny one.' This comes from a lad in a hoodie, grinning from the back of the crowd.

'You don't know that,' says Ginger. 'He's a big boy. He's got my vote.'

'He's no bigger than Nick.'

'Same difference. It's what they've got in their trousers that counts.' She lays a confidential hand on Liz's arm. 'Tell you what, love. Get 'em to send round selfies of their you-know-whats, and then we'll make up our minds.'

Back home Liz transcribes the best of her recorded quotes, and knows none of them will do. Women in real life are always so much cruder than women in the media. There seems to be a general agreement not to admit the fact in public. For whose benefit is that?

This reminds her of the *Stella* commission, a much longer and better paid feature, a project with no brief at all: she's to spin it out of thin air.

As a starting point she types into Google: WHAT WOMEN WANT. Up come references to the Mel Gibson movie of the same name, which she dimly remembers. As far as she can recall, the answer to the title question was that women want Mel Gibson.

She reads on, further down the page.

What women really want: things a guy can do to be perfect for her. This turns out to be 'honesty, caring, and sympathy'. *What women want at that time of the month*: 'honesty, caring and sympathy, with added patience'. So far, so unremarkable.

Then, four Google pages in, she comes upon the real thing.

Turns out women have really strong sex drives: can men handle it?

It's a long review of a book called *What Do Women Want? Adventures in the Science of Female Desire.* The book's author, Daniel Bergner, claims that all the sexologists he's interviewed have reached the same conclusion: women want sex just as much as men do. The body of scientific research conclusively proves, he asserts, that women are not naturally suited to monogamy, and that they're more inclined to want sex for pleasure than for emotional intimacy.

Surely this can't be right. Liz copies out sentences wholesale, already mentally preparing her proposal for Chrissie.

Women may be designed to want multiple partners.

Women's sexual fantasies revolve around strangers.

Salon*'s Tracy Clark-Flory says this book should be read by every woman on earth.*

Liz reads on, about light-beaming plethysmographs inserted into women's vaginas to measure their levels of arousal. The test subjects responded to the images they were shown even when they claimed they weren't responding: images of straight sex, gay sex, copulating apes. The only images that failed to elicit a response were of naked men with flaccid penises.

Can this be true? And, if so, why do we all believe the exact opposite? It's men who want *only one thing*, not women. Ask any woman. She'll tell you she wants an emotional connection. She wants love. The last thing she wants is casual sex.

But maybe she's lying. Maybe we all lie.

Would I like multiple partners? Or, at least, one more than I have? Not at the price of hurting Alan, of course. But put all that aside, assume it could be managed with no consequences, would I do it?

Why not? I have desires. I just choose not to act on them. But the inhibition is stronger than that. I don't even admit my desires. Why?

We women know that if we admit our sexual desires we'll be demonized as sluts. Men don't marry sluts, men rape sluts. So we lie.

We've known for a long time that the fetish of chastity, the requirement that women be sexually pure, is the creation of men. No surprise there. But what if women's sexual desire – or, rather, women's lack of sexual desire – is the creation of men too? What if we've all learned to repress our true nature because men have found it too threatening?

Liz feels a surge of excitement run through her. She starts tapping out her thoughts.

Women crave one-night stands . . .

11

Michael Marcus's ageing Saab drives into the gravelled yard and pulls up beside the barn. Henry sees it arrive through the kitchen window.

'Bang on time. Bad sign.'

Laura has only recently got back, and is unpacking from her Waitrose bag-for-life the elements of lunch.

'He won't mind bagels, will he?'

She's got a broccoli quiche, smoked salmon, cream cheese, a bag of rocket salad. There are chives in the garden. Chocolate éclairs filled with fresh cream, to gratify the nursery tastes of middle-aged men.

'I met Belinda Redknapp by the breads and pastries. She says Tom insists she votes Tory. She told him she wouldn't just to spite him, but she says she will.'

Bang-bang on the door, and their visitor lets himself in.

'How's that for timing?' he says. 'On the button.'

Michael Marcus is a small, neat man with a head of reddish hair that is both copious and thinning. He's wearing a navy blazer over a V-neck sweater, jeans and trainers. He speaks with a breathy softness, articulating every third or fourth word very slowly, as if constantly applying brakes to what would otherwise be a runaway flow of speech.

'I wanted to arrive before *The World at One* because news programmes at election time make me want to scream. They can't not talk about the election, but by now they've nothing new to say. Your roadworks seem to be over at last.'

'It's still a bitch of a drive,' says Henry. 'I always take the train.'

'Saw quite a few orange signs on the roadside.'

'This is Lib–Dem land. Norman Baker's our MP.'

'So what do you think? Is Ed going to make it? Are we going to be ruled by the SNP? Hello, Laura. Good of you to let me invade. Look at those bluebells! You have something precious here, Henry. I don't know why I go on living in London. I started meditating as soon as I hit the M23.'

'You meditate as you drive?'

'It's all about being in the present moment.'

As he speaks he keeps running one hand over the top of his head, rearranging his implausible hair. Henry gets him a beer. He drinks it out of the can while Laura puts lunch on the table.

'If you think of life as a series of peaks and troughs, meditation smooths it out.'

Michael Marcus is not a significant player these days. His little production company survives by underbidding for daytime slots, then hiring directors who can't get work elsewhere at bargain-basement rates. 'Just something to keep you ticking over until the next gig comes along, Henry.' But he has his uses. He took Henry's proposal for a television history of gardens and turned it into an actual commission, even if for a rather different format. The history element dropped out of the title, and Monty Don came on board as presenter. Now it's an amiable trot round the countryside called *English Gardens with Monty Don*. Not quite Henry's vision, but a pleasant enough way of passing the time.

'Have you had a chance to look over my schedule?' Henry says. They're standing in the living room gazing out through the French windows at the garden in young leaf. 'All looks pretty straightforward.'

'Not yet. We're still finalizing Monty's deal.'

'I thought the money had been agreed.'

'Just a few details to iron out. Dickie's woken up and realized he could have a real banker on his hands.'

Dickie, the current channel controller.

'Can't be bad.'

'To be truthful, Henry, I'm happier when I'm below the radar.' He gestures at the view. 'This is Paradise, isn't it? You must be a happy man.'

Henry wants to ask him: Why are you here? Instead he talks about the plans for the shoot.

'I thought we should kick off at Great Dixter. We can decide on the order of transmission later.'

'I do think it's a shame we couldn't sell them on your original idea. The history idea.'

This is a surprise. Michael put considerable energy into convincing Henry that the new format was one to embrace. 'Just think, Henry, we'll bring a whole new audience to the nation's gardens. The programmes will be timeless. They'll repeat them for ever. And Monty is a national heart-throb.'

Over lunch Henry finds himself fascinated by Michael's

greed. He eats everything voraciously, except the smoked salmon. They talk about the election. Michael astonishes Henry by revealing that he doesn't vote.

'It's not that I'm against the democratic process,' he says. 'It's just that I believe each of us is responsible for his own survival. And I mean psychic survival as well as physical survival. What is a government? It's a parent fantasy, a big daddy we can blame for everything that's not right in our lives. Elections give us an illusion of choice over an illusion of control. In reality we have no choice, and governments can do nothing. The economy does what it does, like the weather. I prefer to keep my own umbrella. Or, better still, to learn to love the rain. Though of course I realize my position is riddled with inconsistencies, and driven by my own personal neurotic needs. But isn't everyone's? What do you say, Laura?'

Laura blinks under this stream of speech, delivered in a gentle, almost caressing manner.

'Goodness, I don't know. You sound like Russell Brand. I suppose voting can't make that much difference. But I still do it.'

'I've never heard such dangerous nonsense in my life,' says Henry. 'Of course voting makes a difference! Not just in marginal seats, where a single vote electing a single MP could change a whole government, but every vote. Every vote is counted, you know. The sum totals shift the argument. I'm shocked, Michael, I really am. Don't you want to get rid of this ghastly government?'

'I'm afraid I don't really believe,' says Michael Marcus, smiling as he spreads cream cheese on his bagel, 'that anything of any significance would change if we had a change of government.'

'Of course it would!'

'You don't think our real rulers are Goldman Sachs and Amazon and Google and the bond markets?'

'So to you democracy is a fraud. We're all puppets of global corporations.'

'I'm not a puppet, Henry.' His eyes wide with reproach. 'I'm the master of my own destiny. As you are of yours, if you're willing to accept the responsibility.'

Henry flushes and feels himself to be on the verge of rudeness. He takes evasive action.

'Where's Carrie? Why isn't she having lunch?'

'She says she doesn't want any,' says Laura.

'That's ridiculous.' Henry stands. 'She has to eat.'

'Are you going to make her?'

'Of course not. I shall invite her.'

Henry goes upstairs and taps on Carrie's door.

'Carrie, darling. We're having lunch.'

'I'm not hungry,' she says, through the door.

'Just join us to be sociable, then.'

'I'll be down later.'

'You say that, but you just stay in your room.'

Silence.

'Can I come in?'

Scuffling sounds from within. The door opens a few inches and Carrie's pale face blinks out at him.

'What do you want?'

'Nothing. I've just hardly seen you since you came home.'

'I'll be down later, okay?'

The door closes again. Henry frowns and returns to the kitchen. Laura raises her eyebrows at him, saying, I told you so.

'I don't like the way she spends all her time in her room,' he says.

'She just needs her own space,' says Laura, not wanting to discuss Carrie in front of Michael Marcus.

All through lunch Henry can taste, like bile in his throat, a rising anger that he knows he must control. And yet what is there to get so worked up about? Michael Marcus's self-satisfied pronouncements are too silly to take seriously. Carrie is another matter. There are issues there that will have to be confronted sooner or later.

What is it I'm afraid of? Why did I wake in the night full of fear?

'Do you sleep well, Michael?'

After all, he is a man of my own age, perhaps a few years older, and in my own field of work.

'Do I sleep well?' Michael Marcus is eating an éclair with a fork. 'The simple answer is I hardly sleep at all. Or you could say I sleep most of the time. A true meditative state is a form of sleep.'

God help me. All I want is a little solidarity.

'I thought maybe it was normal for people our age to wake in the night.'

'What is *our age*? People of the same age in years may lead quite different lives. For example, I've trained myself not to worry. Do you worry?'

'Everyone worries,' says Laura. 'I don't believe you don't worry.'

'You're quite right, of course,' says Michael Marcus. 'I worry, as everyone does. I expressed myself badly. I should have said I've trained myself to stand apart from my worries. My worries don't worry me, if you like.'

'Then they're not worries.'

'If that's the way you want to see it, Laura.'

Laura rises a little too quickly, catching Henry's eye.

'Why don't I get George to make some coffee?' She enjoys Michael Marcus's blank look. 'George Clooney.'

'If you have any tea,' says Michael Marcus. 'Camomile, or verbena, or even mint. Then maybe you and I should talk shop, Henry.'

While they wait, Henry asks, 'I take it you're a vegetarian, Michael.'

'I am,' he replies.

'Laura is threatening to join the faith.'

'But not you.'

'No,' says Henry. 'I remain unrepentant.'

'A multi-faith household, then.'

'It's not a matter of faith, as far as I'm concerned. I just like meat.'

Laura, listening, understands that Henry has decided to treat her decision as a joke. 'Faith', in Henry's lexicon, means superstition.

'But you maintain that you have the right to eat other species,' says Michael Marcus. 'Isn't that part of a belief system?'

'No,' says Henry. 'It's part of a menu.'

Michael Marcus smiles. Laura hands Henry his coffee without smiling. Michael has camomile tea.

They take their mugs into Henry's study. Henry opens up the file on his computer that displays his proposed filming schedule. Michael pays no attention to the screen. Instead he stands at the window and sips his camomile tea.

'I want to run something past you face to face, Henry,' he

says, not facing him. 'Dickie's taking a personal interest in the strand. Which is great news. I think I should be able to squeeze more out of him. More filming days, more editing days. Possibly even a longer run.'

'Does that mean I get paid more?' says Henry.

'He wants the money on screen. He's seriously impressed we've signed Monty up.'

'Your doing, Michael. Credit where credit's due.'

'But the core idea is yours, Henry. You brought it to me. In a rather different form, it's true, but it all began with you. And I believe in loyalty.'

Henry suddenly understands what's happening. When they start talking about loyalty you know it's over. He flushes, annoyed with himself that he didn't spot it earlier. Why else would Michael Marcus drive down in person?

'What's going on, Michael?'

'This business runs on personal relationships. We both know that. On the other hand, there are objective realities. My job is balancing the two for the benefit of all.'

'Is this coming from Dickie?'

'Dickie loves the concept. He loves Monty. He wants to get behind it. He sees an opportunity to bring in a whole new audience.'

'I thought we'd already done that.'

'A younger audience.'

'Younger? Kids don't visit gardens. How do you make a series on English gardens younger?'

'It's a matter of style. You employ young directors.'

So there it is. He's being dropped from his own programmes as a matter of style.

'I'm the director, Michael. I created this thing. I brought it to you so that it would be a job for me.'

'I know, Henry. I know.'

'I mean, for Christ's sake, I've taken a big cut in my rate. I do have a track record. I've won awards. I actually do know how to do this.'

'I know. Of course I know.'

Henry sits down in his desk chair and leans his head on his hands. He feels angry and hurt, but most of all he feels defeated. When his original idea for a history series mutated into a low-budget domestic travelogue, Laura persuaded him to stay on board. 'They'll be paying you to get to know the most beautiful gardens in England. What's so terrible about that?' He had even come round to the new format. He was genuinely looking forward to the shoot. He had lowered his sights. He had accepted the harsh demands of the real world. And now this.

'So what's the proposal?'

'It's still your series, Henry. We bring in a couple of new young directors to shoot the programmes. You oversee them.'

'As what? Executive producer?'

'Well, technically that's my role. But alongside me, yes.'

'With what credit?'

'That's something we'll have to sort out between us.'

'How? There's no job there. And speaking of no job, are they proposing to pay me sixty grand for doing fuck-all?'

'No.'

Henry starts to laugh. It's all insane. Why fight it?

'You're tearing up my contract?'

'None of our contracts have been ratified yet. You know that.'

'Oh, hell.'

'None of this is my doing, Henry.'

'No. The illusion of choice. The illusion of control.'

'We don't make the weather.'

Henry looks up and catches in Michael Marcus's eyes something that looks like fear. Why would he be afraid of me? I'm the loser here. But of course that's exactly what he fears. The contamination of failure. He must have been dreading this visit.

'At least you had the decency to come in person.'

'That's how I work. It's all about personal relationships.'

And yet, thinks Henry, we're not friends. That's the cruelty of our business. We use the language of friendship for what is at best a trade, at worst a form of exploitation.

'And anyway,' says Michael Marcus, 'I have a favour to ask.'

'You want me to go quietly.'

'It's about Monty. You had a great meeting with him. He liked you.'

'I liked him.'

'He may be a bit nervous at the idea of a new director.'

'I wouldn't worry about that. Tell him it's a matter of style.'

'We thought maybe you could drop him a friendly email.'

Henry stares. Michael Marcus has the decency to blush.

'You want me to tell Monty Don he's going to be better off without me?'

'No, no, of course not. Just something to say you're behind the new approach. You're excited by it, there's no cause for concern, the same team's in charge. That sort of thing.'

'You want me to drink the poison while praising the emperor?'

'What?'

'Never mind. You've got a fucking nerve, I must say.'

'Here's the bottom line, Henry. If we lose Monty, we lose the commission. Is that what you want?'

'Why do I care? I'm not part of it any more.'

'Of course you are. You're the originator. You're the associate producer.'

'Associate producer!'

'Or whatever credit we negotiate.'

The hangers-on credit. The pity credit. The did-fuck-all-but-has-to-get-his-name-somewhere credit.

Michael Marcus spreads his arms as if he, too, is helpless in the face of forces beyond his control.

'It is how it is.'

'Okay, Michael. You tell me. If you were me – if you were put out to pasture like a geriatric donkey, not to say betrayed and shafted by your own so-called colleagues – what would you do? And please don't tell me you'd *meditate*.'

'What can I say, Henry? You're angry. You have good reason to be angry. But anger is a negative emotion that does most damage to the one who feels it. Meditation helps us to see negative emotions for what they are.'

'Which is what?'

'Clouds on the horizon.'

'Clouds on the horizon?'

'And in time the wind blows, and the clouds sail away.'

It's no good. Any minute now he's going to have to hit him.

'I think you'd better sail away, Michael.'

'Right. Yes. Of course. I understand.' He gives Henry an imploring look. 'What about the email to Monty?'

'No. There are limits. I have my pride.' Suddenly he's shouting. 'If you want a *fucking show trial*, complete with a *fucking staged confession*, you have to start with the *fucking torturers*! For fuck's sake, Michael! Do the thing properly!'

Michael Marcus waves his hands before his face, warding off the torrent of negative emotions.

'Okay. Okay. Just think it over. Please. Yes, I'm going. I'm on my way.'

After Michael Marcus's departure Laura comes looking for Henry and finds him at his desk, tapping out an email.

'What happened there?'

'They've dumped me from *English Gardens*.'

'They can't! It's your idea!'

'They can. They have. Now I'm going to blow it out of the water.'

Laura reads the half-written email on his screen.

Dear Monty. I had been looking forward to working with you on our *English Gardens* series, but today I've been told my services are no longer required. I am to be replaced with 'young directors', as a 'matter of style'. I imagine you can now look forward to quirky camera angles, rapid cutting, and background music with a disco beat, assembled by a graduate of the school of pop video. Just the style for a stroll round Stourhead. All this is the brainwave of the channel controller, or the Great Dickster as he's known—

'You can't say that, Henry!' exclaims Laura. 'Someone'll leak it to the press.'

'Let 'em.'

'You'll never work again.'

'So what's new? I'll have never worked again for some time now.'

'That's ridiculous.'

'Why? Things come to an end. Night falls. Winter sets in.'

'Stop it, Henry!'

'Stop what? I'm standing apart from my worries. I'm being the master of my own destiny.'

'That man is a sad fool.'

'Aren't we all?'

She takes his hands and pulls him up out of his chair so that she can put her arms round him. He feels her body warm against his.

'So just tell me what he actually said.'

Henry tries to speak, but the words don't come. Something big has changed. Instinctively he shies away from this knowledge. He feels the need to be active, to be busy, not to be left alone with his thoughts. This something, this change, has altered the quality of the light. He needs time to adjust his vision.

'It hasn't properly sunk in yet,' he says.

'Is there someone you could call about it? Aidan? Christina?'

Every profession is a secret world, sealed from the gaze of outsiders. Laura understands this. Henry needs to talk his private language of programming and schedules and controllers to fellow initiates. Only then will the outrage done to him take on comprehensible form.

'Yes, you're right,' he says. 'Maybe I'll give Christina a call.'

He gazes at Laura with the eyes of a lost child.

'I keep thinking about what must be going on in the office,' he says. 'Do they all know? I suppose they must. I suppose they must have known before I knew. Oh, hell.'

As his anger fades for want of an object, the wound in him grows.

'You know what this is?' he says. 'This is retirement.'

Bloody third stage of life. Off you go into the forest for a life of contemplation.

'Of course it isn't,' says Laura. 'It's just one project going down. It's happened before. Give it a day or two, then come up with another project.'

'Maybe.'

But he feels defeated. How long can you go on fighting? They wear you down in the end.

'Laura,' he says, 'please don't be a vegetarian. I don't think I can take it.'

'Let's talk about it later,' says Laura. 'When you're feeling better.'

12

All the way home Alan wonders what he's going to tell Liz
about his meeting with Annie Munro. He will tell her about
the meeting, of course. He and Liz are accustomed to sharing
their daily experiences. More than that, he has no one else to
tell, and he wants to talk about the meeting very much indeed.
In talking about it he hopes to come to a better understanding
of his own feelings. But how much can he tell? Liz won't mind
him renewing contact with an old girlfriend, any more than
he minds her occasional lunches with Guy Caulder, Alice's
father. But can he tell Liz that ever since meeting Annie a
fantasy has been growing in his mind, the fantasy of having sex
with her?

Obviously not.

And even if he could share with Liz his desire, he could never
act on it. So what's the point? Better to wait for the whole
flurry of excitement to die down of its own accord.

Except I gave her my number.

Maybe she won't call.

Or maybe she will.

When he gets home he finds Liz hard at work in her study.

'How's your mother?' he says.

'No change.'

He waits for her to ask him about his day, but instead she turns her screen towards him and says, 'Look.'

The headline of the article she's writing reads: WOMEN ARE AS HORNY AS MEN.

'Says who?' says Alan.

'It's a book about the science of female sexual arousal. Isn't that just amazing?'

'If it's true.'

'All the evidence says it's true.'

'Okay,' says Alan.

'You don't sound as excited as you should.'

'I'm not sure what I'm supposed to feel about it,' says Alan.

'You're supposed to feel relief. You're supposed to feel let off the hook. You don't have to pretend to be in love to get sex. Women want a one-night stand as much as you do.'

'Really?'

He's standing there, shifting from foot to foot, staring at the floor, frowning.

'You don't like it, do you?' says Liz.

'I'm just not sure I believe it.'

'Leaving that aside, do you *want* to believe it?'

'I'm not sure.'

'There. I knew it.'

'What?'

'Doesn't matter.'

She turns back to her keyboard.

'What?' says Alan, feeling that he's failed some invisible test.

'I'm working that out,' says Liz. 'Something to do with the way women are raised to feel about sex, and the way men want women to be.'

'Right,' says Alan.

He wanders off, feeling disoriented. In a little while he returns to find her typing fast.

'Shall I knock up something for supper?'

'Oh, would you?'

He finds a pack of ravioli in the fridge, and the makings of a salad. He pours himself a glass of wine. A picture comes unbidden into his mind, of Annie sitting across the table from him in Patisserie Valerie, brushing back her hair. He fills a pan with water and puts it on the Aga hotplate to boil.

She has a husband called Mitchell and a daughter called Ellie and a dog called Pretzel and she lives in Notting Hill. What does the husband do for a living? He must do well to have a house in Notting Hill. He tries to recall the tone of her voice as she showed him his photograph. No overt pride. But then, how did he sound as he showed his pictures of Liz? Neutral. Unpossessive.

Liz joins him at last, desperate for a glass of wine.

'So how was your meeting on the new film idea?'

Alan gives her the abbreviated version.

'Change the title. Change the ending. Otherwise great.'

'You could call it *The Killing of the Beautiful People*,' says Liz.

'Actually, that's not bad.'

'I'd go and see a film called that.'

She's drinking her wine and he's pottering about getting

supper and it's just impossible for Alan not to talk about what's filling his mind. This is the time of day for sharing.

'A funny thing happened today. I was walking down Carnaby Street, and guess who I bumped into? Almost literally.'

'Guy? His office is round there somewhere.'

There's a certain symmetry to the suggestion. Or there would be if Liz still wanted to have sex with Guy.

'Not Guy. Annie Munro. My first proper girlfriend.'

'The one who broke your heart?'

Alan is surprised that Liz remembers. He's been thinking of Annie to himself as the one who got away. But of course Liz is right. She was the one who broke his heart.

'Over twenty years ago now,' he says. 'I haven't seen her from that day to this. But I'd know her anywhere.'

'She hasn't changed?'

'Yes, she's changed. She's got a daughter of eighteen. A husband called Mitchell. But she still looks great.'

How much can he say to Liz? Can he say that he's been thinking about Annie all day? Can he say that all the time he was sitting in the café with Annie he was shaking?

'Why did you never keep up with her?' says Liz.

She's interested, but no more than that. Not jealous.

'I was too hurt by the break-up. I told myself the only way I could deal with it was to cut myself off completely. So that's what I did.'

'When me and Guy split up we went on seeing each other.'

'You're made of stronger stuff than I am.'

'I was an idiot. I should have cut him off. I meant to. But then he'd come round, and we'd end up in bed. It was the only thing he was good at.'

87

'That's the difference,' says Alan. 'With me and Annie it was the one thing I was no good at.'

'What, the sex?'

'Yes.'

So there it is: the simple failure at the root of it all. Not so much broke his heart as discovered him to be a sexual washout. All through today, all the way home on the train, Alan has failed to remember and reflect on this one crucial aspect of their break-up. Five minutes with Liz and out it comes. You'd think it would be the one thing he'd want to keep quiet about. Instead it's entirely the other way. He feels a compulsion to confess the failures of the past.

'I can't believe that, Alan.'

'No, it's true.' He attacks the sealed pack of ravioli with a paring knife. 'I was rubbish.'

'What did you do wrong?'

'Just about everything. I was very nervous. I kept waiting to be told what to do. Then when it happened, no thanks to me, I couldn't hold back. I tried counting. I tried times tables. You know that way of counting where you go One Mississippi, Two Mississippi? I couldn't even make it to the first -ippi.'

Liz laughs.

The water's bubbling in the pan. Alan tips in the ravioli and sets the timer.

'It was torture. You know, sex is supposed to be fun.'

'So is that why she dumped you?'

'Of course it was,' he says. 'She never said so. But you would, wouldn't you?'

'Like a shot. Before you could say Mississ.'

She puts her arms round him and kisses him.

'What a dope you are,' she says.

Then a further insight follows.

'When I met her today,' Alan says, 'all I wanted to tell her was, I can do it properly now.'

Cas appears in the kitchen doorway.

'When's supper?'

'Five minutes,' says Alan.

'Okay,' says Cas, and disappears.

'Is it just me,' says Alan, 'or is Cas slowly losing the habit of speech?'

'I think something's wrong at school,' says Liz. 'I tried to get him to tell me but he wouldn't.'

'I'll have a go at him,' says Alan.

He tries to remember what life was like at thirteen years old. All he can recall is the longing to masturbate.

Liz says, 'So do you want a testimonial from me?'

'What testimonial?'

'Saying you're a great lover. To give your old girlfriend.'

'Yes, please.'

Before him an image rises of Annie opening the envelope containing the imaginary testimonial, and reading it, and looking up from the letter to meet his eyes. In his fantasy her eyes are bright with laughing desire.

This is becoming ridiculous.

'So what are you going to do about it?' says Liz.

'Do about what?'

'Will you see her again?'

'Oh, I doubt it. I don't have any number for her or anything.'

'Shame,' says Liz. 'I'd have liked to meet her.'

Alan knows that what he has just said is technically the truth, but that nevertheless he has told a lie. How can he say that he gave Annie his number?

'If I ever meet her,' Liz says, 'I'll tell her.'

'Tell her what?'

'How good you are in bed.'

13

'So who exactly is this boy?' Mitchell Hamer says to his daughter, Ellie, across the dinner table.

'He's just a boy,' says Ellie.

'He's not a student, is he? Annie says he works in a garage.'

'Everyone's a student,' says Ellie. 'A student's someone who learns things. Everyone learns things.'

'But what do you have in common with him?'

'Dancing,' says Ellie.

'Christ, give me strength!' says Mitch.

Ellie gets up, her plate of shepherd's pie only half eaten.

'Have to go,' she says.

'But you haven't finished,' says Annie.

'I only came to say goodbye to Dad.'

Mitch leaves tonight for Cape Town.

'You can't just walk out like this, Ellie,' says Mitch. 'This is your home.'

'I don't live here any more, Dad.'

Ellie is, as ever, disconcertingly self-possessed. She doesn't get emotional. She just does what the hell she likes. Annie, looking on, seeing Mitch go pink in the face, almost admires her for it.

'And, anyway, I have to meet Franco.'

Franco, the dancing boyfriend.

'You could at least stay to see me off,' says Mitch.

'You're always going off, Dad,' says Ellie. 'It's no big deal. Have a wonderful trip.'

She gives him a quick kiss.

'Bye, Mum.'

And she's gone.

'That girl,' says Mitch, irritably, 'shouldn't treat you like that. She just takes what you do for her for granted. Sometimes I want to smack her.'

'Oh, she's just being young,' says Annie. 'Young people get so caught up in their own lives.'

Mitch's phone pings with an incoming text.

'Praise the Lord!' he says, reading it. 'I've been upgraded!'

He, too, jumps up from the table. It seems dinner is over.

'I'd better sort myself out. The car's picking me up in half an hour.'

Alone in the kitchen, moving slowly about the room clearing away the dirty dishes, Annie realizes how much he irritates her when he says, 'Praise the Lord!' He thinks he's using the expression humorously, he's no happy-clappy evangelical, but even so it's a creepy way to express pleasure. Mitch grew up in a religious family, and although he's long outgrown his childhood faith, some traces linger.

So far she hasn't told him about her encounter with Alan

Strachan. It's not a secret, there's nothing to hide. The opportunity simply hasn't arisen.

She comes to a stop by the sink and, for a brief moment, closes her eyes. She sees Alan before her, sipping his coffee. She sees his eyes on her, and though he says nothing, she knows that he wants her.

She allows her imagination to take the encounter further. They're standing in the street, parting. Suddenly he pulls her close and kisses her. She kisses him back. She can feel his hands on her bum, pressing her against his body. He's hungry for her, he has to have her. She moves her hips against his, just a little, but enough to show him she's willing. He whispers close into her ear, 'Annie, I want to fuck you so much—'

Mitch comes back down, his suitcase packed.

'I wish I wasn't going away just now,' he says.

'I wish you weren't going away.'

She doesn't turn round at once, afraid her cheeks may be burning. What she says is no lie: she hates Mitch going away. Now more than ever, with a number loaded into her phone that she can call with the touch of one fingertip.

It's not my fault, she thinks. He goes away too much, two weeks in every four. The job requires it, but there are other jobs, aren't there? When he worked in the City his hours were so long she hardly ever saw him. Now he's *saving the world* he's in South Africa half the time. *Saving the world* is her private term for his work as finance director for a charity. It's shorthand for *saving everyone else and abandoning me*. He's always saying how happy he is at having got out of the City, but he's still a workaholic.

'I mean because of Ellie,' he says.

'Ellie's fine,' says Annie.

'Don't you think we should check this boy out? I mean, what does Ellie know about him? You know he's Italian?'

'Second-generation Italian.'

'She met him in a club. He could be into drugs. He could be anything. We know nothing about him.'

'She's very keen on him, that's for sure.'

'All a boy wants when he's that age is one thing.'

'Maybe that's all Ellie wants.'

Mitch sits down and lays his hands flat on the kitchen table. This is his I'm-being-serious-now posture. He frowns, which makes his face look lopsided.

'Be serious for a moment, Annie. This boy's not a fellow student, he works in a garage. I wouldn't mind if it was just some passing fancy, but she says it's not.'

'She says she's in love.'

'Well, there you are. I see trouble ahead.'

Secretly Annie agrees with Mitch, but at the same time she finds his concern pompous.

'I'd have thought she'd be more likely to meet a druggie on campus,' she says.

'Get her to bring him home,' says Mitch. 'He needs to know she's got a protective family.'

'What are we supposed to be protecting her from?'

'I know what boys are like.' He looks at his watch, then at his boarding pass. 'I just wish I wasn't going away right now.'

Annie thinks she knows what boys are like rather better than he does.

'Speaking of boys,' she says, 'did I ever tell you about the student boyfriend I had once, called Alan?'

'I wouldn't want to be called Alan.'

'I bumped into him this morning, in Carnaby Street. I haven't seen him for God knows how long. The funny thing is he was just the same.'

Mitch puts away his documents. Annie can see his mind is not on what she's saying. Why should it be? It's only idle chatter.

'You've no idea how pleased I am to have been upgraded,' he says. 'It means I'll get a bed. That makes all the difference. Diane must have pulled strings at the other end. I think she knows someone in South African Airways.'

He looks at his watch again. After all, the time does keep changing.

'Car'll be here any minute.'

'I wish you didn't have this bloody job,' says Annie.

Mitch looks surprised.

'I'm fifty-five,' he says. 'I'm lucky to have it. I won't get another job at this level. I know it takes me away a lot, but we've managed all right with that, haven't we?'

His face is saying, I've been a good provider, haven't I? I've been loyal and trustworthy, haven't I? And at least what I do makes a difference.

'At least what I do makes a difference,' he says. 'Not much, I know, but it's better than nothing.'

'Yes,' she says. 'You're right.'

Another ping from his phone. The car's arrived outside. Mitch seizes his suitcase and heads for the door. He gives Annie a kiss.

'See you in two weeks.'

★

Alone in the house she sits for a while doing nothing. She always hates it when Mitch goes. Somehow she's still not got used to being left, to the physical process of closing the front door after him, and being alone. Tonight she'll feel lonely; by tomorrow she'll have adjusted, and life will go on. She knows her patterns.

Then there's the anger. This is something she's been admitting to herself more and more over recent months, ever since Ellie moved out to live in a university hall. Her anger is unjust and unattractive, she knows, but there it is. She's angry with Mitch for putting his job before her.

It's not that she expects him to be by her side day and night, but the evenings would be nice. At least once a day would be nice. You need someone in your life to tell your day to, for the day to feel as if it actually happened. If there's no one to tell, you start to lose your anchorage. You float about, drifting on strange currents, and after a while you're not sure who you are any more.

This house is too big for me alone, she thinks.

They bought it when Mitch was making more money than they could spend. Back then they'd assumed there would be two children, or three, or four, large families now the luxury of the rich. But after Ellie there had been what the doctors called complications, which took the form of a simplification. One child is simpler than four.

The house has four bedrooms, one of which is converted to her use as an office. She chose the room at the top of the house, where the window looks out over the line of back gardens. Up there, by daylight, she can imagine she's in a tree-house, among the clouds. Mitch was surprised by her choice. 'Such a haul to get up there!' But it's what she likes, the expenditure of effort, the sensation of going somewhere else.

She climbs the stairs now, past the floor that contains their bedroom with its palatial bathroom; past Ellie's room, and the guest bedroom that never has a guest, and the guest bathroom where the shower periodically seizes up due to underuse. Annie has to ask their cleaning lady to run it once a month to keep it functioning. What sort of message does that send? Mitchell Hamer, finance director of Ubuntu Africa, a charity dedicated to building community facilities in the poorest regions of the world, paying a servant to run showers for ghosts.

Actually, Annie rather appreciates that sort of irony. Ubuntu Africa is her rival, her enemy. Because Ubuntu Africa is good and cares for the world, Annie feels herself to be selfish and bad. She's tried to explain this to Mitch, but he was simply baffled. 'So would you rather I went back to investment banking?'

Up in her office Annie opens her screen calendar and looks down the list of jobs to be done. An office block under construction in Clerkenwell requires a large artwork for the lobby. The brief is *edgy but inclusive*. The prospective clients for the office space like to think of themselves as creative. This is the sort of work Annie commissions on a regular basis, acting as intermediary between developer and artist. Not high end, not great art bought for investment, but works supplied to a size and to a price. It's a kind of decoration. The artists in the supply chain are skilful, well paid, and grateful.

One of them, an artist called Fintan Doyle, works on the

scale required for the Clerkenwell job. He also happens to live in Lewes.

Well, would it be so wrong? Make a phone call to an old friend, look him up when you're in his neighbourhood, talk about old times. As for the other fantasy, of course that's ridiculous. He has a partner, and we're both middle-aged.

She tries to remember her time with Alan all those years ago. The details have become hazy, but she retains a strong emotional memory of a life that was both unpredictable and passionate. She remembers thinking how beautiful Alan was when they first met, and she remembers their parting, and how she felt burdened by his pain. The strange thing is that now, after so long, even his pain attracts her. It's as if she wants to find again through him a range of emotions that have become closed to her.

Then there's the new Alan, the man she met in the street. He's sufficiently like the old Alan for her to feel a right of ownership in him, but this is the old Alan made complete.

On an impulse she Googles his name. There's a personal trainer called Alan Strachan. And a film director. And then, there he is: Alan Strachan the screenwriter. She gazes at his list of credits with respect. He's made something of himself.

The way he looked at me. Surely I'm not wrong.

She lets the fantasy begin again. It's only a game. There's no harm in thinking a man wants you. God knows it doesn't happen that often. In a few short years it'll never happen at all. You can't help being flattered.

Why did he give me his number and not ask for mine? Because he wants me to make the first move. That way he can be sure I'm interested without revealing whether he is. Except he revealed it every time he looked at me.

I could go down to Lewes tomorrow, talk to Fintan Doyle about the Clerkenwell job. There's nothing else on.

Oh, yes, it's Election Day. I'll vote before I leave.

14

As Henry Broad gets ready for bed that night he can hear, faint through the intervening walls, the vibrations of Carrie's guitar. Laura is in the bathroom taking off her make-up. After all his plans, he has done nothing today. A certain amount of time on screens, a certain amount of time in the deep armchair in his study, playing music on the radio. He has allowed Laura to think he's been making plans for the future, but there are no plans. He has been holed up like a wounded animal.

The strange thing is that something in him knew this was coming. When he woke in the night filled with a nameless dread, what was it but a premonition? Animals can tell when a storm is coming, they sense the change of pressure in the air. Time to seek the safety of the burrow.

For all his inertia he doesn't feel rested. The blow has fallen, but he remains tensed for the next and far greater blow, though quite what that might be he's unable to say. Just let it end, he thinks. Let the struggle be over. Why must life be so wearisome?

He gets into bed and pulls the duvet close round him. He has a sudden memory of boarding school, and getting to bed, and feeling safe at last.

My bed the fortress. But am I safe?

He called Christina earlier, an old colleague, one he has always suspected had a soft spot for him. At such times one chooses who to call with care. Christina had been suitably appalled on his behalf, which is to say, shocked but not too shocked. These things happen, she said. All careers have downs as well as ups. Don't overreact. But it doesn't feel like a down, it feels like a dismantling. The self so laboriously constructed over long years begins to fall apart. Take this election. Until today he's followed the campaigns with almost hourly interest, and would have called himself well informed. He's certainly been ready with opinions. He can talk freely on the new popular hunger for authenticity, the failure of the mainstream parties to connect with the electorate, and the breakdown of the old political tribes. But all at once he's stopped talking. He's not even sure what he thinks any more. He's not sure he thinks anything. He's not sure who it is that is doing the thinking. It seems to him now, lying in bed waiting for Laura to join him, that all his opinions are no more than borrowings from newspapers, radio programmes, magazines, draped about the tailor's dummy of an otherwise blank self. Headless, faceless, mindless.

But I overreact.

It comes as a shock to discover how dependent he is on the respect of his professional peers. Michael Marcus, for God's sake! The sad has-been they all call 'poor old Michael'. So is it now 'poor old Henry'?

He hears the click of the bathroom light as Laura turns it off, and she's crossing the room to the bed. Now the click of the bedroom light, and the room is dark as she gets beneath the duvet beside him. Her hand feels for his.

'I've not forgotten my promise,' she whispers.

But he has. Now, feeling the kindness of her body close to his, desire returns. He rolls onto his side and lays one arm over her.

'Still here,' she says.

She wriggles beneath his arm, and he realizes she's pulling off her pyjama bottoms. He's filled with gratitude that she should choose in so simple a way to show him that he still exists after all. She must have been thinking of it in the bathroom, she must have been saying to herself, I know what'll cheer Henry up, we'll fuck. No, she would have said 'make love', because love is what it is.

They lie together, folded close, and with one hand she strokes his cock to life. He feels it tingle and grow, and it's like the return of life itself. His cock is saying, What do I care about your career? Just get me started and I'll get on with it. As his erection grows he feels the absurdity of his earlier fears. This Henry, made of the respect of others, dressed in opinions, this Henry, who has turned out to be so fragile, is no more than a puff of air beside his true sexual self. Just let his cock go hard, and all is simple.

He hears Carrie's guitar, plaintive in her room.

'We'll have to be very quiet,' whispers Laura.

It's not how they like to make love, but it'll do.

He pushes close against her, his boxer shorts now half

down, his cock free. For a while their hands do the work, exciting each other, kissing mouth to mouth as they do so. Then he's on top of her, finding his way in, and the fuck proper begins.

'Love you,' he whispers, 'love you,' in time with his thrusts, 'love you.'

Forceful love. Deep love.

And then it starts to go wrong.

'Slowly,' whispers Laura. 'Slowly.'

He slows down. It's going wrong.

Stay calm. Stay in the moment. This is simple. This is something you want. You've been wanting it for days. Take it. Have it. Do it. Fuck your heart out.

But with each thrust he can feel his cock going softer. This is not a reversible process. Neither is it one over which he has any control. His cock has its own mind, and goes its own way.

Why? Doesn't my cock want the big bang pay-off? Isn't that what we're here for, my cock and me? I want it. What's my cock's problem?

'Sorry,' he whispers.

'Give it a moment,' Laura whispers back.

She kisses him, a series of quick soft kisses. Love kisses. Pity kisses.

He moves off her, but stays close.

'Don't know what that's about,' he says.

'Doesn't matter. It'll come back.'

But there'll be no coming back tonight. His cock shrivels steadily, remorselessly, until it reaches its smallest possible size, where it's almost invisible. Like a child hiding under the bed-clothes, playing I'm-not-here. If I can't see you, you can't see me.

He draws his shorts back up.

'Maybe tomorrow,' says Laura.

'Maybe.'

It's not as if it hasn't happened before, but usually there's been a physical reason. Too tired, too boozed. This isn't physical, this is psychological, and he hates that. It's easy to get more sleep, or consume less alcohol, but how do you tell yourself your life's great when it's not?

Sex is supposed to bypass psychology. Isn't it driven by the lizard brain, the most primitive part of the nervous system? What do my hormones care if I'm out of a job? If I'm feeling in need of a treat and I get myself a slice of ginger cake, my hand doesn't go floppy as I raise the cake to my mouth. What's the point of a physical mechanism that operates independently of the will? Who's in charge round here?

What does my cock know that I don't?

That I'm a loser. That I'm finished. That it's all downhill from here. Losers are not wanted in the gene pool. Evolution has found ways of eliminating us. Stop believing in yourself and your cock checks out.

Nature is merciless.

Laura kisses him again, this time a goodnight kiss, and rolls over onto her side. Usually after they've made love she goes to sleep without reading. He waits to see if she'll reach for her book, but honouring the intent if not the act, she turns out her bedside lamp and murmurs, 'Night.'

Henry lies awake and wretched. He sees the red numerals of

the clock. Just past midnight. Election Day has begun. Are they in bed, Cameron, Miliband, Clegg? Are they having sex? Can they get it up? By the end of tomorrow it could be over for all three of them. Lose an election and you lose your erection. So it all comes down to power after all.

Thursday, 7 May 2015

15

As the first light of day begins to flush the eastern sky, the blackbirds start up with their chuckling cries, yip-yip-yippee. Then come the thrushes singing chippy-chippy-ee-you, peep-you peep-you, and the high trills of the robins, water spilling down metal, chink-chink-chink. The light strengthens, and other birds join the chorus, the goldfinches with their hiya-you!, the multiple cheeps of the chiffchaff, the chatter of the sparrows. Not a chorus of praise for the new day, but cries of warning, anger, self-advertisement. The birds are claiming territory, asserting dominion. Peep-you, peep-you! Chink-chink-chink!

The sky turns white and the burning edge of the sun climbs over the rim of the Downs. The early flights out of Gatwick drone high overhead, on their way to Faro, Thessaloniki, Kerkyra. Heavy lorries roll off the A27 onto the Newhaven road to pick up the morning ferry to Dieppe.

In Edenfield's village hall the doors are open already, and John Turner, the presiding officer, is checking the layout of the polling booths. Penny Allsobrook, the poll clerk, has a kettle on in the little kitchen to make a pot of tea. John Turner carries the two locked ballot boxes out of his car to the table where he will sit all through the coming day. The Electoral Commission is strict about poll opening hours, and John Turner wishes to be 100 per cent sure that everything will be ready for seven a.m.

Today will be a momentous day. The *Guardian*'s headline is: IT COULDN'T BE CLOSER. *The Times* predicts: QUEEN TO TAKE CONTROL OF ELECTION AFTERMATH.

'Every single vote counts,' John Turner says.

'Did you see Richard Littlejohn in the *Mail* yesterday?' says his clerk. 'He says voting Labour's like having Jimmy Savile in to babysit.'

'No political opinions in the polling station,' says the presiding officer.

'Don't you start presiding over me, John Turner. If the papers are allowed opinions, then so am I.'

'Opinions finished yesterday,' says John Turner, who knows the rules. 'Today we speak through the ballot box.'

16

First thing in the morning, Liz Dickinson drives from Hamsey into Lewes, and through the town to her mother's house. As usual there has been no change in the night. Karen and Bridget are in the kitchen sharing scrambled eggs on toast. The two carers have become friends, bonded by Mrs Dickinson's mendacious accusations. Bridget is constantly astonished by Karen's tales of her life in Zimbabwe.

'It was their farm,' she tells Liz. 'They'd been there a hundred years, and the blacks came and took it. Just because Karen's family was white! I'm no racist, Liz, you know that, but I say they had no right. Just because you're black doesn't mean you can take anything you want. And they don't even know how to farm! Karen says it'll turn back into bush in five years.'

Liz says, 'You know it's Election Day today.'

'Oh, I don't bother with that,' says Bridget. 'They're all the same. They're just out for themselves.'

Karen has put a little bunch of flowers on the kitchen table. Liz remembers how she once brought her mother flowers on her wedding anniversary. It was never spoken about, but Liz had understood from an early age that 11 June was a day of sadness and mourning, a day on which her mother would be distant and distracted, and busier than usual, without quite knowing what it was she did. One year, when Liz was twelve years old, she brought her mother flowers on the fatal day, meaning to say to her, Look, you still have me. Her mother had burst into tears, and hugged and kissed her. Sometimes Liz could still feel her mother's tears on her own cheeks.

After all's said and done, she did love me. I did grow up knowing there was one person in the world who made me the centre of her life. Then later I had a little girl of my own, and I did the same for her.

Liz feels a sudden ache of longing for her daughter. She wants to phone her, she wants to ask her to come home, she could tell her Granny's come to the end. Except there could be days to go, weeks, months, no one knows. And it would be a lie. She wants Alice for herself.

Only you and me, Addle. We don't need anyone else in all the world.

For eleven years, before she met Alan, it was just the two of them. It frightens Liz sometimes how much she loves Alice. She can feel her skinny little body in her arms even now, clinging to her, defending her even as she sought to be defended herself.

'I'll always love you, Mum. For ever and ever.'

Was it like that for Aster and me? Did she love me with the same bright, burning intensity? Does she still?

She looks over at the shrunken old lady lying so motionless in the hospital bed. Love decays into need, need hardens into tyranny. But there was a time when she was everything to me.

'The nurse is late,' says Bridget.

The district nurse comes every day now, at variable times. She oversees the medication regime, though she does not set the levels of the various drugs. That's the job of the palliative-care nurse.

'Won't be long,' says Karen, seeing Liz looking at her mother. Karen has worked as a carer for many years, and has been present at many deaths.

'Doesn't it get you down?' Bridget is a little morbid in her curiosity.

'Bless you, no,' says Karen. 'By the time they're ready to go you know it's for the best. It's not nice for them in the last days, you can tell from their faces it's hard work. And then it's over, and they can rest.'

Liz looks at her mother's worn face, eyes closed, mouth open, grimly clinging to life. It's been hard work for her for a long time. Her breathing is slow, steady, with a rasp on each exhalation.

Pip-pip-pip-pip-pip-pip. The syringe driver under the pillow starts to bleep, warning that it's about to run out. Each refill lasts for twenty-four hours.

'There you are,' says Bridget. 'I said the nurse was late.'

There's a part of Bridget that feeds on drama, even tragedy. She has no wish for anyone to suffer, but she becomes particularly attentive when things go wrong.

'Does that mean the sedatives will stop working?' says Liz.

'Should be fine,' says Karen. 'The nurse'll be here soon.'

'Let's hope she's in time,' says Bridget, wagging her head as if to say, 'Hope won't peel the potatoes.'

Liz resolves to stay at her mother's house until the nurse comes in order to get her latest estimate of how much longer her mother can live. She knows these estimates are meaningless, but she clings to them even so, seeking markers of any kind in this featureless terrain where days melt into nights.

She settles down beside her mother's bed and watches her sleeping face. So hard not to believe that she'll wake, and look at her, and say, 'Oh, Elizabeth!' It's eternal life that feels natural, and death that's impossible to comprehend.

She puts out one hand and strokes her mother's brow, pushing back a lock of fine white hair. She knows this face so well that it doesn't seem old to her, for all its wrinkles. This is the face of the one person in all the world who has always been there, and always will be there. She can't die. To die is to leave, and leaving is the great betrayal.

Is that why you won't die, Mummy? For me?

The gummy eyes flick open, and there she is, gazing up at her. The dry mouth closes, the lips move. A faint creaking sound climbs up from her throat. Liz is transfixed with terror and love. She withdraws her hand. What she sees in those sharp little eyes is irritation. What she hears in that crackly attempt at speech is a faint echo of the words her mother spoke to her a month ago and more, when she had stroked her hair as she is stroking her today.

What she had said then was, 'Stop petting me.'

Liz's earlier impulse of almost-love is engulfed in a new emotion, of helplessness and horror.

'Look at that!' exclaims Bridget. 'She's back!'

'Mummy,' says Liz. 'Can you hear me?'

The eyes close again. More noises from her mouth, but fading now, as if she's slipping back into whatever depths enfold her. Liz looks on, still in shock.

Did she know me? Surely she did. That beady stare was too familiar. It said what it has always said: My life is unbearable. Why can't you make it better? Self-obsessed to the end, it never occurs to her that Liz, her only child, might appreciate some little sign of love. But it's easier this way, perhaps. The burden of guilt is lifted, or at least lightened.

Go now, Mummy. Just go. It's over.

Aster dreams, and in her dream she sees her daughter Elizabeth. She asks Elizabeth to help her out of bed, because she has become too weak to manage on her own. Elizabeth stares at her and does nothing. Then Aster realizes that her request is foolish. How could Elizabeth help her? She's only a little child. Such a pretty little child, much prettier than Aster was at her age. She's back from school, she'll be wanting her tea and there's nothing in the house. How did that happen?

I must have overslept.

At least I'm a good mother. No one can take that away from me. Rex will have to admit, when he returns, that I've brought up our child well.

When Rex returns he'll look just the same. Not a handsome man, but such a kind face. When he takes off his spectacles to rub at them with his little cloth, his eyes go soft and dreamy. He'll come walking down the path to the front door, and why not? This is his house, the house he paid for. She'll see him coming – she's looked out of the window so often, expecting this moment so often, she'll be ready – and she'll open the door before he can ring the bell. 'You've been gone a long time, Rex,' she'll say.

And he'll say, 'Yes, but I'm back now.'

Help me up, Rex. I find it hard to sit up, I don't know why. I'll put on a kettle for a cup of tea, only I feel so tired. I expect it's some chemical deficiency. I should be given medicine for it, but the doctor does nothing. I'm afraid the National Health Service is not what it was. I've told them I'll pay if necessary, but no one does anything.

I'm so glad you're back, Rex. You can tell those carers to go. They steal things, you know. And they pinch me. Elizabeth won't believe it, but it's true. You know, you look the same as ever. I knew you would. Have I changed much? I'll just rest here for a moment, if you don't mind.

Let's not talk about what happened back then. It's all in the past. But you did make me so unhappy, Rex. You must have known that. That's what I don't understand. Didn't you care that I was unhappy? It would have been easier for me if you'd died. I wish you had died. I wanted to kill you. I wish I had killed you. I want you to die. I want you to go away for ever. I want to know you're never, ever coming back. I don't want to stand by the hall window looking up the front path any more.

I hate you, Rex. You stole my life. You're the only man I ever loved and the only man I ever hated. But I don't want to talk about that. I know you like a quiet life. I'll be quiet, my dearest. I'll be quiet.

The district nurse comes, and sees at once that the syringe driver has run out.

'Oh, my Lord!' she says, as she bustles about with her great box of medications. 'I don't know how that's happened.'

'She woke up,' says Liz. 'She opened her eyes.'

'Did she seem to be in pain?'

'I don't know. It's hard to tell.'

'Well, we'll have her all fixed up again in a couple of ticks.'

The syringe is reloaded, the timer reset. The nurse checks the line to the cannula that is taped to the blotched, withered arm. The old lady sleeps on.

'She was awake in the night too,' says Karen. 'Seemed as if she was struggling to get out of bed.'

'I don't understand it,' says the nurse. 'She's on fifteen milligrams of oxycodone.'

'Should you be giving her a bigger dose?' says Liz.

'That's not for me to say. You'll have to ask the palliative-care team. But it's not right that she's waking up. The medication is supposed to keep her comfortable.'

Over these days of her mother's dying Liz has learned the code and its limitations. The care system accepts a responsibility to remove pain, but not to assist death. This zone between suffering and extinction is called 'comfort'.

'She's a tough one,' says the nurse.

'How much longer do you think it could be?'

'I never thought she'd make it this far, to be honest. I wouldn't like to say.'

Liz wants to shout at her: Tell me! Name a limit! I can't stand this never-ending ending. But she says nothing. The code decrees that all concerned are on the side of life. Life, of course, and comfort.

★

On her way home Liz stops to vote. She had thought she would vote LibDem, as she did last time, but faced by the list of candidates she changes her mind and votes Labour. The election is so up in the air, its outcome so unpredictable, that it feels wrong to vote tactically. This is an election that Labour just might win, and Liz wants to be part of that victory. Norman Baker, the sitting LibDem MP, has a secure majority. The Labour candidate won't be elected for Lewes. But Liz's vote will be counted.

As she leaves the polling station she finds she likes what she's done. It makes her feel part of the onward march of history.

She tells Alan, 'It was a vote for the future.'

17

After breakfast Henry Broad walks down the rutted lane from his house into the village. Bluebells are out in the verges, and the cow parsley is just beginning to unfold its white froth. It's a cool day, a layer of thin cloud screening the sun, but for all that, the spring is dazzling. To one side the line of chestnuts reach out their fresh green fingers, drooping hands asking to be kissed. In the field beyond, the grass is a darker green, richly drenched with dew in the shadow of the church tower. He passes the row of cottages with their neatly tended front lawns, all but one of them second homes, and so comes to the road proper, at the corner by the village shop. He nods at Harold Jones, at his station behind his till. The little sub-post office keeps the shop going, just. Local people these days buy their provisions at Aldi and Tesco and Waitrose. And so along the narrow pavement to the village hall, built in the 1930s in the Tudorbethan style, so long despised, now ageing into dignity.

Others are out on the same errand.

'Morning, Henry. Off to do your duty?'

'Morning, Jim.'

Cars are pulling into the village hall's car park, as party workers ferry aged voters to the poll. The hall doors stand open.
On either side sit party monitors with identifying rosettes, lists
of eligible voters in their hands.

'Morning, Henry. Not such a bad day, after all.'

He goes into the hall. Here, where the village puts on its
annual panto, where the flower show is held, where on Tuesday
evenings women do yoga, the space has been stripped and laid
out for the serious ritual of voting. One long table on the right
is under the command of the presiding officer, John Turner, a
retired accountant now invested with all the gravitas of a high-
court judge. To his right, at another table, sits Penny Allsobrook,
the poll clerk. At the stage end of the hall, four booths have
been erected, modern structures with triangular plastic shelves,
each partly but incompletely screened from its neighbour, like
public urinals. And on the left side, in magnificent isolation on
a trestle table, stand the two ballot boxes. They are securely
sealed, and have slotted lids, but this does not disguise the fact
that they exactly resemble grey plastic waste bins.

Henry comes to a stop inside the doors and gazes at the
scene. The solemnity of the proceedings strikes him for the
first time as absurd. This is fabled democracy in action, this
ponderous process of checking names on lists, of ballot papers
and ostentatious secrecy. He sees it now for what it is, a theat-
rical piece of misdirection to make people believe their opinions
matter. This election will be determined by the voters in the
few dozen constituencies where the result is not a foregone
conclusion; whose votes will have no bearing on the way the
parties form their coalitions; which in turn, once in power, can

do nothing to change the course of events. An illusion of choice over an illusion of control.

Henry is not in a balanced state of mind, but perhaps it takes a little unbalancing to see things as they really are. Who is he going to vote for? And why? Yesterday morning he would have answered in terms of political analysis. Cameron and Osborne have held the line on the deficit; the economy is on the mend. Miliband understands the damage ever-increasing levels of inequality do to the social fabric. Clegg and his LibDems have been a vital brake on the extremes of the main parties. But now he sees what nonsense it all is, what a pompous pretence of knowing how the world works.

Look at Lily Linton, even now huddled in the voting booth, preparing to put her mark on a ballot paper. Lily is a farmer's daughter. She comes from a family displaced in terms of status by the new breed of City workers who have invaded the countryside but have no understanding of country life. Lily will have breathed in resentment of metropolitan elites all her young life. She's incapable of voting Labour or LibDem, though who knows, perhaps her pencil is hovering over the UKIP candidate. Look at Nick Critchell, in his Barbour and Hunter boots, Nick who used to work for Lloyds and now calls himself a consultant, carrying his ballot paper over to a booth. Nick regards anyone to the left of Margaret Thatcher as delusional, because he's so strongly invested in his own self-image as one who has *done it on his own*. He calls welfare 'workfare' and says it creates dependency, which is just his way of advertising his own self-made strength. Look at Julie Sutton, just come into the village hall in her stretch fabric jeans and clinging jumper, which do her full figure no favours. Julie will vote Labour, though she has no love for Ed Miliband, or comprehension of his policies. She and Terry scrape a hard living off the odd jobs provided for cash by the second-home owners. Naturally they resent the unequal division of wealth and hate the markers of privilege. All of them, every one of them, votes instinctively, reflexively, thoughtlessly, driven by the most primitive emotions.

'Hello, Henry. You look as if you're miles away.'

'Oh, hello, Nick. Yes, I suppose I am.'

'Big day. We need the Tories to finish the job. No one wants poor little Ed riding in on the coat-tails of the SNP.'

'Well, we'll know soon enough.'

'Love to Laura.'

'And to Alison.'

Nick strides off, giving genial nods to the party workers by the doors. The Tory worker ticks off his name. Henry watches as old Dick Waller is assisted into the hall. Dick Waller must be close to ninety, but here he is, stick in hand, head held high, doing his duty.

What a joke democracy is. What a game, devised by those who control the levers of power to flatter the rest of us into supposing we make a difference. The ruling class still wage the wars they want, and take the profits, whoever we poor foolish voters raise up or tear down. And how elaborately they've devised the game! The voting in the village hall, the counting of the votes in the town hall, the drama of the winning and losing of seats, the success of this party or that, the triumphal entry of a new man into Downing Street to the giddy heights of government, all to create the illusion of change. But still the banks boom and crash as they did before, the jobs melt away, the price of property inflates and the value of pensions dwindles, just as if some other party had been swept to glory.

And yet I must vote.

Henry realizes he wants to use his vote as an act of violent protest. He wishes there was an anarchist candidate, or one of the satirical parties of his youth, the Monster Raving Loonies. UKIP was a joke once, but not any more. So who gets the votes of the angry, the wounded, the disappointed? How can I show my contempt?

As this thought forms in his mind, Henry understands, with a shock of shame, what is happening to him. Politics as emotion indeed! Yesterday's failures are working their way into his system, like a drug trickled into a vein, slowly reconstructing his idea of himself. Not so long ago he was a well-paid, well-respected member of the opinion-forming classes, who therefore took his own opinions seriously. Now he is unpaid, unlistened-to, unrespected. The very taste of opinions is turning sour in his mouth. No wonder the old become so comically angry. Ours is the anger of the impotent.

Ah, yes! Impotent indeed.

How am I to vote? It would be an absurdity for me to vote.

And yet some deeper impulse compels him to go through the process, like a believer who has lost his faith but still drops to his knees in church. Henry may be angry, but he has no wish to draw undue attention to himself. So add this, too, to the tally of magical forces that give the zombie democracy its appearance of life: emotional identity, tribal habit, social conformism.

He goes to the long desk and hands over his voting card. John Turner acknowledges with a smile the time Henry has spent looking about him.

'Made your mind up, then?'

He tears the ballot papers carefully from the book.

'White in the box with the white label. Yellow in the box with the yellow label.'

Henry carries his ballot papers the few paces to a booth, with its high shelf and its short pencil on a string. He stares at the list of names on the white paper. In the past he's put his cross by Norman Baker of the LibDems, following the Lewes pattern of tactical voting that has virtually eliminated the Labour vote, but has kept the Tories out. This time, however, the LibDems have been in coalition with the Tories. A vote for Norman Baker is in a sense an endorsement of the present government.

Is that what I want?

Henry stares helplessly at the second, yellow, ballot paper. It offers a list of district councillors, none of whose names mean anything to him. Even if they did, he has no idea any longer what he wants. None of the parties embodies his hopes. None of the leaders excites his admiration. So, after a further moment of indecision, or lack of decision, he leaves both ballot papers unmarked, folds them in half and then in half again, and posts them through the slots in the ballot boxes. White into white, yellow into yellow, as instructed.

As he leaves the hall the party workers smile and nod, while studiously refraining from asking him how he cast his vote. The secrecy of the ballot is a pillar of the glorious tradition of British democracy. Henry has no desire to tell them that even now his papers lie blank in the boxes, mute witnesses to one citizen's loss of faith.

18

Driving down to Sussex, Annie Hamer feels absurdly excited.

Getting closer. Getting closer.

Visiting artists in their studios is the part of her job she most enjoys. She likes the company of artists, for all their moodiness and egocentricity, and she likes playing the fairy godmother. But as the A23 approaches Brighton, as she turns off the A27 into Lewes, it's Alan Strachan who fills her mind.

Will I call him?

She's going to wait and see.

This is an odd way to look at the matter, as if she's someone else whose actions are unpredictable to her. When in the middle of a long morning at work she goes down to the kitchen to make a sustaining cup of tea, she often says to herself, as she descends the stairs, 'I wonder if I'll have a cookie too.' There's a kind of cookie she likes very much, it's called Chewy & Fruity, and it comes in a box of a purplish colour. Her policy, as a rule, is that she doesn't snack between meals, but every now and again the longing for a cookie overcomes her better self and she reaches up to the high shelf where the purplish box lives. She keeps the cookies high up so that she won't take one without knowing she's doing it. So now, when the action unfolds, the hand reaches up, the fingers extract the cookie from its nests of packaging, and she looks on with the air of a neutral observer. 'I see I've decided to have a cookie today.'

When was the decision taken? As early as the moment she rose from her desk chair, three floors up? Or just now, as she entered the larder, which also holds the tall fridge, to get milk for her tea? And what causes her to give in to temptation today, when she didn't give in yesterday? It happens so quickly, the fatal decision. One moment there's no knowing what she'll do, the next moment she knows with absolute certainty that the decision is taken, and very soon now, unstoppably, chewily, fruitily, the cookie will be in her mouth.

But odd even so that should see her visit to Sussex in this light. There's virtue of a kind in resisting the temptation to snack. What virtue is there in deciding not, after all, to visit an old friend? The fact that she hasn't yet made her decision alerts her to its nature. Calling on Alan would be an act of self-gratification, and she's not sure she deserves it.

Deserve! Why does everything have to be deserved? Why must pleasures be earned and paid for? No answer, other than that's how it feels. You can tell yourself a hundred times a day that it's your right to have what you want, but you still don't believe it. You have no rights. You have no innate value. Your only worth lies in your capacity to be useful to other people.

Female thinking. This is how we've been raised to feel. All women are charity workers in their everyday lives, selflessly slaving for the good of the needy, the clamouring, suckling tribes of People Who Aren't Me. This is why Annie harbours such a strong secret resentment of her husband's work. He gets congratulated – he gets paid, for God's sake! – for doing good to others.

The thoughts come and go as she drives down Lewes High Street, past the ornate war memorial. Why is calling on Alan like filching a cookie? Because it's a selfish desire, of no bene-fit to anyone else. The desire for what? For admiration. For that look she caught in his eyes in the coffee shop in Soho.

Extraordinary how such knowledge is transmitted by such infinitesimally small signs. Like the tremor on the far reaches of the spider's web when a gnat's wing vibrates as it comes near: the spider awakes. Annie has no memory of a particular look in his eyes, or a smile, certainly there was never a compromis-ing word; and yet she knows it, and has been feeding on the knowledge ever since. Alan Strachan desires her.

There's no sin in taking pleasure in that. At forty-four years old, after twenty-one years of marriage, you no longer expect to arouse the desire of strangers. And, of course, Alan is no stranger. He's both known and unknown. Familiar enough to be safe, different enough to be exciting.

Round the one-way streets to the edge of town, to the area by the river known as the Phoenix Quarter. Here, in a motley collection of old iron-foundry sheds, the artists of Lewes have built their colony, like rooks in the treetops. They have no security, one gunshot and they'd flutter away, but for now the developers, with their *vernacular styles* and their *affordable housing*, are caught in the toils of the planning system, and the colony is thriving.

She climbs iron fire-escape stairs to an upper level, where a windowless wall extends the width of the old foundry. Overhead the roof is of pitched glass, through which streams the white light of day. The space is far too big for even an artist with a penchant for outsized canvases, and much of its expansive floor is empty. The artist himself is at work in one corner. He's a stocky man in jeans and a red check shirt, with a beanie hat pulled low over his head. He must have heard his visitor enter, but he doesn't turn from his canvas. He's painting a street scene, a meticulously rendered row of shops with parked cars and passing pedestrians, and in the middle of the street a gaping hole that glows with fire, like the entrance to Hell.

'Fintan,' says Annie.

Fintan Doyle turns, takes a look at his visitor, and resumes his painting.

Annie studies the work.

'I like it,' she says. 'Is it a commission?'

'No,' says Fintan. 'Get thee behind me, Satan.'

'I am behind you.'

'Good.' He turns to her with a grin. 'Always liked that one. Jesus saying to Satan, Get behind me. Cover my back, Satan. You're on my team, Satan.'

He starts cleaning his brushes.

'I may have a commission for you,' says Annie.

'You want a coffee? It's only instant, but I make it with real boiling water.'

'As opposed to what?'

'Hot tap.'

'Do you want me to make you a present of a coffee percolator, Fintan?'

'Don't bother. It'd only get nicked. This is a creative community round here, which means no one has any money. We survive by borrowing. I love borrowing. Do you borrow?'

'No,' says Annie. 'Never.'

'Ah, you poor deprived rich girl.'

He has a tin containing digestive biscuits. Annie declines this treat also. She explains the commission.

'It's for the lobby in a reconditioned office block where each floor will be let to a different client. The artwork has to present a unifying theme. It has to say, Wow! And it has to say, Now!'

'Wow *and* now,' says Fintan, pursing his lips.

'Six by four metres.'

'Fucking Ada! How'd you get it in the door?'

'Strong colours. Something to cheer them up as they come in to work.'

'When do you want it by?'

'Ten thousand.'

'You must want it soon.'

'Six weeks.'

He raises his coffee mug as if in a toast.

'Here's to corruption!'

'You'll do me a sketch first?'

'I'll dance a jig in a nightdress if that's what you want, my darling. That was pounds?'

'It was.'

'Ah, you lead me astray with your fancy money.'

'I suppose someone paid Michelangelo.'

'The pope paid for the lad. If you were the pope, my work would be art. But not being the pope you lead me astray. You are a scarlet woman. God bless you.'

★

After leaving Fintan's studio, Annie sits for a few moments in her car, waiting to see what her next move will be. She will call Alan, or she won't. He'll answer, or he won't. She'll visit him, or she won't. They'll see more of each other, or they won't. She'll have sex with him. Or she won't.

At each fork there's only one route that leads from the beginning to the end. The first act, the phone call, does not propel her inevitably to the last act, the sex. And yet it does.

She makes the call.

He answers. He invites her over. He gives directions. It's all very natural and there's nothing out of order about it, and it's pardonable vanity to stop in a layby on the way and touch up her face. She wonders what Alan's partner will be like. From the picture he showed her she looks nice.

She finds the house easily: a low, russet-tiled farmhouse surrounded by crumbling outbuildings. There are wild flowers everywhere, pushing up between brick pavers and in the cracks in walls, pink ragged robin and white ox-eye daisies.

She pulls her car to a stop beside another parked car, but doesn't get out. The house door opens, and Alan appears, alone. She gets out. He's looking at her the way he did before. Now, seeing him again, she knows she's right.

'So you found it,' he says.

'Yes. No trouble.'

'Come on in.'

He leads her into the low-ceilinged kitchen and offers her yet more coffee, which she declines. It turns out that Alan's partner isn't there.

'She's gone to her mother's,' Alan says. 'Her mother's dying.'

'Oh, I'm so sorry.'

'The sorry bit is that she could go on dying for years.'

Annie tells him about her artist, and how he says she's leading him astray with fancy money. Alan says he knows all about being led astray by fancy money. Annie then gives him her standard speech about how there's nothing wrong with talented people getting paid for their work, and how the idea that working for money demeans an artist is a hangover from the nauseating fear the Victorians had of trade.

'Back then if you had something to sell you couldn't be a gentleman. Well, sod that. Who wants to be a gentleman any more?'

All the time she's talking he's watching her, and the way he watches her makes her glow. The kitchen window at the back looks out over the fields towards the long line of the Downs. A single tractor is toiling up and down a distant field.

'I'm okay about being paid,' says Alan. 'The bit I don't like is being told what to do.'

'You think if you were free to do exactly what you liked you'd do better work?'

'Yes,' says Alan. Then, 'No, probably not.'

'I have this theory that art thrives on restrictions,' says Annie. 'Tell an artist to do as he pleases and you get a self-indulgent mess. Tell him it's got to be four feet square and red and done by Tuesday, and you get a masterpiece.'

Alan's smiling at her. She catches a sudden glimpse in his face of the beautiful young man he once was. She wants to kiss him.

'Four feet square and red and done by Tuesday,' he says. 'That's exactly the sort of job I'd like to do. Where have you been all my life?

'You're the one who ran away, Alan.'

His eyes widen.

'I did not run away, I was dismissed. I withdrew with dignity.'

'You sulked.'

'What was I supposed to do? I was suffering.'

So quickly, so easily, they're back in the past. The past when, for a while, they were lovers.

'I'm sorry,' she says. 'I was confused.'

'Oh, I'm not blaming you,' he says. 'I would have dumped me.'

'No, you were sweet, and clever, and interesting. I was just too young to handle it. We were both too young.'

'And I was a wimp.'

'I don't remember you being a wimp. I remember you being rather ardent.'

'Too ardent, right?'

They're looking into each other's eyes, remembering. He's so unafraid now, she can't get used to it. The sweet boy she once knew, and this new directness, this feeling of force coming out of him.

'Let's face it, Annie, I was a lousy lover.'

'You were not!'

'It's okay. It was a long time ago. I'm not the guy I was then.'

'No, seriously, Alan, that's not the way I remember it.'

It is the way she remembers it, but at the same time it was never the sex that mattered, even then. And she's well trained in the habit of protecting the menfolk.

'And anyway, I expect I was rubbish in bed too.'

'Not at all. You were amazing!'

You'd think from the look on his face that it all happened yesterday.

'Dear God!' he exclaims. 'I remember our first time like it was yesterday. I couldn't believe you were letting me do it. I thought, Now I can die. Nothing will ever be better than this.'

'Oh, Alan.'

She's moved by the intensity of his memory, and also aroused. It makes her feel young again, and sexy.

'No one had ever wanted to please me the way you did.'

She tries to remember what it was she did. I must have stroked his cock, she thinks. That's the usual procedure.

'And then' – he's rushing on, swept by the torrent of memory – 'and then that was it for me. I couldn't stop myself. Nothing much for you, but everything for me.'

'No, it was lovely for me too.'

'I never gave you a chance.'

She gets it then, and realizes with a shock that he must have minded about it from that day to this. It's so not what she remembers that it's an effort to take his concerns seriously. She remembers how he seemed always to be watching her with wounded eyes, wanting more than she was able to give. But not this sex bother. Even then she'd thought, It'll come right in a while.

'I promise you, Alan, I mean it when I say it was lovely for me.'

'But I didn't do anything to make it lovely.'

Then she has a real full memory. It hits her with such a shock that tears come to her eyes.

'Yes, you did,' she says. 'You trembled in my arms.'

'Did I?'

'It made me cry.'

'I didn't know that. I don't think I was looking. I felt so ashamed.'

'God, men!' she says. 'It's all about performance.'

'Did you really cry?'

She knows he can see the tears on her cheeks. All she wants is to take him in her arms. Instead, she brushes the tears away.

'All a million years ago,' she says.

They can't go on talking like this, they both know it. He offers to show her round the garden. The garden is wild and full of secret places and looks like no one does anything to it at all, but Alan tells her they have a gardener who comes two days a week. The leaves on the trees are bright and fragile. Between the trees the ground is thick with bluebells.

'First it was the snowdrops,' says Alan. 'Now it's the turn of the bluebells. Then we'll get the apple blossom. It's like a firework display in slow motion.'

He leads her right round the house back to the front yard, and shows her his workroom. It's warm and cluttered with books and papers. Posters of his films are pinned to the walls.

'I'm so impressed, Alan,' Annie says. 'I Googled you after we met. I had no idea you'd done so much.'

'Nor has anyone else. Screenwriting is like cathedral building. You do it for the greater glory of God.'

'But you must be proud.'

'I'm proud I'm earning my living.'

'I never even knew you'd become a screenwriter. I thought you'd become a teacher.'

'I was a teacher, for about fifteen years.'

'Why did you never answer my letter?'

She says it before she realizes what she's saying. A letter she wrote twenty-four years ago. Until this moment she would have sworn she'd forgotten all about it.

He doesn't pretend not to know what she's talking about.

'You said in your letter you wanted to be friends. I didn't want to be friends.'

'Didn't you want to see me again one day?'

'Yes. When I'd sorted myself out.'

'Sorted yourself out?'

'Got better at sex.'

Back to the mechanics again.

'And did you?'

'Eventually,' he says. 'Growing older helps.'

'But you still never came to find me.'

'Actually, I did,' he says. 'But you were off somewhere.'

She thinks back. That must have been the year she spent in Paris.

'I expect I was in Paris.'

'There you go. You were off leading a glamorous life in Paris.'

'I was miserable.'

'Now she tells me.'

'You know what I think?' says Annie. 'I think being young really sucks. I'm well past forty and I like myself so much better now than I did then. I think I'm a better person in every way.'

'Me too,' says Alan. 'And the sex is better, too.'

They both laugh. She avoids his eyes.

'The trouble is,' says Annie, 'the sex may be better, but it doesn't look as good. I mean, I'm not in bad shape, but I wouldn't dare show my naked body in public.'

'That's the big secret, isn't it? Sex is supposed to be for the young, but they don't enjoy it the way we do.'

Now she looks at him, and her look says: So? Are we going to do anything about it? But then she speaks, and it seems to her to be someone else speaking.

'Sounds like you have a good relationship.'

'I do. Liz is the best. I'm lucky to have her.'

'I'm lucky to have Mitch.' Annie knows how to be loyal too. 'He's one of those men who's deep-down decent, you know?'

'What does he do?'

'He's the finance director for an aid charity called Ubuntu Africa. Ubuntu means we all belong to each other. He's in Cape Town now.'

'Lucky him. He gets to do something really worthwhile.'

'Yes.'

Through the workroom window Annie sees a car driving into the yard. She looks at her watch. They speak quickly.

'I'd better be getting back.'

'Where did you say you live?'

'Clarendon Road. Notting Hill.'

'My agent's offices are near there. Just off Portland Road.'

'Look me up. We're at number ninety-two, up at the less smart end.'

They go out to the yard. Liz is getting out of her car. Alan introduces them and Annie thinks what she thought when she saw Liz's picture: what an attractive person she is.

'Come in and have a cup of tea,' Liz says.

'Oh, no, I must be getting back.' Annie's already hunting for her car keys in her bag. 'I only looked in for a moment because I had business in Lewes.'

'You must make a proper visit some day,' says Liz.

'I will,' says Annie. 'You have such a beautiful house.'

Then there's nothing left to stay for, so she drives off.

All down the narrow Sussex lanes heading back to the main road, her mind is full of Alan and the way he looked at her. She thinks of how she remembered him shivering naked in her arms, and she shivers now. She thinks of how she'll sleep alone tonight. She wishes Alan would come and join her in her bed. That's a bad thought to have but she doesn't care. It's not as if anyone else knows.

I could give him such a good time. I really could.

19

'Do you realize,' Henry says to Laura, 'that for all three party leaders, today is make or break?'

'That's what elections are, isn't it?'

'No, I mean, this will be the end of the road. For at least two of them, after this their political career is over.'

'I expect they'll heave a sigh of relief.'

'But just think,' says Henry, wanting her to feel it as he feels it. 'For five years you've been in a position of real power, you've been in the news every day, everyone's heard of you, what you say is listened to and analysed, you have staff to run your office, you have a car and a driver, you're doing something that really matters in the world. Then you wake up one morning and it's all gone.'

'They can go on being leaders of their parties, can't they?'

It's not something Laura's ever given much thought to.

'They can, but they won't. Cameron and Miliband will be booted out, and Clegg will resign.'

'How do you know?'

'That's not the point,' says Henry. 'All I'm saying is, what must it feel like to be them right now? Your whole future is hanging in the balance. The chances are that right now, today, is the highest you'll ever get, and from now on it's all downhill. And it's not as if they're old, any of them. Cameron's not fifty yet. Miliband's barely forty. They've got half their lives ahead of them.'

'They'll be all right,' says Laura. 'They'll get jobs in the City, or in Brussels, or somewhere. They'll make heaps of money and write their memoirs and give lectures. You don't need to worry about them.'

Henry doesn't know how to get Laura to understand that there's something bigger and deeper here, something that affects everybody. All your life you're on an upward path, it's so taken for granted you don't even realize it. From when you're a tiny child, every day, every month, every year brings with it some advancement. Things get better. You grow taller, you master new skills, you discover where and how you're going to make your mark in the world. All the time, you're *becoming*. From each step on the staircase you're climbing you can see more, and more people can see you. Maybe there are times when you can't take the next step, but you still know it's there, waiting for you. It's so deep in us, the belief that tomorrow will be better than today. However much philosophers urge us to live in the present, we don't, we live for tomorrow. The present moment just isn't enough. It's too disappointing, too *known*. But tomorrow – tomorrow can be anything. It can be everything. It's hope itself. How can anyone live without hope? Then one day you look about you and you know you've reached the top of the staircase, and the next step is down.

What do you do then? It's too soon to die. You have almost half your life still to live. But you're on the way down.

Henry sees the party leaders going through the motions with their professional good humour, and it seems to him to be a ghastly charade. Today must be a day of torment for all three of them. After the relentless pressure of the campaign, suddenly they have nothing whatever to do but wait for the axe to fall. Caught in that stillness, barred from speaking truthfully to a single soul, half paralysed between dread and glory, what else can they do but brace themselves for failure? Too soon for the magnanimous speech of concession. Too soon for the display of grace under fire. Only silence, and waiting, and public lies, and private fear.

'Have you voted?' Laura asks Henry.

'In a way,' he says.

'Try to get Carrie to vote. I know she won't.'

Henry says nothing to this.

'Are you all right, darling?'

'Probably not,' he says.

Laura is fishing for her car keys in her bag.

'I don't understand how things disappear in my handbag. You'd think there wasn't enough space. I'll get this stupid meeting over as soon as I can. I've no idea what he wants now.'

Laura's wearing a smart black trouser suit, like a politician. She's been summoned to another meeting by Sir Christopher Vickery. Or perhaps he's Lord Vickery. Henry, shabby in jeans and jersey, feels he hasn't been keeping up.

'I may go out on the Downs,' he says. 'I want to do High and Over.'

Laura gives him a kiss as she goes.

'Everything's going to be all right,' she says. 'Tell Carrie she has to vote.'

Henry goes upstairs and stands outside the door to Carrie's room. He's feeling strange. Everything is not going to be all right. There are no sounds from within. What does Carrie do all day?

'Carrie?'

No answer. Perhaps she's asleep. He knocks.

'Carrie?'

A listless voice answers.

'What is it?'

Henry's in no state to deal with a sulky child. He struggles to hold back a rising wave of anger.

'You have to vote.'

'Not going to,' says the invisible daughter.

'No, Carrie.' His voice sharper now. 'That's not good enough.'

Footsteps shuffling across the room. The door opens, but only a few inches. Carrie's sleep-bleared face peers out at him.

'What?'

'You have to vote, Carrie. You're over eighteen.'

'No, I don't.'

Something in her voice, the dulled, affectless tone, the casual lack of respect, tips Henry over the edge.

'Yes, you do!' he barks. 'You do have to vote!'

You do have to leave your room! You do have to live your own life! Why should we have to tiptoe round you all day? Why should we feel guilty because you're unhappy?

'Pull yourself together, Carrie! Get dressed, for God's sake! It's after lunch and you're still in your pyjamas! What's the matter with you?'

She stares at him. He knows he shouldn't be saying these things but he can't stop himself.

'Apparently you're going through some sort of bad time, though I don't see what can be so bad in your life, but whatever it is you won't make it any better by never getting out of bed. So put some clothes on and go down to the village hall and bloody well vote!'

She's still looking at him as if she doesn't understand a word he says.

'Hello?' he says roughly. 'Anyone home?'

'Why do you care if I vote or not?' she says at last.

'It's what we do when we're grown-up, Carrie. It's how we show we accept some responsibility for our world. You can't stay a child for ever.'

What am I saying? I'm the one who left my voting paper blank. I'm a fool and a hypocrite and I'm making my own daughter hate me. Of course she can stay a child for ever. She'll always be my baby.

But he can't stop himself.

'I don't know what you do all day in your room all by yourself, but it can't be so important that you can't spare ten minutes to walk down the road and make a mark on a piece of paper.'

'Who am I to vote for, Dad?'

'I don't know! You have to decide that for yourself.'

'But it's all so stupid.'

'What's stupid is never getting out of bed! What's stupid is never leaving your room! Laura's worried to death about you. You don't come down to meals. You don't talk to us. How do you think we feel? I'll tell you how we feel, we feel stupid! So maybe you're right, maybe everything's stupid, and we should all just give up.'

He's shouting now. He's out of control. Worst of all, he's letting his own pain into his voice. Carrie stares at him, biting her lower lip. They used to call it her squirrel face when she was little.

'All right, Dad,' she says. 'I'll vote.'

He feels as if he's been punched in the stomach. He sags back against the banister railing. Her capitulation spills all his anger, leaving him empty, weightless.

'Oh, Jesus,' he says.

'Dad! Are you okay?'

'No,' he says.

His legs can't hold him. He lets himself slip down until he's sitting on the landing carpet, his back against the banisters.

What have I done? Oh, what have I done?

She comes out of the doorway and kneels down beside him, frightened.

'What is it, Dad? What happened?'

'It's nothing.'

'Are you having a heart attack?'

'No. No.'

'I should call a doctor.'

'No, I promise you, I'm okay. Just a moment of giddiness.'

'Has it happened before?'

The flat tones are gone. She's concerned for him. He feels a flood of love for her. This must be what I wanted, he thinks. How pitiable we all are, how helplessly in the grip of vanity. She cares for me, and nothing else matters.

· He pulls himself upright again and smiles for her so she can see there's nothing to worry about.

'One too many beers over lunch.'

She gazes at him, trying to understand, wrinkling her brow.

'Nothing to worry about.' His voice firmer now. 'And look, forget I said all those things. I don't really care whether you vote or not.'

'Would you like me to make you a cup of tea?'

'Yes. That's a good idea.'

'Give me a minute and I'll get dressed.'

Henry goes downstairs and puts on a kettle. While he's waiting for Carrie to come down he takes several deep breaths, and splashes some cold water on his face. He doesn't want to disgrace himself again.

Carrie appears in jeans and a T-shirt, her hair pulled up in a twist on the back of her head.

'Are you sure we shouldn't call a doctor?' she says.

'Yes, I'm sure.'

'Where's Mum?'

'She had to go out to a client.'

They drink their tea sitting across from each other at the kitchen table.

'Is there anything I can do?' says Carrie.

He knows then exactly what he wants from her.

'Come on a walk up the Downs with me.'

Carrie looks into her tea.

'But if you'd rather not, that's fine.'

'All right,' she says.

'Really? You'll come?'

He hadn't expected her to agree.

'Yes.'

'I promise I won't get at you. I won't say anything at all, if you'd rather.'

'No, that's okay,' she says. 'You say anything you want. Just so long as I don't have to talk.'

'You don't. You don't have to say a word. Just be there. Keep me company.'

Henry feels his energy returning. He's done the impossible. He's got Carrie out of her room. Laura will be pleased.

20

'The children have departed,' says Christopher Vickery, leading Laura out onto a sheltered patio beyond the French windows. 'Repellent, aren't they?'

Laura can't help laughing at that. He smiles to see her laugh, watching her through rimless spectacles perched on his grand beak of a nose. Now that they're alone together she becomes aware of how tall he is. She barely comes up to his chest, even in her heels.

'They can't plead the excuse of a broken home. Their mother didn't leave till Henrietta was of age.'

He speaks with the ironic detachment of one long accustomed to human depravity.

'Your house must be over there somewhere,' he says, gesturing across the river valley.

'Yes,' says Laura. 'Under Mount Caburn.'

'Too close to the main road for me.'

'It is noisy.'

'You have children?'

'Two. Grown-up now.'

'Bearable, are they?'

'Mostly.'

'And you and—'

'Henry.'

'You and Henry have stuck it out?'

'So far.'

'Such an implausible notion, isn't it? That two people who are attracted to each other in their youth should be suitable companions for each other thirty or forty or fifty years later. Primrose was perfectly right to leave me. Everything I had to say to her had long been said. We bored each other.'

'You're lucky you were able to be so civilized about it,' says Laura.

She realizes she's playing with the rings on her fingers, always a sign that she's nervous.

Why am I nervous?

'There were occasional lapses of decorum,' he replies, his eyes fixed upon her. 'I am human too.'

'Aren't we all?'

Where is this leading?

The retired judge sees the question in her eyes and becomes businesslike.

'I have made my decision,' he says. 'I have decided to donate my library to the University of Sussex. I am not a pelican. I see no need to pluck out my own feathers for the benefit of my young.'

'That's wonderful news,' says Laura. 'Would you like me to let the librarian at Sussex know?'

'Do whatever is appropriate.' Still those steely eyes looking down on her, from behind the glint of his spectacles. 'But I'm concerned about you, Laura. You charge a commission. In the case of a donation, you get nothing. That does not seem right.'

'Please don't worry about that at all, Christopher. I'm thrilled that your library will be available for scholars, and I know the university will be too.'

'Even so, you're entitled to be paid for your professional services. You must appreciate having an income of your own, to do with as you please.'

'Oh, anything I make goes into the family kitty,' says Laura.

'Had I asked you to sell my library on the open market I calculate you would have earned a fee of at least twenty thousand pounds. But you've made no attempt to dissuade me from making it a gift. I respect that. I admire it.'

'Thank you, Christopher.'

'I admire *you*, Laura.'

This is so pointed that Laura feels herself blush. Surely, she thinks, he can't be coming on to me?

'You're a very beautiful woman.' Still those grave, judicious tones. 'I state that as a simple matter of fact. Beautiful women are not uncommon. Primrose was beautiful in her way. But you are also an honourable person, and that is far less common.'

'This is all very flattering, Christopher,' says Laura, 'but if you knew me better you'd start to see through me in no time.'

'I would like to know you better,' he says. 'One of the few benefits of maturity is that we have earned the right to speak our minds. Also we appreciate that time is limited. We are past the days of false modesty. So I tell you very simply, Laura, now that our business relationship is coming to an end, I would like to see you again.'

His calm self-satisfaction leaves Laura speechless.

'Let me take you out to dinner,' he says. 'I'm a member of the Garrick.'

'I don't think so.' Laura struggles to find the right words. 'I don't think that's a good idea. No, I'm sorry.'

She feels like a teenager receiving an unwanted advance, terrified of giving offence.

Christopher is unabashed.

'How long have you been married, Laura? Twenty-five years?'

'Oh, more.'

'Aren't you bored with each other yet?'

Once again Laura is silenced.

'Yes, I know,' says Christopher, 'we're not supposed to ask questions like that. All marriages are supposed to be innocent until proved guilty. But, really, it doesn't make sense, does it? A moment's thought tells us that everyone would choose to develop other relationships if they could. And why not? What's wrong with the adventure of getting to know other people? Are we to be imprisoned in a cell for two for the rest of our lives? Marriage is a useful arrangement for having children, it has all sorts of economic advantages, but once the children have grown up and left home, and the mortgage has been paid off, what's left? I take the view that our time of life is a time of reinvention. The hard slog is over. We can be young again.'

He speaks in such reasonable tones that Laura hardly knows how to make sense of her reaction.

'I don't know what to say,' she says.

'I hope at the very least,' says the judge, 'that it's pleasant to know you're admired.'

How can she say that she finds his admiration creepy? He

seems to be so far past the days of false modesty that he's forgotten he may have reasons for true modesty.

'I think I must be out of practice,' she says.

'Oh, come now. I can't be the first man to tell you he finds you attractive.'

'Once you're married,' says Laura, 'once you have children . . .'

Her voice tails away. She thinks of Nick, her long-ago boyfriend, who reappeared after half a lifetime with a similar proposition. What is it about men that makes them believe their attentions must be irresistible? It's quite apparent that Christopher thinks he's flattering her.

'Believe me,' says Christopher, 'marriage and children are no bar to other relationships. Remember, I've sat on the bench for many years.'

'Well, yes,' says Laura, fumbling for a way out. 'The thing is, Henry and I get on rather well in our way.'

'And long may it last. All I suggest to you, in all humility, is that there is room in our lives for more than one companion.'

'Companion?'

'I believe the word means one with whom you break bread.'

'At the Garrick.'

'If that appeals.'

Laura is beginning to recover her equilibrium. She's also becoming aware that she feels angry. This pose of urbanity is fraudulent, a cover for something more manipulative. He may be a foot taller than her, but she won't be overawed.

'You're a man who believes in plain speaking,' she says.

'And why not?' He smiles. 'That way we all know where we are.'

'Not quite,' says Laura. 'You say you want to invite me to dinner at the Garrick. As a companion.'

'Yes.'

'And then what?'

'Must there be a further motive?'

'No, of course not. I'm sorry, I think I've misunderstood. It's just that back when I was single, and men asked me out to dinner, they usually wanted to sleep with me afterwards. But, of course, I was so much younger then, and so were they.'

'And did you sleep with them?'

'When I liked the look of them well enough.'

'Why should anything have changed?'

He's doing that intense eye-contact thing again. Someone must have told him that he mesmerizes people. He doesn't mesmerize Laura.

'Oh, I see. So you are hoping I'll sleep with you afterwards?'

His face jerks back in shock. It's an involuntary movement, and he recovers his poise quickly, but now Laura knows he's on the run.

'You believe in plain speaking too,' he says.

'That way we know where we are.'

'Don't you think some things are better left to be discovered, over the course of time?'

'Time is limited,' says Laura.

He frowns. Laura is playing his lines back to him. The situation is no longer under his control.

'I think it would be misleading to say as much as you suggest,' he says. 'I'm hoping for adventure. An adventure can take many forms.'

'So long as it's with someone beautiful.'

He gazes at her, and now there's a new look in his eyes: more respectful, more wary.

'I do hope I haven't spoken out of turn.'

'I can look after myself,' Laura says.

'So I see.'

'I think maybe you've grown a little too accustomed to getting your own way.' She speaks gently. The moment of danger is past.

'The besetting sin of judges,' he says.

He holds out his hand and she lets him take hers. It's an odd gesture, as if they're adversaries shaking hands after a match.

'I was right about you,' he says. 'You're an honourable person.'

'Or just conventional.'

He keeps hold of her hand.

'Don't think too badly of me,' he says. 'I'm not really some kind of ageing Don Juan at all. I just get a little lonely at times.'

He releases her hand and turns to go back into the house. With his back to her he says casually, 'I wanted to make you a payment, to compensate for the loss of commission.'

'That's a very kind thought, Christopher,' she says, 'but it's not necessary. Sussex will be delighted by your donation, and that'll probably bring me goodwill and further work down the line.'

'You won't take my money?'

'Not as a gift, no. Gifts never come free, do they?'

At the front door, as she's leaving, he says, 'I wish I'd met you thirty years ago. I wouldn't have let you get away then.'

21

Carrie looks out of the windows as they drive, turning this way and that as if everything she sees is new to her. Henry keeps his eyes on the road ahead and wonders what she's thinking, but doesn't ask. The long shoulder of Firle Beacon keeps them company on the southern horizon. This is a familiar route, the school run to Underhill. How many times has he come this way, with Carrie and Jack bickering in the back? At the time he had grumbled about it, one of the chores of being a parent. Now it hurts to think of those days when the children were young, and his days were full.

He sees the turn-off ahead, with its sign they always laughed at, saying SCHOOL SLOW. He glances at Carrie and sees she too has turned to look.

'Still there,' he says.

But it's not there. That was another life. A new generation of children now troops into the assembly hall, and younger parents lean against their parked cars waiting for the end-of-school bell.

So many doors have now closed. The long office building in Shepherd's Bush by the railway line where he began his career is now a hotel. Even the mighty Television Centre, so modern when he was young, so glamorous, is soon to be turned into flats. Better that way. Let the waters close over the unre-visitable past.

Carrie aged ten, her solemn face shining in blue light. He's sitting on a bench in the barn theatre watching her in a school play, *Charlie and the Chocolate Factory*. She's Violet Beauregarde, the girl who chews gum. The part calls for her to stick her gum behind her ear, and it gets tangled in her hair. Later Laura has to cut her hair to get it out, and Carrie cries bitterly.

At the time it was just one of those things you do, you make time to go to the school play. All the other mums and dads are doing the same thing. You feel nervous for your child, and proud, and you sneak a look at your watch and wonder what time you'll get home. There are always more important things to do, more urgent calls to make. But, really, this is it. Watching your daughter, awkward in the blue light, this is what you do it all for. And now it's over.

They drive on past the familiar entrance, and all his heart and soul wants to turn up that bumpy drive, and pull into the puddled car park, and see the little children come running over the lawns.

'Do you remember being in *Charlie and the Chocolate Factory*?' he says.

'I had to turn into a blueberry,' says Carrie.

The road sweeps them away, pass the great corrugated asbestos roofs of Middle Farm. They drive between walls of trees until Selmeston, where the road rises and the trees fall back and a wide vista of hills and plains opens up ahead.

'So where's this walk?' says Carrie.

'Not much further.'

Henry is a practised walker. He knows where to park, and what routes to follow so that you never suffer the indignity of retracing your steps. This walk that he's chosen today is not long, perhaps an hour and a half, but it leads to one of the finest views in England, and Henry is a connoisseur of views.

They turn off the main road at the roundabout by Drusillas Park Zoo and head for Alfriston. There are lambs in the meadows, and on the higher fields, broad bands of yellow rape. A brisk wind is chasing clouds across a blue sky: a good walking day.

Now they're into narrow lanes, where passing oncoming cars is difficult. A stone bridge carries them over the river Cuckmere, which will be their companion for much of the walk. Then the lane takes them up the far side of the valley, past high windowless flint walls and handsome country homes, into the village of Litlington.

They leave the car in the car park beside the Plough and Harrow.

'Better zip up your coat,' says Henry. 'It can be quite nippy up top.'

Carrie does as he suggests. She's wearing Laura's coat, with the collar turned up so it hides her mouth. Henry pulls on a wool hat over his bald head. They walk round the pub and down the path that leads to the river. There's a cherry tree in full pink blossom, and a clump of ashes with ivy-covered trunks, so the valley is still hidden. Henry wants to tell Carrie this is how the best walks work, they withhold and tease, they demand tribute and spring surprises. But Carrie is silent, and doesn't meet his eyes.

Out of the trees, they emerge into the valley proper, and climb up onto the levee that bounds the river's southern side. The river is narrow here, the water mud-brown, fringed by biscuit-coloured reeds. The well-trodden path on the levee is hard dry earth hemmed in by brambles and cow parsley. It follows the river, winding in a long meander across the valley floor to Cuckmere Haven.

Henry points to the hill that rises steeply to the west.

'That's what we're climbing,' he says.

The hill is made of two headlands that meet at the top, where a triangle of bushes and trees form a shadowy region, inescapably like pubic hair. On one headland, a tattoo on a thigh, is the chalk image of a white horse.

'Is the horse prehistoric?' says Carrie.

'No,' says Henry. 'It's nineteenth century.'

The tide must be high. The river is almost level with the grassy banks, its surface reflecting the bright light of day like a shining path. The longer grasses ripple in the wind, golden tips above darker blades. The salt smell of the sea comes to them on the wind.

Now that they're away from the houses, and away from other people, the real walk can begin. It takes a kind of solitude to be granted the rewards of walking, which come with the shedding of self-awareness. There's no one to see you, no one to judge you. After a while you even cease to judge yourself.

And yet he's not alone. Here's Carrie, stumping silently along beside him, her face in her coat. She gives nothing and asks nothing. Henry finds this fits his mood well. It's not unlike going for a walk with a dog.

'Not so bad after all, is it?' he says.

'No,' says Carrie. 'It's all right.'

When the children were little and they came on walks, they ran about. They gambolled. When does it stop, the gambolling?

'Do you remember rolling?'

'Yes,' says Carrie.

She may not be saying much as she walks, but this does not mean Carrie is unaware of the familiar stranger by her side. As they follow the turns of the river, and sometimes he's ahead and sometimes he's by her side, all the time she feels the tug of the link between them.

Why did he collapse like that, on the upstairs landing?

She can feel it growing in her, a complicated emotion made up of fear and memory and love. Her father is so deep a part of her life that she rarely notices him, or thinks to ask him if he too has troubles. But when he sank to the floor and she said, 'Are you all right?' his answer was 'No.' So he's not all right.

This is both frightening and liberating. Carrie can't begin to know how to ask what's wrong, it feels almost sacrilegious. Also it's embarrassing. But if he's sad she wants to comfort him. She wants to take his hand, now as they head towards the lower slopes of the hill, and squeeze it.

Funny old Dad, with all his opinions.

Carrie has no opinions any more. That's all dropped away, along with the old childish belief that things are the way they are for a reason.

'Do you remember rolling?' he says.

Yes, she remembers rolling. They used to do it on the Glynde side of Mount Caburn, where the close-grazed downland slopes gently to the village. Her father would trot along beside her in case she rolled too fast. His protective presence was just another part of the accommodating world, along with the bouncy turf, along with gravity itself. She remembers the blue sky swinging past, and the scary thrill of being out of control, and the bumps and scratches on her arms. She doesn't remember him, not really. But he was there.

He's always been there.

They've reached the bridge. The wind on the surface of the river water makes it appear to ripple downstream, but the high tide is driving it upstream, as the floating debris of twigs shows. They linger for a moment on the bridge, looking down at the water. Then they cross and climb the steep chalk track out of the river cutting.

At the top, the wind now on their backs, they begin the long ascent of the hill proper. The barns of Frog Firle lie below them, historic buildings as lovingly maintained as any church. The grass at their feet is speckled with daisies, and the occasional lone buttercup. They pick their way through cowpats.

'We'll get to the view soon,' says Henry.

The higher you climb, the further you see. Such a simple instance of cause and effect, and so morally fitting. The greater the effort, the greater the reward. Until the day they change the rules on you.

Carrie recalls, as if with an effort of will, that Henry has a thing about views. Why should it be so hard to think of her father as a person with likes and dislikes, hopes and fears? It strikes her then that she doesn't think of him as a person at all.

He exists rather as a necessary part of her world, like the ground on which she walks. You don't ask the ground what it's feeling.

She sneaks a quick peek at him as they climb. He looks funny with that wool hat on his head. His face is so familiar to her it's almost invisible, but she takes in the deep set of his eyes, the angular line of his jaw. His cheeks are pink with the exertion of climbing, his breaths coming faster, as are her own.

What a kind face he has. A face all his own, like no one else's. People say Jack looks like him, but Carrie knows the truth. She's the one who takes after her father. She'd be much prettier if she took after her mother, but she has Henry's eyes, Henry's cheekbones.

She feels a sudden violent clutch of love for him. Why isn't he all right?

Halfway up the rising field they stop to get their breath back. Below them now lies the Cuckmere Valley across which they walked, the river snaking back and forth on its journey south. Between distant humps of cliffs they glimpse a thin silver line of sea. A band of sunlight is crossing the land towards them from the east, lighting up the fields of rape, glinting on the roofs of cars as they pass along the hedge-hidden road on the far side of the valley.

'What happened, Dad?'

He sighs and shakes his head. Of course he knows at once what question she's asked. He sets off climbing again, and Carrie stays close by his side.

'Just a bit of annoying news,' he says. 'They don't want me to do the gardens series after all.'

Carrie has never asked herself about her father's work. She knows what he does, and she knows he likes doing it, and there seems nothing more to be said. From time to time he's complained about the failings of colleagues. But he's always been busy, always interested in what he's doing. It has never seemed to be a precarious existence, as her own is precarious. He's been talking about this gardens series for months. How can he not be doing it?

She wonders what to say. There's not much point in asking questions about what's happened, it's not a world she understands. And, anyway, she doesn't want to ask questions. She wants to make him feel better.

'I'm sorry,' she says.

'Yes. It's thrown me a bit.'

They climb higher, steeper. In the next valley the brown and green stripes of Rathfinny vineyard come into view, making corduroy patterns on the hillside. The cloud shadows march over the land, promising the coming of the laggard sunlight.

'I expect something else'll turn up,' says Henry.

Then, turning to Carrie with a sweet smile, he adds, 'Actually, I don't.'

'Oh, Dad.' And she really does take his hand and holds it as they walk.

She feels him interlace his fingers in hers, and squeeze them. She wants to tell him how much she loves him but she just can't find the words.

'I could keep on trying,' he says. 'Writing outlines, submitting proposals, waiting for a stroke of luck. But even thinking about it makes me feel tired. It's like chasing a train, you know? The faster you run, the further away it gets.'

He's never talked to her like this, not ever. She can think of nothing at all to say in reply, so she squeezes his fingers instead.

At the almost highest point of the hill, just before the cap of trees, he calls a stop. They're both breathing hard now. From here they can look down on the whole valley, the zigzag of the river now gleaming a dull turquoise, the sea a deep silver bowl.

'Best view in England,' Henry says.

As they stand there the clouds pass at last, and the slow-moving sunlight reaches them. Now the Downs on the far side of the valley are in cloud shadow. Carrie lifts her chin out of the collar of her mother's coat, into the warm sun.

'Is this the top?'

'Not quite.'

They walk on through a kissing gate into the trees. The final rise is a narrow path between blackthorns and brambles, bending in and out of pools of sunlight. They pass the path that branches off to the car park and the Seaford road, and follow the main track until it comes out of the trees. The white horse is now on the steep slope to their left. Already the ground is sloping downhill.

'So was that it?' says Carrie.

'Yes. That was it.'

Going down now there are steep steps cut into the hillside, held in place by timber risers. They're still holding hands, and so can help each other not to stumble as they descend. Carrie feels overwhelmed with emotions she doesn't know how to express. All she can think is that she wants to put it in a song. How they climbed a hill in shadow and came out into sunlight. How her father told her he was sad. How there was a view that went on for ever, but the hill had no top to it. How she held his hand and he squeezed her fingers. How she loved him so much it hurt.

22

Liz has said nothing at all about meeting Annie, which makes Alan nervous. It's true she has a lot on her mind. But the longer the subject remains unbroached, the more it seems to him to loom between them.

She emerges from her study at last, and finds Alan in the kitchen, doing nothing in particular.

'I feel distracted,' he says. 'It's this election. I have the feeling that normal service has been suspended. We're all holding our breath.'

'This election, and my mother,' says Liz.

'Any developments?'

'No.'

'Can't go on for ever.'

'Karen knew an old lady who went on like this for two years.' She heads for the fridge. 'Am I allowed a glass of something, or is it too early?'

She holds up a bottle of wine, silently asking him if he wants a glass too.

'I'll have a beer,' says Alan. 'So what did you think of Annie?'

'She's beautiful,' says Liz. 'You didn't tell me that.'

'For her age. She is nearly fifty.'

Liz gives him a curious look.

'So how come she showed up?'

'She commissions work from artists. She was visiting an artist in Lewes.'

'I bet she was only doing that as an excuse to look you up,' says Liz.

'I did wonder,' says Alan. He feels oddly relieved. He wants it to be true, and he wants not to have to lie to Liz.

The front door slams. They hear the sound of a car driving away. The clatter of Cas's shoes as he runs upstairs. Liz meets Alan's eyes.

'You said you'd talk to him.'

Alan takes a can of beer out of the fridge, pops it, drinks.

'Now's as good a time as any.'

He heads up the stairs, beer in hand. He finds Cas lying on his bed, still in his school clothes, gazing at his iPad. Alan comes into the room uninvited and settles himself on the upright chair by Cas's desk. He sits there drinking his beer in silence.

After a while Cas speaks.

'So?' he says.

'So what's going on, Cas?'

'You tell me.'

More silence. Alan finishes his beer.

'I told you about my aliens story, didn't I?' he says.

He and Cas often talk movie plots. Other dads take their teenage sons to football matches. Alan and Cas critique popular films. On the whole Cas is more generous in his responses than Alan: for example, the work of Christopher Nolan. Alan holds that Christopher Nolan has never yet made a film that has a coherent story. Cas says Christopher Nolan is a genius.

'Yes,' says Cas. 'It's good.'

High praise.

'I think it's good,' says Alan. 'But I think they're going to make me mess it up.'

'Don't let them.'

'It's not as easy as that. I can't make the film myself. I need them to get the money. So if they say I have to make changes so they can get the money, it's not helpful for me to say no.'

Silence. Then, 'Why are you telling me this, Dad?'

'Would you rather I didn't?'

'It's a trick, isn't it?'

'What sort of trick?'

'The kind where they put an informer in a cell with a suspect. The informer tells his secrets to get the suspect to trust him.'

'I'm not telling you secrets.' But secretly Alan marvels, both at his son's perception and at his grasp of movie-plot beats.

'You're telling me you're having a bad time. So I'm supposed to tell you I'm having a bad time.'

'Are you?'

'Mum sent you, right?'

'Yes,' he says.

'I'm fine.'

'You're too bloody smart for me, I'll tell you that.'

'How smart?'

'How smart? I don't know. You want me to grade you?'

'Am I a genius?' says Cas, from the bed.

'A genius? I don't know that I'd go that far.'

'Me neither.'

This is a strange turn for the conversation to take. Why would Cas ask if he's a genius? Alan wonders if his son is afraid he's autistic and, if so, how to raise it. He doesn't seem autistic to him: just private.

'If the informer-in-the-cell trick doesn't work, what comes next?'

'Threats,' says Cas. 'Then violence.'

'Of course. Violence.'

He thinks of Stuart saying, 'A man who does nothing is not a hero.'

'I think my producer would like me to put more violence into my plot. Especially at the end.'

'The hero sacrifices himself to save the aliens, right?'

'Yes.' Alan is touched that Cas remembers.

'It's kind of been done, Dad.'

'So what do you suggest, genius?'

Cas says nothing. Alan begins to worry that he's hurt him.

'Look, maybe you're right,' he says.

Then Cas starts talking.

'It's no big deal,' he says. 'I'm getting some grief from a moron at school, okay? I wrote this essay, and Miss Mills liked it and read it out in class, and this kid Kieran Kelly put his hand up at the end and said, "Miss, that's genius!" Now when I come into a room they all whisper, "Genius!" Whenever I speak they stare at me and say, "Genius!" It's become a thing. It's spread to the upper year groups now. It's just a joke.'

But his eyes are bright, hurting.

'Jesus, Cas! Doesn't it make you want to kill the lot of them?'

'No. Only Kieran Kelly.'

'Is he seriously stupid?'

'Not at all. He's smart.'

Alan can't think of any way to make the situation better.

'If it's any consolation,' he says, 'life gets better once you're past forty.'

'Can't wait,' says Cas.

23

Driving back from Rodmell to Edenfield, Laura remembers she hasn't voted yet. She stops at the village hall to do her duty. As she collects her ballot papers and takes them to one of the booths she has a memory of the first time she voted, in the 1979 election that brought Mrs Thatcher to power. It was a thrilling day: at last she was allowed to play her part in the national drama. That excitement is long gone. Even though this election is the most closely fought for years, it has failed to engage her. She feels guilty about this, and doesn't talk about it, even to Henry. It's not that she doesn't care what happens to the country. But somehow, over the last few years, politics has ceased to involve her. She feels like a spectator asked to offer an opinion on other people's quarrels. As far as she can tell there's something to be said on both sides. People keep saying you can't trust politicians any more, but to Laura the problem lies elsewhere. She's willing to believe they mean what they say, but she can't get any kind of a grip on what it is they're saying. They behave as if they differ violently, but they seem not to differ much at all. They produce figures to support their policies, and other figures to show their opponents' policies are wrong, but all the figures cancel each other out. What are we supposed to think?

I'm not stupid, Laura tells herself. But either I've missed something, or everyone else is just pretending. It's like certain kinds of art these days. Everyone applauds but you can't see it, so you keep quiet. You tell yourself, It's not for me, so how can I judge?

But still she does her duty. It's like herd immunization, or chain letters. You don't want to be the one who breaks the link.

As she stands in the polling booth, pencil poised over the ballot paper, she realizes she's going to vote Green. This comes as a surprise. Her parents always voted Conservative. Henry has always voted LibDem, the tactical vote in Lewes that has kept the Tories out. The Green Party has no chance, but in voting for it she's voting against business as usual. Its very powerlessness attracts her. The world of power says to her, Things have always been as they are. There's nothing to be done about it. Misery, cruelty, greed, these are realities that can never change. To think otherwise is sentimentality. But Laura has begun to think otherwise.

She puts her cross against the Green candidates on both ballot papers. It feels like a public declaration. Of course no one is watching, and no one knows what she's done, but to her it's a great silent shout.

Turning off the road into their home yard she sees that Henry's car is gone. She goes into the house, slips out of her heels and puts on a pair of flats. Then she calls upstairs, 'Carrie! I'm back.'

There's no answer, but Carrie never does answer when called. She's always playing music in her room, and can't hear. It's one of the many ways her presence in the house is disturbing. Laura likes to know if she's alone or not. Carrie lives among them like a ghost.

She goes upstairs and knocks on Carrie's door.

'Carrie? Are you in there?'

She opens the door. The room is empty, and in a mess. The bed not made, clothes on the floor, as are her laptop and her guitar, and two used mugs of coffee. This is a person who lives on the floor.

Laura sits on the bed and looks round the room. Carrie must have gone with Henry on his walk. This is a good sign, surely? Laura's worry about her daughter is undefined but deep. Her solitary existence, her unhappiness, feels like a reproach.

This is the room she's lived in for almost all her life, the room in which she was a little child. An anxious, secretive child, but also enchanting, somehow unpredictable. The markers of those childhood years are everywhere. The string-puppet princess she called Magnificker, insisting on the spelling, hangs over a jar of glitter pens. Cocktail umbrellas, a brief craze, festoon a pin-board. One shelf is packed with small framed photographs, the kind given as presents between school friends. There stands Carrie, grinning bravely between now nameless small girls. There's a photograph of Laura, too, with Henry beside her, in the days when he had hair. On one wall is pinned a Roy Lichtenstein poster of a weeping woman drowning, saying, 'I don't care! I'd rather sink than call Brad for help!'

Such a room should make Laura proud. This is the baby she

has raised, and protected, and ushered into the world. This is her achievement, isn't it? Or if not exactly her own creation, this is certainly the work to which she has devoted half her life. But any pride she feels is overlaid by worry. The project is not yet finished. Carrie is not happy.

She remembers then how Michael Marcus said she must stand apart from her worries. How do you do that? She pictures her worry, in the form of Carrie, sitting cross-legged on the floor, not looking up, as she so often does. There, Laura tells herself, I'm here and my worry's over there. But then her imagined Carrie lifts her head and looks at her with such suffering in her eyes that it makes Laura flinch.

Why do men say such things? They seem to live in an entirely different mental space, where they lead grander mental lives. Now, at the time of the general election, this verbal pomposity has become epidemic. They attack each other with their opinions as if they alone have in their hands the making of the world. Is it something to do with testosterone? Or is it just the way the culture's formed us, that men are at ease with abstract terms while women cook the dinner?

No, that's showing my age. It's all changed now. Girls outperform boys at school. Some women even out-earn men at work. And yet I still catch myself switching off when men start talking like the op-ed pages. Am I just stupid after all? Why is my train of thought always so easily distracted?

Take Christopher Vickery. A clever, articulate man, he weaves a web of grand statements about 'all marriages' and 'our time of life', but all he's trying to say is, 'I fancy you.' It isn't about stupidity, it's about style. Men use abstract language as a defensive wall. Christopher Vickery was just protecting himself.

At least until the end when he said he was lonely, and suddenly, for a brief moment, a real person appeared before her.

All conversations are disguised versions of the same primitive exchange of needs. Do you respect me? Should I fear you? Do I have power over you? Do you love me? Women are more at ease with the language of emotions; or, at least, less afraid.

But maybe that's just another social construct. Is Carrie less afraid?

Are we to be imprisoned in a cell for two for the rest of our lives?

The old judge's words have unsettled Laura in many ways.

Once the children have grown up and left home, what's left?

But Carrie has not left home. She's not happy. She still needs me.

As this thought forms, something catches in Laura's throat. Her mind, reacting more slowly, traces the self-accusation that has wrenched her body.

Is worrying about Carrie my way of holding onto her?

No. No! Not true! I want her to leave home. I want her to live her own life. I want to be told this bad time she's going through is over, and she'll go back to being strong and happy all by herself. I want her not to need me, truly I do.

She pictures Carrie as she has seen her so many times, alone with her guitar before an audience, strong and beautiful, singing her songs. Her songs that are clear and true as running water. That's my daughter, out in the world.

And me? Where am I? I'm sitting in the room she filled with her body and spirit for so many years, and it's empty now. The room has become a museum. The bright, prickly person who made it has gone. Jack left long ago. I have no children, and am no longer a mother.

Laura would never say this to her girlfriends, or even to Henry, because it sounds like an admission of weakness, but she knows it to be true. For the last twenty-six years, first and foremost I have been a mother. Being a mother has dominated every other aspect of my life, including my marriage and my job. I have lived for my children.

This is shocking. Worse, it's ridiculous. She feels as if she's come upon herself trapped in a cliché. To shake herself free of such thoughts, she gets up from Carrie's bed and leaves her room, closing the door softly behind her.

Downstairs she thinks she'll make a cup of coffee, then realizes the dishwasher has been run and needs emptying. Hardly conscious of what she's doing she opens the dishwasher door, feels the gush of heat on her face, and lifts out the cutlery basket.

'We can be young again,' says Christopher Vickery.

Laura doesn't want to be young again. It feels like bad form, old people trying to be young. It feels like ingratitude. And, anyway, it's only code for having sex. The judge wants to prove he's sexually potent. Men are so simple: if they can still do it, they're still young.

She thinks then of Henry last night. He hates it when the sex goes wrong, but it always comes right again later. Her instincts tell her to make light of it, not to add to the pressures on him by making him think she minds.

Do I mind?

Laura's thoughts dart here and there as she separates the knives and forks, the spatulas and the teaspoons. Does Henry want sex to prove he's still young? She pictures his pleading face and answers herself, No, Henry wants sex the way a dog wants his dinner. It's an intermittent but intense hunger that comes upon him every week or so. He's told her as much. One of the advantages of making love with the same person for thirty years is that you get to know what's really going on.

Putting away the bowls and plates, Laura finds herself wondering what would have happened if she'd responded differently to the judge. Suppose she'd had dinner with him at the Garrick, and afterwards gone with him, suitably intoxicated, to some little flat in Marylebone or Bayswater. How would matters have proceeded? Her imagination recoils at the thought. She can't imagine herself saying to the judge, as she says to Henry, 'Do this to me. And now do this.' They would have fumbled in silence, like teenagers. He would have achieved some sort of gratification, and she would have had to pretend. Do people still do that, in their fifties?

To her annoyance she finds that one of her favourite handmade bowls has been dishwashed, and has chipped. That must be Henry being careless, clearing up too fast. He never notices that sort of thing.

How unfair it is that men can have orgasms so easily. It doesn't seem to make much difference who they do it with, a prostitute will do as well as a wife. Or even a blow-up doll. It's more like shopping than love. Except when it doesn't work, of course. How would she feel if it never worked again? The thought flashes by, and is gone.

How is Henry now? Is Carrie confiding in him as they walk over the Downs?

Laura feels a tiny pang of jealousy. I'm the one she needs. There's no one knows her as I do. I've lived for you, Carrie, for you and Jack. I've made you. You're mine.

She lets herself run on like this for a few moments to get it out of her system, like a crying jag. Then puts George to work on her coffee and pulls herself together.

I'd rather sink than call Mum for help!

So that leaves Mum standing on the shore, wondering what happens next. All very well talking about reinvention, but reinvention as what?

I'm not going to be a bloody forest-dweller, I can tell you that for a start.

Henry's car comes crunching over the gravel. The front door opens and closes. Footsteps on the stairs. Henry appears in the kitchen.

'Where's Carrie?' says Laura.

'Gone to her room,' says Henry.

'How was the walk?'

'It was good. Quite a wind, up top.'

She gives him a look and he shrugs, understanding.

'She's fine.'

'Did she talk?'

'No. There wasn't much talking. She knows I'm feeling a bit down. She held my hand.'

Laura nods and says no more, but inside she wants to cry. It's such a long time since Carrie held her hand. It's not fair.

'After you'd gone I got cross with her and shouted at her about staying in her room and not voting and I don't know what. Then I fell over.'

'You what?'

'Well, more like slid down. To the floor.'

'Henry! Are you all right?'

'Yes, I'm fine. I suppose I just got myself too worked up. Carrie was very sweet, actually. I think that's why she said she'd come on the walk.'

'Do you think you should have yourself looked at, darling?'

'Maybe.'

'Will you promise me? Have a proper check-up?'

'Yes. All right.'

'You say that, and then you never do anything.'

'No, I will.'

'So that's why she held your hand.'

'Yes. I suppose so.'

Laura reaches out to hold his hand.

'I went and sat in her room,' she says. 'I don't really want her to leave home at all.'

'Me neither,' says Henry.

He hasn't asked her about her trip to Rodmell. He's forgotten.

'You know I was called back to the Vickerys'?'

'Oh. Yes.'

'The old man's decided to give his library to Sussex.'

'After all you've done?'

'I don't mind. But that's not why he wanted to see me. He propositioned me.'

'He did what?'

Henry has been mooching distractedly about the kitchen. Now he comes to a stop and pays attention.

'He told me I was beautiful and said he wanted an adventure.'

'The old goat!'

'I don't actually know how old he is. Seventy, I'd guess.'

'What about me?'

Of course Henry's first concern is himself. His woman, his dignity, his honour.

'Christopher believes there's room in our lives for more than one companion.'

'Well, fuck him! Companion, for fuck's sake! He's got a nerve! What did you tell him?'

Henry's gone pink in the face. He's more upset than she expected.

'I don't remember exactly what I said, but he got the message.'

'Extraordinary!'

'Don't worry. He's no competition, I promise. He said he was lonely.'

'Tough,' says Henry, mercilessly. 'Not our problem.'

'And I voted on the way home. I voted Green. I expect you think I'm wasting my vote, but I feel better for it.'

'It's not personal therapy, Laura. You're voting for the next government.'

'So who did you vote for?'

He stares back at her in silence.

'Henry?'

'What?'

'Are you all right?'

'Did you really vote Green?'

'Yes, I did,' she says. 'Is that a problem for you?'

'Yes,' he says.

But he's leaving the room, making for the refuge of his study, not waiting to talk about it. But then quite suddenly he stops, and without turning to look at her, he says, 'I left my ballot paper blank.'

'Blank!'

'I didn't vote at all. And while we're on the subject I'd like to say that I like meat, I see nothing wrong in eating meat, and I don't relish the prospect of spending the rest of my life being made to feel guilty about it.'

And off he goes, shoulders hunched. Laura lets him go. He's angry. He's probably been angry for days.

He likes meat. He wants meat.

It's infantile, this cry of 'I want'. But Laura can't find it in herself to be angry back at him. She doesn't want him to fall over again. She knows she's in the right as far as the argument goes, but he's not arguing. He's crying like a baby who wants to be fed. He's expressing pure desire. Desire is never wrong, any more than the weather is wrong. It's just there, and has to be dealt with. Deeper than reason. Driving reason before it.

So what is it I desire?

For a moment Laura catches a glimpse of something else, something big and important, of which all her arguments about eating meat form only a surface shimmer. Then it slips away again, out of reach.

24

Cas announces that he's going to stay up all night to watch the election results. Liz doesn't want him to because he has school the next day. Alan's view is that it's not worth it.

'It's going to take for ever to sort this one out. Remember last time? We didn't know who'd won for five days. This time they're saying it could take a month.'

'Can't I see some of it at least?' pleads Cas.

'Stay up for the exit polls. Then if you're that interested, get up early tomorrow. It'll be much more interesting in the early morning.'

'I'm not getting up early,' says Cas, looking at his father as if he's mad. 'Staying up late's fun. Getting up early sucks.'

So they all settle down just before ten to watch the election coverage on the BBC. David Dimbleby shows off the studio tricks for the night, a virtual Downing Street with a path to the door of Number 10, and the virtual inside of Big Ben's four clock faces doing duty as swingometers. Then the real Big

Ben bongs out the hour, and the figures for the exit polls are revealed.

> Conservative   316
> Labour   239
> LibDem   10
> SNP   58

Alan gapes at the screen.

'That can't be right.'

'Why not?' says Cas.

'They were supposed to be level-pegging. The Tories are miles ahead.'

The pundits in the studio are all expressing surprise too. Either the exit poll is faulty, or the opinion polls throughout the election campaign have got it wrong. No one will know for sure until the first marginals declare, between one and two a.m.

'That's it, Cas,' says Liz. 'Up you go.'

'But I want to see what happens.'

'You want to sit here for four more hours being told no one can predict the result?'

'Yes.'

But after ten more minutes, Cas gets bored.

'I can't believe it's all done on paper and counted by hand,' he says. 'If people were allowed to vote on their phones it'd all be over by now.'

'Go to bed, Cas,' says Liz. 'We'll be up soon.'

Cas goes on up.

'If this turns out to be real,' says Alan, pointing at the screen, 'it means the same bunch carries on.'

'And what does that mean?'

'Hard to say,' says Alan. Then, 'Actually, this is embarrassing.'

'What?'

'I've just realized I'm reacting to it all as if it's a story. As soon as the exit poll came up I started to feel excited, because it's a reversal of expectation. I'm a drama junkie.'

'We all are,' says Liz.

'But it's so immature. I mean, I should have an opinion on who I want to be in power based on how well they'll run the economy or something. And here I am thinking, If Ed loses, what will he say to his brother?'

On the screen Jeremy Vine is demonstrating in his virtual Downing Street how close to the door of Number 10 the two parties will get, based on the exit poll. A clicking carpet of hexagonal blue tiles rolls down the street, almost to the door. The red tiles stop a long way short.

'How long are you staying up?' says Liz. 'I'm calling it a day.'

David Dimbleby reminds the nation yet again that the exit poll is only a poll, and nothing is yet certain.

'I'll come now,' says Alan.

Undressing in their bedroom, Liz says, 'I keep thinking about your old girlfriend.'

'Thinking what?'

'What it must have been like for you, her showing up like that.'

'It was strange,' says Alan.

Liz goes into the bathroom and makes a long buzzy noise with her electric toothbrush. When she comes out she says, 'So was it nice strange?'

'Yes, I think it was,' says Alan. 'I felt like I was laying a ghost.'

'How long was she here?'

'Half an hour or so.'

'Did you get round to the subject of past failures?'

Alan can hear the curiosity in her voice clearly enough, but he sticks resolutely to the tone he's chosen, of neutral disclosure. He doesn't want to do anything to encourage the waiting fantasy.

'The funny thing is she didn't seem to remember that.'

'You mean your sexual performance wasn't the centre of her entire existence?'

'All right,' says Alan, taking her place in the bathroom. 'You can laugh.'

While he's cleaning his teeth Liz says something he doesn't catch. He's thinking to himself, I've got nothing to hide. Why am I acting so guilty?

'What was that?'

'Oh, I was just saying men should really display their erections to each other. They're the ones who're impressed by that sort of thing.'

'I thought your new book told you women like that sort of thing too.'

Now they're getting into bed. Liz wriggles about to create warmth. Alan turns out the light. In the darkness Liz says, 'Actually, women do like that sort of thing too.'

In the darkness Alan says, 'I think Annie was just being polite about not remembering.'

'After all, she did dump you.'

'Exactly.'

'So now you've laid her ghost,' Liz says, 'do you want to lay her?'

'You've been planning that line.'

'So do you want to?'

'No, I'm not planning to lay her.'

'I said do you *want* to.'

Alan doesn't answer. He feels Liz's hand reaching for him under the duvet.

'You're allowed to want things,' she says.

Her hand on his thigh.

'Yes, I suppose I do want to,' he says.

'Well, you're not to.'

He rolls into her arms. She feels for his cock and finds it well on the way.

'You could always pretend I'm her.'

'I'd never do that!'

'I don't mind. So long as it's a secret. And so long as it's not real.'

She's stroking his cock as she speaks, feeling it grow hard.

'And so long as I can watch,' she adds.

'You want to watch me with another woman?'

'Yes,' she says. 'And I want to be the other woman.'

'I just want it to be you,' says Alan.

'Liar.'

As they make love she imagines another woman in his arms, a woman with no name. Then she imagines she has another man in her arms, equally anonymous, and this stranger is fucking her just as Alan is fucking her, but not being Alan she owes him nothing. He desires her and wants her for his pleasure alone. She feels the heat of his body, the body that desires her body, and her own desire rises up to meet his. She's actor and spectator, she's herself and other, she's the object of desire and the source of desire, she's fucking and fucked—Now she's shouting, no words, just the breaking out of the wildness in her, the letting go of restraint. He makes no sound at all. It's as if he's not there.

All for me, Liz thinks.

After they've finished and she's lying hot in his arms, she says, 'That was research.'

'If you say so.'

'But it doesn't mean I'm a slut.'

'Why would you be a slut?'

'Because I want sex.'

'Oh, that sort of slut. That's the kind I like. In fact, it's the kind I love.'

'Even if I was so slutty I wanted to have sex with other men?'

'Ah.'

'Not that I'm planning to.'

Alan's silent for a while.

'Would I be allowed to watch?'

Friday, 8 May 2015

25

Henry rises early and pads downstairs in his dressing-gown to turn on the television. At times like these the radio won't do. For all his newfound cynicism about the process, he feels the need to see the changes as they happen, to be part of the national experience. Like everyone else, he watched the exit polls last night with disbelief. Now he has returned to the fray, like a motorway ghoul, cruising ever more slowly past the fatal pile-up.

It's just after six. He's in time to see George Galloway, expressionless beneath his gangster hat, go down to heavy defeat in Bradford.

'It's a new day,' says David Dimbleby, 'and Britain is waking up to a familiar face in Downing Street. The latest forecast puts the Conservatives at 325 seats, one short of an absolute majority.'

An absolute majority! The LibDems are being destroyed. Nick Clegg calls it 'a cruel and punishing night'.

Ed Miliband says, 'This has clearly been a very difficult and disappointing night for the Labour Party.'

Cruel and punishing! Difficult and disappointing! The world has become a mirror in which Henry sees his own emotions reflected back to him.

Nick Robinson, the BBC's political editor, says, 'It's as if an electoral firing squad has felled a whole generation of Labour leaders.'

Laura appears in T-shirt and jogging bottoms, still sleepy.

'What happened?'

'Tory triumph,' says Henry.

David Cameron tweets a picture of himself hugging his wife, crushing her face against his.

Norman Baker has lost Lewes.

'Norman Baker lost!' exclaims Laura.

The Green candidate has come fifth. She expects some jibe from Henry, but he says nothing. She pads over to the worktop and feeds a pod into George.

Andrew Neil predicts there may be three leadership elections on the way, as Ed Miliband, Nick Clegg and Nigel Farage are all forced to resign. Paddy Ashdown has said in the night that he'll eat his hat if the exit polls prove to be right. Andrew Neil now presents him with a hat to eat.

Henry tears himself away from the television to shower and get dressed. As he dresses his mind is on the fallen leaders who have now, so unexpectedly, joined him in the shadows. Their glory, such as it has been, is now passing away. Whatever else they do for the rest of their lives, they'll never have the same power again. Are they bitter? Are they broken?

Am I?

He has been avoiding his office computer ever since Michael Marcus came to lunch, now almost forty-eight hours ago. He knows he can't prolong his angry silence much longer. There are arrangements in place that will have to be cancelled; that perhaps have already been cancelled without his knowledge. At the time of Michael Marcus's visit he had been too proud to go into the exact details of his new status. Was he out of a job as of two days ago? Had new directors already been hired? How is he to present himself to the production office? As a ghost?

Now, like a reluctant swimmer advancing cautiously over the pebbles into a chilly sea, he enters his study. The computer is asleep, its screen black. Black but shiny, it forms an actual mirror, in which he sees himself unflatteringly reflected. Instinctively he holds himself straight, conscious of a growing tendency to slouch. But then he thinks, No one's watching. I can slouch as much as I like.

This is why people need jobs. Your job is what links you to the world. You get up in the morning and you make yourself look clean and presentable because there are people to meet, places to go. Take that away and your spine softens, your flesh sags, you lose a certain quality that could be called uprightness. In evolution the first stage after the apes that we recognize as distinctively human is called *Homo erectus*. So, seeing himself mirrored in his computer screen, Henry Broad stands tall.

Of course it's all about sex. The parallels are ready and waiting, to jeer and torment. They say the loss of a job can lead to the loss of libido. Libido, the desire for sex, not to be confused with potency, the ability to have sex. This is a cruel distinction, thinks Henry. To desire but not to be able to perform. He desires now. He feels it in every part of his body. But, come the moment, he slouches. All in the mind, they say, those who study such things, and right now his mind is thoroughly rattled. *Sorrows come not single spies but in battalions. Untune that string and hark what discord follows.* Or, to put it in non-Shakespearean terms, I'm fucked.

He reaches out one hand and taps the space bar. The screen jumps to life. A column of emails, all relating to arrangements that will now, presumably, have to be unarranged. Their problem, not mine.

And an email from the Arch Meditator, from yesterday.

Thanks for lunch. Sorry to have been the bearer of bad news. These decisions are way above my pay grade, as you know. On the matter of the reassuring message from you to Monty Don, I'm sure your present feeling is No Fucking Way. But I still want to ask you to do this. If Monty pulls out you gain nothing, but we lose the project and the whole team is thrown out of work. I can't believe you would want that. I accept that there's nothing in this for you (unless you count the matter of karma: what goes around comes around). Sorry to have to push you but time is of the essence. We have to talk to Monty about these changes soonest. So if you can drink the poison while praising the emperor, as you with your abundant historical knowledge put it, do it today. The Romans would have called it virtue.

Karma, for fuck's sake, thinks Henry. You can't believe I want the whole project to go under? Try harder. One out, all out.

My abundant historical knowledge goes further than the Romans. When General Paulus lost the battle of Stalingrad, Hitler promoted him to the rank of field marshal. This was a signal. Field marshals were expected to commit suicide rather than be taken prisoner. Paulus refused to 'enter national immortality', saying, 'I am a Christian. I have no intention of shooting myself for this Bohemian corporal.' The day after his promotion he and his staff surrendered. He lived for another fourteen years, ending his days in a Dresden library as the chief of the East German Military History Research Unit.

So what's the moral of that? If it's a choice between national immortality and a library in Dresden, I take the library.

Meanwhile there's a draft email waiting on the computer that must be completed and sent, or rewritten and sent, or deleted with no message sent. The first flush of righteous anger has long passed, but Henry is not yet ready for magnanimity. The only course open to him is procrastination.

He shuffles into the living room, ostentatiously slouching, and settles down once more before the soap opera of national crisis.

He watches as Nigel Farage loses. 'I've never felt happier,' he says. But he doesn't look happy.

He sees Nick Clegg arriving with his wife at the ICA in Pall Mall. In his resignation speech he calls the results 'immeasurably more crushing and unkind than I ever feared'. A little later Ed Miliband resigns, saying, 'I am truly sorry I did not succeed.' There's a surprise.

Then come helicopter shots of Cameron's car passing through streets cleared of traffic, on his way from Downing Street to Buckingham Palace, down a Mall draped in Union flags, a brutal image of power and privilege.

To the victor go the spoils.

And the losers? Custom requires them to go with a good grace. The decent phrase, the throwaway joke, the distant echo of Roman virtue. But imagine how it would be if a defeated leader spoke as he truly felt. 'My friends, this is a bitter day. My hopes lie in ashes. My life lies in ruins. I'm wounded because I know this is a rejection of me personally, and I'm angry because I don't believe I deserve it. I leave you to join the ranks of the living dead, among the forgotten politicians and ageing celebrities being wheeled slowly backwards, their eyes still fixed pitifully on the past, towards the shore of the Lake of Oblivion. Today you're kind enough, or ghoulish enough, to listen to me. Tomorrow the waters will close over me. I shall be a long time drowning.'

Carrie comes in. She's barefoot, her feet make almost no sound on the carpet.

'Do you have any idea what's happened in the election?' he says.

'No,' says Carrie.

'It's a political earthquake,' says Henry. 'Miliband's out. Clegg's out. Farage is out.'

'I don't see that it makes any difference,' says Carrie.

'It does to them.'

Carrie leaves. A little later Laura appears from her study, cappuccino in hand, and watches the screen from behind him.

'Anything new?' she says.

The television is telling them that Ed Miliband's last act as leader will be to attend the VE Day Seventieth Anniversary at the Cenotaph. Nick Clegg will be there too. They'll lay memorial wreaths.

'You couldn't make it up,' says Henry.

'Does it depress you?'

'I wish it depressed me more. I think I've become addicted to sudden loss of power.'

'Oh, Henry. I wish you'd stop this.'

'Have I become boring? I expect I have. Don't worry, I'll lay my wreath soon, and then do the decent thing and slip away.'

Self-pity, the least attractive of all human traits.

But why not? We live in the age of the selfie. Self-help for a creed, self-abuse for pleasure, self-harm for punishment. What's a little self-pity between friends?

26

Aster Dickinson, motionless in bed, thinks she can hear the cars passing down Edison Crescent. That means she's on the front side of the house, and must have been put to bed in her father's dressing room. This room is not at all like her mother's pretty boudoir. The furniture is immense and made of mahogany, and the smell is of cigar smoke and bay rum. Her father's hairbrushes have no handles. There's a boot rack for his huge leather shoes and a wardrobe for his jackets, which are made of tweed and cloth and linen.

When cars pass outside, their headlights throw beams on the walls. Silvery windows appear with wavering surfaces that travel slowly across the room. Each time they get almost as far as the high bed where she lies, but then they disappear.

Miss Brownlow says Mummy's coming to collect me from school, and when I see her I'm not to say, 'Where's Daddy?' But when she drives up in the Benz I say it first thing. 'Where's Daddy?'

The cemetery is bright and hot and filled with the sound of

birds. I'm to drop my posy of flowers into the grave, onto the coffin. The flowers make a soft sliding noise and fan out on the shiny lid. There's a tall soldier with a bugle hanging against his side on a cord. When he plays it everyone cries. It's like the signal to cry. But I don't cry.

In the orchard, right in the middle, there's a big old apricot tree. Its branches spread sideways, like a candlestick. It grows apricots, first green then golden amid the dark leaves. There's a place in its branches where you can sit exactly as if you're in a chair. I can hear the wind hissing in the leaves. I hear it now.

Has everyone gone? I don't know how it is, but people always seem to leave me. I haven't made a great success of my life. Did I ask for too much? All I've ever wanted is not to be left alone.

Pull me up, Elizabeth. Sit where I can see you. My father died when I was young, you know. You get frightened after that. Mummy said, 'Be a good soldier.' I have tried, but sometimes it's been too hard. Forgive me if I've been a bad mother. Having a baby scared me, to tell the truth. I never really knew what to do. But I have loved you, my darling, more than all the world. You're all I have left. Tell me you love me. Come and give me a hug. That's all I want, really. Someone to hug.

27

Alan Strachan has arranged to have lunch with his agent in London. It's something he's been meaning to do for a long time. Elaine is important to him, in a sense his entire livelihood depends on her, and yet all their dealings are by phone and email.

'I'm coming up to make sure you really exist,' he tells her on the phone.

And for another reason, one that he tells no one, not even himself. Instead he fills his mind with the minutiae of his journey, playing a series of private games that lock down his attention without costing him any real emotional effort.

To this end, on reaching Lewes station he leaves his car in the station car park without paying and displaying a parking ticket. He has never yet returned to find a plastic-wrapped notice on his windscreen, and already calculates that he's saved more in daily rates than he'll have to pay out in a fine. It's a small foolishness, which makes his heart beat a little faster each time he returns to reclaim his car.

On the platform he positions himself where the front doors of the front coach will open, an easy calculation if you know the formation of the train. There are small blue-and-white signs that tell the driver where to stop: 4-Coach Stop, 8-12 Coach Stop. The illuminated display screens tell the number of coaches, as do the loudspeaker announcements. There's a further clue. The tea trolley, which joins the train from Eastbourne here at Lewes, is always wheeled to the place on the platform where the front-most train doors will open. Alongside the trolley man or woman there's a member of the station staff carrying a fold-up ramp. While waiting for the train to arrive they chat in a language Alan doesn't recognize, perhaps Latvian or Estonian. Sometimes, perfidiously, a train promised as being made up of eight coaches arrives with only four, and pulls to a stop far down the platform. At such times the trolley, the fold-up ramp and Alan have to scamper down the platform; and, of course, at such times Alan fails to secure his preferred seat.

This should not matter, but it does. Alan likes to sit in a window seat with a table, facing the direction of travel, in a coach where the seats are laid out two by two at either side of the aisle. There is another kind of coach in every train in which the aisle is narrower and there are three seats on one side and two on the other. Not only are the seats themselves narrower, they're harder and have no armrests. In the normal way of things the lead coach is of the more comfortable kind, but you can never be sure. When Alan enters the train and finds himself among the inferior seats he walks back down the train until he reaches a superior carriage.

Of course, none of this is of the slightest importance. A seat is a seat. At some times of day you count yourself fortunate not to have to stand. But it's just one of the games he plays, by which he is forever achieving tiny victories, or enduring tiny defeats.

Today he gains his desired seat. Now comes the defence of territory. He likes to be able to stretch out his legs under the table, so it's best to have no one in the seat opposite, at least as far as Gatwick. The travellers who get on the train at the same time as him usually understand this. Today a very small, bent old lady comes shuffling up the aisle to the pair of seats facing him and with considerable difficulty installs herself directly in front of him. Both other seats of the foursome are free. She then takes out a snippet of newspaper and starts to do a Sudoku.

Alan moves to the aisle seat beside him, so that he can stretch out his legs. He moves in a clattery fashion, hoping she'll realize why he's moving, but she seems not to notice. She has thick grey hair cut like a helmet, and a face so remarkably wrinkled that she seems to possess every possible expression at once. Her concentration on her Sudoku is absolute, but unsuccessful, in that her pencil makes no marks. From time to time she utters a sharp grunt.

Partly victorious, partly defeated, Alan allows his mind to look ahead as far as his coming lunch with Elaine.

'Of course I'd love to see you,' Elaine said on the phone. 'But I can't help wondering why.'

'It's time I set eyes on your new assistant,' Alan said.

'Hannah's been with me over two years now.'

The agency is situated in a mews behind Portland Road, Notting Hill, which means, when coming from Victoria, that he has to submit himself to the indifference of the Circle line. The platform from which the westbound Circle line trains depart also hosts the westbound District line trains. These green trains are showered on happy suburbanites in abundance, some to Wimbledon, some to Richmond, some to Ealing Broadway. But the yellow trains that go to Notting Hill and Paddington are released only reluctantly, and at long intervals. Today Alan watches five trains go by before he can board. Another miniature defeat.

Elaine has offered to take Alan out to lunch, even though it's he who has requested the meeting. She's booked a table at Julie's, where she's been going for years. Elaine is large and motherly in appearance, though not in personality. Their stroll up the street to the restaurant is slow and majestic.

'Did you stay up to watch the election?' she asks him. 'What a shocker!'

'I saw the exit poll. Then when I got up this morning, it was all over.'

'To tell you the truth,' says Elaine, 'I'm secretly relieved. We'd have been paying mansion tax. Both Geoffrey and I vote Labour, because you do, don't you? But this morning we both felt as if we'd dodged a bullet.'

'Wasn't it St Augustine who said, Lord make me virtuous, but not yet?'

'He said, Give me chastity, but not yet.'

'Oh, right,' says Alan.

Then as they settle into one of Julie's characterfully cramped tables, Elaine says, 'I hope you're not going to sack me.'

'Good heavens, no,' says Alan. 'What would I do without you? I could never ask for the fees you get for me.'

'It's getting harder,' says Elaine. 'Is Stuart asking you for an outline on your sci-fi thing?'

'Yes,' says Alan.

'Don't give him anything. He hasn't agreed terms yet.'

Alan does in fact have a reason for seeing Elaine, though it's nothing new. As he tucks into his steak-and-kidney pie, he puts before her his perennial lament, the lack of control he has over his work. Elaine sighs over her salmon and pea fishcakes.

'What can I say, Alan? It's how the business works.'

'You don't think I should write a spec script without a contract, and then offer it with the condition that they make no changes?'

'There's two defects in that plan, my dear. They might not want it. And if they do, they'll change it anyway.'

'So do you think I should set up as a writer-producer?'

'Do you want to?'

'No. Not at all. How about writer-director?'

'Do you want to?'

'No,' says Alan, glumly.

'The system will never change, my dear, so long as they're the ones with the money. Mel Gibson made his Jesus film with his own money, I believe. Kubrick's first film was financed by his uncle, who owned a drugstore. Do you have an uncle with a drugstore?'

'No,' says Alan.

'Have you put aside substantial sums from the money you made on the dog movie?'

'No,' says Alan.

'Then I suggest you go on as you are, but maybe write poems on the side. That shouldn't take long, and no one will interfere with them.'

'All right, Elaine. No need to be bitchy.'

'I'm just looking after my fifteen per cent.'

'I thought it was ten per cent.'

'Who's not been reading his contracts?'

'I never read my contracts. That's why I employ you.'

'Of course it is. You are the talent. The talent doesn't worry its little head over nasty numbers.'

Alan thinks of Annie's outburst about Victorian gentlemen and their fear of being tainted by trade.

'You're perfectly right, Elaine,' he says.

He's managed up to now to block thoughts of Annie; or rather, since he knows perfectly well what he's doing, to keep such thoughts behind a closed but by no means locked door. But now the door has opened, the image of Annie is back, and his heart is beginning to beat faster.

So he's planning a visit to an old friend. There's nothing he needs to keep secret about that. And yet the plain fact is, he has not told Liz.

What is there to tell?

This is, thinks Alan, the real secret. He does not yet know what will happen when he makes the call in Clarendon Road. Most likely nothing at all. He's already admitted his desires to Liz. There's something humiliating about a desire that is not met by an answering desire. This uncertainty, more than any waiting guilt, stops him letting his imagination reach too far ahead.

One step at a time.

'So is it back home to Sussex now?' says Elaine.

'Soon,' he says.

28

Henry taps on Carrie's bedroom door.

'Come on. Time for the laying of the wreaths.'

Carrie appears, blinking. She seems to have been asleep.

'Do I need to see it?'

'We all need to see it. It's called closure.'

They gather in front of the television, Henry and Carrie and Laura, and watch the memorial service at the Cenotaph. In London, judging by the umbrellas over the waiting veterans, it's raining. A suitably sombre grey early afternoon.

The hour strikes. A gun fires over the Thames. Buglers play the Last Post. Banners are lowered to trail the ground.

'Don't you find it comforting?' says Henry. 'Take the long view and we're all dead.'

Prince Andrew lays a wreath, or perhaps it's Prince Edward. Hard to tell through all the gold braid. Then there they are, the three leaders, all in dark blue suits, all the same height, all holding wreaths of red poppies. They move together in unison, forward to the Cenotaph, up the step, bend to lay the wreaths, back down the step, bow the head.

'Have they rehearsed this?' says Henry. 'If so, when?'

Sad organ music accompanies this slow dance of death. Two of the leaders are laying wreaths on their own graves.

'Guess which two aren't enjoying this,' says Henry.

'We do know who they are, Dad,' says Carrie.

There follows a hymn.

> *Time like an ever rolling stream*
> *Bears all its sons away*
> *They fly forgotten as a dream*
> *Dies at the opening day . . .*

The rain holds off. The three leaders depart through the arched doorway of the Foreign Office. One is victorious, two are defeated, but they're all going to die.

'Death the great leveller,' says Henry. 'People forget. We need more death around.'

'Honestly, Dad,' says Carrie.

'Imagine being Nick Clegg. Or Ed Miliband. This is brutal public humiliation. How do you survive that? You spend weeks having everyone cheer everything you say, you're the big man in every room you enter, and then boom! Overnight you're nothing. You're history. You're a footnote to history. No one wants you around. You're an embarrassment. What on earth do you do? You want to crawl into a hole and die. But instead you've got another forty years to go.'

Laura and Carrie say nothing. Henry doesn't mind. He's talking mostly to himself.

I've just witnessed a half-death, he thinks.

'You know what? We're going to have to get used to this. We all live so long, we don't just have one life, we have two. And we have two deaths. There's the full death that comes at the end, but before that there's the half-death. Half of us dies, but half lives on. That's what's just happened to Miliband and Clegg. And here's the question. What do they do for the rest of their lives?'

This idea of the half-death strikes him as rather original.

'So what you're saying,' says Carrie, 'is that when important people stop being important, they feel bad.'

It doesn't sound quite so original put like that.

'Yes, I suppose so.'

'The thing is, Dad, most people don't feel important ever.'

'Everyone has their own little world where what they do matters. For a while at least.'

'Actually, no. There's a whole lot of people who feel that nothing they've done has ever mattered, and nothing ever will.'

Laura turns to Carrie in dismay.

'Do you feel that?'

'Sometimes.'

'But it's not true, Carrie. What you do matters to us. Matters a lot. Tell her, Henry.'

'Of course it does.'

'I know that,' says Carrie. But gently, as if afraid of hurting them, she adds, 'You're my parents. I'm like an extension of you. If I fail, it's like you're failing yourself. That's why I matter to you.'

'No, Carrie. No.'

Laura feels bewildered. What she's saying can't be true. If it is, there's no such thing as love.

'We love you,' she says.

'I love you too, Mum. Forget I said it.'

Then Carrie's getting up out of her chair.

'Where are you going?'

'Upstairs.'

To her room. To the land where she's all alone.

'Carrie,' Laura says. 'Tell us what we can do.'

Halfway out of the door, not looking back –

'Just don't let Dad die.'

'I certainly won't,' says Laura. 'I'm making him go to the doctor.'

But they've played the Last Post, Henry wants to say. I've died my half-death. I've laid my wreath. Time like an ever-rolling stream bears all its sons away. Ed and Nick and me.

29

The Telegraph Group's offices are right by Victoria station, which makes it easy for Liz to look in on Chrissie Charteris and talk over her feature in person. Of course, it could all be done on the phone, but Liz feels the need to get away from Sussex, where her mother's dying seems to fill every room. If the end comes at last, she can be back home within an hour or so.

Riding the long escalator from the lobby, up to the steel and glass quadrangle that perches on top of the Sussex line platforms, she envies Chrissie her metropolitan life. This is a world where people carry passes, where the elect sweep by with a nod to the security guard and the lower orders like herself must sign their names in the register.

At the top of the escalator, before a further set of barriers that leads to the newsroom, there is a wide high-ceilinged atrium known as the Sky Bar. Here, on low black leather couches, people sit talking in soft voices beneath a cloud-white glass roof. This light from above may be daylight or it may be artificial light, it's impossible to tell. The effect is of brightness without a source, and of space without freedom.

Liz gives her name, and settles at one of the small round tables that cluster by the coffee bar. She takes out her iPad and opens the file she sent to Chrissie, which is her first draft. As she re-reads it, a tall silver-haired man, crossing the atrium, sees her and comes to her table.

'Liz Dickinson!' he says.

Liz looks up.

'Hello, Graham.'

Graham Martin-Smith, once one of her bosses in the days when she had bosses, has since risen to great heights, though Liz isn't exactly sure what title he goes by these days.

'You look so grown-up, Graham.'

He's wearing an expensive suit, a shirt with double cuffs, a silk tie.

'Have to look the part,' he says, smiling at her. 'What a night, eh?'

'I expect you're all happy.'

'Like waking from a bad dream. But maybe you don't see it that way.'

'I voted Green,' says Liz. 'As a result our LibDem MP lost to the hated Tories. I feel personally responsible.'

'The hated Tories.' Graham gives her a fatherly smile. 'Admit it, Liz. You're much more comfortable having people in charge who allow you to feel morally superior but let you keep your money.'

'What money is that?'

'I take it you're here because you're doing something for us.'

'For *Stella*, I hope.'

She feels his gaze upon her. She remembers an office jaunt to Monaco with him, where they all drank far too much, and he banged on the door of her bedroom.

'So what is it?' He gestures at the iPad.

'A feature on what women want,' says Liz.

'What's the answer? Isn't it supposed to be shopping and fucking?'

'Just fucking, really,' says Liz.

Graham raises his eyebrows and purses his lips, like an expert art buyer appraising a painting.

'I shall have to take a look at that,' he says.

Shortly after he's gone, Chrissie appears.

'Sorry, sorry. It's been a long night. You want a coffee?' They go back many years, Liz and Chrissie, to the time when they were both gossip feeders for the *Standard*'s Londoner's Diary. 'The ad department's just told us we're up-paging. How soon can you get your feature finished?'

'Monday?'

'That would be great. What do you want? Latte?'

They settle back at the round table with their coffees.

'So you like it?' says Liz.

'Love it,' says Chrissie. 'It's what my editor calls a zeitgeist piece. Her only question was, do we say *randy* or *horny*?' She grins at Liz. 'You always were the sexy one.'

'Me? I could tell a few stories about you.'

Chrissie sighs. She's been divorced for years now.

'All I do these days is work. I've just survived the fourth round of cuts. Life doesn't get any easier, does it?'

'Tell me about it,' says Liz. 'Here I am, writing about sex, and my mother's dying.'

'Oh, Liz.'

'No, it's all right. She might be dying, but she might not.'

'Life and death, I guess.'

'Something like that,' says Liz. 'But you know, waiting for her to die does something to my sex drive.' Lowering her voice, 'It makes me randy, or maybe horny. Is that a terrible thing to say?'

'You know what Betjeman said before he died? He was asked what he most regretted and he said, "Not enough sex."'

'You know I'm going to have to do interviews to flesh this thing out?' says Liz.

'Of course.'

'How about I start with you?'

'Oh, no. I'm far too old. I'm practically past it.'

'You are not too old!' exclaims Liz. 'You're forty-seven, same as me.'

'Ssh!' Chrissie looks around in alarm. 'They think I'm thirty-nine.'

'I don't just want to write about how women want sex. I want to write about how *older* women want sex.'

'No, Liz, no. Not the O-word.'

'What do you want? Milfs? Cougars?'

'No one admits to being old until they're dead. Call them grown-up women.'

'I'm so sick of this youth fetish,' says Liz. 'I know young people are more beautiful, but older people have better sex. It takes years to get comfortable with your body. It takes years to work out what you want, and to get up the courage to ask for it.'

'And by the time you get there, there's no one to do it with.'

'Oh, Chrissie. Don't say that.'

They gaze at each other helplessly.

'It's just another of life's design faults,' says Chrissie. 'Like underarm hair and childbirth.'

'But I'm right, aren't I?'

'Easy for you to say, honey. You've got a man.'

'All right,' says Liz. 'But how about this? From the age of sixteen to the age of twenty-two I had sex with a dozen guys, more. I even managed to get myself pregnant – and I never once had an orgasm. Now I'm forty-seven years old, I really know how to enjoy myself, and I have sex with just one guy. Does that make sense?'

'So you're saying you'd like to have an affair.'

'Not just one. Lots. Wouldn't you?'

'I'm available.'

'So we're no different from the guys, after all.'

Chrissie thinks about that.

'Wearing my editorial hat,' she says, 'I can hear my readers saying, How do you have an affair without fucking up your marriage?'

'Honestly,' says Liz.

'Honestly?'

'It's not the sex that does the damage. It's the cheating.'

'I hope you're writing all this down.'

'The other day Alan bumped into an old girlfriend, from long before he knew me. She's our age, but she still looks great, I've seen her. I could tell from the way he talked about her that there was still something there. So I asked him straight, Do you want to fuck her? And he said, Yes.'

'But he's not going to do it.'

'No, he won't do it. But what if it was the other way round, and it was me and an old boyfriend? Would I do it?'

'No. You wouldn't.'

'I'd damn well think about doing it. There's been too much dying in my life recently. I need some living.'

Chrissie picks up Liz's iPad, opens Google, and taps some words into the search bar.

'Have you heard about Regrets of the Dying?'

'No.'

'It's this blog written by a nurse who cares for terminally ill patients. She made a list of the five things they said they most regretted. Here it is.'

Liz looks at the list on the screen.

1. I wish I'd had the courage to live a life true to myself, not the life others expected of me.
2. I wish I hadn't worked so hard.
3. I wish I'd had the courage to express my feelings.
4. I wish I'd stayed in touch with my friends.
5. I wish that I had let myself be happier.

'Nothing about sex,' says Liz.

'It's all about sex,' says Chrissie. 'Sex is about all those things.'

'Oh, Chrissie,' says Liz, copying down the list in her notebook. 'You are as wise as you are beautiful.'

'So how come I'm on my own, girl?'

Her phone shivers.

'Oh, God. I'm going to have to go. So you'll get me the piece by Monday lunchtime?'

'I'll do my best.'

30

Alan Strachan walks up Clarendon Road half in a dream, and comes to a stop outside number 92. It's a tall white stucco terraced house, with steep steps to a high ground floor. The plane trees in the road are just coming into leaf. Across from the house stands a pub called the Clarendon, its woodwork painted a smart blue-grey. But higher up, at roof level, an older name cut into the plasterwork reveals it once to have been called the Britannia.

As Alan stands looking at it, a young woman is herding two small children into a neighbouring house: a nanny, not a mother. The cars parked outside are expensive, new, clean.

Then the door at which he's gazing opens, as if yielding to the pressure of his longing, and there she is.

So it's happening, this adventure. He wants to believe he's done nothing to will it. Things happen, and he responds.

She's wearing jeans, a white T-shirt, and a long, loose-knit cherry-coloured cardigan. She's smiling at him.

'You look like you want to buy the house,' she says.

'I couldn't afford it.'

He climbs the steps to the front door.

'You saw your agent?'

'Yes,' he says. 'She gave me lunch at Julie's.'

'Very nice. It's Nando's for us.'

Inside, the house is handsome, a little shabby.

'We bought it twenty years ago, when we had money,' says Annie, apologizing for not living up to the post-code. 'It feels very empty with Ellie away.'

He follows her downstairs into the kitchen, which occupies the whole lower ground floor. A shaggy black dog lumbers out of his basket to investigate the visitor.

'That's Pretzel. He's getting old.'

'Aren't we all?' says Alan, scratching the dog behind his ears.

'Coffee? Wine?'

'I don't suppose you've got any beer?'

'Sorry, no.'

'Coffee would be great.'

She doesn't ask him why he's come, and he offers no reason. They're formal with each other, unsure how to behave. Alan looks at the photographs and postcards on the pin-board by the fridge: Annie and Mitch against various foreign backgrounds, Ellie as a little girl. Annie is very photogenic. Unable to look at her directly here in the room, he admires her photographs.

'How did you and Mitch meet?' he asks.

'We were on the same graduate course.'

'So, not long after I knew you.'

'No, not long. A year or two.'

He wonders if there was anyone in between. It seems hardly possible that there was him, and then there was Mitch.

'So when is he back from South Africa?'

'Two weeks.'

She brings him a mug of coffee. It's good, rich and strong.

'Good coffee.'

'Mitch is fussy about coffee. He's taught me how to do it properly.'

Alan feels paralysed. There are things he wants to say, but to say them he needs permission, and he doesn't know how to ask. So he looks round the long room, and out through the French windows to the little garden at the back, and makes polite conversation.

'I suppose this would once have been a modest house for a modest family,' he says. 'Now it must be worth millions.'

'It's bigger than it looks from the outside. If you count the attics it's got five floors. Lots of stairs to keep me fit. I have my workroom right at the top.'

'So you can pretend you're going out to work.'

'Yes,' she says, pleased he understands. 'Exactly.'

'That's why I work in an outbuilding. Work space has to be separate from home space.'

For a moment there's silence as they drink their coffee. The silence is dangerous. They need words as a modesty panel, to give decent cover to their thoughts.

'Would you like a tour?'

'If it's not being too nosy.'

'I don't mind. Other people's houses are always fun.'

Now that they have a project they relax a little. Annie starts to move about, showing off her home.

'So this is the kitchen. We live down here, mostly.'

'The television is the clue,' says Alan. 'The screen is where the heart is.'

The modest-sized flat screen stands on a dresser, facing a long, deep sofa.

'I'm not sure it's like that any more,' says Annie. 'There's a bigger one upstairs.'

She leads him up to the raised ground floor. Following her he's acutely aware of her legs. She has good legs.

'This is the living room.'

'Where you don't actually live.'

'Exactly.'

And so on up: a master bedroom, with its connected bath-room; Ellie's room, also with a bathroom; a guest bedroom, where there stands a wide and untouched bed.

'Not that we have many guests. My brother lived there for a while.'

'Robbie?'

She's surprised that he remembers, as is he. Sometimes things long buried in memory just pop out. He met Robbie only once: an annoying teenager who affected cynicism.

'He died,' she says.

'I'm sorry.'

'Coming up for ten years now. You probably never knew, but he suffered from serious depression. Mitch was wonderful with him. He let him live here. Supported him. But you can't make people go on living when they don't want to.'

On up ever narrower stairs to the attic.

'And this is what I grandly call my office.'

Alan looks at the tidy desk, the wooden filing cabinet, the stack of archive boxes.

'You're very organized.'

'I think being organized is what non-creative people do as a substitute. We create order.'

'It's what creative people do too. Make shapes out of the shapelessness of life.'

He looks out of the dormer window. She comes to his side to see what he sees. He can feel the heat from her body.

'Don't you love my view? That's the communal garden behind Elgin Crescent. I can't go into it, but every day I look at it, so it's as if I do own it in a way.'

Descending the many stairs again, Annie leading, and so not able to see his face, she says, 'I dreamed about you last night.'

'I hope it was a good dream.'

'It was a strange dream. The kind I haven't had for years.'

Alan wants to ask if it was a sex dream.

'Was it that dream about sitting an exam, and you don't know the answers?'

'No,' she says, 'but it was from student days. I was in bed with a man in a single bed, and I kept thinking I was going to fall out.'

So, a sex dream from student days. I was there, he thinks.

They go back down to the kitchen.

'Who was the man in the bed?'

'You.'

'In bed with you, but not having sex.'

'We were, in a way. We were going to. But I kept almost falling out of bed. And then I woke up.'

He sees her reflected in the black mirror of the TV, and can tell that she's blushing. The heightened colour in her cheeks excites him.

216

'Sounds like you were trying to get away from me,' he says.

'I didn't actually fall out.'

'Even so. We didn't manage to do it.'

'Honestly, I don't know what I'm doing telling you my sex dreams. I am almost fifty.'

'You're forty-four. Same age as me.'

'I might as well be fifty. Men go for younger women, everyone knows that.'

'That's to show off to other men. For simple pleasure, give me a woman of my own age.'

'Like Liz.'

'Exactly. Liz is three years older than me.'

'Mitch is nine years older than me.'

And so, like conscientious chaperones, the absent partners return.

'How long have you two been together?' says Alan.

'Twenty-two years.'

'You win. Liz and I have been together fifteen years now.'

For a moment neither speaks.

'Funny to think,' says Alan, 'that if I hadn't been such a dud in bed we might have made a go of it, you and me.'

'I told you.' She raps him lightly on the arm with one hand. 'I didn't care about that.'

'It's what you dreamed about.'

'In my dream,' she says, speaking slowly, as if reluctantly, 'you did try to make love to me, and I tried to stop you. But I couldn't.'

'But it still didn't happen.'

'No. I woke up.'

What Alan wants to know but can't ask is, Was it the young

me in the dream, or the old me? Did I fail, in the dream? Do you dream of me as a sexual failure? 'I tried to stop you,' she says, 'but you were too strong for me.'

'It sounds like I was raping you,' he says. 'That's not like me at all.'

'No, of course not. Dreams are such a muddle, aren't they?'

A silence falls again. Just as he's given no reason for coming, now he tells her, without explanation, 'It's time I was going.'

She makes no attempt to detain him.

'You and Liz must come to dinner when Mitch is back.'

'And next time you're down our way, give us warning and we'll feed you.'

They stand before each other, in that moment of parting where it's now customary to exchange a kiss on the cheek, but they don't kiss. The absent kiss fills the space between them.

He goes quickly.

Later, on the train home, Alan returns to the story of her dream. In the dream she behaved properly in resisting his sexual advance, but at the same time she wanted him to overpower her resistance. After all, both people in the dream, both herself and him, were her creations. Both desires, to resist and to submit, belonged to her. So what does that mean? That she wants to make love with me, but wants it not to be her fault. Which exactly describes my own case.

At this rate we'll get precisely nowhere. Perhaps that's what we want, the adventure of the journey but not the danger of arrival. At least this way no one gets hurt.

31

When she gets home Liz finds Alan is not yet back. She calls
Bridget and learns that there's been no change. The palliative-care
nurse has phoned to say she won't be there till after five thirty
or six. Her mother sleeps on. At this time on a Friday Liz usually
goes to a Pilates class at a friend's house, a class made up of
middle-aged women like herself. She has it in mind to question
the others on the subject of her feature. She might as well go to
the class and head on to her mother's afterwards, in time to catch
the nurse.

Life must go on.

She calls Bridget again and tells her she'll be with her by six.
Then she changes and drives to the old Sussex barn in Plump-
ton, part of the estate of her friend Penny Worth, where the
class is held.

The trainer, Mickey, is Australian and in her twenties. Penny
Worth herself, handsome, decent, generous with her money
and her time, is a year or so younger than Liz. Her husband
runs a private equity fund, and is rarely at home. The rest of

the class is made up of Rachel Quinn, an elfin artist in her fifties, the only one among them fit enough to follow the trainer move for move; Jane Hammond, who is undeniably plump and no longer pretends otherwise; and Laura Broad, mother of Alice's boyfriend Jack. There is a tacit understanding within the group that the weekly class is not competitive, either in fitness or in beauty. The tone is one of wry regret at the extent to which they fall short of physical perfection.

For an hour they lie on their mats gazing up at the rafters of the old barn, and inhale and exhale upon instruction.

'Tighten that T-zone,' calls Mickey. 'Keep it engaged!'

They push down on their pubic bones, they retain their pelvic stability, they squeeze their glutes. In the exercise that requires them to press a sprung ring between their knees and rock from side to side, Liz, whose mind is full of sex, imagines the ring as the sights of a gun, and the gun is pointing straight between her thighs.

'Legs into tabletop position!' calls Mickey. 'Now we're going to work those abs!'

Their hair is twisted off their faces; they all wear leggings and singlets, unembarrassed by the way such clothing reveals the ungainly parts of their bodies that they have learned, in the rest of their life, to disguise. This is a conspiracy of honesty.

When the class is over, and Mickey, the alien from Planet Youth, has departed, they pull on fleeces and gather in Penny's kitchen to drink fresh-squeezed orange juice and to gossip. For a little while they talk about the election, treading carefully, unsure of each other's politics.

'I never thought Norman would lose his seat,' says Laura.

'It's my fault,' says Liz. 'I voted Labour.'

'I didn't know you were a socialist, Liz,' says Jane.

'Just trying to get my youth back,' says Liz.

Then she tells them how she's been commissioned to write a feature about women's sexual desire. The members of the Pilates class meet each other's eyes apprehensively. No one wants to appear ridiculous.

'The less I think about that sort of thing the better,' says Penny. 'It's not like I'm going to wake up one morning and find I'm young again.'

'Yes, but that's just it,' says Liz. 'Why do we think of sex as being only for the young?'

'I don't,' says Penny, 'but I'm married, aren't I? I'm not in the market any more.'

'But would you if you could?' says Jane. 'That's what Liz is asking.'

'Would I cheat on George? No, I wouldn't. I don't do that. I'm not a cheater.'

'What if it wasn't cheating?' says Liz.

'How can having sex with another man not be cheating?'

'If your husband knows about it,' says Liz.

'If I did it and George knew about it, he'd kick me out of the house.'

'There are couples who do it,' says Rachel. 'Who have open marriages.'

'I'd love to have an open marriage,' says Jane, wistfully.

Penny is astonished.

'You want Oliver to screw someone else?'

'I was thinking more of my side of it,' says Jane.

'Start with an open marriage,' says Penny, 'and you'll end with a divorce.'

'Closed marriages end in divorce too,' says Laura.

But Jane is liking the idea the more she thinks about it.

'As far as I'm concerned,' she says, 'I'm all for it. The problem isn't cheating, or divorce, it's finding a man who wants to have an affair with me. It's easy for men. They can be small and fat and women still seem to want them. But for us, you have to get your man while you're young and then you have to hold on tight and pray you make it through to old age.'

'That is so true, Jane,' says Penny. Her husband comes into the small and fat category. 'If I were to start having affairs, George would say, Whoopee, and the next thing I know he's dumping me for a younger model.'

'So we have to be faithful,' says Liz, 'to stop our men leaving.' She's taking notes.

'Of course,' says Penny.

'And is it the same for men?'

'Men are different,' says Penny, firmly. 'Don't ask, don't tell. That's what my mother taught me.'

Rachel has been listening with a puzzled look on her face.

'What do you think, Rachel?' says Liz.

'I think it's so interesting,' says Rachel. 'I don't know that we're so different to men. I think we all want the same thing, really. We all want love, and security, and companionship. But we want adventure too, and flattery, and excitement. The thing about having an affair is it really boosts your morale.'

'Are you speaking from experience, Rachel?'

Rachel acts like she hasn't heard Liz's question. She's appealing earnestly to the group.

'You must have felt it, that sinking feeling when you look at your husband and think, I'm never going to have sex with anyone but him for the rest of my life.'

This produces a burst of laughter. Even Penny laughs.

'So what do you do about it?' says Liz.

Rachel blushes.

'I'm not telling,' she says. 'Sorry. I just can't.'

'Does Jonathan know?'

Jonathan is Rachel's much older husband, an academic at Sussex University.

'Jonathan knows as much as he wants to know,' says Rachel. 'It's been a bit bumpy. But we're okay.'

Jane is agog.

'Where did you do it? That's always what I want to know. In my fantasy we do it in a luxury hotel. I think I want the luxury hotel almost as much as the sex.'

Then Penny starts talking, in a quite different tone of voice. She sounds as if she's in a dream.

'I was propositioned once, not so long ago. It was at the hunt ball. He's an old friend, a very attractive man, actually. He was rat-arsed, course. He said, Penny, you're the only decent-looking woman here. Will you be offended if I tell you that you drive me wild with desire?'

She repeats the remembered words with slow care. Clearly she's relived the moment many times. The others listen in awe.

'I told him no, no woman objects to being desired. It's a compliment. I told him I was touched and grateful. So then he said, Penny, come with me into the bushes and let's fuck.'

The others gasp.

'Oh, my Lord!' says Jane. 'Did you?'

'No,' says Penny.

'I bet you wish you had,' says Jane.

'Sometimes,' says Penny.

'Why not?' says Liz. 'Sex is supposed to be fun.'

Penny comes out of her trance as abruptly as she entered it.

'It's no good talking like this,' she says. 'All it does is stir things up, and then where are you? You make your bed and you lie in it.'

'And he snores,' says Jane.

'So is this what you're writing about, Liz?' says Rachel. 'About wives having affairs?'

Liz then tells them in more detail about the book she's found, and how it claims women are just as randy as men, only they're unable to admit it. They talk for a little while about whether they believe this or not.

'Do you believe it, Liz?' says Laura.

'I don't know,' says Liz. 'I find it so hard to know why I believe the things I believe. Mostly I just want to please everyone.'

'In the end,' says Penny, her equilibrium regained, 'it's a matter of dignity. That's why I didn't go into the bushes at the hunt ball. Someone might have seen us, and I would have scratched my bum on the ground, and got dead leaves stuck all over my dress. I'm as game for a good time as anyone, I hope, but I do have my pride.'

As they leave Penny's house Liz suggests to Laura that she stop off for a glass of wine on her way home.

Pouring the wine, she says, 'You were very quiet back there.'

'Oh, I'm too old for that sort of thing,' says Laura. 'Though I was actually propositioned yesterday. By a client of mine.'

'There you go. Were you tempted?'

'Not remotely. Mind you, he is very old and very pompous.'

'Did he just come straight out with it?'

'There was some padding about to prepare the ground. Then he asked me if I was bored with Henry, and said, "Are we to be imprisoned in a cell for two for the rest of our lives?"'

'Crikey!'

Laura gives a helpless shrug. She realizes she's playing with her rings.

'It seems to me I'm better off just not thinking about that sort of thing.'

'Men think about it,' says Liz.

'Yes, you're right. Henry says when he starts thinking about sex he can't think of anything else until he's done it.'

'So why don't we think about it?'

'We're different,' says Laura.

'Are we?' says Liz. 'I thought that. But then I thought, Why am I thinking that? Because it's impossible to believe that women have desires like men? I mean, what if we're at the stage gay men were at a hundred years ago? If you were gay, you didn't ever hear of anyone else being gay, you thought you were the only one, so you had to be a freak. Then times change, and it turns out millions of others want what you want, and you're normal. Maybe it's like that now for women and sex.'

'Maybe,' says Laura. 'But I don't see what's to be done about it. I mean, if I started carrying on like that—'

'You'd lose Henry.'

'I'd *hurt* Henry. He doesn't need it. Especially right now.'

'Of course. I'm not talking about what we might *do*. I'm talking about what we might *want*.'

'I'm a lot older than you, Liz. I'm almost fifty-seven. That makes a difference.'

'I don't see why.'

'We all talk about sex as if its only point is pleasure. But its actual function isn't pleasure, it's making babies. The pleasure's there to lure us into having the babies. So maybe when that's no longer possible, something changes.'

'Or maybe,' says Liz, 'when you know there's no risk of getting pregnant any more, that's when you're free to have as much sex as you want.'

'Maybe,' says Laura.

'But you're still not buying it.'

'I suppose I'm still adjusting. My life keeps on changing. For years I was fertile and trying not to have children. Then I was fertile and having children. Then I was raising children. Then the children left home. Now I'm not fertile any more, and I've got no children. What am I good for? As far as evolution's concerned, I'm done. It's over.'

'Fuck evolution,' says Liz. 'My mother gave up when she was my age. She's been on her deathbed for forty years. I'm not giving up.'

'But Liz, what are we supposed to do?'

'What does anyone do? What do the men do? Keep living!'

'The men go on being fertile. For them sex is still part of the life force. I'm not part of the life force any more.'

Liz stares at Laura. She takes Laura's hands in hers and fixes her with a solemn gaze.

'Are you truly telling me you feel your life's over?'

'No, not at all. I just feel that it's not about me any more. Now, for the first time in my life, I can stop thinking just about myself and my family. I feel like I've got more to give than ever.'

'And more to take.'

Laura laughs guiltily at that.

'Yes, you're right. I'm not so good at taking.'

'But you're still part of the life force, okay? The life force isn't only about babies. And, anyway, what are babies? They're just tiny old people at an early stage. We're the rock'n'roll generation, girl. We're going to grow old in style. We're going to party till we drop!'

'Oh, Liz.'

She gives Liz a hug.

'We're the pioneers,' Liz says. 'No one's been where we're going before. We're healthy, we're liberated, and we're financially independent. So let's invent the future!'

Liz's phone rings. It's Bridget, to say the palliative-care nurse has arrived. Liz looks at the time. She's late.

'Oh, God,' she exclaims to Laura. 'Back to the deathbed.'

32

When Liz enters her mother's house she finds Kim, the nurse, is accompanied by her supervisor, an older woman called Megan.

'Kim told me how things are going here,' Megan says. 'I thought I'd best see for myself.'

Megan is stocky, with cropped hair and no make-up. Her eyes are a startling blue. She takes in the situation with a few searching glances, then assumes control. From her brisk questions Liz understands very quickly that she's come with a particular object in view, but that it is not to be named. A strange feeling creeps over her, of relief mixed with something close to awe.

'We were up in the night again,' says Karen.

'Up in the night?' Megan pounces on the information. 'Up how?'

'Not out of bed,' says Karen. 'We wave our arms about.'

'Any sign she's in pain?'

'Who's to say?'

'Course she's in pain,' says Bridget, way ahead of Karen. 'What else do those noises mean?'

'Noises?' says Megan.

'Like little screams.'

Megan studies the paperwork, tutting softly to herself.

'Dose on the low side.'

'I didn't want to take any risks,' says Kim.

'Quite right.' Megan turns her frank blue eyes on Liz. 'Kim here's fairly new, but me, I've been round the block a few times. I'm a little more robust.'

Her eyes asking Liz as she speaks: Are you up for this?

'She's not woken properly for days,' says Liz. 'I can't bear to see her suffering like this.'

'You'd be happy for her to go?'

'Oh, yes,' says Liz. She wants to cry with gratitude. This is the first time any medical professional has spoken what's hung in the air for so many days.

'Other relatives?'

'Only me.'

'Right.'

Megan turns her attention back to the log book, which details the medication regime. She speaks to Kim in matter-of-fact tones.

'Increase levothoxine to fifty. Midazolam to thirty. Oxyco-done can go up to thirty too.'

'Thirty?' says Kim, taking notes, brow furrowed.

A knock on the door and the district nurse comes in. It's at once clear that she's not here by chance. Megan has arranged this.

'I'm upping the dose,' says Megan, neutrally. And to Liz, referring to the district nurse, 'Jennifer here will sort out the prescription for you. She knows the score.'

'We go back a long way,' says Jennifer. She takes in the new dosages. 'I'll phone this lot through to the pharmacy right away. Is there someone who could pop in and pick it up?'

Liz is about to offer, but Bridget is already on her feet.

'I'm on my way,' she says.

It's as if everyone's been waiting for this moment, the plan long agreed, requiring only the firing of the starting gun. Only poor cautious Kim looks a little sorry for herself.

'She did seem to be comfortable,' she says.

Megan glances at the sleeping old lady for the first time.

'There's comfort and comfort,' she says. 'Nobody's saying you did anything wrong.'

She and Liz talk about the election. Megan is a staunch Labour supporter.

'I can't stomach those Tories,' she says. 'You think they ever use the NHS? Don't make me laugh. It's private hospitals for them, just like it's private schools and private planes and private islands for their holidays. I wish they'd just get themselves a private country and leave the rest of us in peace.'

'So you're a fan of Ed, are you?' says Liz.

'I don't know about fan. He does look like Wallace from *Wallace and Gromit*, you have to admit it. But he's gone now.'

Bridget phones from the pharmacy. There's some problem with the pharmacist about a legally controlled drug. Megan speaks directly to the pharmacist, using a medical language that sounds to Liz like code.

'That'll be all right,' says Megan, after the call.

'I'm so glad you've come,' says Liz. 'It's been going on so long. I just want it to be over.'

'I see it all the time,' says Megan. 'Mind you, I don't believe in euthanasia. That's not my job. My job is to manage things so there's no unnecessary pain.'

'Of course,' says Liz. 'I understand.'

Megan reaches for her bag.

'Jennifer will follow through as soon as your carer's back. She'll give the new dose right away.'

Jennifer nods. 'Right away.'

Megan offers Liz her hand as she goes, an odd, almost formal gesture. Her grip is firm, her gaze full of kindness.

'I know she can't hear what you say, but you may like to make your goodbyes.'

Not long after the palliative-care team have departed Bridget returns with the new prescription. Jennifer fills a syringe and searches the sleeping old lady's arms for an accessible vein. Liz, watching, feels a last tremor of fear that the nurse will be unable to administer the drug, but then the needle is in, and the syringe is emptying. She wants to ask, 'How long now?', but that would break the conspiracy of silence. Jennifer withdraws the needle and dabs at the puncture.

'Poor old thing,' she says. 'Won't be long.'

'By the morning, do you think?'

'Some time in the night.'

Of course they've said much the same every day this week, but Liz has faith in Megan. The dosage figures mean nothing to her, but that handshake, and that look told her everything.

She phones Alice.

'You may like to come home and say goodbye to Granny.'

Nothing to do now but wait.

33

To the general astonishment of the Broad household, Jack phones to announce a brief appearance at home. He's calling from the train. His homecomings are so rare these days that Laura likes to celebrate with a better than average meal, but it's too late, there's no time. She inspects the contents of the fridge. There's leftover chicken, carrots, beans, peppers. Ginger and noodles on the larder shelves. She can make a stir-fry. But will that make him feel sufficiently loved?

Henry is surprised in more prosaic ways. Why is he coming? What does he want? Is he to be met at the station?

The answers turn out to be simple enough. Alice is coming down to Sussex because her grandmother is dying. Jack has decided at the last minute to come down with her and see his family. Alan is to meet them at the station, deliver Alice to the house in Lewes where the dying grandmother lies, and bring Jack on to the Broads' house in Edenfield.

'So, is Jack getting a vegetarian dinner?' says Henry.

'I'm making a stir-fry,' says Laura. 'I can add some chicken for you and Jack.'

Then Jack's arriving, and he's in the hall, and Laura has him in her arms. She looks small and fragile beside her grown son.

'Poor Alice,' says Laura. 'Is she very upset?'

'I don't think so,' says Jack. 'She never liked her grandmother. She's doing it to be with her mum.'

He sounds subdued.

'You're tired, aren't you, darling? Did you stay up all night to watch the election?'

'Most of it,' he says. 'Plus I'm always tired these days.' And turning to Henry with a smile, 'You should have warned me, Dad. Working for a living is exhausting.'

'Until it stops,' says Henry.

'Wasn't it horrific? The election, I mean.'

'It did have a certain ghoulish fascination,' says Henry.

'All those smirking Tories! Where do they find them? Men in chalk-stripe suits with combed-back hair. They must have a factory somewhere, bolting them together out of redundant bankers. And did you see the woman who beat Ed Balls! One of the smartest economists in politics pushed off-stage by a former beauty queen!'

'Really? The one who clutched her hands and looked up to Heaven?'

'She's a former Miss UK or something. We're turning into Berlusconi's Italy.'

'Henry, give Carrie a shout,' says Laura. 'Tell her Jack's here.'

'Is Carrie still at home?' says Jack.

'Still up in her room,' says Laura.

Jack can tell by the look his parents exchange that all is not well with Carrie.

'What's she up to at present?' he says.

'We don't know,' says Laura.

'Nothing,' says Henry.

'She's a bit of a worry, to be honest,' says Laura.

'Now, how about a drink, Jack?' says Henry, taking down a bottle of wine.

Carrie has heard the car drive up, and has heard the exclamations of delight that greet Jack's appearance. The prodigal son has returned. Except that in the Bible story the prodigal son is a wastrel, who doesn't deserve his parents' joyful welcome, whereas Jack is leading a life of respectable industry. There's no parable to tell the story of the wastrel who stays home.

Carrie has always had a conflicted relationship with Jack. He's been there all her life, forever more capable, forever too far ahead for her to be able to catch up. He's always been so mature and responsible that there's been no room left for her to grow up. By his side she's always felt half formed, chaotic. She marvels at the straightforward way he lives his life. How is it possible to decide to be a teacher, and then to become a teacher, and for that then to be your life? How is it possible to decide you love one person, and go on loving them, until at last they give in and love you back? Compared to her own volatile existence, Jack seems to be made of rock. She believes him to have as little idea as a rock would have of what it's like to be her. For years now their meetings have been friendly but superficial, running on the residual inertia of their shared childhood.

She can hear voices rising up from the kitchen. She knows she'll have to go down and greet him. She's just gathering her strength for the encounter when she hears footsteps climbing the stairs, and there comes a knock on her door.

'Carrie?'

She feels a stab of panic. Not here, not in my room. This is her place of refuge, the space within which she is unobserved, and so unjudged.

She opens her bedroom door just wide enough to allow her to slip out and close it behind her.

'Hello, Jack.'

He stares at her, not understanding her defensive manoeuvre.

'Are you coming down?'

'Soon,' she says.

But instead she crosses the landing and goes into his room. She understands there must be a reckoning between them, and she chooses what is, in effect, neutral space.

'Where are you going?'

He follows her in. The room is as orderly as a tomb. The bed is made, the duvet uncreased, the pillows undented. Various reminders of Jack's young life are arranged on the shelves: Lego creations, coils of cable from outmoded electrical devices, kitsch ornaments from travels abroad. Nothing has been touched for years.

'God,' says Carrie, 'your room is so depressing.'

'Yes, well.' He looks round, frowning. It's clear to her he doesn't even see it any more. 'Why have we come in here?'

'So as not to be in my room,' says Carrie.

'Are you coming downstairs?'

'Maybe,' she says.

'Carrie,' he says sternly, big-brotherly, 'you know all this staying in your room really bothers Mum.'

'What have you come home for?'

'We're not talking about me, we're talking about you.'

'I'm not the interesting one, Jack. You're the interesting one.'

'Oh, sure.' To her surprise he sounds angry. 'You think I don't get it? All this shutting yourself away in your room, it's just to get attention.'

'Yes, I expect it is,' says Carrie.

'Well, it's just not fair on Mum. There's nothing wrong with you.'

'Isn't there, Jack?'

'Stop it, Carrie! Stop it at once! I know all about how you put on a sad face and make everyone sorry for you. I'm not sorry for you.'

'Thank you, Jack.'

'Oh, for God's sake!'

He looks like he wants to hit something.

'You shouldn't bother with me,' she says. 'You should give up on me. I'm a hopeless case. You've got your life sorted, you've got a job, you've got a girlfriend. Go on without me, Jack. I can't keep up any more.'

'What do you know?' he says. 'What do you know about me?'

He's pulling faces in the oddest way. It's as if different versions of himself are fighting to take over his expression. Then she sees his jerky gaze take in one of his long-ago Lego models, a home-made hybrid of a castle and a spaceship. He stares at it as if it has a secret to impart. Carrie remembers how he used to play with his Lego for hours. She used to want to play with it, too, and sometimes, grudgingly, he would allow her some of the simpler pieces.

'Dad collapsed,' she says.

'What?'

'He was on the landing, shouting at me. Then he just collapsed. He got right up again.'

'You mean he fell down?'

'Yes.'

'When was this?'

'Yesterday.'

'Has he seen a doctor?'

'I don't think so. He seems fine now.'

Jack starts to pace about, his fists clenched before him, putting on the man-look that says something needs to be done.

'He should have a thorough health check,' he says. 'He's always been useless at seeing doctors.'

'I think it's about his work,' says Carrie. 'It's gone wrong.'

'What's gone wrong?'

'He's been pushed out.'

'Oh,' says Jack.

Now he's at a loss. Doctors can't fix that.

Laura calls from downstairs.

'I need some help! Where are you all?'

'We'd better go down,' he says.

'I'll come later.'

'No,' he says. He gives her a quick look that isn't from Jack-the-fixer at all. It's far more unsure, a silent plea.

'Please,' he says. 'For Mum.'

But it's not for Mum, it's for him. His tone of voice tells her so. For some reason he needs her with him downstairs. So she comes, for him.

'Carrie, darling,' Laura says, the novelty of Carrie's appearance in the kitchen outshone by the novelty of Jack being in the house at all, 'could you lay the table?'

Henry is reading the paper, drinking wine.

'Dad, what's this about your job?' says Jack.

'Ah, yes. I was going to ask you all for some advice.'

Henry gives Jack a concise version of Michael Marcus's visit, ending with Michael's request that he send a reassuring email to Monty Don.

'If I'm going to do it,' he concludes, 'I need to do it pretty much now.'

'They've got a bloody nerve!' says Jack. 'I should just tell them to sod off.'

Carrie, quietly laying the table, wonders at Jack's angry response. It's as if the wrong has been done to him personally.

'Laura thinks I should just move on,' Henry says. 'Put it behind me.'

'People can't be allowed to get away with behaving like that,' says Jack.

It's like he's in school, thinks Carrie. A child has broken the rules and must be punished. Except the world doesn't work like that. There's no teacher, and there are no rules.

Jack adds, 'Especially if it's making you ill.'

'Oh, I don't think it's making me ill. But I do feel I've been messed about.'

'Honestly, Dad,' says Jack. 'You owe this jerk nothing.'

He helps himself to wine, not thinking to get any for anyone else.

Slowly and thoughtfully, Henry lays out for them the fruit of his reflections.

'Whatever I do to them, it seems to me it's not going to get me what I want. I'm not going to change them, or turn them into better people. So you could say I should think only of what's best for me. How can I act so that I get some benefit out of this mess? I can do some damage to the project as an act of revenge, but once the satisfaction of hurting the people who hurt me has passed, I'm still in the same place. So maybe I'm better off asking myself what exactly it is that hurt me.'

Carrie, listening to every word, knows the answer. But she's no longer used to speaking out.

'Being swindled out of your job,' says Jack.

Henry looks across the room straight into Carrie's eyes. He knows I know, she thinks.

'What hurts,' he says, 'is finding out you don't have the power you thought you had. Finding out other people don't rate you as much as you thought they did. That's what hurts.'

'Oh, darling,' says Laura, busy paring ginger.

'But they're wrong, Dad,' says Jack. 'You've won awards.'

'It's all right,' says Henry. 'I'm not asking for sympathy. I'm just trying to think my way through this thing. It seems to me that whatever I do next, the object must be to show that I'm worth more than they seem to think.'

Don't be like them, Dad, thinks Carrie. Don't play their game.

Ever since they went on the walk earlier she's had this strange feeling of connection with him, as if she has only to look at him to know what he's feeling.

'I don't want to be like Michael Marcus,' he says. 'I want you to be proud of me. I want to be proud of myself.'

'I think you know what you want to do,' says Laura. 'You might as well get on with it. I'll put the stir-fry together when you're done.'

Carrie sees the look between them. Mum knows too. She's known all along what he'll do. The one left out is Jack.

'Get on with what?' Jack says.

'I'll do it now,' says Henry. 'Then it's over and we can all forget about it.'

He goes to his study to send his email.

'Do you realize what he's just done?' says Laura. 'Do you realize how unusual that is? He just sat there in front of all of us and said he was hurting. Nobody does that.'

'He's amazing,' says Carrie.

'Will he be all right?' says Jack. He speaks humbly. He's stopped trying to make things right.

'As much as anyone ever is all right,' says Laura.

'I'm not all right,' says Carrie. 'I'm a terrible worry to my parents.'

Laura comes over and kisses her.

'It's true,' she says. 'I hate to see you unhappy.'

'But it's all right now, Mum. Don't you see? Dad's made it all right to be unhappy.'

'It's all right for me to be unhappy,' says Laura. 'But you're my baby. I can't bear for you to be unhappy.'

'You have to, Mum. You have to bear it.'

'So you're unhappy,' says Jack, 'because Mum's unhappy that you're unhappy. What about me?'

'Are you unhappy too, Jack?'

'Maybe I'm struggling a little. Maybe I'm really struggling quite a lot.' Suddenly he can't stop himself. 'Teaching's hard, it's relentless, it wears you out. Half the time I feel as if I'm wasting my time, nobody's interested, but if I don't deliver the results the whole school suffers, so I have to deliver. My year-thirteens sit their first A levels next Friday and they're all having breakdowns. It's like their entire future depends on it, it's life or death, which it isn't, but you start to believe it. You want to know why I've come down tonight? I had to get away from the madhouse. I had to come somewhere where you don't even know it's exam time, and you don't, do you? Why should you? Who cares about stupid exams anyway? Why would anyone get suicidal over an exam? Except they do, and they come to me to save their lives and I can't, because I'm drowning too.'

Henry comes back into the kitchen.

'Done,' he says. 'Can't get it back now.'

'What did you say?' says Laura, from the stove.

'I was gracious. I wished them all success. I was like a twinkly-eyed grandfather giving his blessing to the young folk. Now I can move on.'

'We're all going nowhere, Dad,' says Carrie.

Henry looks at her in surprise. He sees the expressions on their faces, and realizes something has changed.

'What happened?'

'We're drowning,' says Carrie.

'Stir-fry's ready,' says Laura.

The food is in a great metal wok, with the chicken in a separate pan. Laura puts it down before Henry, so he can serve it. She speaks to him as she takes her place at the table.

'Jack's having a hard time at work.'

'Sorry to hear that, Jack,' says Henry. 'How bad is it?'

The wok wobbles as he serves. He adds chicken to Jack's plate in heaped spoonfuls.

'I'll survive,' says Jack.

Then, unexpectedly, he smiles.

Jack's remembering his castle spaceship, and the time of absolute absorption in its making, and how when it was finished he'd sat and gazed at it for a long time. He remembers thinking, Yes, that's what I meant to do, and now it's done. Later, he thinks, I may go to my room and build something out of Lego.

34

Liz decides to make supper for everyone in her mother's house, now Alice is coming. There's an odd mix of provisions in the kitchen, some left over from the time when the old lady was still eating and some brought by Karen for her own consumption. Liz lines up the most promising ingredients: three onions, half a dozen eggs, a half-empty bag of basmati rice, an unopened pack of mushrooms, and from the freezer a bag of frozen peas. There's no wine in the house, but there's a bottle of Baileys and a bottle of Harveys Bristol Cream sherry. Judging by the supply in the fridge, Karen drinks Diet Coke.

Her mother was no gourmet cook, even in her younger days. Liz remembers many meals of sausages and mash, or cheese and potato pie. On Sunday there was always a roast. They sat at this same kitchen table, Liz on the far side from the stove, her mother serving, her movements formal, almost stately. Liz remembers always being hungry, and always being impatient. The unspoken tension at meals was that her mother wanted them to last as long as possible, and Liz wanted them to be over quickly. At the time she had supposed this was because meals were boring and she had better things to do but now, looking back, she knows she was in flight from her mother's insatiable emotional demands. Mealtime for Aster was a daily celebration of her private religion, which was the family. With Liz before her, she was a mother, and at this table, feeding her child, her life had purpose and meaning. The many little rules she enforced, inherited from her own very different childhood, had become the ritual elements in a secular service: you don't start eating until everyone is ready; you don't gobble; you hold your knife and fork just so; you make conversation; you finish what's on your plate; you say thank you; you ask to get down.

Liz puts a pan of water on the stove to cook the rice. There comes a quick tap on the front door and all at once her own daughter Alice is before her. Alice in jersey and jeans, hair tied back, wide eyes anxious, always so much taller than she remembers, as if when they're apart she becomes a little girl again. Her own darling Alice, arms reaching out, unexpected, dearly welcome.

'I'm not too late, am I?'

'No. She's still here.'

Liz takes Alice through to the room where her mother lies on the hissing hospital bed. Bridget is sitting at the card table playing patience. Alice stands a moment looking down at her grandmother. She stoops and touches her brow with her lips.

'It's me, Granny,' she says. 'Alice.'

Liz looks on.

Alice turns to her.

'Can she hear me?'

'We don't know.'

244

Bridget shakes her head.

'She's somewhere else now,' she says. 'Far away.'

Back in the kitchen, Alice says, 'I used to hate her so much. There doesn't seem much point any more.'

'She wasn't so bad to you, was she?'

'I hated her because she was horrid to you. She was always criticizing you. Mostly about me. I was turning out bad and it was all your fault.'

'Poor Mummy,' says Liz. 'She really did get dealt a rotten hand. When you think about it, all that fuss about behaving properly was just her way of coping. Did you know that when her father died her mother told her to be a good soldier? A little girl of eight, being a good soldier.'

'I don't care,' says Alice. 'She was a miserable old bat.'

'Oh, Alice. I'm so glad you've come.'

Alice helps Liz to make dinner, chopping the onions and putting on a pan to fry them. They have a glass of sweet sherry each as they work. Alan has promised to bring wine when he joins them later, with Cas.

'I thought we could eat in the study,' says Liz. 'Someone has to be there to watch over Mummy, so we might as well all eat together. Bridget and Karen have been saints. I want to say thank you to them as much as anything.'

In the short time they have alone together, mother and daughter, they catch up on each other's lives. It won't be the same when the others are here.

'Will it be hard for you when she does die?' asks Alice.

'I don't know,' says Liz. 'I really don't. Right now all I want is for it to be over, but who knows?'

'I'll hate it when you die.'

'Then I won't die. Actually, darling, I will, because there'll come a time when you're fed up with me not dying. But let's not talk about that. Tell me how things are for you.'

'Well. I've been promoted.'

'Darling! Congratulations!'

'And I'm supposed to be on a plane tomorrow morning to Copenhagen. I'm on the Lego account.'

'Lego? Is that good?'

'Well, it's one of our biggest. And it impressed the hell out of Jack.'

'How is Jack?'

'Really, really stressed. His students have exams and he's giving them extra coaching all the hours there are. He's at work at eight tomorrow morning. It's crazy.'

'Can't he just say no?'

'These are his students, Mum. He feels responsible for them.'

'So you can't stay the weekend?'

'I'll stay as long as you need me.'

A clatter in the hall, and Alan and Cas are with them. Cas is filled with morbid curiosity.

'Is Granny going to die tonight? How will you know? Will she make a noise?'

'What noise? What are you talking about?'

'It's called a death rattle.'

'I've no idea,' says Liz. 'You'd better ask Karen.'

Alan carries the kitchen chairs through to the study and they lay places round the square card table. There's six of them, with Bridget and Karen, and not enough room, but they manage. Alan has forgotten the wine so they drink the sweet sherry.

'It's a bit odd to have it with dinner,' Liz says, 'but it's very good sherry in its way. Mummy was always very particular. It had to be Harveys Bristol Cream.'

'She liked her Baileys best,' says Bridget.

Liz raises her glass.

'Here's to Mummy,' she says. 'A good soldier.'

They all turn to the old lady, sleeping on the breathing bed.

'I never knew she was a soldier,' says Karen.

'I just mean she did her duty as she saw it,' says Liz.

'We're talking about her as if she's dead,' says Alice, 'but she's only sleeping.'

'She's on her way now,' says Bridget.

'How will you know when she goes?' says Cas.

'You just know,' says Karen.

Liz goes into the kitchen to dish out the fried rice. Alan follows to help. It's the first moment they've had alone together.

'How was Elaine?' says Liz.

'Very relieved she won't have to pay mansion tax.'

'You must have had a very long lunch.'

'I called in on Annie afterwards. She lives near Elaine's office.'

'Oh, right,' says Liz, keeping her attention on the fried rice, scraping the best crusty bits off the base of the pan. 'How was that?'

'It was good. I didn't stay long.'

When they join the others in the study, Cas is telling Alice the plot of Alan's proposed new film, *The Human Disease*. Both Cas and Alice take a semi-professional interest in Alan's ventures. Alice is unconvinced by the ending.

'You can do better than that.'

'They want a different ending,' says Alan, 'so I suppose I'll have to.'

'I told Kieran Kelly the plot of your film,' says Cas.

'What?' exclaims Alan. 'The boy who's been bullying you?'

'He's not been bullying me.'

'The one who laughed at you for being a genius.'

'Oh, that's all stopped,' says Cas. 'Miss Mills told Kieran he had a natural flair, so now he's decided to be a writer like you.'

'Like me!'

'He asked me what sort of money you made writing films,' says Cas. 'I told him millions.'

'But I don't make millions.'

'Some do,' says Cas. 'You told me.'

Karen has been examining the bottle of Baileys.

'What is it?' she says to Alice, not wanting to interrupt the conversation.

'It's a sort of alcoholic milk shake,' says Alice.

Karen pours herself a small glass and sips it.

'Oh, that is nice! No wonder she liked it.'

'I'll tell you what,' says Bridget. 'I'll miss her when she's gone. But she was that strong-willed. You couldn't tell her.'

'She was a selfish beast,' says Alice. 'Everyone had to run round worrying about her.'

'But you know, darling,' says Liz, 'it was only because she was unhappy.'

She looks over at the bed where her mother lies. She's both present and not present.

'You say what you think,' says Karen, approvingly, to Alice. 'English people never say what they're thinking.'

'In my ad agency,' said Alice, 'they all say they've voted Labour but actually they've voted Conservative.'

'How do you know?' says Alan, interested.

'It's hypocrisy pride. Very on trend.'

'Mummy always voted Tory,' says Liz. 'She said it was her duty to her class.'

'I'm servant class,' says Karen, now on to a second glass of Baileys. 'We're called carers but really we're servants. Funny when you think about it. Back in Zim it was us who had the servants.'

'You're not a servant, Karen,' protests Liz.

'Oh, I don't care. Just as long as no one's chopping me up with a machete, I'm happy.'

'Who was chopped up with a machete?' says Cas. 'Someone you know?'

'My brother-in-law,' says Karen.

'What, chopped up dead?'

'That's enough, Cas,' says Liz.

'Chopped up dead,' says Karen.

'Too much dying going on,' says Alice. 'How can you carry on with ordinary conversations when someone's dying?'

'There's always someone dying somewhere,' says Cas. 'One hundred and eight people die every minute.'

'Who says?' says Alan.

'It's a fact.'

'But it's different when you know them,' says Alice. 'I've never known anyone die before.'

'She's not gone yet,' says Bridget.

They all pause and look across the room at the old lady lying so still in her bed. They hear the hiss of the air mattress.

'You know what, darling?' says Liz. 'This could go on for ever. I think you should say goodbye to Granny, go back with Jack tonight, and catch your plane in the morning.'

'But what about you?'

'I'll be fine. I'll call you if anything happens. I don't want your life to come to a stop. Alan, you can take them to the station, can't you? And, Cas, it's high time you were in bed.'

'But I want to stay for the dying,' says Cas.

'There's nothing to see,' says Karen. 'One minute they're there, the next minute they're gone.'

35

Alan's visit, in which nothing was said and nothing happened, has left Annie in turmoil. All the time he was in the room with her she felt as if she was standing on the edge of a cliff, and with one short step, less, with the movement of one little finger, she would start to fall.

And then he was gone.

By the evening she realizes her solitude is doing her harm. Alone in the house she fantasizes all she could have done with Alan, and then, regaining her senses, is overwhelmed with shame.

What's the matter with me?

Too much time, too little to do. But what is there to do on a Friday evening? Then she recalls one of her artists, a Russian exile called Tatiana Malova, saying to her, 'You must visit me, but come in the evening. In the day I work. In the evening, I get lonely.'

She's not yet been to her studio. It's somewhere improbable, like West Ealing.

She gets out her phone.

★

The canvas is big, it almost fills one side of the studio. The work in progress is fully sketched but only half painted, in a parody of high Renaissance style. A blue sky populated by angels looms above a Madonna and child. Kneeling before the Madonna is a thickset man in a dark grey suit.

'A commission, I take it?' says Annie.

The artist stands beside her, a tiny woman of about sixty, in paint-stained overalls, a red bandanna around her head.

'Russian gentleman,' she says.

'I hope he pays extra for the angels.'

'I don't like to do. But he gives so much money. I must live.'

Annie looks round the small studio space.

'Can I see the work you do for yourself?'

Tatiana pulls out a sequence of black-and-white photographic portraits, ranges them alongside a large partly painted canvas. The photographs are all of women, all of them middle-aged or older. They face the camera with the same defeated gaze. Their faces are cruelly real, harrowed.

'My widows,' says Tatiana. 'In Russia, men die young. It is land of widows.'

'You took the photographs?'

'Yes.'

'They look so sad.'

'It is sad to be woman.'

Annie moves slowly down the line of faces, meeting the eyes of the women in the photographs. The canvas is a half-finished painted version of the faces, huddled together, mutely testifying to a world of loss.

'I think your clients don't want like this,' says Tatiana.

'No,' says Annie. 'I think they'd rather have the angels.'

'It is for you to tell me. My widows pay me nothing.'

Driving home, Annie is haunted by the faces of Tatiana's widows. Russian women in London are young and beautiful. It's hard to imagine them turning within a few years into those lost souls with their downcast eyes and withered cheeks. No doubt their wealth will shelter them from the harsh wind for a while. But whether young and desired or old and unwanted, the terms of life are the same: they live on the sufferance of men.

I don't want that for Ellie, she thinks. I want her to have her own life. I want her to live on her own terms. What does that take? Five hundred pounds a year and a room of one's own, said Virginia Woolf. And more than that: a dream of one's own. A vision of a life that extends beyond attracting and keeping a man.

Have I achieved that?

For all her roster of clients, for all her ranks of grateful artists, Annie knows that her business is no more than an accident. She didn't grow up dreaming of selling second-rate art to property developers. It came about by chance, by the accident of introducing an artist friend to a friend of Mitch's in the City. From there it's grown into a small business, which gives her valuable income and a reason to go out of the house, but it's not what you'd call a passion project. So where does the passion go?

This is dangerous territory. Passion belongs to youth. With the passing of youth comes the time of responsibility, marriage, motherhood. But motherhood, too, passes. What then?

She's driving into her home streets now. She turns off Lad-broke Grove into Lansdowne Crescent just as a car pulls out of a residents' parking space opposite the church. At this time of night residents' parking spaces are hard to find, and she takes it. The walk back to Clarendon Road will do her good.

A short, fat, square-faced woman is wheeling a bike out through the gates in the iron railings round the church. She gives Annie a friendly wave. It's Angela Southcott, the associ-ate vicar of St John's. Annie and Mitch are parishioners, and make occasional appearances at church events. Annie waves back as she passes, smiling as she does so. She remembers Angela Southcott telling her in the middle of a chaotic church fête how she had divined God's purpose in giving her what she calls her 'warthog face'. 'People are so afraid of each other,' she said, 'so afraid of being mocked or judged. But they take one look at me and feel much better about themselves.'

As she lets herself into the house she wonders what she can make for supper, and realizes she doesn't feel hungry. Her mind is still full of Tatiana's widows, images that have somehow been joined by the cheery ugly face of the vicar on her bike. Angela Southcott gives much of her time to visiting old ladies in care homes, whom she calls 'my witches', meaning they have magical powers. Widows and witches: the fate of the ageing female.

Pretzel comes pushing at her legs, asking to be fed. Annie opens the back door to let him out into the garden, but he doesn't want to go. He's become like a lifer, a prisoner so institutionalized he doesn't want to leave his cell.

I want to leave my cell.

She realizes what she wants more than anything is a glass of red wine, a big glass. And some Pringles. She knows her taste for Pringles is debased, and mostly she has it under control, but tonight she's alone, there's no one to see. And why not? So she goes back out and walks down to the corner shop and buys a tube of Sour Cream and Onion Pringles. She also buys a six-pack of Stella. It's good to have beer in the house.

Back home she settles down on the kitchen sofa with her bottle of wine and her Pringles, turns on the television with the sound off, and proceeds to get a little drunk. After a while the wine has the required disinhibiting effect, and she allows herself to think about Alan. His image, or the idea of him, has been close by all along, like a face pressed against a window. She's avoided letting him back in, because where can it lead? What's to be done about him?

For simple pleasure, he said, give me a woman of my own age. I cried. I actually cried. All because I remembered how he trembled in my arms.

It astonishes her how powerful the feelings are.

He called himself *a dud in bed*. He said *the sex is better now*. This glimpse of his shame from all those years ago moves her. She wants to make amends. Add to this that other glimpse, like warm sunlight seen through the crack of an opening door, which is his desire for her, and she feels her whole body tingling in response all over again.

Come over and fuck me, Alan. I'm on my own tonight. No one need know.

No sin in pretending. I'm only talking to myself. It's not as if anything's actually going to happen. We widows, we witches, are allowed to dream.

Her phone jiggles with an incoming email. It's Mitch.

```
Problems here, coming home early. Booked on a
flight Saturday night. See you Sunday.
```

Sunday! That means tomorrow, Saturday, is the last day she'll be on her own. Whatever might have happened with Alan now won't happen.

Her marriage is safe.

Only now that the threat or promise has been removed does she admit to herself how very real it had become. Never more than a fantasy, but it came close, so close. She shivers with fear at the thought. It's been like a madness, something beyond her power to control.

And now Mitch is coming home. Mitch will keep her safe. She emails back:

```
Sorry about the problems. Happy you're coming
home.
```

As soon as the message has gone, she feels the beginnings of regret. Is this to be all? She's seen Alan twice only, and something has begun that has not yet run its course. Whatever it is, Mitch has no part in it. Once he's home his presence will change everything.

But they still have one more day. They have tomorrow.

She makes the call before she can have second thoughts, and he picks up. He's driving. He's just dropped someone off at the station. He pulls in so he can talk.

'Mitch is coming home early. He'll be home on Sunday. I don't suppose you can spare some time tomorrow.'

'I don't think so.'

WILLIAM NICHOLSON

'Could be any time.'

'All depends what happens here. I'll call you in the morning.'

That's all they say to each other. All the important information is contained in what they don't ask, and what they don't answer.

36

Now that the others have gone the house is quiet. Bridget and Karen clear up the dinner, then Bridget leaves.

'You go too,' Karen says to Liz. 'I'll call you if needs be.'

'I'll stay a little longer,' says Liz.

Karen goes into the sitting room where she has her laptop, and Liz settles down in the chair near the hospital bed. She wants this time alone with her mother, even though she has nothing left to say to her, and as far as she knows her mother doesn't know she's there. The hollowed-out face lies motionless on the pillow, the lights of the syringe driver winking away beside it, the air mattress hissing as it rocks her in sleep.

Liz looks at her mother's face, but she can't see it as it is now. Instead she sees the face she's known all her life, a face that has endured so many years of loneliness. She sees the refusal to be bowed, and the quick anger at the slightest hint of disrespect. Not a good soldier, perhaps, but a fighter certainly. But the waste of it! That so much of a life should be lost to anger and regret.

She realizes then that, of course, she's thinking of herself. Her mother's dying is her own dying. She is looking on the end of life and asking herself, Has it been well lived? Has it been all it could have been?

Aster had been a good-looking woman in her day. How was it that she married so late, and that the marriage was so short-lived? How was it that for the forty years and more since Rex left her she found no other partner? If she could speak now, if she could offer her own regrets of the dying, what would she say? Surely she would say, I wish I had been loved more. I wish I had loved more. But this is not the lesson she has taught her only child. Liz has been raised in the shadow of betrayal. Even now, loving Alan as she does, there remains a part of her that she will not give away. Rely only on yourself, her mother taught her. Be ready for the day they leave. But all by herself, in fear of turning into her mother, she has taught herself another lesson. I am the source of my own strength. I am the purpose of my life. My happiness does not depend on the caprice of another.

I was nursed on the bitter milk of abandonment. I have raised my own child on the sweet milk of independence. No wonder Alice is so much at a loss to find herself so steadfastly loved. Each one of us fights the war gone by. I've equipped my daughter with obsolete armour. And if one day she has a daughter, she'll make the same mistakes, and try to protect her from dangers that have become no more than a memory.

She closes her eyes and listens to her mother's breathing. The breaths come slowly, with long intervals between them, but on they come. Liz feels how easily she could slip into sleep. It's been a long day. For some reason she finds herself recalling how

Penny Worth wouldn't go into the bushes, saying, 'In the end it's a matter of dignity.' We fear shame more than loneliness. What nonsense that is! You get to the end of your life and look back and know that all that counted were the times you escaped the little bubble of self and came close enough to another person to touch and be touched.

Karen comes in.

'How are we?' she says.

She goes to the side of the hospital bed. Liz senses at once from her sudden stillness that she's become alert. She sees Karen stoop low, putting her ear to the old lady's lips. Then she straightens up and turns to Liz.

'We've gone,' she says.

Gone? But I've been here all along. How could I not have known? How could such a significant event have taken place unnoticed?

'Are you sure?'

'Oh, yes. I'm sure.'

Liz goes close to the bedside. Her mother lies just as she's been lying for so many days, moving gently with the rise and fall of the air mattress. Her eyes are closed, her mouth is open, but it's true, she's no longer breathing. Only the bed continues the illusion of life.

'Mummy?' she says.

Karen takes her hand and squeezes it.

'I'm sorry,' she says.

'No, it's all right,' says Liz. Then, thinking how absurd that must sound, she says, 'It's all for the best.'

'Shall I call the night nurse?' says Karen.

'Is that what we have to do?' says Liz.

'They have to verify the – verify what's happened,' says Karen.

They have to verify the death. There's been a death. But such a quiet death that it's hard to believe.

Liz understands there's a procedure to be followed, and she's grateful. This is no time for novel initiatives. So Karen calls the night nurse. Then she calls Bridget.

'She asked me to tell her,' she says to Liz.

'Of course,' says Liz. 'She would have liked to be here.'

'At least you were here,' says Karen.

Except I wasn't, thinks Liz. I haven't been here for my mother for a long time. People say it as if it's the last consolation: 'At least I was with her at the end.' But Liz was within inches of her mother when she died, and didn't even know it. Now she has no idea how to behave. There should be ritual actions to perform, and ritual words to speak, to bridge the awkward gap between life and death. She should be laying out the body, whatever that means, and having the neighbours round, and making them cups of tea, and hearing them say, 'She looks so peaceful now.'

She doesn't look peaceful. She looks worn out. Liz lets her gaze linger on the familiar features, hoping to stir a memory that will bring with it a stab of love, and so perhaps some tears. But she feels nothing at all.

I don't think I believe it yet. Any minute now those cross little eyes will open and she'll say, 'Pull me up.'

She calls Alan. He says he'll come over, but she says no, stay with Cas, there's nothing to do here.

'But you,' he says. 'How are you coping?'

'I'm fine,' she says. 'I think I'm in denial or something. I don't really believe it's happened.'

She doesn't use the word *death* or *died*, not out of fear at their finality, but in case it turns out not to be true.

Bridget comes, and bends over the bed in her turn. When she rises, her face is wet with tears.

'She's taken up that much of my life, she has. I'm sure I don't know what I'll do without her.'

Bridget's tears shame Liz, who has no tears.

'Am I to ring Cooper's?' Bridget asks.

'Cooper's? Oh, yes. Yes, of course.'

Cooper's are the undertakers from Lewes.

The night nurses arrive, two of them, carrying the proper forms. They examine the old lady in a respectful but business-like way. Then, while one of them removes the syringe driver, the other goes through the form.

'It's what we call an expected death,' she says. 'The GP saw her within the last two weeks, so we've no need to get her out to sign the certificate. I can verify the death myself. All you have to do is pop into the register office sometime in the next week or so.'

She signs the form, and gives a copy to Liz. So now her mother's death is verified but not registered. That just about describes Liz's feelings.

Before they depart, the night nurses unplug the hospital bed. The hissing sound ceases. The silence fills the room. Liz is flooded with an overwhelming sensation of release.

Gone at last. The fear of her, the weight of her, gone for ever.

You wore me out, Mummy. You and your unhappiness.

She calls Alice to tell her. Like Alan, Alice's concern is all for the living.

'Are you grieving, Mum?'

'No. I should be, I know.'

'Just think, Mum. You've been a single daughter and a single mother. You've had to cope with both of us. And you've been amazing.'

'She was a single mother, too, and in a far harder time. She never got over Rex leaving her.'

'All right,' says Alice's faraway voice. 'We can be sorry for her now. But you should be proud. You did everything right.'

Two men from Cooper's come, both in dark suits, white shirts and black ties.

'What do you need me to do?' says Liz.

'Nothing at all, Miss. We'll do it all. You can call the office in the morning and sort out the details.'

They open the back of their black van and bring out a folding stretcher and a black bag.

'Maybe you'd like to step into another room, Miss?'

Liz chooses to go out into the garden. It's a cool, clear night. She walks slowly up and down the lawn in the bars of light falling from the kitchen window. She thinks about the men from Cooper's, and how they must sit waiting somewhere, in their black suits and ties, ready to respond when the phone rings. What do they do while they wait? Play cards? Watch old movies?

Suddenly she stops and bends over. It's come like a pain in the gut: not grief, but loss. Death has locked her mother away for ever, and now a last secret hope must die, too. It's something Liz has never consciously admitted to herself, an absurd little deathbed scenario, complete with touching last words. In this fantasy Aster can still just talk. She takes Liz's hand in hers and

says, 'I know I've been critical of you, Elizabeth, but under-
neath I've always been so proud of you.'

The longing of the little girl she once was, the little girl she
outgrew long ago. But here she is, after all these years, wanting
the most powerful person in her private universe to tell her
she's done well after all. Words that were never spoken, and
now never will be.

On my own now.

The men from Cooper's come out of the house carrying the
stretcher between them. On it lies a long black bundle. They
load the stretcher into the van, and the van drives away.

Back inside, Bridget and Karen are stripping the hospital
bed.

'The hospice man will come to take the bed away first thing,'
says Karen. 'It's top-of-the-range, this one. Can't afford to leave
them empty.'

Liz looks round the study. All through her childhood this
has been the cold room, the unused room. The room that had
she had a father would have been his den. Then for a few weeks
it became a dying room, and that paradoxically filled it with
life and purpose. Now it's slipping back into emptiness.

'I'm so grateful to you both,' she says. 'You've been wonderful. I don't know what we would have done without you.'

The *we* is her mother and herself. Her mother, whose life is
now over, and can be judged. So long as you have a future
anything is possible: times of suffering can be counted in the
balance with times of peace yet to come. But death draws a
line. The account is closed. No victory for Aster at the end. A
sad and lonely life ended by a sad and lonely death.

What am I, her child, to make of that?

The answer comes out of her like an explosion.

I will live. I will live!

It's past one in the morning when she gets home. Alan is awake, waiting up for her. He takes her in his arms and at last she cries. She doesn't attempt to explain, but she's not crying for her mother. She's crying because her resilience is all used up. She's crying over the waste of a life.

She sleeps deeply, and dreams. In her dream she returns to her mother's house to find her in bed, drinking a cup of tea. Stunned to see her alive after all, she tries, stammering, to explain that she really had appeared to be dead. Her mother brushes the matter aside, not interested in ascribing blame. 'At least those awful carers have gone.' And so they have. In the dream Liz then tries to make phone calls, to Bridget, Karen, to ask them to return, but the phone isn't working properly. She gets no answers. Her mother complains about the recent consignment of logs. 'They're far too small,' she says. 'They burn in no time at all.'

'But, Mummy, we get them to cut them small so they're not too heavy for you to pick up.'

'Look, you see, the fire's gone out.'

She looks, and the fire has gone out. The grate is dark and empty, even of ashes.

Saturday, 9 May 2015

37

Death is bossy, but Liz Dickinson is stubborn. She knows she should go round to her mother's house first thing and start the process of sorting out her affairs. Also she must go into Lewes to the registrar's office in Southover Grange and register the death, but are they open on a Saturday? Also, she must speak to the funeral directors, decide on a date for the funeral, and book a slot with the crematorium. Her mother had always been definite about that. She did not want to be put in a hole in the ground. This, Liz irritably imagined, was part of her refusal to accept the possibility of her own extinction. Liz wanted to snap back at her, Why are you so afraid of being buried alive? You've been buried alive for over thirty years.But Liz performs none of these obsequies. Instead she decides to sit at her desk and write the feature article for which she will be paid a thousand pounds. This is her way of claiming her own right to live, against her mother's demands, which continue after death.

The female scorpion, she writes, copying from an article in the *Atlantic Weekly*, which in turn takes it from the book under review, *has to wait forty-eight hours before being ready to have sex with the same partner again, but only an hour and a half to have sex with a different partner.*

It's fine that it's a scorpion. You don't mess with scorpions. If a female scorpion gets off on variety in sex, why can't we? To hell with stand by your man. Aster stood by her man even after he was long gone, faithful to an empty bed, and what did that get her?

This is not about my mother. But it is about empty beds. It's about loneliness, and wanting someone to hold in the night.

Alan puts his head round the door.

'You okay?'

'So far.'

'Anything I can do?'

'Not right now.' Then, turning to let him see she really is okay, 'Today's my first day of freedom, and I'm bloody well having it.'

'Good for you.'

She presses on with her article:

Alongside the lingerie ads on the walls of the Underground I'm now seeing a lot more of men wearing only their pants. I've even heard of David Gandy. Does this mean that at last the admen have woken up to the secret power of women's lust?

Alan reappears.

'I've just had a call from Stuart on his way to LA. He wants to know if I could make a brunch meeting. I told him your mother just died.'

'A brunch meeting in LA?'

'In Terminal Five.'

'You want to do it?'

'It could be useful. But it's not vital.'

He's telling her he wants to do it but won't abandon her.

'Go. If you want to go, go.'

'What about you?'

'I'm not the one who's died. I'm free, so you're free too. We get to live our lives now. If that means brunch at Terminal Five, which isn't my idea of fun, then hey, go for it.'

Someone calls from Cooper's. No, says Liz, no dates yet fixed, but, yes, there'll be a cremation. No, she doesn't want an open coffin for those who loved her to pay their respects.

Who is there who loved her? The funeral will be a modest affair. There have been friends and neighbours over the years, but one by one they dropped away, worn out by Aster's anger. What's the use of being the faithful one, the virtuous one, if it turns you into the angry one?

We're as greedy as men, she writes. *We like getting drunk as much as men. Why wouldn't we be as randy as men? The answer, of course, is that we are, but we pretend we're not. Somewhere deep inside we know that if we let on to men how much we like sex — all kinds of sex, sex with all kinds of partners — the men would take fright. They'd realize they can never satisfy us. They'd fear we might take our pleasure with them and then eat them. And we might.*

38

It feels strange to be in Heathrow and not about to fly. Alan makes his way past the long lines of check-in desks and rides the escalator to the upper level, self-consciously aware of his lack of luggage. But really, these days, an airport is just a shopping mall, a place where busy people suffer imposed leisure, and so feel permitted to spend money on themselves.

Or to hold meetings. This is the true mark of the high achiever. Stuart is on his way to Los Angeles and has some issues to discuss with Alan about his project.

To Alan, it's as if an invisible hand is moving him across a board, in a game that can't now be stopped. It's no longer necessary for him to take any decisions. He has only to play the part that life is dealing him.

He finds Stuart is already installed in a window corner of Carluccio's, with his iPad and a substantial late breakfast before him.

'Thought I'd get on with it,' he says, as Alan pulls up a chair at his table. 'My flight's in just over an hour and I'm not through security yet. Good of you to trek out here. Better face to face.'

Stuart has ordered fried eggs, grilled pancetta, toasted panettone and coffee. Alan asks for a croissant and a coffee.

'It's worth getting it right,' says Stuart. 'I'll be seeing a few people in LA who might go for this.'

He's checking through Alan's outline. He reads from his screen.

'*The Dying of the Beautiful People.* Not sure the title's quite right yet but the core idea is great. Can't go far wrong with beautiful people.'

He does a little serious eating, then scrolls through the notes before him.

'Let me remind myself.' A quick flash of a smile. 'I had the children do me some notes.'

'It's all right, Stuart. I know you don't have the time to do your own thinking.'

'Or the brains,' says Stuart.

They've worked together before, which makes the process more human, if not any easier.

'Mysterious deaths, great. Uprising, great.' He's nodding as he scrolls. 'Jeopardy, great. Issues to flag up. One, humour. Two, the ending.'

'Humour?'

'Oh, you know. Maybe the technology malfunctions. Maybe the machines have their own agenda.'

'This is bloody Jean-Claude and his comic robot, isn't it?'

'Probably. Could be darkly comic?'

'I'm not having a fucking comic robot, Stuart.'

'Okay. Moving on.'

Alan's croissant comes, complete with little jars of jam. He hunts through them for marmalade.

'Clementine marmalade? What's that? Marmalade's supposed to be made from Seville oranges.'

Stuart is moving on.

'The hero sacrifices himself in silence. That's quite passive.'

'Self-sacrifice is passive, Stuart. Think Jesus on the cross. Not an active move.'

'You're right there.'

Then he looks up and his brow furrows, as if he's pushing out a serious turd. He's having an idea of his own.

'But after the crucifixion, didn't Jesus rise again? Isn't that his big ending? Whoosh! Up to Heaven like a rocket!'

'My hero can't have a resurrection, Stuart. The whole point of my story is that humans are destroyers, by and of their very nature. He has to die, and he has to stay dead.'

'Sure, I see that. But this is the climax. Can't he *die bigger*?'

'You want a shoot-out? You want him to go down guns blazing?'

Stuart has now finished his eggs and ham. He turns his attention to the toasted panettone.

'How's the marmalade?'

'Gutless,' says Alan.

'I want him to die like a hero. Help me here. I'm in CAA telling them the story so they'll give me one of their A-list stars, and I say he dies at the end, and they say, Okay, how?'

'Fine,' says Alan. 'I'll get something for you by the time you land.'

'Tomorrow's soon enough. I fly back Monday.'

He thumbs his notes up the screen.

'Oh, yes. We want to skew younger. Your lead characters are mostly in their forties.'

'So's half the audience, for Christ's sake. Haven't we grown out of making movies for teenage boys?'

'Remember Cyrus Blavatnik? Cyrus used to say, "Stuart, never forget, we see movies in the dark. What else happens in the dark?"'

'Sex,' says Alan, who has heard this many times before.

'Movies are about sex.' Stuart shuts down his iPad with a snap. 'No one wants to have sex with middle-aged people.'

39

Annie sits waiting in the kitchen, slowly drinking a mug of coffee, listening to the sound of cars passing in the street outside. Pretzel lies at her feet, occasionally raising his head and nudging her leg. She strokes him without looking down.

He'll be here soon. He called to say he was on his way. When he comes we'll talk a little about this and that, and then I'll tell him what's been happening to me. I'll tell him about my fantasies. Then the madness will pass.

'I wanted to have an affair with you. I've no idea why.'

He'll say, 'Me too.'

That's all she wants to hear, that's what she wants made real: that he desires her. Once said it needn't be acted upon. It can be their secret, a warm thought for cold nights. Their unfinished business will be finished, and they can each return to their lives with no damage done.

This is Annie's plan, arrived at after a sleepless night. Perhaps she even believes it.

An age goes by. The doorbell rings. Time begins.

There he stands on the doorstep, at first with his back to her, like some casual caller. Then he turns as the door opens, and meets her gaze. A slight lift of the shoulders that says, 'Here I am.' No greeting peck on the cheek. Already beyond that.

He follows her downstairs.

'How was Terminal Five?'

'Unreal.'

The dog pushes at their legs.

'Liz's mother died last night.'

'I'm sorry.' Does that change anything between us? 'Doesn't Liz mind you being away?'

'She's back at work. She's writing about how women want sex as much as men.'

'What?'

Annie thinks she must have misheard.

'Not what most people think. But who knows?'

He's not looking at her. It's as if he's afraid to look at her. But he isn't asking, 'Why am I here?' He knows why he's here.

'So Mitch is having work problems.'

'Yes. He'll be home early tomorrow.'

And this is our last day.

'Just as well,' Alan says.

'That's what I thought.'

'I've found it quite confusing, meeting you again.'

'Me too.'

'Human nature, I suppose. You lose something, you want it back.'

She can feel the nervous intensity that radiates from him, it's almost a physical sensation, like heat. So much energy can't be contained for long.

'Even if it's old and tired,' she says.

'You're just the same to me, Annie.'

He says it so simply. She wants to reach out her arms, hold him, kiss him.

'Look at us,' she says. 'Just standing here.'

'I can't stay,' he says. 'I've just looked in for a moment on my way home.'

'On our last day.'

'Just to say goodbye.'

He wants the same as me. He wants to be told it's true.

'Goodbye,' she says, knowing he won't go.

'Goodbye, Annie,' he says, not going.

He holds out his hand. Such a strange, sweet gesture, almost formal: *asking for my hand*. She puts her hand in his. He holds it lightly, then tighter, as if afraid she might withdraw it. Holding his hand, looking into his smiling eyes, Annie is flooded with joy. Now it will happen. Now it can't be stopped.

'Am I allowed a goodbye kiss?' he says.

She moves towards him. The dog lumbers up, sensing their intimacy, jealous, pushing at her legs. As she takes a step towards Alan she stumbles over the dog and falls into his arms. Her weight catches him off-balance, and he, too, falls. They tumble together onto the sofa, her body on his, his arms round her, his breath on her cheek, his lips on her skin.

They kiss. Not pretending any more.

His hands on her body, pushing under her shirt. She pulls it off for him, and her bra. His hands on her breasts, his mouth on her nipples. Her hand on his belt, unbuckling. The ridge swelling beneath.

He wants me.

'Upstairs,' she says.

So much freedom. So much power. Never when they were young could it be this way. Youth is so full of fears. Now, fully grown, Annie is fearless.

In the guest bedroom she undresses for him, offering her naked body to his desire. His desire is her desire; exciting him excites her. His gaze makes her new again.

His body is unknown to her, his touch unfamiliar. This her first time, this her virginal infidelity, fills her with a wonder that she knows will never come again. The shyness and the showing, the otherness and the being so close, the shock of fulfilled desire, all this is precious, never to be forgotten.

'I want this,' she says to him. 'I want this so much. I want this.'

Not *you* but *this*. I'm using you and you're using me. I thank you for that. I love you for that.

Don't speak, my darling. Don't think. Just fuck me.

40

Laura is at her desk answering emails when Carrie appears in her study doorway.

'Come and see.'

Laura follows her upstairs to her room. Carrie stands back so she can enter first. For a moment Laura doesn't know what it is she's being shown. Then she sees it: Carrie has tidied her room. It's not a very successful job of tidying, but the floor is now visible.

'I decided to have a clear-up.'

Laura finds herself touched almost to tears. It's something to do with the gap between Carrie's pride and the actual achievement. It makes Laura feel Carrie is her little girl again.

'That's wonderful, darling. What brought this on?'

'I don't know, really.'

Laura sits down on the bed, where the duvet has been pulled into something resembling its proper place. Carrie sits down beside her. Together they survey the room.

'Now I can start my life again,' says Carrie.

She speaks brightly, bravely.

'Has it been so bad up to now?'

'Pretty rubbish.'

'Oh, darling. What did we do wrong?'

'No, Mum. You're not to do that. You're not to take over my life.'

'All right. I'm sorry.'

The new forceful Carrie is mollified.

'After all, you are my actual mother,' she says. 'You did sort of make me. That's strong stuff. I mean, you're wonderful and everything, but I don't want to turn out like a mini-you.'

'You'll never be that, Carrie. You're not like me at all. You're so much braver than I ever was.'

'Braver? I've done nothing.'

'All I ever wanted to do was please people, and be pretty, and have them need me. You're not like that at all.'

Laura realizses as she speaks that part of her envies her daughter. She envies her her truculence, and her refusal to smile.

'I should have been more selfish,' she says.

'Like me.'

'You don't feel you have to please people.'

'No. I just sit here on my own having a shitty time.'

They grin at each other. Carrie takes her mother's hand. Laura thinks, She held Henry's hand. Now it's my turn.

'You're changing, Mum.'

'Am I?'

Laura looks at Carrie's pale face, so vulnerable, so unyielding, and she aches with love for her. She doesn't want her to be having a shitty time. She wraps her free arm round Carrie and holds her close.

'Maybe I can start my life again too,' she says.

'Not too much,' says Carrie.

'What would be too much?'

'Leaving Dad.'

'Oh, no, I don't think I'd do that.'

They sit together in silence. Laura is thinking how surprising it is that they're saying these things to each other, but if this is what they're to say, she wants it to be the truth. Carrie is her little girl, now grown into a woman as much as she, Laura, is a woman, and she deserves the truth.

'Not that it's easy being married,' she says.

'I always thought you and Dad have the perfect marriage,' says Carrie. 'I know I won't have a perfect marriage.'

'We don't have a perfect marriage,' says Laura, firmly. 'We have a marriage that works.'

'And a nice house, and nice jobs, and money. You've got it all. I'll never have the life you've got.'

'What are you talking about?' Laura's taken aback by Carrie's sudden bitterness. 'Why won't you?'

'Everything's different now. Jobs are different. Men are different. You're the generation that's had it all. Everyone knows that.'

'Well, I'm very sorry. What do you want me to do about it?'

'Nothing,' says Carrie. 'There's nothing you can do about it. Just don't expect me to match up, that's all.'

'Don't expect you to have a nice job and a good marriage?'

'Don't expect me to have any kind of job, or any kind of marriage.'

'All right,' says Laura. 'I won't.'

'Liar.'

'Well, I'll try not to.'

Carrie presses herself against her, her soft body making up for her hard words.

'The thing about marriage,' Laura says, 'is that it's not really about love at all. It's about habits. No one tells you that. It's much more like having a job than it's like having an affair. Your husband's your co-worker. He's the person you do things with.'

This idea has only formed in Laura's mind as she's been speaking.

'So you don't really love Dad at all?'

'Yes, I do love him. I'm all bound up with him. He's the person I tell things to.' Suddenly, ridiculously, she thinks of the way Henry snores. 'He's the noises of someone else in the house.'

Carrie doesn't laugh. She's touched.

'Romance is so time-consuming,' says Laura. 'Being married is different. It's having someone else in the house, but you don't have to stop living your own life.'

'I think that does sound romantic,' Carrie says wistfully. 'I love it that you and Dad are solid. I just don't think it'll be like that for me, and I don't want to disappoint you.'

'You could never disappoint me, darling. All I want is for you to be—'

'Don't say it!'

'All right. I won't.'

'Don't even think it.'

'What am I to think?'

'Think I'm someone who isn't you, and never will be you, who's never going to settle down, and never going to amount to anything, but who's fine with that.'

'I'll try.'

'See? I've tidied my room. I can't be a total loser.'

Later Laura thinks of all the things she could have said to Carrie and didn't. So many thoughts are rising to the surface, these days, things she's always known but hasn't before exposed to the light. You go through life telling yourself the same comforting story until one day, for no good reason, you say, No, it's not like that at all.My life is held together by a web of habit. I get up in the morning at the same early hour, even though there are no children to take to school. I talk to Henry over breakfast about nothing much. I have work meetings, and meetings with friends, at which nothing of any importance is said. I go to the supermarket, I cook meals, they're eaten, and it's as if they'd never been. I talk to Henry about nothing much, and we go to bed, and we sleep. And so it goes on, day after day, this life of nothing much. And it works.

This is the wonder. Not that so much triviality should be sufficient to give meaning to a life, but that the entire fragile machinery of my life works. There's so much that could go wrong. The clocks could stop. The boiler could break down. The power could fail. My lungs could stop breathing. My heart could stop beating. Henry could die.

This is my marriage. The deep machinery of my life. But it's not my entire life.

41

Cas has been waiting impatiently for Alan's return. The moment he steps through the door he accosts him.

'Dad! You're needed!'

Alan seeks out Liz in her office to let her know he's back.

'I'll keep going, if you don't mind,' she says. 'I'm almost done.'

Already, so soon, the drama of the death is slipping into the past. Everyone has present concerns.

'That's fine. Cas wants me for something.'

Cas has got his new friend Kieran Kelly with him, the one who wants to write films. Kieran is a bulky youth with a pale complexion and eyes that are always darting about as if he expects to be ambushed.

'I saw *Rockefeller*,' says Kieran. 'Did you do that?'

'Yes,' says Alan.

'And *The Winter Raiders*?'

'Yes,' says Alan.

Kieran nods, offering no opinion on either film.

'I might write films,' he says.

'Kieran's got an idea for your new one,' says Cas.

'Well, I could do with some ideas,' says Alan, gamely. 'I saw my producer earlier, and he's still not happy with the ending.'

'That's because the ending's no good,' says Kieran.

'Maybe you should think of being a producer,' says Alan.

'No,' says Kieran. 'I want to be a writer.'

The boy is impervious to sarcasm. Alan decides, for Cas's sake, to play it straight.

'Why not?' he says.

'Tell Dad your idea,' Cas says.

A crafty look comes over Kieran's face.

'If I tell you my idea,' he says, 'and if you use it, then everyone will think it's your idea.'

'Yes, I suppose that's true,' says Alan.

'And you get all the money.'

'It doesn't seem fair, does it?'

'So make me an offer,' says Kieran.

'That's not so easy,' says Alan. 'After all, until I've heard your idea, I don't know what it's worth.'

'I'll settle for ten per cent,' says Kieran.

'For world rights? And no shared credit?'

'I hadn't thought of that,' says Kieran. 'Is that where you get your name on the screen?'

'Yes.'

This gives Kieran pause for serious thought. Cas looks on, impressed at his professionalism.

'I'd like my name on screen.'

'Then you need to have contributed at least one third of the screenplay,' says Alan. 'That's the rule, set by the Writers Guild of America.'

'All right,' says Kieran. 'I'll just take the money.'

'Assuming I use your ending.'

'You're the witness, Cas,' says Kieran.

'Sure,' says Cas.

'Ten per cent?' says Kieran.

'Ten per cent,' says Alan.

Thus reassured, Kieran reveals all.

'Your beautiful aliens,' he says, 'they're beautiful, and they keep dying, right? It turns out that humans are killing them with a sort of human disease, right? So at the end the aliens have to destroy the humans, right?'

'Right,' says Alan.

'So my idea is, right at the end the beautiful aliens turn out to be – zombies.'

'Zombies?'

'Right. Zombies. The living dead. They're alien zombies.'

'Why?'

'Why?' Kieran looks at him as if he can't have quite understood. 'Zombies are cool.'

'Oh,' says Alan. 'Okay.'

'So what do you think, Dad? Might you use it?'

'I'll have to think about it,' says Alan.

'Ten per cent of a million is a hundred thousand,' says Kieran.

'I don't get paid that much,' says Alan. 'And fifteen per cent goes to my agent, and five per cent to my attorney, and one and a half per cent to the Writers Guild, and then you turn dollars into pounds, and you deduct income tax, and you end up with about a quarter of what you got paid.'

'A quarter!' Kieran is deeply shocked. 'That is so sad.'

42

Annie has no train to catch, no place to go. She remains alone, at the scene of the crime.

Have I done wrong?

It doesn't feel wrong. It feels right, inevitable. She has no regrets. But somehow she needs to understand what has happened. She needs to get it fully under her control before Mitch comes home.

Her body is still nervously alive, made supersensitive by the physical memory of his body. So much of making love consists of skin contact that hers feels as if it's burning. No great novelty in the lovemaking, except that today she held a stranger in her arms, and the stranger's intense desire for her awoke her own desire.

Not a stranger: sweet Alan, grown into a man.

But what is to be done now?

She needs to talk to someone. She needs advice. She remembers the vicar on the bicycle waving to her, and sees it as an omen. Angela Southcott is intelligent, and she's discreet. Also, this sort of thing could be said to be in her line of duty. She was a psychotherapist before becoming a priest. 'I'm doing the same job as before,' she likes to say, 'only now I don't get paid for it.'

Funny, ugly little Angela on her bicycle: healer of souls.

Annie looks up her number and calls her. She's spending the day in Grenfell Court, a council-run care home nearby.

'I'm here till seven,' Angela says. 'Feel free to come on over if you want.'

Grenfell Court is a drab yellow-brick block set back from the road behind a strip of mown grass. The front door is security locked, but it opens when she buzzes. The hallway inside is clean and bleak. The Filipino care worker who lets her in tells her where to find the day room: down a passage, through fire doors.

The day room is square and light, with a dozen armchairs ranged round its walls. Four old ladies occupy four of the chairs, all apparently independent of each other. A fifth old lady is in a wheelchair. Angela Southcott sits beside her, taking notes.

She looks up as Annie enters the room and gives a nod to indicate that she'll be with her soon. Annie sits down in one of the empty chairs. The old ladies gaze at her and smile, but say nothing. There's a picture on one wall, a print of Constable's view of Salisbury Cathedral from the Meadows. Annie dimly remembers that Constable painted the picture after the death of his wife. The stormy sky is said to reflect his emotional state, and the somewhat colourless rainbow his token symbol of hope. Here among the silent old ladies it offers little promise. She recalls Tatiana's widows. Was that only yesterday evening? It feels an age away.

Why is it always women who are left alone at the end?

Then the lady vicar is on her feet and beckoning to her.

'Let's get ourselves a snack,' she says. 'They have a little canteen where they sell Rice Krispie cakes.'

As Annie follows her down another hallway, Angela Southcott waves one hand at the passing scene.

'Would you like to live here?' she says.

'No,' says Annie. 'I'd rather die.'

'They all make the same mistake. They care too much about hygiene. A real home isn't as clean as this. I'm on a campaign to establish messy care homes, full of clutter and muddle. And if that means a few germs cause a few old people to die a few years sooner, so much the better.'

The canteen is tiny, and unmanned. Angela helps them both to tea and Krispie cakes.

'I really shouldn't be bothering you,' Annie says.

'Makes a change from the witches,' says Angela.

Over her cup of tea Annie tells her story, reporting all of it truthfully except the detail that the lapse from marital fidelity took place earlier that same day.

'I knew it was wrong,' she concludes. 'I mean, the Church would certainly say it's wrong.'

'Oh, the Church,' says Angela, pulling a face. 'The Church hasn't anything sensible to say about sex at all. After centuries of using church law as a tool for men's control of women I think a period of humility and silence is called for.'

'Oh,' says Annie. 'Right.'

'Can we forget about me being a vicar? It just makes me

cross every time I think about it. Here you are, coming to me filled with guilt because you've acted on a sexual desire, and all I can think is how for centuries the Church has told us that Eve was the first sinner, and hers was the first sin. Really! What nonsense! Only a man could dream up such self-serving tosh!'

'Right,' says Annie.

'Let's clear away the rubbish, shall we? Sex in itself is good, not bad. That has to be so, doesn't it? God made sex, sex makes us. What's not good is the use of sex to cause suffering. So it's no different from all the other parts of our life. No different from making money, or driving a car. If you drive your car into a bus queue, that's bad. But driving isn't bad.'

'Yes,' says Annie. 'I suppose so.'

'So the question for you is, who are you hurting?'

'Well, Mitch. Or I would be if he knew.'

'He doesn't know?'

'Oh, no! I couldn't tell him! You know Mitch. He's the kind of person who gives back the change if he gets too much.'

'And you think knowing you were having an affair with another man would hurt him?'

'Terribly.'

'Why?'

'Why?' Annie gazes at Angela in bewilderment. Surely the question hardly needs asking. 'Well, it's a betrayal, isn't it?'

'A betrayal of what?'

'My marriage vows. His trust in me.'

'Do you feel differently about him because of having an affair?'

'Do I?' Annie considers. 'You know, it's very odd, but I think of him more lovingly because of it. I think it makes me mind some things less.'

'Because he's not having to carry the entire burden of satisfying all your needs.'

'Maybe. Yes, I suppose so.'

'People make such extreme demands on each other, don't they?'

She beams at Annie, and eats her Krispie cake.

'But Angela,' says Annie, 'are you telling me it's all right to have an affair?'

'I can't tell you that, Annie. How do I know? All I can do is get you to see clearly what's at stake here. Get away from the sex side of it and look at the love side. Are you more loving or less loving?'

'Oh, more!'

'Then Mitch will see that.'

'But I can't tell him. I can't.'

Angela looks grave.

'Why is that, Annie? Why would Mitch not want you to be as fulfilled as possible?'

'But – but – but—'

'But he's a man? And men own their wives' sexuality?'

Annie gazes back at that square, ungainly face, and sees the bright twinkle of intelligence in Angela's eyes.

'You're a very unusual vicar, Angela.'

'Actually, I'm not. You'll find most women priests think this way. We've been tempered in the furnace of the most sexist institution in the land. We know how churchmen have built their prestige, even their identity, on the subjugation of women. You come to me with a tale of female desire, of desire satisfied, and it makes me want to cheer. But I ask you again, who are you hurting?'

'I don't want to hurt anyone. I don't mean to hurt Mitch. But I will, I just know it.'

'So your solution is not to tell him.'

'Yes. I think so.'

'What you're doing, this affair, it's important to you. It's changing you. But you want the one person who's closest to you of all people in the world to know nothing about it.'

'So you're saying I should tell him?' says Annie, humbly.

'I'm saying if you love someone you don't lie to them. You don't cheat them. You don't treat them as too weak to bear the truth. Mitch isn't a child. Men deserve to be treated with respect, too.'

'Yes,' says Annie. 'Yes, you're right.' She sighs a long sigh. 'But it frightens me, even so.'

'It'll frighten him too,' says Angela. 'Take it slowly. He may choose not to know. He has that right, too. But at least give him the choice, to know or not to know.'

Annie nods, taking it all in.

'Do you want your Krispie cake?'

Annie shakes her head. Angela's plump hand reaches out and scoops it up.

43

Alan's first instinct has been to tell Liz what has happened, but the moment hasn't arisen. Cas is there with his friend Kieran, then Liz becomes tied up with making decisions about her mother's funeral, then it's dark and Alan has to drive Kieran home. They're not safely alone together until they're upstairs getting ready to go to bed.

Liz is ostentatiously tired.

'God, what's happened to me? Do you think it's because I'm not grieving?'

'You've worked all day.'

'Oh, yes. I suppose it's that.'

So Alan resolves to put off his confession until tomorrow. Or maybe longer. Maybe for ever. What good does it do talking about it?

Then when they're in bed and the lights are out he hears himself say, 'I saw Annie today.'

This takes him by surprise. Now what?

For a moment Liz just lies there in silence. Then she says, 'So that's what took you so long.'

'I went to her house. Her husband's coming home tomorrow.'

'And?'

Of course Liz is only guessing. Sometimes it feels like she can read his thoughts, but she doesn't really know. It's not as if he's going to leave her. But he and Liz have the habit of honesty, and Alan sees with sudden clarity that this is his only chance. If he doesn't say it now, it will never be said. Then one day, maybe far in the future, the secret will come out, and Liz will say, But I thought we trusted each other. Have I been wrong for so long? We do trust each other. That doesn't mean we don't hurt each other.

So Liz says, in that way she has of knowing everything, 'And?'

And Alan answers, 'Yes.'

There it is. A short confession, but a full one. No excuses.

Liz lies there by his side, silent. She has her eyes open, looking up at the ceiling.

'Liz?'

'I suppose you want to know what I'm feeling.'

'Yes,' he says.

'Threatened.'

He knows that voice: Liz being honest. She wants to track her responses truthfully, not use them in a blame game.

'Scared, because maybe it was better with her than with me.'

'No—'

Then she starts to cry.

'Oh, God! I thought I'd be so good at this. I knew this was going to happen. Did you have to do it?'

'I'm not even sure why I did.'

'Oh, please! You're not a child.'

'I'm sorry—'

'No, not that. You're not sorry. You wanted to do it, and you did it. You want to know how that makes me feel? It makes me feel like shit.'

'I'm a fool. I should have kept my mouth shut.'

'So where did you do it?'

'Her house.'

'Her bedroom?'

'A spare bedroom.'

'Fuck you, Alan! I don't want to have these feelings! I don't want all this anger!'

'What can I do, Liz?'

'You know what this does to me? It turns me into the fucking wronged woman! I hate that!'

She turns to look at him, her face wet with tears.

'Are you going to do it again?'

'No.'

'Why not? You liked it, didn't you?'

'Because I won't.'

'How do I know that? You might want to run off with her.'

'I won't. I promise.'

He makes a move towards her, he wants to dry her tears, but she pushes him away.

'No! I refuse to be a *fucking victim*.'

Her accusation against her mother. She won't be like her mother. She dries her tears herself, taking deep breaths.

'Tell me what it was like,' she says. 'Tell me what happened. Make me understand why you did it.'

So he tells her. How the desire had been building and building in him, and how Annie knew it, and how they hardly talked at all. Liz wants to know about the sex, but he's not good at talking about that. All he can say is, 'It was nothing special.'

'But did it make you feel good?'

'Yes,' he says.

She wants to know who undressed first, and what her body looks like. She wants to take possession of his adventure. Alan's afraid to admit too much pleasure in it, because he wants to save her from hurt, but she doesn't want to be saved.

'Is her body better than mine? Did she do things for you that I don't do?'

His answers are too timid, too non-specific.

'Don't protect me, Alan. I need to know all of it.'

'But why? What's the point?'

'So there are no surprises. I don't want there to be secrets which make you do things I don't understand. I want to feel what you felt. I want to want what you want. Then it won't frighten me.'

Little by little she gets it out of him, and so forms a picture for herself of his sexual obsession.

'It's your victory over the failure of the past, isn't it?'

Alan hesitates before he replies. He wants to repay Liz's honesty with his own honesty. Yes, it's sweet to return to the field of defeat as a conqueror. But mostly it's the electric charge of desire. The potent sensation of knowing your desire is reciprocated.

'She wanted what I wanted,' he says.

How could he resist? It all comes down to chance and opportunity. He wants her to feel how intensely exciting it was for both of them. There is no other excuse.

'Are you sure you won't do it again?'

'Sure,' he says.

She moves closer to him in the bed. His arms reach over to embrace her. They kiss.

'Are you still angry?' he whispers.

'Yes,' she says.

She feels for his cock.

'I don't think I'll be much good,' he whispers.

He never was a twice-a-day man.

'Doesn't matter,' she says. 'We can just play.'

He knows then what it is she wants to play. She's Annie and he's fucking her. It's come over her as a compulsion. She's super-aroused.

'Touch me,' she says. 'Touch me all over. Like you did with her.'

He strokes her all over, running his hands up the sides of her body to her breasts, and back down the middle.

'What did she do? Did she do this?'

She's sliding her hand over his cock. It's hard now.

'Did you lie on top of her? Lie on top of me.'

They make love. After a little while he feels his cock shrinking inside her. But she's not interested in what's happening to him. She's a long way from being done. She takes his hand, moves it between her thighs.

'Touch me. More. Harder.'

His finger finds the right spot, and the sensation builds in her, making all her body vibrate. Then after a while she needs to take control. She pushes aside his hand so she can rub herself harder and faster.

'Ah! Fuck! Ah!'

Her orgasm hits her like a train, causing all her body to buck with the power of it.

'Oh, God! Oh, God!'

It rolls on and on, her limbs shuddering, and then slowly dies away, leaving her limp and gasping, filmed in sweat.

'Oh, God! Oh, God!'

He strokes her gently as she lies beside him, still trembling.

'That was strong,' she says.

She can't explain, and doesn't try. This one was for her, her body's pleasure is all her own. The beautiful selfishness of sex. He can't take that from her by fucking someone else.

'Will you do something for me?' she says.

'Yes,' he says.

'Sleep in the other room.'

So he gets out of bed and crosses the dark hall to the spare bedroom, where he spends the rest of the night alone.

Sunday, 10 May 2015

44

Annie wakes to a sensation of dread.

Mitch will be home in less than two hours. His key will turn in the lock, he'll drag his suitcase into the hall, he'll call out her name. Her first welcome-home kiss will be a lie. Her first loving words will be a lie. What she's done shuts her away from him and forces her to live out a pretence. Surely he'll sense it and say to her, You're different. Something's changed. What is it? And then she'll have to tell him. And then—

But of course he'll notice nothing. She's being foolish. How can he know? He'll only know if she tells him.

But I am going to tell him.

Her moment of panic passes. But it leaves its mark. She has seen, in her imagination, his hurt, accusing face. She has sensed his pain. She doesn't want to sit in the house and wait for the sound of his key in the door. Better to be there at the airport to greet him. Better to speak out before he begins to suspect. Better to say, 'I told you at the first opportunity.' Then if there are any recriminations they can take place in the car driving home, and she won't have to see his face.

The plane lands early. She's barely stationed herself by the rails in front of the Arrivals doors when she sees Mitch coming out. He's walking with two others, a tall black woman with a head of tight grey curls, and a small tanned white woman. All three wheel carry-on cases behind them. They're talking earnestly, and Mitch, not expecting to be met, does not look up.

Annie calls to him.

'Mitch!'

He's astonished. He greets her with a beaming smile, visibly touched.

'Annie! How sweet of you.'

He takes her in his arms and kisses her. Then he introduces her to his colleagues, Janetta, the director of Ubuntu Africa, and Diane, the chief fundraiser.

Annie offers to drive them all into town, but the other two plan to go directly to the office in Hackney.

'It'll be quicker for us on the Piccadilly line,' Diane says, her eyes squinting as she speaks, as if looking into the light.

In the car driving home Mitch explains the crisis that has cut short his trip. A change of minister in the South African government has resulted in a big cut to the grant they receive.

'The new minister claims it's part of the ANC's Africanization policy, but we're eighty per cent African. The grant we're losing is going to another development charity, which just happens to be run by the new minister's wife. It's absolutely blatant, but there's nothing we can do about it. So as of yesterday we're five million rand short.'

Annie listens, and expresses sympathy, as he pours out his anger and his fears for the future. This is no time to be revealing sexual indiscretions.

'We could lose everything, Annie. All the training centres, all the staff. It's having no notice that really screws us. We just have to hope DfID bails us out.'

The Department for International Development is Ubuntu's other major funder.

'I'll have a quick shower and change, and then I'll have to get into the office, too, I'm afraid. I know it's Sunday, but we need to set up an emergency meeting as soon as possible.'

Once in the house he parks his suitcase at the foot of the stairs and goes into the kitchen for a cup of coffee.

'Good of you to come, Annie.'

'I knew how tired you'd be.'

'We got upgraded on the return as well. Flat beds all the way. BA likes to call its business class Club Class. Doesn't that just say it all?'

He's making the coffee his own special way, grinding the beans just so, tipping the grounds into the paper cone.

'The whole idea of a club is you're in and everyone else is out. If Ubuntu means anything it means we're all in it together. There's something about the whole idea of clubs that's divisive.'

'But you liked getting the flat bed.'

'Yes.' He sighs, and smiles at her. 'We're all hypocrites. But I'd rather have ideals and fail to live up to them than have no ideals at all.'

'Oh, Mitch.'

'What?'

'That's such a Mitch-ish thing to say.'

And in that moment, watching him fuss over his coffee-making, she feels a great tenderness towards him. He seems to her to be as earnest and as helpless as a little boy.

He goes upstairs to shower. Annie, sitting drinking coffee in the kitchen, tells herself this isn't the right time. He's worried about work. Then she tells herself there never will be a right time, and the longer she leaves it the harder it will get. Do it now, in the middle of the work crisis, and at least he'll have something else to distract him.

So she goes upstairs and is there sitting on the side of the bed when he comes out of the shower. Seeing his naked body, she feels a second pang of tenderness. He's a good man, she thinks. I'm going to hurt him. Why would I do that? He never needs to know.

Angela said, If you love someone you don't lie to them. But not telling isn't the same as lying, is it? She tries to think how she would feel, if it was the other way round.

I'd feel angry. I'd feel it's not up to him to decide what I'm to know and not to know. I'm not a child.

'Oh, hello.' He's surprised to find her there.

'I know you have to rush out,' she says. 'There's something we need to talk about.'

'Oh?' he says, pulling on his clothes. He sounds wary all of a sudden. Perhaps he guesses.

'I was going to leave it to a better time. But there never is a better time, is there?'

'Christ, Annie,' he says, buttoning up his shirt. 'What is it?'

She knows now she's going to tell, but she'll tell it obliquely, at first at least. As Angela said, he may choose not to know.

'Well,' she says, 'it's about you and me. And how we trust each other. And what we do that maybe we shouldn't.'

Mitch comes to a stop, his shirt not yet buttoned to the top. He stands motionless, his head bent as if in prayer.

'I've been dreading this,' he says.

Annie is too surprised to say anything.

'I suppose I knew you'd find out some day,' he says.

He goes on standing there, half dressed, his fingers still on his shirt buttons, head down, now with the air of a supplicant. Annie feels dazed. The reversal is too sudden.

'I'm such a fool,' he says.

'Mitch,' she says, finding her voice at last. 'Please—'

But he interrupts, now looking at her, his voice urgent, frightened.

'The one thing, the only thing, you have to believe this above everything else, I love you and only you. Nothing's changed in my feelings for you.'

'Right,' she says, dazed.

'Tell me you believe me.'

'What's this about?' she says. 'I don't understand.'

He comes to sit beside her on the bed: just like the way she was going to tell him in the car, side by side. He sits there, his socks not yet on, his bare toes pressed to the floor.

'I'm such a fool,' he says again. 'You get into these things so easily, and then you can't get out. It's all such a cliché. I feel humiliated telling you.'

He falls silent for a moment, and she's about to speak, when he presses on, speaking now in a rush.

'You're a long way from home, you go to a party, you drink

too much, there's someone there who's available, you think – you don't think, you just *do*. And then it's done, and it can't be undone.'

'Who?' says Annie.

'You met her at the airport. Diane.'

Annie pictures her in her mind's eye: the trim figure, the tan, the squinty eyes.

'It's just a physical thing,' Mitch says. 'I'm not in love with her. I don't want to run off with her. God forbid! It's just one of those stupid things men do. I should have put a stop to it long ago.'

Long ago?

'What do you mean, long ago?'

'I kept meaning to. But I suppose I thought, It's all far away, Annie will never know, what's the harm? But of course these things always come out in the end. And you know what really drives me crazy? This isn't like me. This isn't who I am.'

'No,' says Annie.

'The me I am with you, that's the real me.'

He feels for her hand. She lets him take it.

'I'm sorry,' he says. 'I'm so, so sorry.'

She has no words. He waits for her to speak, but she says nothing.

'Do you hate me?' he says.

'No.'

'Are you going to leave me?'

'No.'

He starts to weep, tears of shame and relief.

'Thank God,' he says. 'Thank God. I swear to you nothing like this will ever happen again. Ever, ever.'

'You'd better finish getting dressed,' she says.

'Yes.' He snuffles as he weeps. 'I have to go to the office. We're in mid-crisis.'

'So I gather.'

He looks at her and she gives him a small smile. He smiles back, his damp eyes craving more forgiveness than she can offer.

'Give me a hug,' he says. 'Please.'

She puts her arms round him. He clings to her, his cheeks wet on hers. Just like a small boy.

After he's gone Annie sits in the kitchen, doing nothing, staring at the grain of the wooden table top. It forms thin bands that stream round the knots like force fields. The knots are like planets – no, like solar systems. If you travelled far enough away our whole world would look like this, our whole universe. To an astronomer in a far-off galaxy we must be infinitely small, and our concerns of no significance at all.

Mitch has been having sex with another woman. Mitch is sorry. Mitch wept.

None of this seems quite to fit together. If he had an affair it must have been because he wanted to. It must have excited him. He must have looked forward to their times together, anticipating the coming pleasure. Why else do it?

She's imagining Mitch as if he's herself. She's the one wanting the affair. She's the one having it.

So don't I mind?

There's something here that she minds very much indeed, but she can't put her finger on what it is. It's not the simple fact of infidelity, it's something more oblique. Meanwhile, until she's made her own confession to Mitch, it's as if all her reactions must remain provisional. She may turn out to be angry, but she doesn't yet have the right.

Ellie calls. She wants to bring her new boyfriend over.

'Dad's back,' says Annie. 'He came back early. He's got a work crisis.'

She says come over for supper. She'll cook something nice.

'Do your stir-fry beef,' says Ellie. 'All I ever eat is pasta. And don't get cross if Franco says he wants to watch the football.'

'Is he likely to do that?'

'It's like his god. He's almost converted me.'

Annie realizes she's asked them over this evening because she doesn't want to be alone with Mitch. She can't put off making her own confession for long, but she needs more time. The rules of the game have changed.

45

Today's the day I begin the rest of my life.

Carrie lies in bed, awake but not yet up. She loves this time of day, when lingering in bed feels like an indulgence, but has not yet become an illness. Roughly speaking, up to lunchtime is acceptable. After that you need a sick note.

She's made some basic arrangements. A phone call to an ex-boyfriend so she has somewhere to stay. Beyond that the future stretches before her, empty but no longer quite so frightening. Randall was surprised to hear her voice, but also pleased. He may have expectations. That's his problem.

I don't have to please people. Especially boys.

Carrie lies in bed and thinks about boys. Boys and men. That other race which has always felt so alien to her. You don't realize until you really think about it how many allowances you make for them. They forget your birthday. They don't listen when you talk. They don't notice when they hurt you. They do cruel things without seeming to notice. Oh, that's just boys, you say.

Then they become men, and nothing really changes. The boy who took all the orange Smarties becomes the man who has sex and never calls. It's like they lack the capacity for feeling what others feel. The better ones are trained to a point where they have manners, and behave well, but it doesn't come instinctively, the way it does with women. They're just not that interested in anyone but themselves.

Boys don't have friends. They have mates: they go to the pub together, to the match, to the war. But they have no real interest in each other.

He's just not that into you.

That's the least of it. Face it, girls. He's just not that into anyone. The male sex is dysfunctional.

So muses Carrie, lying in her warm bed on a late Sunday morning. And yet, she thinks, there's Dad, in his funny woolly hat, talking about chasing a train and never catching it. There's Jack, suddenly not all right after all, saying, 'I'm drowning, too.'

They barely have the words, when the time comes, and they want to talk. These alien creatures, these boys, these men, she feels it now: they're not so different from us, they just don't have the words. They don't know how to look inside and report on what they find there. So when it goes wrong, the inside part, they're bewildered, lost.

It was watching Jack in that brief moment when he cracked open that revealed this to Carrie. 'I'm struggling,' he said. And all at once, instead of the usual anger that male lack of awareness induces in her, she felt pity. It was as if she was watching a dumb animal caught in a trap. This is a novel perspective. Her older brother has always been more sure of himself than her, more articulate. He's always been the focus of attention in the family. Some psychic law of primogeniture has granted him privileges denied to her. And yet there he stood, his face twisting with pain, trying to tell her that his life was not working as it should.

Jack never calls her. He never texts or emails to let her know how he's getting on, or even, Heaven forbid, to ask how she's getting on. He's always busy. That's the male default state: busy. Work is sacred. Family is a support system. Sex is recreation. Love is – what? Do boys do love? Passion, yes: passion as resisted desire, passion as chase and conquest. But love, the slow interplay of thoughts and feelings, that's for the womenfolk. To men it sounds too much like gossip. Yes, there's a good indicator. Show me a man who likes to gossip and I'll show you a man who can love.

And yet Jack came upstairs to find her. He undertook the mission to venture into uncharted territory – for what did he know of her unhappiness, how deep and dark the terrain might prove? He came to carry her back to the castle, the princess who had wandered out into the forest and got lost. He may have been cross and graceless, he may have said, 'Stop it, Carrie!', as if reprimanding a naughty child. But he came, which is caring of a kind. And then he said, straight out of the heart of his pain, 'What do you know about me?'

The primal question: what do you know about me? Not enough, Jack. You tell me so little. But I want to know. And I want you to know about me, too. That's why I write songs. That's all my songs are, Jack. They're me telling what it's like to be me. All you have to do is listen.

Out of this dance of thoughts, which have filled Carrie's

mind since Friday evening and now it's Sunday, a new ambition has grown. Carrie wants to write songs for the boys.

Such a simple idea, but it has brought her back to life. Maybe only a few will listen. Maybe only one or two will understand. But this is more than strumming a tune to pass the time. This is a mission.

I am an evangelist, thinks Carrie.

She's been writing a song for her father. She's trying to say how once he was everything to her, and then nothing, and how all along he was always there. She has fragments.

> *When I close my eyes I see*
> *How tall you were*
> *You sheltered me*
> *You sheltered me*
>
> *Because you held my hand so tight*
> *I never feared the night*

And –

> *I thought all men were made like you*
> *It isn't true*
> *But if I trust this shitty world*
> *Where faces lie and hearts are cold*
> *And beauty fades and hope grows old*
> *And love is fairyland*
> *It's all because there's someone who*
> *Once held my hand.*

WILLIAM NICHOLSON

She joins them for lunch, and tells them she's leaving.
'What? Today?'
'I thought you'd be pleased.'
'Where will you go? What will you do?'
This is her mother, protective, panicking. She has visions of
Carrie sleeping on the streets.
'She'll be fine,' says her father.
So who loves me more?
'I'm going to sleep on Randall's couch. I'll be okay, Mum.
Really I will.'
She wants to be gone now. After days of hiding she's ready
to run. She doesn't want to be a cause for worry any more.
She wants to be invisible.
When it's time to leave, her mother gives her a close hug.
'You're wonderful, Mum.'
'Me? What did I do?'
'You know.'
Henry drives her to the station.
'You know we're always here,' he says.
'Yes, Dad. I know.'
She wants to tell him how seeing him fall on the landing has
made all the difference to her, but she doesn't fully understand
why, and can't find the words. In her song it's his steadfast
strength that sustains her. In life it's his weakness that has set
her free.
No, that's too grand. There was no lock on the door.
We ask too much of men, she thinks. They must be our dads
for ever, able to swing us up in their strong arms. But then they
stagger against the banisters, and fall to the floor. Down to the
floor, down where I live.

'Keep in touch,' he says in the ticket hall.

He too hugs her, a long, tight hug. This is where she should say how much she loves him, but still the words don't come.

'Love you, darling,' he says.

'I'll call,' she says.

She shoulders her rucksack and picks up her guitar case. She goes through the ticket gate without looking back.

When my song's finished, she thinks, I'll come home and sing it for you.

46

Mitch still hasn't come home when Ellie arrives. Annie hugs her specially close, as if she might lose her soon, and says nothing about the designer rents in her jeans. She gazes on her fresh young face with wonder.

'You're so pretty, Ellie!'

Franco, the Anglo-Italian boyfriend, is loitering in the hallway.

'Come on in, Franco,' says Ellie. 'This is my mum.'

Franco gives her a wordless nod. He's a slender, good-looking youth, in a leather bomber jacket, tight jeans and red Converse shoes. Annie sees at a glance that he cares about his appearance: he has his own sense of style. He looks restless, as if he wants to be elsewhere.

'Franco's a massive fan of Italian football,' Ellie says. 'They're playing now.'

'Lazio against Inter,' says Franco.

'Go on, then,' says Annie.

Ellie takes Franco upstairs to the living-room TV, then comes downstairs to rejoin her mother. The sounds of the game come floating down to them.

'You don't mind, do you?' says Ellie. 'He'll come back down to eat.'

'Don't you want to watch with him?'

'No. I want to stay here with you.'

'Help yourself to a drink,' Annie says. 'Take one to Franco.'

'You don't have a beer, do you?'

'As it happens, I do.'

Ellie goes to the fridge and finds an unbroken six-pack of Stella.

'Magic.'

She takes a beer up to Franco. Annie pours herself a glass of white wine and stands drinking it, feeling like a criminal. Then she sets about dinner.

Ellie says, 'So? What do you think?'

'He seems quiet.'

'He can talk when he wants to talk. But he says most of the time he can't be bothered.'

'I hope he can be bothered to talk to you.'

Ellie puts her arms round her mother, her sweet face shining with happiness.

'I love him so much, Mum. He's so adorable. And he loves me.'

'Lucky girl.'

'He's just perfect. Franco says it's fate. You know I met him at this club? He's the most amazing dancer. Then I walked right past his garage, and there he was! Fate!'

'What does he do in this garage?'

'I don't know. Fixes cars. But he's really smart, Mum. And he wants four children, same as me.'

'Hey, slow down. Aren't you getting in a bit deep here?'

'Of course I am,' says Ellie, her eyes sparkling. 'I'm in over my head.'

'I just don't want you to get hurt, darling.'

'Why should I get hurt? We love each other.'

'Well,' says Annie, 'it's just that first love affairs don't always last. Mostly they don't last.'

Ellie unhooks herself and moves away, hurt.

'Why say that? And anyway, it's not true. Lots of people fall in love and marry and stay together for the rest of their lives. It's not unusual. I bet it's what happens most of the time. Just because it didn't happen to you doesn't mean it won't happen to me. Look at Dean and Inge. They've been together since school, and they're your age.'

'Yes, but Inge did have that affair.'

'What do you want me to do, Mum? Love Franco less, in case it goes wrong later?'

'No, darling. Of course not.'

She hears the front door open.

'There's Dad back now.'

Supper round the kitchen table is a curious affair. Mitch is tired and has a cowed air about him. Whenever his eyes meet Annie's they ask, silently, Is it going to be all right? Ellie is nervous and talks brightly, her eyes checking to see if her parents approve of Franco, and he of them. Annie, caught in the midst of all this, is overcome with the sensation that she's not really there at all, that she's been replaced by an actor who looks like her, who might be found out at any moment.

'So you work in a garage?' says Mitch.

Franco nods. Then, aware that more is required, says, 'Yes.'

Ellie amplifies: 'He's going to start his own business.'

'Doing what?' says Mitch.

'Whatever pays,' says Franco.

'Franco's going to be a millionaire by the time he's thirty,' says Ellie.

'Million's nothing these days,' says Franco. 'Everyone in this street's a millionaire, just from their houses.'

'True enough,' says Mitch.

'So what do you want to make money for, then?' says Annie.

Franco gazes at her, puzzled.

'So I've got money,' he says.

'Yes,' says Annie, 'but money's not . . .'

She stops, confused. She thought she was saying something self-evident, but in the face of Franco's blank look, she begins to doubt.

'I mean,' she says, 'people usually want money to get them something else.'

'I want money to get me rich,' says Franco.

Annie looks to Mitch for help, feeling out of her depth.

'But Franco,' says Mitch, 'being rich isn't the end of the story, is it? You have to do something with the money. Having it just piling up in the bank doesn't give you anything.'

'If I had money piling up in the bank,' says Franco, 'it'd give me a great feeling. I'd feel rich. I'd feel like I could have anything I wanted.'

Annie watches Ellie watching Franco as he speaks and, to her surprise, sees on her face a look of pride.

'Franco doesn't think like us,' Ellie says. 'I didn't get it at first either. I thought he was being all shallow and, like, materialistic, wanting just to make money. So Franco said, What does your dad do?, and I said, Works for an aid charity, and he said, So where does the money for the charity come from? Someone has to make it, right? Like, all you do is spend it?'

'Fair point,' says Mitch.

'So we need people to get rich,' says Ellie, 'for the charities, and the art, and everything that we care about – I mean in our family, right? Like, I'm studying art history, which is great, but someone has to pay for the art, and the university, and for me to study. Right?'

Surely, thinks Annie, Ellie never used to say *like* and *right* all the time.

'You're converting her, Franco,' says Mitch.

'When you're together,' says Ellie, 'it's important to have the same values. Like, you and Mum have the same values.'

'But you have to be true to yourself, too, Ellie,' says Mitch. Then, meeting Annie's eyes, he blushes and falls silent.

'Oh, Franco and me are different,' says Ellie. 'Franco drinks beer. I don't like beer. Franco thinks art's a waste of time.'

'No, I don't,' says Franco.

'Well, you did,' says Ellie, giving him a loving look, touching his arm. 'It's me converting you, there.'

'I've got nothing against art,' says Franco. 'It just comes later, right? First you buy a nice car, then you buy a nice house, then you maybe buy a boat or a plane, then you buy a football club, then you buy art.'

'The ultimate consumer luxury,' says Mitch.

'That's it,' says Franco, nodding. 'Art's a luxury.'

Ellie is delighted. It seems to her that Franco has won his point, and gained the respect of her parents.

'See?' she says. 'You don't start out liking the same things. But you grow together.'

After Ellie and Franco have gone, Mitch helps Annie clear the table and wash up. Annie knows he wants to talk about the crisis between them.

'Did you sort things out at work?' she says.

'We managed to get a meeting with the Department set up for tomorrow,' he says. 'Really I should be preparing for it.'

'Go and work if you need to, Mitch. I can do this.'

'There's something I have to do first,' he says, looking at his watch. 'Something more important.'

This means *save the marriage*. But why should he look at his watch? Are they running to a timetable?

I'm so irritable, she thinks. What right have I got to be irritable? I suppose it's because Mitch is using his I'll–fix–it voice. He's going to *fix the marriage*. This is what men do when things go wrong. They fix them.

'What did you think of the boyfriend?' she says.

'I give it six weeks.'

'Why? Because he works in a garage?'

'He's a novelty. The novelty'll wear off.'

Oh, thinks Annie, but it's fun while it lasts.

Then the clearing up is done and he's looking at her as if he's going to make an announcement and she's to pay attention.

'We're not talking about it,' he says, 'but it's *there*. It's *here*. The elephant in the room.'

'Elephant?'

She finds herself smiling, as if this is all faintly comic. She sees Mitch flinch.

'So I'm going to do something about it,' he says. 'I'm not going to let this come between us.'

'The elephant?'

Why am I being so flippant? I don't feel flippant. It's not appropriate.

But she can't help herself. She's no longer fully in control.

'I'm going to prove to you,' he says, 'that it's over, and in the past, and that we – that is, you and me – we're as strong as ever.'

As opposed to *we* – that is, him and her. Or *we*, me and him. The other him. So many permutations. But Mitch is going to fix it.

'I talked to Diane today,' he's saying. 'She understands. She accepts. I want you to know that. So now' – he takes out his phone, glances at his watch – 'I'm going to call her, and she'll tell you herself.'

Annie waves her hand before her face, waving it away, this clumsiness, this embarrassment.

'Please, Mitch. There's no need.'

But he's made a plan. Probably they synchronized watches. He makes the call.

'Diane? It's Mitch. I'm here with Annie. I'm putting you on speaker.'

A thin, bleak, far-off voice sounds from the phone.

'Mitch?'

'You're on speaker,' Mitch says, like a teacher prompting a child. 'Annie's here with me.'

'Oh,' says the disembodied voice, the voice of the elephant in the room.

Annie stifles the impulse to giggle.

God, what's the matter with me?

'Like I said earlier,' says Mitch, speaking a little more slowly and clearly than is natural, 'I want both of you to hear me say this. I love Annie. I won't do anything to hurt our marriage. Whatever we had, it's now over. I mean you and me, Diane. Not you and me, Annie.'

No, no, don't giggle. Look solemn. The elephant is being sent out of the room.

'That's what we agreed, isn't it, Diane?'

'Yes,' says the disembodied voice.

'It was never serious between us, was it?'

'No,' says the disembodied voice.

'And now it's over.'

'Yes, Mitch.'

Poor elephant. A sad circus animal, kneeling on command.

'Annie's hearing everything we're saying,' says Mitch. 'I want this all to be out in the open between us. Annie, do you want to talk to Diane yourself?'

Annie shakes her head in mute alarm.

'She's shaking her head,' says Mitch to the phone.

'Is that it?' says the faraway voice.

'Yes,' says Mitch. 'That's it. Bye, Diane.'

'Bye.'

Mitch ends the call. He turns to Annie with a look of triumph in his eyes, and sweat beading his brow.

'There.'

'Oh, Mitch,' says Annie. 'What must she be feeling?'

'She's fine. She's got her own life. Look, let's forget about Diane. My priority is rebuilding my marriage.'

'The thing is, Mitch,' says Annie, 'I don't think it's as easy as that.'

'I'm not saying it's easy. I'm just saying I'm one hundred per cent determined to do it.'

He's standing four-square before her, for all the world like a fighter ready to take on all comers. Now is the time for her to tell him there's a second elephant in the room; now, before a gap opens up between his decisive, almost surgical action, designed to heal them, and the discovery of a second alien growth. If she doesn't speak now, what will he say later? Now, this evening, she's still able to plead that she's in shock at his revelation, that there's hardly been a moment, that she always meant to tell him on his return. But the moment has come, and she can't speak.

'I don't know what more I can do,' he says. 'But if you know, then tell me, and I'll do it.'

His phone rings. He checks the caller and pulls a face at Annie.

'Janetta. I have to take this.'

She nods, waves him away to his call.

'Janetta,' he says to the phone. 'Yes, of course . . . When did you hear? . . . Do you want me to fill him in on the figures?'

He walks away, talking on the phone. Annie finds she can hardly stand. She sinks onto a chair and rests her head in her hands.

Adultery is so tiring.

Monday, 11 May 2015

47

Aster Dickinson kept her papers in a desk in the study. She had no idea which were important and which were not – 'Rex dealt with all of that' – so she kept them all. When Liz opens the desk she finds impossible heaps of electricity bills and council-tax demands and letters announcing winter fuel payments. And there, on the top of all the rest, is a brown A4 envelope on which is written: MY FUNERAL. The lettering is erratic, written within the last few months, Liz guesses. Inside is a sheet of paper with words crawling slantwise across it.

> *I wish to be buried in the graveyard of St Mary's, Edenfield.*
> *I wish my gravestone to read:*
> > *Here lies*
> > *Aster Dickinson*
> > *Loyal wife of Rex*
> > *Loving mother of Elizabeth*
> > *'She did her duty.'*

Liz gazes at the paper. No date, no signature. Why buried after all? Why Edenfield, a village four miles away? Then she remembers. It was there that her mother met her father. He had been billeted in a farmhouse there in the war – the house where the Broads now live – and had been back on a sentimental visit. They had actually met in the churchyard. Some friend of Rex's, wounded in the Dieppe raid, had later died and was buried there, and Rex was looking for his grave. Aster was at her little easel, painting a watercolour of the church and Mount Caburn beyond. She used to paint a lot before she was married, and afterwards too. But when Rex left she put away her brushes and never painted again.

That must have been fifty years ago. And yet here she is, only a few months back, scratching her wishes, biro in her arthritic hand, as if it had all happened yesterday.

Liz understands. Her mother wishes in death to reclaim the moment when she met a man who loved her. And surely she was right. On that afternoon in the churchyard he must have thought, How lovely she is, we could be happy together. After all, he did marry her.

She did her duty.

My poor cheated mother, starved of love, refusing to be beaten, ever ready to spot a slight, quick to anger, armed against pity, nursing deep within herself this secret memory of the time she was loved.

The time they made love.

Almost unthinkable now, and yet Liz herself is the living proof. Aster and Rex, naked in each other's arms. Aster submitting her fearful body to the invasion of sex in her love for her husband. No way of knowing that she was fearful, of course, but it must have been so: a thirty-six-year-old virgin, who had never believed herself to be attractive to men. And having made him the supreme gift of herself, she believed them to be united till death. They have been united till death, in her mind.

Loyal wife of Rex.

What price a wife's loyalty today?

But no, thinks Liz, that's not how it is any more. In her mother's day, loyalty was understood to be the price paid for security. For the home, the children, the income that sustained them. But loyalty was never expected to buy happiness. It was always a deal struck in a marketplace. So how has it come to be dressed up in all the finery of moral laws?

Alan has been disloyal.

Earlier this morning Liz completed her feature on WHAT WOMEN WANT and sent it off. Chrissie has cleared space for it in the magazine this coming Sunday. These last few days have been filled for Liz by death and desire, and everything, everything has changed. The world no longer looks the same.

I'm a mortal creature hurtling towards extinction. I'm as driven by sexual desire as any man. Why do we punish men for what we want for ourselves? If we could only speak the truth, women and men both, we wouldn't be so afraid.

It's men who fear. It's men who seek to control women, with their laws and their moral codes and their structures of shame. But if we're to break free of this control, if we're to demand the freedom to act on our desires, then we must give men the same freedom. Is so much freedom possible?

It seems to Liz, sitting among her dead mother's papers, that she has a vision of how the world might be if we only spoke the truth. It's a world that blazes with adventure, but perhaps it burns too brightly. Perhaps it will make us mad, so much freedom. Perhaps we'll cry out for new laws.

And she thinks again of her mother's wasted life and swears, Never again! Let no more women's lives be so starved of joy.

So now I suppose I must arrange a churchyard burial in Edenfield.

She bows her head. So much to do. From beyond death her mother continues to make demands on her. She did her duty. She expects me to do mine.

She's about to leave when, on an impulse, she goes upstairs to her childhood bedroom. Her mother has preserved the room just as she left it, thirty years and more ago. She hasn't entered the room for a long time, resenting the message it's designed to send, that she's still a child, still under her mother's control. But now, with the end in sight, the room has lost its power to hurt her.

It's clean and tidy and lifeless. Everything special to her she removed long ago, leaving only the shell of a self she no longer recognizes. The blue duvet cover patterned with clouds, the amber-painted walls, the shelf of books, mostly birthday gifts, which she may have read long ago and no longer remembers.

Then her gaze falls on a curious item on the chest of drawers. It belonged once to her grandfather, and was claimed by her mother after her father's early death, and so it has passed down to Liz. Aster had presented it with great solemnity, indicating that with this gift came an ineradicable bond. For this reason Liz had always disliked it and hidden it away. But evidently her mother had discovered it and restored it to a place of honour.

It's a miniature ebony signpost stuck into a small piece of granite. It has two silver arms, one saying LONDON, the other saying EDINBURGH. A silver plaque set into the granite reads:

> *Give over yer blathering*
> *Aboot yer mooter-car.*

It had meant nothing to the ten-year-old Liz to whom it had been entrusted. Now, gazing at it, she can begin to decode some of its layers of reference. Her grandfather had found it amusing. Perhaps he'd been given it because he was over-proud of some car bought some time in the 1930s. The joke had been shared with his little daughter; he would have read out the words in a comic Scots accent. So its meaning lay not in the signpost, or the motor-car, but in the shared amusement of father and daughter; a father who died when Aster was only eight years old.

Now that the end has come, Liz is released to think of such things. As her mother's power wanes, pity comes to take its place. Why could she not have shared the joke with her mother? Why not allow her the happy memory of her own childhood? She wants to go back downstairs right away and tell her, saying, 'It's so funny, Mummy. Give over yer blathering.' But, of course, it's too late now.

★

ADVENTURES IN MODERN MARRIAGE

Back at home she finds Alan alone in the kitchen. She knows he's waiting to have *the talk* and she doesn't want to have it. She's still in a state of denial about her own feelings. It's as if, now that her mother has died, she has become a different person. No, not different so much as temporary. All permanence has melted away. She must begin the process of building a new self, but not yet. Let the storm subside first.

She tells Alan of her mother's last wishes.

'She's not here any more,' he says. 'She'll never know.'

'I feel I should at least try.'

'She wasn't a parishioner of Edenfield. I doubt if they'd let you. Graveyards are tight for space, these days.'

Ever practical, like a real man. And he's right. In the end the decision won't be emotional, it will be administrative.

No administrative solution for our shared life. Once the law would have limited the choices, but no more. Our hard-won freedoms leave us exposed to the storm winds of our desires.

'Liz,' he says. 'We have to talk.'

'I know. Just not yet.'

She's afraid of saying things she'll regret later. It's like sending emails. You can draft messages filled with anger and self-pity, and your finger hovers over the SEND button, but so long as they remain unsent they're part of your argument with yourself. Once you press SEND they can't be recalled. They exist, on the record, for ever. In the same way, whatever words she speaks to Alan will live in his memory from that day on. An instinct of self-preservation tells her not to speak, not even to start speaking, because once she's started, who knows what will burst out?

But of course she knows what's waiting inside, building up pressure, pushing for its moment of release. It's the force that lays waste the world: anger.

48

Today, Annie says to herself. Today, when he gets back from work, however tiring his day has been, I will tell him.

She practises the conversation in her head.

'Mitch, you know how you had something to confess to me? Well, the ridiculous thing is . . .' Is it ridiculous? Better to say *shameful*. They can both be shamed together, by their parallel betrayals. Except she doesn't feel ashamed. This is what scares her: that she won't sound sorry enough.

When she told Mitch she wouldn't leave him, he wept. The more she thinks about this, the more it feels out of character. Who was he weeping for? Himself, presumably. Her reassurance banished some deep fear. The fear of losing her? A voice whispers in her ear that Mitch's fear has very little to do with her. He fears showing himself in public to be a bad man. If a man can deceive his wife, is he to be trusted with money donated by well-meaning folk to a charitable institution?

But Mitch is not a bad man. This affair of his changes nothing. Annie wonders at herself for not feeling more outrage.

Perhaps, she thinks, I'm still in shock, and haven't yet accepted the reality of it. But somehow actions that have taken place so far away lack the power to harm her. He might as well have told her he'd been dining with a stranger, down there in Cape Town. What's that to her? It's another world, where he leads another life.

Would I react this way if it weren't for Alan?

Mitch wept for his sins. Annie feels no impulse to weep, either for him or for herself. Again, she finds herself puzzling over Mitch's tears.

Back when they first met his most attractive quality to her had been his self-containment. He was a good-looking boy, but no more so than many. In those days boys hung about Annie, causing her to use up most of her energy in letting them down gently. A pretty girl raised in the habit of pleasing others is caught in this trap almost daily: you smile on a boy, and do what you can to make him feel good, and shortly he starts feeling too good, and you have to disappoint him. So by some cruel mechanism of nature all the charms with which you've been blessed end up causing pain and anger.

Into this world of smiles and tears strode Mitchell Hamer, with his air of one who had other concerns on his mind. Annie was recently back from a year in Paris, where she had been unhappy and lonely. Mitch clearly admired her, but he made no moves towards her. He was hard-working, ambitious, very clear in all his statements. Of course, he was older than she was, and she liked that too. He felt like a grown man among boys. He'd been working for a bank for five years before embarking on his master's programme. And he was rich, at least compared to her.

Embarrassing to realize, looking back, what a difference that made. He didn't splash his money around. But he had a car. He paid the bill in good restaurants. He took real holidays, in pretty boutique hotels. Annie found all that side of things restful.

But best of all, Mitch gave her the feeling that he didn't need her. Enjoyed her company, yes, but she could come and go as she pleased, it was all one to him. This was even more restful than the money. It was like having a walker. She felt able to call him up when she felt bored or lonely and say, 'Take me out somewhere. I need to be given a good time.' And he did.

Then one day he said to her, 'You know you're going to marry me, don't you?'

She had been astonished. But then, thinking it over, she had said to herself, Of course.

He still made no moves.

'I'm waiting,' he said. 'When you're ready, you'll come to me.'

It sounds like a poor strategy to win a beautiful young woman, but it turned out to be irresistible. There he was, strong, solvent, secure in himself, patient in love. He had to do no more. The one giant fact that he was waiting for her exerted a pull, like the force of gravity itself. Helplessly, gladly, she fell towards him.

And now, over twenty years later, he tells her of his secret life apart from her, and he weeps. What will he say when she tells him her secret? Will there be more tears?

He's late home. Waiting for him, growing ever more nervous, telling herself she's not nervous, Annie drinks far more wine than is her usual custom before supper. As a result, when at last she hears his key in the door she finds she's swaying when she stands up.

He's rubbing his face as he comes into the kitchen. He looks drained.

'Not a good day,' he says.

Silently she pours him a glass of wine and hands it to him. She has resolved to get to her confession quickly. There's to be no more false bonhomie. But what can you do when he looks so beaten down?

'We're going to have to lose staff,' he says. 'We've done the best we can, but there's no other way.'

'I'm sorry, Mitch,' she says.

'It's all come too quickly. Usually you can plan for these things. Donors give notice, you find new sources. But this – it's like an execution.'

He stops rubbing his face and gives her a weary smile.

'Sorry. Last thing you want to hear about. How are you?'

'I'm all right.'

'Look, I'm going to have to spend half an hour or so dealing with emails. Do you mind?'

'No, that's fine,' she says. 'I'll have supper ready in half an hour, then.'

Left alone, Annie turns on the radio to block out her thoughts. Supper's ready, and has been for a while. The first moment of his return has passed. Is it now too late? Should she put off her confession? But the thought of passing another twenty-four hours with her secret heavy upon her is unbearable. She feels as if she has a stone in her mouth.

As he comes back into the kitchen she hurries out the words

before he can speak; before they slip once more into the deep channel of commonplaces.

'There's something we have to talk about, Mitch.'

She turns at once to the stove and carries the dish of lasagne to the table, needing actions to free her from eye contact.

'Can't it wait?' he says. 'I've had enough high drama for one day.'

More high drama to come, Mitch.

'I've put it off too long already,' she says.

He gazes with melancholy eyes at the plate of lasagne, lasagne she has made herself, not bought from Marks & Spencer. Mitch has always loved her lasagne. Even at such times the habit of pleasing drives her on.

Please and rebel. Rebel and confess.

'If this is more about Diane,' he says.

'No, it's not about Diane.' Sitting down before her own plate. 'It's about me.'

'Do you mind if I start? I'm starving.'

'Go ahead. Eat.'

He goes ahead and eats. Annie doesn't even touch her food. She feels giddy. The cliff edge is before her. Now she must jump.

'While you were away,' she says, 'I met an old boyfriend. We bumped into each other in the street. I hadn't seen him for almost thirty years. We got talking.'

Mitch eats steadily, but he's listening. Now Annie's begun she finds it's easier than she feared. The stone is out of her mouth.

'We fixed to meet up, and catch up. And so we did. And then we met up again. And then – well – I slept with him.'

Mitch stops eating. He looks up from his plate, bewildered. 'You slept with him?'

'Yes.'

'Why?'

'I wanted to. So did he. So we did.'

'Yes, but why?'

Mitch's absolute incomprehension aggravates Annie. This has the effect of making her feel less guilty.

'I suppose I was flattered,' she says.

'Yes, but you actually slept with him!'

'Yes. I did.'

'I'm sorry, Annie,' Mitch says, now back to rubbing his face. 'I'm not following this at all. I find it hard to believe what you're telling me.'

Maybe this is a form of denial, Annie thinks. Maybe he's not letting himself understand in case it hurts too much.

'I know it seems to be a big thing,' she says, 'but it isn't. He's happily married, like me. It was just a one-off.'

'Happily married!'

Now Mitch is shaking his head, spreading his hands in the air. He's performing the part of a man who has met a mystery.

'Were you drunk? Did he force himself on you?'

'No, no,' says Annie, irritation growing. 'It was nothing like that. It was just something that came up, and I thought it would be fun.'

She knows as she says it that this will make it worse, but she can't stop herself. His reaction demeans her. He seems to think it inconceivable that she should accept the attentions of another man.

'Fun!'

'Sex can be fun, Mitch.'

'But – but – but what about us? What about me?'

'You were away.'

You were away fucking Diane, the elephant in the room. But Mitch seems not to have made the connection.

'What difference does it make that I was away? We're married! You're the mother of my child! I trust you implicitly. Christ, I just can't believe this!'

'You were away with Diane, Mitch!'

But Mitch doesn't seem to hear her. He's showing signs of falling apart. He has pushed the hair on the back of his head about so much that it stands out like a ruff.

'I feel like the world's gone mad,' he says. 'You meet some man in the street. You bring him into our home. And you have sex with him.'

'Mitch—'

'I simply don't understand what you thought you were doing.'

'I was doing what you did with Diane!'

He stares at her. Understanding dawns.

'Is that what this is about? To get back at me?'

'No! I didn't even know.'

'So what's it got to do with me and Diane?'

'For fuck's sake!' says Annie. 'If I've done something wrong, then so have you.'

He stares at her for a long moment, like a man just woken from a deep sleep. Did he even hear her?

'Who is this man?' he says at last.

'His name's Alan. He was my boyfriend in my first year at Bristol.'

'So he's your age?'

'Exactly my age.'

'Does he make a habit of this sort of thing?'

'I've no idea,' says Annie. 'Does Diane?'

'What?' says Mitch.

'I haven't cross-questioned you about Diane.'

Mitch waves his hand in the air between them.

'Stop saying Diane. This isn't about Diane.'

But she's put him off his stride. He frowns and attempts to get back on track.

'One good thing,' says Annie. 'This means you don't need to feel so bad about Diane.'

'What? Why?'

'It shows we're both capable of straying.'

'Yes, but Annie – I mean, come on – can't you see?'

'See what?'

'I'm a man! This is what men do! It's different for men!'

He's giving her an anguished look, a look that says, Surely you know that. But she doesn't.

'How's it different for men?' says Annie.

'Everyone knows it! Men use pornography. Men go to prostitutes. For men, sex is like scratching an itch. It isn't emotional. It isn't personal. It's just a physical need. But for women – women are different. Women don't want impersonal sex. Women want love.'

'Does Diane want love, then?'

He blinks at her, struggling to fit the pieces of his thoughts together. Annie can see from the look on his face that he's not trying to be clever. This is what he believes, in his deepest being.

'The point I'm trying to make,' he says, 'is that I don't want love with Diane.'

'Do you want love with me?'

'Yes! Yes!' He seems to think she's got it now. 'That's what I been trying to tell you! For a man, there's the one you love and marry and have children with, and that's serious and for ever. And anything else you get up to is just – just—'

'Scratching an itch.'

'I know it sounds crude. But yes.'

'And you don't think women might feel that way too?'

She's keeping it general, not saying, 'Mightn't I feel that way?' There's only so much he can take at a time.

'No, I don't,' he says. 'For women, sex is something that enters deep into them. It's something that has long-term consequences. Women have babies, not men. Sex for women is always serious.'

'So you think what I did with Alan was serious?'

'That's what scares me,' he says.

'Okay. Look at me.'

Reluctantly he meets her eyes. She speaks slowly and clearly.

'What I did was just for fun. It wasn't deep or serious. It was just sex. Not love. Not marriage. Just sex. You're totally wrong about women. We like sex too. We're no different.'

'Really?' he says, not believing her.

'Just give it time,' she says. 'Let the idea sink in. You'll see I'm right. You've told me what you did with Diane was just physical. Well, it's the same for me.'

'The same for you.'

He sounds dazed. The fight's gone out of him.

'I know it's a shock,' she says. 'But it's actually not a big deal at all.'

'Isn't it?'

He wants to believe her. His eyes ask her to make him believe her.

'Come here,' she says. 'Give me a hug.'

She holds him in her arms.

'We're grown-ups,' she says. 'We don't own each other. But we're making a life together. We owe each other the truth.'

'The truth,' he says, clinging to an idea he's accustomed to believing in. 'Yes, the truth.'

He holds her tight.

'I'm not letting you go, Annie. I'm not letting you go.'

49

Mitch sleeps poorly, and wakes at two in the morning. He knows he won't go back to sleep. He lies restless in bed, his mind tormented by all that Annie has said. It seems to him that she hasn't understood the enormity of what she's done to him. She calls it *fun*, but it's a kind of fun that makes him unable to breathe. The more real this impossible act becomes to him, the more it feels like an assault. It's as if she and this unknown man have committed this offence against him, without regard to his pain. It's a kind of mugging.

Ever more agitated by these thoughts, he looks on Annie sleeping beside him with growing horror. How can she sleep? Is she a monster? Then, frightened by such thoughts, he wants to wake her, he wants to hear her voice.

'Annie? Annie?'

She stirs, and wakes.

'Sorry,' he says. 'I can't sleep. I'm having a bad time. I have to deal with this.'

'What?' says Annie, drowsy from sleep.

'This man,' says Mitch.

'Oh, Mitch.'

'I can't get past it. I never thought you'd do this to me.'

'I didn't do it to you,' Annie says wearily.

'I keep seeing you in bed with him. It stabs me. It's like being knifed. I can't stand it.'

'What do you want me to say, Mitch? Do you want me to say it never happened?'

'Yes. Say you didn't do it. Say you made it up to punish me. Tell me it never happened.'

'Would you believe me if I did?'

'Oh, Annie!' He cries out to her in his pain. 'If only we could go back. If only you hadn't told me.'

'Mitch,' she says, trying to speak soothingly, 'Mitch, this is just a nightmare you're having. It's not real. What happened is such a little thing. It's you that's turning it into a nightmare.'

'It is a nightmare,' he says. 'I can't get the pictures out of my head. And it makes me so - so worked up.'

Then it comes to him, the simple truth of what he's feeling.

'I'm just so *angry*, Annie.'

Her voice hardens.

'With me?'

'With you,' he says. 'With him.'

'You don't have the right to be angry. I wasn't angry with you.'

'Maybe not. But that's what I feel.' He's proud of his discovery. He's a man again. 'I'm angry.'

'Then you're going to have to get a grip on yourself,' Annie says.

Mitch hears this and his anger swells. He's asking for sympathy, for reassurance, and all he gets is character training.

'Get a grip on myself?'

'It's the middle of the night. You wake me up to tell me you're angry. You expect me to sympathize?'

'I don't expect anything,' he says.

'Go to sleep, Mitch,' she says. 'And let me sleep.'

'Fine,' he says.

He gets out of bed, pulls on a bathrobe, dignified in anger.

'Fine,' he says. 'You sleep.'

He and his anger leave the room.

50

Henry lies in bed, once again unable to sleep.

All day he has scoured the papers for news of the defeated leaders. In *The Times* he found a sad picture of Ed Miliband with his wife Justine, in the garden of the Lord Palmerston in North London. She's giving him a questioning look, and he's looking rueful, beneath a canopy of spring leaves. 'Former colleagues race to disown his strategy and politics.' So not just defeat but burial. Not just burial, but erasure from history.

As for Nick Clegg, he's disappeared so completely that even his disappearance is no longer news. After the ceaseless clamour of attention for five years, nothing. Into the silence.

And it's all my fault.

Henry knows this is absurd, but he's tormented by the conviction that his one unmarked ballot paper has single-handedly destroyed two political parties, and betrayed a hapless nation into the hands of the greedy and the selfish. Hatred and lies have overcome compassion and honesty, all because he failed to hold the breach. Of course, in the real world of cause and effect this is nonsense. But there's another world, a night world driven by invisible forces, and in this world Henry feels as if he's been swept away by the same hurricane as the fallen leaders.

His obsession with their fate is not a healthy one. He's hungry for their pain. He's killed them, and now he wants to share their punishment.

I suppose I'm having some kind of a breakdown.

We who suffer the half-death belong together. We don't love each other, but we understand each other. This is the great divide: not left and right, but up and down. We who are down are legion, and we demand tribute. Give us the fall of the mighty, show us feet of clay, regale us with tales of corruption in high places. Find us cellulite on the thighs of the beautiful and darkness in the hearts of the famous. Bring us disasters and wars, drown us in the sorrows of strangers. Let us believe that all are losers, all, and all are burning with us in the modern Hell where we're punished not for our sins but for our failure.

Laura stirs in bed beside him, then half wakes and slips out to go to the loo. When she returns to bed she catches a glint on Henry's cheek.

'Henry? What is it?'

'Nothing,' he says. 'Can't sleep.'

'Have you been crying?'

'I don't know. Have I?'

He brushes away tears.

'Night thoughts,' he says.

'Is this about losing the job?'

'I suppose that's what started it.'

'What else?'

'Well, you know. The sex thing.'

'Yes, I know.'

She doesn't say, Don't be silly, none of that matters. She knows it matters.

'And I didn't vote. I feel like it's all my fault. Stupid, isn't it?'

'Very stupid.'

'I think I might be having a breakdown.'

'Let's hope it's just a small one.'

Her voice so sane and comforting.

'Am I good enough for you?' he says.

'Yes, my love,' she says. 'We're just about good enough for each other.'

Tuesday, 12 May 2015

51

In the morning when Annie comes down she finds Mitch dressed for work, finishing his mug of coffee. He looks up at her, hollow-eyed, reproachful.

'Just promise me one thing.'

It's evident that he's been arguing with her in his head all night.

'What's that?'

'You'll never see him again.'

'Mitch, he's a friend.'

'Friend!' cries Mitch. 'Friends don't have sex!'

'They can do.'

'So you are going to see him again?'

'I'm not saying I'll have sex with him.' She resents even being pushed this far. 'Of course I'll see him again.'

Mitch rises, and takes up his briefcase. He stands before her, head high, in a posture of solemnity.

'I ask you not to,' he says. 'For the sake of our marriage. I've ended it with Diane. You heard me. All I'm asking is that you do the same.'

'Is Diane a friend of yours?' says Annie.

'A friend?'

'Do you enjoy her company? Apart from the sex?'

Mitch shrugs, irritated.

'She's all right.'

'Then you can go on being friends with her, can't you?'

'No,' says Mitch. 'I can't.'

'Why not?'

She knows it's a form of goading, like poking a bear with a stick, but she can't stop herself. He's become so pompous.

'You know as well as I do,' he says. 'Sex changes things. I can't be friends with Diane any more. And you can't be friends with this man. You're just being naive, Annie.'

'Am I?'

He can't take that look of hers. And seeing the way he flinches and turns away, Annie knows they've not reached the end yet, whatever the end is. Mitch thinks the end is mutual forgiveness, and the promise not to stray again. Annie wants to say to him: *I don't want to be forgiven. I want to be understood.* But for now there's a wall of anger between them, shutting out the light.

'I have to go,' he says abruptly. 'I do have other concerns, believe it or not. I ask you to think about what I've said.'

He leaves the room with rapid steps. The front door slams behind him. He has so managed matters that he's had the last word, for now.

What happened to strong, silent Mitch? What happened to the man who loved her but didn't need her?

Then she thinks, in a moment of illumination, this isn't about me at all. This is about his self-image as a man. No, that sounds like something superficial, like a passing vanity. This goes to the core. It's about his very identity as a man.

That's what we're up against, we women who claim the right to desire. We're dismantling the identity men have so laboriously built over the centuries. This idea of women that Mitch has, it's nothing to do with how real women are, and everything to do with how men need women to be. His manhood is defined by my womanhood, by the fantasy of womanhood he's been given. My sexual freedom emasculates him.

No wonder he's helpless with rage. No wonder he declares so self-importantly, 'Think about what I've said.' The stakes are high. He might as well say, Do you want a husband who is not a man? How do I answer that?

I want to say to him, Trust yourself more. You're stronger than you know. We're growing up now. We can dare to tell each other the truth. And that's not the end of love, it's the beginning.

52

WHAT DO WOMEN WANT? BELIEVE IT OR NOT – SEX!

The headline looks more aggressive on the dummy printout. Liz gazes at it, spread out on Chrissie's desk: two pages, broken up by big-type sub-headlines – WOMEN LIKE PORN TOO – WOMEN LIKE CASUAL SEX – WOMEN AS RANDY AS MEN.

The *Stella* team sit in a row of desks by the windows, on the periphery of the vast newsroom. At the centre is a ring of desks where the editors sit, known as the Circle of Hell. At the far end two floors of glass-walled offices rise up, where men in shirt sleeves can be seen gazing down on the newsroom. The great space is eerily quiet.

'What do you think of the artwork?' says Chrissie.

The illustrations Chrissie has found to break up the text are black-and-white line drawings of naked embracing couples.

'Where on earth did you get them?'

'Remember *The Joy of Sex*?'

'That's a million years ago.'

'The guy who wrote it based the format on cookery books. The illustrations have become iconic. I gave the art department *The Joy of Sex* as a reference, but told them to keep it clean.'

She nods towards Art, the other side of a potted plant, and just before the rows of desks that house Fashion, Beauty and Luxury.

'I see you've hedged your bets,' says Liz, touching the weasel words in the headline. 'Believe it or not?'

'That's Graham.'

'Graham? Does he have any say in Editorial?'

'No, never. But he actually came and asked to see this one. He loves it. He wants you to look in on him before you go.'

She points across the newsroom to one of the offices in the glass wall.

'He's up there.'

Liz picks up the two-page spread, as if to get the measure of its sheer size.

'Can you do one for me? I want Alan to see it before it's out on Sunday.'

Alan the betrayer. The one who must be punished.

'Take that one. I'm done with it. I'm already two weeks on.'

Liz folds the pages, and puts them into her bag.

'It's going to be big, Liz,' says Chrissie. 'Most of all online. You're going to get monstered by the trolls, you know that.'

'I'm a bigger monster than any troll,' says Liz. 'I'm Shiva the Destroyer.'

'I thought Shiva was male, and had a huge phallus.'

'So?'

★

Graham's office has its own outer office, with a pretty young PA. Liz introduces herself.

'Is he in?' says Liz. 'He wants to see me.'

'Yes, sure,' says the pretty young PA. 'Go on through.'

Graham jumps up, putting down his phone, and beams at Liz.

'Here she is! The heroine of the hour!'

'I can't believe you have an office with a secretary,' says Liz. 'It's like being on the set of *Mad Men*.'

'Can you see me at a desk down there?' He spreads his arms wide, displaying the newsroom, like God looking down on his creation. 'I'm the boss these days, Liz.'

'You always were a survivor, Graham.'

'Last of the old gang,' he says. 'Frank Kelly's packed it in, gone off to moulder in the Dordogne.'

He crosses the room to close the door, which Liz has left open.

'Read your piece,' he says. 'It's sensational. I've talked to Chrissie. We both agree we should get you back on exclusive contract.'

'Thanks, but I'm fine working the way we do.'

'I haven't named any figures yet.'

'I'm just not a company animal,' says Liz. 'It suits me to be free to work when and where I like.'

'I understand. But we're going to do all we can to keep you to ourselves.'

He turns round the screen on his desk to face her, and keys up the digital version of her feature.

'This,' he says, gesturing at the screen, 'is probably the most compelling piece of journalism we've ever printed. Women as randy as men. It's shocking. It's sexy. It's honest.'

'And it's true. Believe it or not. Which I'm told is your contribution.'

'Yes, I did put that in,' he says. 'I felt some qualification was needed. After all, it's not established scientific fact.'

'It's true, Graham.'

'Because you found a book that says so?'

'Because the book reports on a wide range of studies that say so. Because nearly all the women I talk to say so.'

'And because you say so?'

'Yes.'

'But not all women would agree.'

'Not all women know what they want.'

'But you do.'

'I think so, yes. I try to be honest with myself.'

'Honest, indeed.' His eyes are fixed on hers. He seems to be trying to read her mind. 'This is a blazingly honest piece, Liz. I admire you for that.'

'Thank you, Graham.'

'So tell me something. You say women want casual sex as much as men. When you want casual sex, where do you go?'

'I don't go anywhere,' says Liz. 'It's not something you buy in a store.'

'No, of course not. Not until they open brothels for women.' He gives a pleasant laugh at the absurdity of the notion. 'No, it happens between friends, doesn't it? Colleagues. We all know about office affairs.'

'Of course,' says Liz.

'So next time you're in the mood' – he gives another pleasant laugh – 'you know where I am.'

Liz gets it at last. The anger in her rises. Of course Graham would take it all personally. He's a good-looking man now into his sixties, he's spent his working life having affairs. To him all her feature says is, Come and get it, boys. 'Are you propositioning me, Graham?'

'I'm just letting you know I'm willing to stand in line and wait my turn. I'm not proud.'

'You want to have sex with me?'

He blinks a little at the direct question, but it doesn't wipe the smile off his face.

'Only if the prospect pleases,' he says. 'I know I can't compete with the young bucks.'

'Your place or mine?' says Liz.

The smile freezes.

'That was quick.'

'I do have one condition,' says Liz. 'Your wife has to know.'

'My wife?'

'I don't cheat, Graham.'

He moves away from her, heads back behind the defensive palisade of his desk.

'You've not met my wife, have you, Liz?'

'You think she wouldn't like it?'

'It would hurt her deeply. I wouldn't dream of doing that to her. I'm simply not that cruel.'

'You wouldn't dream of having the affair? Or you wouldn't dream of telling her?'

'What she doesn't know doesn't hurt her. My wife is a wonderful woman, but she's fifty-eight years old, for God's sake.'

'Graham, when I'm fifty-eight I hope to be enjoying an active and varied sex life. Have you ever talked to your wife about sex? How do you know she wouldn't like a really hot affair?'

Graham goes red.

'This has all turned rather personal, hasn't it?'

'You're the one who made it personal. Sex with me is personal, Graham.'

'I'd just rather keep my wife out of it.'

'Will you let her read the paper on Sunday? Will you show her my feature and say it's the best piece of journalism you've ever printed?'

'I don't know what point you're trying to make here, Liz. If you're angry because you feel I took advantage of you in some way, then I apologize.'

'I'm not angry,' says Liz. 'I'm shocked. I'm shocked that you can read twelve hundred words about women's sexual desires and not notice that it might tell you something about your own wife.'

'I asked you to keep my wife out of it.'

His voice has turned sharp.

'Here's what I suggest, Graham,' says Liz. 'When the Sunday edition comes out you wrap it in a plain cover with a label saying: NOT SUITABLE FOR WIVES. Unmarried women can read it, and divorced women, and sluts and whores, because there has to be someone for men to have their affairs with. But God forbid we should let the wives have any fun.'

Graham is tapping his fingers on the desktop, frowning.

'This is always where it goes wrong,' he says. 'It's a good feature, Liz. You've done a fine job. Then you have to take it one step further, and you're lecturing, and hectoring, and preaching, and it all turns angry, and aggressive, and ugly. Why do you have to do that? Why do women have to do that? You're equal to men now, God knows. That battle's won. But it's never enough, is it? No, on you go, you angry women, telling us to feel bad, feel ashamed, go down on our knees, beg forgiveness. Well, I'm sorry I've got a dick, okay? I'm sorry I like using it. I'm sorry I came on to you. It won't happen again.'

Liz gazes at him, shaking her head.

'It's not all about you, Graham,' she says.

'I'm relieved to hear it.'

He's not looking at her any more. The charm offensive is over.

'So I'm not coming round to your pad for a quickie?'

'It seems not.'

She leaves, closing the private office door behind her.

53

Laura says don't go, but Henry is curious.

'Why would Michael Marcus want to give me lunch?'

'Guilt,' says Laura.

Michael Marcus's invitation is to lunch at the Dean Street Townhouse. He has, he says, a proposal to put to Henry. An apology is not worth the journey, but a proposal is another matter.

Their table is at the back, in the area used for afternoon tea. The main dining room is fully booked.

'And this is supposed to be the era of austerity,' says Michael Marcus, rising to greet Henry.

They sit on low, small armchairs, and eat off a low, small table. It feels like they're in a doll's house.

'I appreciated your email,' says Michael Marcus. 'It's been a miserable business. But you come out of it well, Henry. Dickie calls you the last of the true gentlemen.'

'Let's forget it, shall we?' says Henry, feeling his neck prickling.

'Of course, of course.' He makes a motion with one hand, as if throwing something over his shoulder. 'There,' he says. 'It's gone.'

Henry wants to say, It's not gone, it's lying in a broken heap on the floor behind you. But he's promised himself not to get angry. His own anger exhausts and humiliates him.

'I want to tell you a story,' says Michael Marcus.

This, too, annoys Henry. 'Oh,' he says, 'is it bedtime?'

'A true story,' says Michael Marcus, smiling patiently. 'You come into it at the end. Or so I'm hoping.'

That's to keep him listening. Ah, well, at least he gets a lunch out of it.

'Last autumn I spent a very unusual week on a retreat in Dorset. It was a Buddhist meditation retreat, with the focus on Tantric teachings and techniques. It was extremely enlightening, but that's another story. I made friends there with a remarkable woman called Farah, who grew up in Pakistan. She and I still meet, when the opportunity arises. We continue to explore the Tantra, which I might say is limitless, a journey without end.'

'Hold on a moment, Michael,' says Henry. 'Isn't Tantra all about sex?'

A picture is surfacing in his memory of marathon love-making sessions.

'It's a route to enlightenment,' says Michael Marcus, gently. 'It's about weaving together the physical and the spiritual to become one with God.'

'Through sex?'

'Yes, through sex. Sex isn't the goal. Enlightenment is the goal.'

'Of course,' says Henry, 'of course, but isn't the way you do it by going on and on and never coming?'

'On the contrary. Tantric techniques lead to the full body orgasm.'

'Golly,' says Henry.

'To return to my story. Farah, of course, knows that I run a television production company. Recently she asked my advice. Her son Tariq, who is a student, has spent many weeks in Balochistan taping video interviews with young men, Pashtun and Balochi, talking about martyrdom. You know, of course, how real this topic is, how live, though perhaps that's an unfortunate choice of words. For us, martyrdom is a quaint relic of the Middle Ages. In the *madrasa*s of Pakistan it's an open door to Paradise.'

Henry listens, wondering why Michael Marcus is telling him this. At the same time another part of his mind is trying to picture the small, ageing, weasel-faced specimen before him engaged in prolonged non-orgasmic sex with a lady called Farah in Dorset.

'Tariq,' Michael Marcus continues, 'has taped over thirty hours of young men talking about martyrdom, in Pashto, of course, or Balochi. Farah tells me they speak very frankly. These are not militants, you understand. These are ordinary young men. But what comes through, so Farah tells me, is the extraordinary allure of martyrdom. This is something we in the West simply don't comprehend. And Farah believes, as do I, that Tariq's tapes could form part of a documentary on the subject.'

Now Henry begins to understand.

'Have you set it up anywhere?' he says.

'No,' says Michael Marcus. 'As yet all I have is the broad idea, and the tapes. What we need is someone to craft a much fuller proposal. The tapes themselves are not very dramatic. But the subject matter – well, I think you can see for yourself.'

Henry's mind has already started working. Thomas à Becket. Joan of Arc. Nine/Eleven. The martyrdom videos posted by jihadis before they blow themselves up. A highly provocative juxtaposition.

'No money, I take it,' he says.

'Not yet. But it has a good chance of being picked up, wouldn't you agree?'

So this is Michael Marcus's peace offering. *English Gardens* has been torched. Perhaps Henry can pull a hot coal from the ashes. Still, it's a good idea. It appeals to Henry's knowledge of history, and of religion. Do the jihadi martyrs actually believe the promise of Paradise? It's a question he's never seriously addressed before. To the modern Western mind it seems too childish: that anyone would choose to die to gain entry to a dated fantasy version of Heaven.

'These tapes,' he says. 'They show that young Pakistanis today buy the Koranic picture of Paradise?'

'Of course. The words of the Prophet come from God. How could they not be true?'

'Seventy-two virgins and all?'

'Oh, it gets much better than that,' says Michael Marcus.

He takes out a notebook and turns the pages.

'Listen to this. It's not from the Koran itself, it's from one of the Hadiths, the reported teachings of the Prophet. You're perfectly correct about seventy-two young women, that's seventy *houri*s plus two wives, who will be given to each chosen one who enters Paradise. All of whom,' he reads from his notes, 'will have "appetizing vaginas". But most importantly' – he reads again – '"The penis of the Elected never softens. The erection is eternal."'

'Dear Lord!' says Henry, awed.

'We can laugh,' says Michael Marcus. 'We can mock. But if you're a young Muslim man with extremely limited outlets for sexual expression, that's a prospect worth dying for.'

'Of course it is,' said Henry.

'So what do you say? Would you like to give it some thought? It struck me it might be rather up your street. I remember the show you did years ago on iconoclasm, with Aidan Massey.'

How long ago was that? Fifteen years at least. You have to give it to Michael Marcus, he doesn't forget. He's a living archive of British factual television.

'Let me get this straight,' says Henry. 'There's no money. There's no expression of interest from a commissioning editor. There's just a lady from Dorset, and some tapes I won't understand.'

'That's correct,' says Michael Marcus.

'So I'm to take this on as an act of faith.'

'That's rather neat, Henry. Yes, I offer it to you to make of it what you will.'

In the latter part of his career Henry has found himself obliged to accept work at lower rates of pay. Now he's being offered work for no pay at all. Why not stay at home and read a good book? But old habits die hard. For all his adult life he's had a project to work on. It isn't only about pay.

They order, and eat, and Henry finds himself marvelling at Michael Marcus. He must be pushing seventy, but here he is, tucking into a cheese soufflé, brokering a television series, and pursuing the full body orgasm.

'Michael,' he says, 'do you mind if I ask a rather personal question? It's about your Buddhist retreat in Dorset. Is it theory or practice?'

'Oh, practice,' says Michael Marcus. 'Very hands on.'

'And you don't find yourself, well, flagging?'

'Ah, yes,' says Michael Marcus. 'Everyone always wants to know that. How does one keep it up?'

'Well, yes.'

'The first thing to say is that Tantric sex does not depend on having an eternal erection. That's why we talk about a full body orgasm. The Western conception of sex is ridiculously penis-centred, you know.'

'I expect it is,' says Henry, 'but I don't see how we men are to manage an orgasm without one.'

'Then you'd better come on one of the courses.'

'I'm afraid I'm a little past it,' says Henry. 'Forget about eternal erections. I wouldn't get to first base. My Tantric partner would be drumming her fingers and yawning.'

'Oh, we've all been there,' says Michael Marcus. He reaches into his inside jacket pocket and brings out a plastic-covered card, on which four round beige pills sit in plastic bubbles.

'Take one of these,' he says. 'You'll get to first base.'

Henry examines the pills.

'This isn't Viagra. Viagra's blue.'

'It's much the same. It's called Levitra. Take one half an hour before, preferably on an empty stomach, and you're in business.'

Henry is riveted. Can it really be so easy? Of course he knows all about Viagra – who doesn't? – but he's never yet met a man who admits to using it. Michael Marcus seems to be entirely relaxed about it. This alone has a powerful effect. Simply by taking out his pills and showing them, he has broken down several small barriers of secrecy and shame and male pride.

'What's it like?' he says.

Henry has never been a pill popper. He fears the effect of alien chemicals on his body.

'You get a bit flushed,' says Michael Marcus. 'That's all, really. Try one.'

He pops one of the little beige pills out of its plastic bubble, wraps it up in a paper napkin, and gives it to Henry.

'That's eight quid's worth. Don't lose it.'

Henry's on the point of refusing it, but then he thinks: Who am I kidding? I'm almost sixty. Why wouldn't I need a little help?

'Thank you, Michael,' he says, pocketing the paper bundle. 'You never know when it'll come in handy.'

Then he blushes. Why am I making myself out to be some sort of Lothario? It'll come in handy, if at all, with my wife. No bragging rights in having sex with your wife.

'You want to know what I think about Islamic fundamentalist terror?' says Michael Marcus, lowering his voice. 'Al Qaeda, and Islamic State, and Boko Haram, and all the rest? I think it's all about sexual repression. You've got a creed that's medieval in its sexual puritanism. You've got a surrounding culture that flaunts pornographic images. You've got young men boiling with testosterone. And you've got a Paradise that promises everlasting sexual gratification. Add them all up and what do you get? Violence as a stand-in for sex. Then violence as a gateway to sex. Then sex.'

Henry thinks of all the paintings of the early Christian martyrs, so often portrayed at the moment of death, faces shining in ecstasy. St Sebastian, his naked body pierced by arrows, his beautiful face gazing upwards to his reward. Martyrdom as fetish: just another way of intensifying the orgasm.

'I expect you think I'm being racist, or Orientalist,' says Michael Marcus. 'Maybe I am. But Farah tells me we make the same mistake over and over again. We underestimate the power of faith.'

'You know, Michael,' says Henry, 'I really think you might be onto something.'

Michael Marcus is pleased.

'So you'll give it some thought? Maybe buzz me over something?'

'Why not?' says Henry, fingering the paper-wrapped pill in his pocket.

54

'I've had a rethink about the ending,' says Alan Strachan. He's back in the conference room with Stuart and Jean-Claude and the pretty young woman who writes everything down and has a name he still hasn't registered. 'He doesn't die.'

Stuart nods, waiting to hear more. He's back from LA, where he claims to have tried out Alan's idea and met with some interest. Some, but not enough.

For the last two days Alan has felt as if his life has been suspended. A great pause has come upon him. This floating state turns out to be intensely creative. Somehow, via a route he can't follow, his personal crisis has fed into his story. He no longer wants his hero to sacrifice himself for the greater good.

'The core idea doesn't change,' he tells the meeting. 'It's still a story of humans causing beautiful aliens to die, by invisible acts of oppression. They're still killing the beautiful aliens by forcing them into a psychic straitjacket. I shouldn't have to spell out the metaphor, but I will. This is what black people feel: I'm not black, I'm a person, I'm unique, I'm me. It's what gays feel: don't stereotype me, don't think that being gay describes all of me. It's what old people feel, and disabled people. Everyone who gets reduced to a category feels this. They all want to say, "See me as I am, not as you label me." That's the core idea, and I don't want to lose it.'

He watches the pretty girl's fingers dancing over the keys of her laptop. How on earth does she keep up?

'So my hero finally realizes how he's killing the beautiful aliens. He can stop stereotyping them. He does stop. But how can he make up for the damage he's done? My first answer was, he sacrifices himself. Like Jesus, he takes on himself the sins of all humanity, and pays the price. But I've had a better idea.'

He sees their attentive faces waiting on the revelation. This is true storytelling, he thinks. Make them hungry for resolution. What he does not tell the production team is how the simplistic ideas of a school friend of his son have jolted him into a new approach. Zombies! Ridiculous to turn beautiful aliens into zombies, of course.

But even as he had rejected the absurdity he had found himself staring at its obverse: 'beautiful aliens' is as lazy a generic label as 'zombies'. He, the author, the creator of the story, has been as guilty as his space travellers of an act of psychic oppression.

'Who are these beautiful aliens?' he asks the listening team. 'What do we know about them? How will we cast them? How will we dress them, and make them up? So far I've given one description only: they're beautiful. But is beauty always the same? Do they all look alike? Once people start to become individual in our eyes, do they become less beautiful? Imagine a catwalk procession of fashion models. We can hardly tell them apart, because all we see is their beauty. But in fact every one of them is unique. What if their beauty is a kind of mask, and when the mask falls away what we see beneath is quite different, infinitely varied: sweetness, ugliness, courage, malice, hope, stupidity, fear? When the masks fall away what we see is *complexity*. We see *individuality*.'

The pretty girl has stopped tapping at her keyboard. Stuart is twisting about in his chair as if he needs to go to the men's room.

'Yes, yes, yes,' he says. 'But how does the story end?'

'Our hero comes out of hiding,' says Alan. 'The great crowd of beautiful aliens has gathered outside to kill him. He climbs up onto a high rock, and he makes a speech that changes everything. "From the first moment we met you," he says, "we've called you the beautiful people. But you're not beautiful. You're all different. You're funny-looking. You're fat." He's pointing at them as he speaks. "You're wrinkly. You've got a big nose." And as he points – you! you! you! – the faces of the beautiful people change before our eyes. They become individual. They become real. It's a giant transformation scene. The human invaders, of whom he's the last, have so wanted the aliens to be beautiful that they've projected their dreams onto them. Now he sees truly. He sees them as they really are. And so at last the danger is over. He's not killing them any more. The mission is accomplished. He can go home.'

The pretty girl is gazing at him with tears in her eyes. Alan finds this disconcerting.

'Incredible!' says Jean-Claude.

'It's a bummer,' says Stuart. 'Who wants beautiful people to turn out to be ugly?'

'What would you know?' says Stella. 'Ugly people think beauty's the answer to everything, and it's not.'

Stuart stares at her in astonishment.

'Where did that come from?' he says.

'It's so unfair.' Stella is turning pink, rising from her chair. 'You have to be beautiful or you're worthless, so you make yourself beautiful, and then it's like nobody wants to know anything more about you. So then you feel worthless anyway. It's all so stupid and small-minded and cruel. I think Alan's ending is amazing and you should make the film just the way he says, and if you do, nobody will ever have seen anything like it and that – that will be beautiful!'

Too agitated to continue, she scoops up her laptop.

'I'm sorry.'

She leaves the room.

'Extraordinary,' says Stuart. 'What was that all about?'

'Don't be a fuckwit, Stuart,' says Alan.

Stuart gives a sigh of exasperation.

'I can't sell a movie where beautiful people end up ugly.'

'Not ugly. Real.'

'This is the movies, Alan. Who wants real?'

'I'll tell you what,' says Alan, 'I'll write the first draft for nothing. Then you see if it sells.'

Stuart stares at him.

'For nothing? You'd really do that?'

'Yes,' says Alan. 'But you don't own it. If someone else offers me more, they get it.'

'But I've invested time in this project. I've talked it up all over town.'

'For that you get first look.'

'First look? Is that a promise?'

'Yes, Stuart. I promise.'

'I mean, what do I know?' says Stuart, helplessly. 'Maybe ugly is the new black.'

55

Annie is already there, sitting in the café waiting for Alan. Her anxious eyes greet him, full of questions. He kisses her cheek, the kiss of a friend.

'Thank you,' she says. She's thanking him for responding so quickly to her message: *Must talk*.

He's expecting her to tell him, We shouldn't have done it. We mustn't do it again. 'Mitch is having an affair,' she says.

'What?'

'I was all set to tell him about you and me, and suddenly he started confessing. It's been going on for some time. In South Africa.'

She looks into his eyes, searching for the right reaction.

He doesn't know what to say. Is this good or bad?

'Are you all right?' he says.

'Oh, Alan, what a mess it's all turning out to be.'

She puts her hands out for him to hold.

'Have you told Liz?'

'Yes,' he says.

'How did she take it?'

'Not great. She's angry.'

'I told Mitch last night. He went crazy. He can't deal with it at all.'

'Even though he's been cheating too?'

'He says it's different for men. He's asked me never to see you again.'

'If that's what you want,' says Alan.

'No! It's not what I want!' Her response is fierce and immediate. 'How dare he tell me who I'm to see and not see?'

'You'd think he'd forgive you,' says Alan, 'if he's been having an affair too.'

'I don't want to be forgiven,' says Annie. 'I want to be understood.'

Alan is impressed. It's like Stella in the production meeting saying, 'Ugly people think beauty's the answer to everything.' How come women see so much more clearly than men?

'Sometimes I think men just can't understand women,' he says.

'Or don't want to,' says Annie. 'Mitch needs me to be someone I'm not. I didn't know that until all this happened.'

'How bad is it between you two?'

'It's bad. But honestly, Alan, it feels more like he's a child having a tantrum than anything real. I think he cares more about how it looks than about what I might be feeling.'

'What are you feeling?'

'I'm not sorry we did it.' Her hands are squeezing his. 'Are you?'

'No,' he says.

'But you're not about to leave Liz. And I don't want to leave Mitch.'

'No.'

'So I suppose we both have to do what's called patching things up.'

'Does that mean not seeing each other again?' he says.

'Maybe.'

'I want to see you again.'

'Are you willing to meet in secret? And cheat and lie?'

'No.'

'Nor me. I'm being straight with Mitch. But, my God, it's hard work! Men can be so primitive.'

'You know who you'd really get on with?' says Alan. 'You know who'd understand everything you say? Liz.'

'Maybe one day,' says Annie.

'I mean it. She's writing about all this. She'd be great. On the other hand, she did say she wanted to kill you.'

Annie looks wistfully at Alan.

'Seems to me you two get on pretty well.'

'I think we did,' says Alan. 'But I may have fucked it up.'

'Me too.'

'So is that it? We sinned and now we get punished? That would be the way the story ends, if this was a studio movie.'

'To Hell with that,' says Annie, suddenly fierce again. 'If my marriage to Mitch can't cope with this, it's not much of a marriage. I'm not sorry. I refuse to be sorry. I'm glad we did what we did. If it pushes Mitch and me into knowing each other a whole lot better, then that's a result. And if it busts us up, well, there's life after marriage, right?'

56

Mitchell Hamer has had a bad day. He's accustomed to being in control of his work, but for most of the day he's felt as if the organization is unravelling before his eyes. Diane has resigned, with immediate effect. Janetta has called him in to talk about it. It turns out what he had supposed was a secret affair has been known to all of them.

'Diane's very distressed,' says Janetta, gravely.

He wants to say, My wife's cheated too. But he can't. He has to hang his head and accept the unspoken admonishment. Diane, Janetta implies, is sacrificing her career to his marriage.

All through the day Mitch feels aggrieved, while knowing he's guilty. It seems to him that life is being unfair to him, that the punishment is not equal to the crime. Yes, he's been unfaithful to his wife. But look at the price he's asked to pay: he must break off all relations with Diane, in a manner he knows hurts her deeply; he must endure the disappointment, if not the outright censure, of his colleagues; and he must live with the humiliating secret that his wife has had sex with another man.

By the end of the working day this last torment, which has caused him such anger, is giving rise to fear. What if Annie were to leave him? The possibility is unthinkable, but once thought it becomes unbearable. All the way home, riding the crowded Central line from Bethnal Green to Notting Hill, he punishes himself with visions of life without her. Memories of their years together come tumbling out at him, as if he's opened some overfilled cupboard. How is he to be parted from her without ripping out half his life? It seems to him impossible to unmake all that he and Annie have made together.

By the time he's walked from the tube station to the house he's in a very different frame of mind from when he set out in the morning. Then he had said to Annie, 'I ask you to think about what I said.' Now it's he who has done the thinking.

Putting his key in the front door, opening the door, entering the familiar hall, a new dread seizes him: what if she's already left? But her voice calls from the kitchen.

'That you, Mitch?'

When he goes into the kitchen there she is, as she always has been, already pouring him a glass of wine.

She hands him the glass without speaking.

'So I'm back,' he says.

Stupid thing to say: as if he had ever contemplated not coming back.

'Me too,' she says, not meeting his eyes.

He wonders if she's waiting for him to say sorry again. Surely it's her turn to say sorry. Instead he says something he had no idea he was going to say.

'I don't want to lose you, Annie.'

'Don't you?' she says.

'I know I've been stupid. I've not handled this at all well. I'm not very good at this sort of thing, really. I don't know what to say, or what to do. I just kind of biff about in the dark.'

He has hit the right note. He senses her softening.

'Biff about in the dark?'

'Yes.'

'You were so angry this morning.'

'Yes. Well. There's been a lot of stuff going on in me. I'm sorry. I feel ashamed.'

'Me too.'

She says it simply, as if it's just one of life's accidents.

'I've tried all my life to be' – he stumbles over the old-fashioned term – 'to be a good man. I've tried to live the right way. But it turns out I'm not a good man after all.'

'Oh, Mitch.'

Her voice has now softened, too. As he senses the return of her love for him, he's released to go further.

'That's not who I'm supposed to be,' he says. 'Weak-willed. Selfish. The sort of man who treats women badly. But somehow it turns out I am. How did that happen?'

'How do any of us end up doing the stupid things we do?'

She's saying us and we. His fear begins to recede. She's not going to leave him.

'I suppose we go a little crazy,' he says.

'We want adventure,' she says. 'That's not so terrible.'

'Isn't it?'

'That's all I wanted,' she says.

'So you don't want to leave me for him?'

'Never,' says Annie. 'I never wanted that. Nor does he.'

'Nor did I. Nor do I.'

He feels as if they're swearing an oath. He wants to swear an oath. He wants to bind her to him for ever and ever.

'Sex is such strong stuff,' she says. 'Sometimes it's stronger than we are. But it's still only sex. If every time we felt a bit horny we had to fall in love and get married, well, we'd all have to have an awful lot of marriages.'

He marvels at her words – 'a bit horny' – and at her manner. She's smiling now. Is it all really so unimportant?

'Only sex,' he says, as if trying out the idea.

'We're bigger than that, aren't we, Mitch?'

'I want to be,' he says.

'Come here, then.'

He goes into her arms and she hugs him close.

'Let's try to be honest,' she whispers. 'Loving and honest.'

'Loving and honest,' he repeats.

'We're strong enough to let each other have our own lives, aren't we?'

'Our own lives together?'

'Yes, Mitch. My own life with you. Your own life with me.'

'Yes,' he says, 'yes, that's what I want.'

'Twenty-one years together.'

'And Ellie.'

'And Ellie,' she repeats softly.

'We'll make it work, Annie.'

He kisses her, and she kisses him back.

The doorbell rings.

'I'll get it,' he says.

She hears him opening the front door as she refills their glasses. She hears him utter an exclamation of surprise. A woman's voice says, 'Can I come in?' Mitch says something too low for her to hear. The woman's voice sounds clear, filled with pain. 'I'm leaving. I want to say goodbye.'

Annie goes into the hall. There's Mitch, blocking the front doorway. In the frame of the doorway stands the small tanned woman she saw at the airport.

'Please just go,' Mitch is saying, very low. 'Annie's here.'

Diane's face is lined with anguish.

'It's all right, Mitch,' says Annie. 'Say goodbye. You owe her that.'

'Annie!' says Diane. 'Oh, Annie, I'm so sorry.'

'That's enough,' says Mitch.

'I'm going,' she says. 'I'm getting out of your life. I'm doing what you want. I'm on my way to the airport.'

She's speaking to Mitch but her frantic eyes are on Annie.

'Look!' she says, gesturing to the street behind her. 'The minicab's waiting.'

'Please, Diane,' says Mitch.

'Won't you – won't you . . . ?' Diane starts to weep.

'Give her a goodbye kiss, Mitch,' says Annie.

Mitch gives a small awkward shake of his body. Diane falls into his arms, and kisses him.

'Goodbye, baby. Goodbye, my love.'

Mitch receives her kisses while at the same time contriving to keep his body from the waist down apart from hers. Annie watches this act of contortion, this demonstration of love that withholds love. As the embrace ends Diane turns her tear-stained face to Annie.

'Just so you know,' she says, 'I'm not some little tramp. I adore him. I thought he adored me. I'd never have let it go so far if I hadn't believed that you and he—'

'Please, Diane,' says Mitch. 'Don't make things worse.'

'I want her to know I'm not a home wrecker,' says Diane. 'I have my pride.' She speaks to Annie again. 'He told me the passion had gone out of his marriage. You know he lives with me, when he's in Cape Town? He has done for three years now. We've bought furniture together. I thought we'd end up together for ever.'

Mitch goes deep red.

'I never said that,' he says.

'Oh, Mitch!' says Diane. 'What about our song?'

'That's enough,' he says.

'He serenaded me.' Diane speaks past him to Annie. 'We rented a beach house, right on the sea. He sang for me, our special song, "Born Free". Born free to follow your heart.'

She's weeping again as she speaks.

'You have to go,' Mitch says. 'You'll miss your flight.'

'For God's sake,' says Annie.

She retreats to the kitchen. She hears sounds of sobbing from the hall, and Mitch's low voice. Anger is rising within her.

The front door closes. Mitch rejoins her.

'I didn't need that,' he says. He gulps at his wine. 'She's gone,' he says.

Annie moves away from him.

'I'm sorry you had to see that,' he says.

'What about her, Mitch?'

'You don't have to worry about her. She won't be back.'

'What have you done to her?'

He looks at her wide-eyed, injured.

'You know,' he says. 'You know everything.'

WILLIAM NICHOLSON

'You told me it was just physical. You told me it was just sex.
She thought you were going to be together for ever.'

'I never said that. I swear.'

'So why did she believe it?'

'I never made any promises. That's just her fantasy.'

'Where does the fantasy come from, Mitch? What did you
say to her?'

'I didn't say anything.'

'You had sex with her! You must have said something! What
did you say? Did you say, I really want to have sex with you,
but it's only physical, and I don't love you?'

'Of course not.'

'So what did you say?'

She wants to scream at him. He's moving his head from side
to side, acting out with his body his urge to escape her anger.

'You know how it goes,' he says. 'You can't just say, I want
you for sex. No one says that. So you go a bit romantic. It's
just a game.'

'Romantic how? She thought you adored her.'

'It's just a way of speaking. It's a way of saying, You're really
gorgeous, I really fancy you. It's what you do. I'm not proud
of myself, Annie. I've already admitted what I've done. What
did you expect me to say? I want sex with you but I don't love
you?'

'So instead you said, I do love you.'

'I didn't say it.'

'No. You sang it. For fuck's sake, Mitch, you bought furniture together!'

'Furniture! That's a joke. A bedside lamp. One bedside lamp!
That's what we bought together.'

387

Annie feels as if her anger is choking her.

'A bedside lamp!'

'Not exactly setting up house.'

'I can't take this. Sorry, I just can't take it.'

She runs up the stairs to their bedroom. She has no plan, only that she has to get out, away from him. She pulls out a small overnight case and starts packing a few essentials.

Mitch follows her.

'What are you doing?'

'I'm going.'

'Going where?'

'Away,' she says.

'Annie, please.' His plaintive little-boy voice. 'I thought we'd agreed we were going to make it work.'

Annie hardly knows what she's pushing into the suitcase. With every passing minute the rage in her grows.

'You've lied to me,' she says. 'You've lied and lied. You lied to her, saying you loved her. You lied to me, saying you never loved her. All you've done is lie.'

'But you did it too.'

'I did it, but I didn't lie! I never told Alan I loved him. I never told him we'd be together for ever.'

'Where are you going?'

'I need some space. I feel so angry, Mitch.'

'But you're coming back?'

'I don't know.'

'You have to come back. I've ended it with Diane. She's gone.'

'Oh, I'm so sorry, Mitch.' Her voice bitter with sarcasm. 'If you'd known, you wouldn't have had to break up with her at all, would you?'

'I didn't mean that. You know I didn't.'

'If you hurry maybe you can get to Heathrow before she boards her flight. It would be just like in the movies.'

'I don't want Diane! I've never wanted Diane!'

'*That is a lie!*' She really is screaming at him now. 'You cheated on me, and now you're cheating on her!'

She closes the suitcase with sharp clicks, and marches downstairs.

He comes running after her.

'Please, Annie. Please.'

He pulls at her sleeve.

'Let me go!'

'Where are you going?'

'I'll call you.'

She goes out of the front door, pulling it shut after her. Mitch yanks the door open again and stands at the top of the steps watching as she goes to her car and drives away.

He sinks down on the doorstep and puts his head into his hands.

'Oh, fuck, fuck, fuck,' he says to himself.

57

Liz brings the printout of her *Stella* feature home and it's lying for all to see on the kitchen table, so Cas sits down and reads it. Then Alan comes home and finds Liz and Cas in deep discussion about how girls are or are not different from boys.

'We can't go on now that Dad's here,' Cas says. 'He'll start telling me the facts of life or something creepy.'

'I will not!' protests Alan.

'Yes, you will,' says Cas. 'You'll think it's your fatherly duty to give me advice about growing up.'

'Aren't fathers meant to give advice?'

'Not any more, Dad,' says Cas. 'We get all that stuff online.'

'That's just the mechanics. What about the psychology?'

'We get that from *Keeping Up With the Kardashians*.'

'What?' says Alan.

'It's a TV reality show,' says Liz.

'Those shows aren't real,' says Alan. 'They're scripted.'

'Oh, wow, Dad,' says Cas, rolling his eyes. 'Now you tell me.'

Alan gives up.

'You're too smart for me, Cas. There's nothing I can teach you.'

'How's the beautiful aliens?' says Cas. 'Are you going to make them be zombies?'

'Not zombies, no. But there's going to be a big transformation scene.'

He describes the new ending, and tells them how the production assistant cried when she heard it, and said, 'You have to be beautiful or you're worthless.'

Cas is impressed.

'That is seriously cool, Dad. Do you think the movie'll get made?'

'Who knows?'

'Beautiful aliens who turn ugly is pretty much the same as zombies, I'd say.'

'It is not.'

'Which means you owe Kieran ten per cent.'

'I do not!'

'I'm going to tell him.'

Cas disappears to commune with his phone.

Alan, left alone with Liz, gestures at the printout.

'Looks great.'

'Chrissie's boss told me it's the most compelling piece of journalism he's ever printed. Then he made a pass at me.'

'Is that good or bad?' says Alan. 'I feel like I don't know any more.'

'I'm going to have a lapel button made that says, *Yes, I want sex, but not with you.*'

Alan smiles, then lets the smile fade.

'You're still angry.'

'What do you expect?'

'Tell me what to do, Liz.'

'I have no idea. Go back in time. Behave differently. Think you can do that?'

She moves away, starts picking out the elements of supper.

'I saw Annie after my meeting,' he says. 'We had a coffee in Soho. It turns out Mitch has been having an affair in Cape Town.'

Liz speaks without looking round.

'Great. Now they can forgive each other.'

'I said that. She said, I don't want to be forgiven. I want to be understood.'

'That's good,' Liz says.

'I told her she should talk to you. I told her you'd understand.'

'How did that go down?'

Cas comes back in.

'I have to go over to Kieran's,' he says. 'Okay if I stay the night? Okay if I bike?'

'Yes, you can stay over,' says Liz. 'No, you can't bike. You've got no lights and it's getting dark.'

'So what do I do?' says Cas, looking tragic. 'Get a bus? Which doesn't exist?'

'I'll drive you,' says Alan.

'Why do you have to spend the night at Kieran's?' says Liz.

'It's called having friends, Mum.'

'All right, that's enough,' says Alan. 'I've said I'll take you.'

Shortly after they've left, a phone buzzes, and Liz realizes

Alan has left his phone on the kitchen table. She picks it up, sees an unidentified number, and answers.

'Alan's phone.'

She hears a woman sobbing at the other end.

58

Mitch is crying with hurt and frustration, but he's also hungry, so as he cries he makes himself a fry-up. Three rashers of bacon are sizzling in the pan as he cracks an egg over them, and due to his tears he lets the egg spill over the bacon.

'Oh, fuck!' he says.

The second pan containing baked beans starts to bubble, spitting orange spots over the stove surface. He fumbles for the knob to lower the gas and it goes out.

'Fuck!' he says again.

He tries to scrape the rapidly solidifying egg off the bacon, using a kitchen knife. The egg shreds.

'Fuck, fuck, fuck!'

He doesn't hear the front door open.

'Mum! It's me!'

Ellie comes into the kitchen and sees Mitch at the stove, his back to her.

'Dad, where's Mum?'

Mitch turns and she sees his tear-stained face.

'Dad? What's the matter? What are you doing?'

'Making supper.'

'Where's Mum?'

'Out,' he says.

Ellie goes to the stove and sees the mess in the pan.

'This is a total bollocks.'

She takes over, doing her best to extract the bacon from the egg.

'You should have sent out for a pizza.'

Mitch sits down at the kitchen table and puts his head into his hands.

'So where's Mum?'

'I don't know.'

'You don't know?'

'We had a bit of a row. She walked out.'

Ellie turns off the gas under the pan and comes to the table where she can look at Mitch properly.

'She walked out! Why?'

'Long story.'

'Hey, hey,' says Ellie. 'I live here. I'm your daughter. I need to know what's going on.'

Mitch starts to cry again.

'I just want her to come back.'

'Dad! This is horrible! Call her.'

'I've tried,' says Mitch. 'She doesn't answer. Oh, God, I'm so sorry, Ellie. It's all my fault.'

'Why? What have you done? Have you been shagging some-one in Cape Town?'

'Yes,' says Mitch, miserably.

'Oh, for fuck's sake!' Ellie doesn't sound so much shocked as irritated. 'Franco said you would. He said it's what everyone does on business trips. I said not you. I said you're not like that.'

'Mum too,' says Mitch, into his hands.

'Mum too what?'

'She had a thing with some man,' mumbles Mitch. He wants Ellie to know, but he doesn't want it to be him who's told her.

'Mum did?'

Now Ellie is shocked.

'How do you know?'

'She told me.'

'Did she do it to get back at you?'

'No,' says Mitch. 'She didn't know about me.'

'So why did she do it?'

'I don't know, Ellie.' He looks up at her, pitiful, damp-cheeked. 'I'm having a really hard time over this. I just wish she'd come back.'

'Is that where she's gone?' says Ellie. 'Has she gone to him?'

'I've no idea.'

His face, his voice, his posture are all calling for help. He's telling Ellie that he's in no state to sort the situation out.

Ellie rises to the call, becoming businesslike.

'This thing in South Africa. Was it serious?'

'No,' says Mitch. 'Not at all.'

'You still love Mum?'

'Yes. This is killing me, Ellie.'

'So what's she doing walking out?'

Mitch gives a helpless shrug.

'This is horrible, Dad. We have to do something.'

She pulls out her phone and calls Franco.

'My mum's walked out on my dad and no one knows where she's gone and she won't answer her phone.'

She listens, then turns to Mitch.

'Her phone's still on, right?'

Mitch gives a lift of his shoulders.

'Should be,' he says.

'Yes, it's still on,' Ellie says to Franco. Then, 'Really?' Then, 'I'm up for that.'

She ends the call.

'Franco says if she's got the phone on he can track her.'

'Track her!'

'He says it's easy. His boss at the garage has the app.'

'You can't do that, Ellie.'

'Watch me.'

'No, no. Leave her to come home when she's ready.'

But his face is raised and his eyes are bright.

'Dad, she cheated on you and she walked out on you. She needs to be told she's acting like a selfish bitch.'

This is so exactly what Mitch believes that he has nothing to say.

'I'm not going to sit here on my arse,' says Ellie, 'and watch this family fall apart.'

59

When Alan gets back from taking Cas to Lewes Liz has some unexpected news.

'Your girlfriend called.'

'What?'

'On your phone. She's walked out on her husband. She was crying. She said you told her I was a good person to talk to.'

'Yes,' says Alan. 'I did.'

'Well, she's coming here.'

'Here!'

'I said we'd give her supper. And a bed for the night, if she needs it.'

Alan looks dazed.

'Why?'

'I'm not sure.'

Alan blinks and shakes his head. He feels scared.

Liz says, 'You can always call her and tell her not to come, if you want to.'

'I don't know what I want. What's supposed to happen when she comes?'

'I've no idea.'

'Are you going to shout at her?'

'I might.'

'She was really crying on the phone?'

'I think it was more anger than anything. She said there's no one she can talk to.'

'I don't understand, Liz. What do you want out of this?'

'I don't know,' says Liz.

She does know, but she doesn't want to talk about it. When Alan told her he'd had sex with Annie she experienced many reactions, but the dominant one has come to be the sensation of exclusion. She feels shut out. Shut out from what matters to him, and shut out from the fun. She doesn't want to be the person outside the window peering in at the party.

Then there's the whole matter of control. You don't realize it, but in any long-lasting relationship you establish a balance of power, a network of levers and pulleys that keeps the two of you in balance. You know how to hurt each other, and how to soothe the hurt. You know how to please each other, and most of all you know that you matter to each other. This is the ground on which you stand. Then along comes an affair, and in a single seismic shock you discover that there's a part of his life in which you don't feature at all. Your power is gone.

Half understanding this, Liz reaches out to Annie to draw her towards her, into her world, where she will become real to her. And when she comes, what then?

★

399

It's half past nine by the time Annie drives into the yard of the Hamsey house. She sits for a moment in her car, summoning up the courage to get out. Now that she's here she feels as if she must have been mad to come. At the same time the pressure of the outrage within her is so intense that she must tell someone. She must vent the accumulated anger.

How dare he? Absurdly it's the bedside lamp that tortures her. The bedside lamp they bought together, and placed beside the bed. The bed in which they lay together, and made love.

She hears the sound of the front door opening. Alan comes out into the yard. Annie dabs at her face, and gets out of her car.

'I'm so sorry, I'm so sorry,' she says.

'Come on in,' says Alan. 'Supper's ready.'

Annie bursts into tears. The sheer normality of it overwhelms her. Supper's ready!

As soon as she enters the kitchen and sees the table laid for three, and smells the rich aroma of a pot of chilli con carne, and sees Liz's interested gaze take her in, she feels the madness start to recede. Life goes on.

'I shouldn't be here,' she says to Liz. 'I just didn't know where else to turn.'

'It's okay,' says Liz. 'Alan's terrified.'

'Sorry, Alan,' says Annie. 'I bet you wish now you'd never bumped into me in the street.'

Alan looks to Liz.

Liz says, 'Don't look at me.'

'This is difficult,' says Alan. 'I've lost track of what's my fault, and what I'm to do about it.'

'Let's eat,' says Liz.

Over supper Annie tells her story. She tells how Mitch confessed to his fling, which was *only sex*. She tells how she confessed to her own extramarital adventure.

'You said you'd tell Liz. So I thought, Why not tell Mitch?'

She describes how Mitch reacted with wounded fury, because *it's different for men*; and how later they were reconciled. Then the *other woman* appeared, and Mitch's story turned out to be a pack of lies.

'He told me it was nothing, just sex, and all along this woman's thinking they're going to spend the rest of their lives together. I just thought, How dare he? How dare he!' She trembles with anger as she relives the moment. 'And then when the affair gets embarrassing for him he just says it's over and she's not to see him again. He made her say it on the phone, with me listening! I know you must think I'm mad, but it's seeing the way he's treated her that really does it for me. She came to our house! She really loves him! It's not just sex. Why did he tell me it was?'

'But he doesn't want to go off with her,' says Liz.

'No. He says not. He says I'm the only one he loves.'

'Do you believe him?'

'I suppose so,' says Annie. 'But I don't know who he is any more. When I told him about – about . . . you know— Sorry, this is all really strange, talking to you like this.'

'About you and Alan,' says Liz.

'About me and Alan, he went through the roof. He kept saying I'd stabbed him. I've never seen him so angry. He's this quiet, rather serious man, he doesn't get angry. It was frightening.'

Liz says, 'I haven't made a pudding, but I thought I'd do us all a mug of cocoa.'

'Cocoa!' says Annie.

'Liz thinks hot cocoa cures all ills,' says Alan.

'You are amazing,' Annie says to Liz.

So Liz puts a pan of milk on the Aga to heat up, and mixes some chocolate powder in the bottom of a jug.

'Is he still angry with you?' she says.

'I don't know,' says Annie, 'and I don't care. Different for men! You can say that again! It's different for men because they think they're the only ones who want sex.'

Alan pushes over the printout of Liz's article.

WHAT DO WOMEN WANT? BELIEVE IT OR NOT – SEX!

'Liz's latest,' he says.

Annie takes in the headlines.

'My God!' she says. 'Is this true?'

'You tell me,' says Liz.

Annie reads on.

'I wish Mitch could see this.'

'It'll be in the *Sunday Telegraph* this Sunday,' says Liz. 'Bring him a copy in bed.'

'If I'm home.'

Liz pours hot milk into the jug and stirs.

'Does he know where you are?' she says.

'No,' says Annie. 'I don't want him to know. I'm not going home till I'm ready.' Then, seeing the flash of anxiety on Alan's face, 'Don't worry. I'm not moving in.'

Liz brings them over mugs of cocoa.

'Oh, my God,' says Annie, breathing in the smell. 'I feel like a little girl again.'

She blows on the steaming mug.

WILLIAM NICHOLSON

'You're welcome to have a bed for the night,' says Liz.

'You are amazing,' says Annie, again. 'Why don't you hate me? I'd hate me, I'm sure, if I was you.'

'I do hate you,' says Liz. 'And I hate Alan. Maybe I even hate myself. But what do I do then? Hating's not much of a plan. Did Alan tell you my mother just died?'

'Yes.'

'She believed marriage was for life, and when my father left her that meant her life was over. So she had forty years of living on after her life was over. All my life I've sworn I'll never do that. I have a life whether I'm married or not. And, for the record, Alan and I are *not* married. So if you think the way I think, and something like this happens, it doesn't stop your life in its tracks. I won't let it. My life goes on.'

They drink their cocoa in silence. A strange silence, but a welcome one, sitting here, all in the same room.

Do I mean it? Liz thinks. Hasn't it stopped my life in its tracks?

She looks at Alan and sees the way he frowns into his cocoa, and she knows so exactly what he's thinking that she has nothing to fear. He's like a child caught scrumping apples. No excuse, no defence, only that sullen look that says, What if I did? But he's not a child. Men aren't boys. We're all grown-ups, responsible for our actions. All he has to do is speak the words Annie spoke: *I don't want to be forgiven, I want to be understood.*

Alan sees Liz watching him, and he wants it all to be over. But at the same time he thinks how beautiful they are, these two women he has loved. He can't silence the low whisper of male pride that says: I fucked them both. He blushes as this thought

403

passes through his mind. It's one thing to give way to temptation. It's something else when you catch yourself taking pride in it.

I deserve to be punished, he thinks. But he's still not quite sure why.

Now Liz is talking to Annie. They're talking about sex and men, prompted by WHAT DO WOMEN WANT?

'We want the sex,' Liz is saying. 'We just don't want the men.'

'You need a man for sex,' says Annie. 'Unless you're a lesbian.'

'Shall I leave now?' says Alan.

'You're not getting it,' says Liz. 'I want a man for the sex, and I want you for everything else.'

'Aren't I a man?' says Alan.

'Yes, you're a man. But you're also Alan, the person I share my life with, and know best in the world.'

She sees he's not getting it. She turns to Annie.

'Do you get it?'

'Yes,' says Annie.

'You're not going to leave Mitch, are you?'

'No.'

Annie drinks her cocoa and ponders. To her surprise, she finds most of her anger has gone.

'But I don't know why I bother with him. He's lied. He's been cruel to Diane. He's behaved like a spoilt child with me. Why *do* I bother with him? I suppose because I know none of that's really important. It all comes from his immaturity. Almost a kind of innocence. He's just not very evolved. But at the same time he's sweet and caring. He has high moral standards. I know that sounds unlikely, but he has. He's reliable, and hard-working. And I want to say he's *good*. But in the end it just comes down to this feeling that, good or bad, for better or worse, he's mine. We've thrown in our lot together, you know? Does that count as love?'

'Yes,' says Liz. 'It'll do.'

60

Franco drives the red garage pick-up at alarming speeds down the night roads. Ellie sits beside him, and Mitch beside her, all three squeezed onto the bench seat in the cab. Ellie holds the iPad and calls out the directions as they go.

'I knew a guy,' says Franco, 'he bought a derelict farm somewhere down this way. Cost him three hundred grand. He spent a hundred on it, did it up. Sold for a million.'

'Next left,' says Ellie.

'Will the tracker take us right to the house?' says Mitch.

He's watched the blue dot all the way, the marker that represents Annie in her hiding place. Just seeing it helps to ease the turmoil within him. She's not lost: she's with the blue dot.

'Not right to the house,' says Franco. 'Within fifty metres.'

'Fifty metres! That could be a whole street.'

'Except it's not a street, is it?'

They're coming off a main road into a narrow country lane.

'Railway crossing coming up,' says Ellie. 'Then it's a right soon after.'

The pick-up jolts over the railway crossing.

'Where the fuck are we?' says Franco. 'How do people live out here? There's no lights.'

The two dots on the screen are converging: the red dot that is their position, and the blue dot that is Annie. As they make the right turn and drive down an even narrower lane they see the lights of a solitary house ahead.

'Has to be it,' says Franco.

They pull up by the entrance to the house's yard.

'That's Mum's car!' says Ellie.

'Gimme five, girl!' says Franco. They slap hands. 'I call that a result!'

Now that he sees Annie's car, Mitch becomes afraid. He sees himself through Annie's eyes: the cuckolded husband, chasing her to her lover's lair, to assert his marital rights. It doesn't look good.

'I don't think we should do this,' he says.

'We're here now,' says Ellie. 'We're not going home without Mum.'

He and Ellie have different agendas. Ellie is angry, because Annie has broken up the family, or threatened to. Mitch is just lost. He wants the terrible ache inside him to go away. He wants Annie back.

'I can't go in,' he says.

'Well, I can,' says Ellie.

'Don't tell her I'm here,' says Mitch. 'Just bring her out.'

'Come on, Franco,' says Ellie.

'What am I supposed to do?' says Franco.

'Back me up.'

Mitch stays in the cab of the pick-up as Ellie and Franco cross the yard and knock on the front door of the main house. The door opens to reveal a tall, thin man with unkempt hair. He hears Ellie say, 'We've come for my mum.' He hears the man say, 'You must be Ellie.' Then they go into the house and the door closes.

Annie follows the voices into the hall. She sees Ellie, and is stunned.

'Ellie! What are you doing here?'

'Me?' says Ellie. 'What about you? What are you doing here, Mum?' Her voice rises as she loses control. 'What's going on, Mum? You cheat on Dad, you walk out on him, you don't tell him where you've gone – he's falling apart! What are you doing here? Are you trying to destroy our whole family? Why would you do that?'

'Ellie! Darling!'

Annie tries to take her daughter in her arms but Ellie won't let her. She goes into a corner, like a wild animal. She presses her face to the wall.

'Get away! Don't touch me!'

She starts to sob, violent, wrenching sobs.

Franco looks on in awe.

'Jesus!' he says.

Annie says, 'Please, Ellie.' She tries to soothe her again.

Ellie reacts with fury.

'Keep away from me!'

Liz, now watching from the kitchen doorway, says, 'Come into the kitchen. Everyone's welcome.'

Alan says to Franco, 'You want a beer?'

'Cheers, mate,' says Franco.

Alan and Franco go into the kitchen. Ellie stays pressed into her corner, back to everyone, sobbing.

'I'm just in the kitchen, darling,' says Annie.

She follows the others. Liz gives Franco some of the leftover chilli. Franco settles down at the table to eat, and seeing the printout of Liz's feature, he pulls it over and starts to read.

Annie is shaking. Alan gives her a full glass of wine.

'How on earth did she know where I was?' says Annie.

'Tracked your mobile,' says Franco.

'What do I say to her?'

Before anyone can answer, Ellie appears in the doorway. She's got a second wind.

'Look at you!' she says. 'You people disgust me! Get out of there, Franco! What are you stuffing your face for? Let's go, Mum! We're going back to Dad.'

Annie looks at her in anguish.

'Ellie, darling—'

'I don't want to hear it, Mum. Not here, in front of these – these—'

'Just a minute,' says Liz.

'And you can keep your mouth shut!' screams Ellie.

'There's a few things you need to know,' says Liz.

'I don't have to listen to you.'

'*Shut up!*' Liz's voice is suddenly so loud that it makes Ellie gasp. '*Shut the fuck up and listen!*'

Liz has become magnificent. Her authority is so immense that Ellie, who has been in a state of hysteria since entering the house, is completely overawed.

'First,' says Liz, 'your dad's been having an affair for three years – three whole years! – with a woman who thought he was going to leave his wife and marry her. Got that?'

Ellie stares back at her, mute.

'Second, your mum had a boyfriend when she was your age. Him. Alan. My partner.' She points at Alan. 'They had a love affair back then. It ended. They met again a few days ago. She slept with him once. Once! Got that?'

Ellie nods.

'Third, she told your dad what she'd done. And Alan told me what he'd done. No one cheated. They just had sex. And guess what? Sex is fun. People like it. It's not disgusting. It's not hateful. It's one of the ways we share love. Got that?'

Ellie nods, mesmerized.

'Fourth, your mum is amazing. She's beautiful, and she's sexy, and she deserves a life of her own. Your dad doesn't have to fall apart just because she wants a bit of fun. And neither do you. You should be proud of her. You should be so lucky as to be enjoying sex as much as she does when you're her age. Got that?'

Ellie's head is now bowed in silence.

'And last of all, I've got a mother too, only she died three days ago. She wasn't the best mother in the world, and she messed up her life, and she messed up mine too, and that's all I ever saw. But now she's dead I'm starting to see what a battle her life was, and how bravely she fought it, and I want to tell her. I want to say, I'm proud of you, Mum. And I can't. It's too late. Don't let that happen to you. Tell your mum – tell your mum—'

She breaks off. She's biting her lower lip to stop herself crying.

'Just tell her you're proud of her.'

She turns her face away, starting to cry.

Alan goes to her and kisses her. Liz lets him wrap her in his arms.

Annie's eyes are on her daughter.

'It's true,' says Annie. 'Everything she says is true.'

Mitch, sitting in the cab of the pick-up, is growing cold and frightened. He wishes he'd never come. He dreads facing Annie. If it was his car he'd drive away, but he can't. The emotions of the last two days have exhausted him, but he knows, sitting in the cab in the cold and dark, that there's one thing he's sure about. He does not want to lose Annie.

I love you, Annie. I can't live without you. Don't leave me.

But no one comes out of the house. She's in there with her lover and his daughter, and the whole situation is so humiliating he wants to creep into a hole and die.

Why don't they come out?

Then a new fear seizes him. Annie has told Ellie all about the hideous scene with Diane, and now Ellie hates him too. He's not just losing his wife, he's losing his daughter. Mitch starts to panic. What can he do?

A gust of rain passes, pattering on the windscreen before him. The blurring of the world outside intensifies his feeling of loneliness. It's no good. It's unbearable.

I'd rather be humiliated than alone.

He gets out of the cab and crosses the yard in the rain. The front door isn't fully closed. He pushes on it and it opens. He goes into a narrow hall. Voices come through an open inner door, and a smell he doesn't at first recognize. The scene that greets his gaze is unexpectedly domestic: they're sitting round a kitchen table, drinking cocoa. And there's Annie, looking so beautiful it makes him want to cry.

He stands in the kitchen doorway, aware that all talk has ceased and all eyes are on him. All he sees is Annie. He speaks only to her.

'I'm so sorry for everything,' he says. 'Please come home.'

Annie doesn't answer for a long moment.

'All right,' she says at last.

Then everyone starts getting up from the table and bustling about. Oddly, no one asks him who he is. They all act as if they've met before. Annie takes his hand as if he's a child come down in the night who has to be put back to bed.

'Come on. I'll drive you back.'

Franco is entranced by the revelations in the feature on what women want.

'Can I get this online?'

'Take it,' says Liz.

'Can I? Cheers. Wait till I show the lads at the garage.'

Alan starts clearing the table. Ellie sits with her hands cupped round a mug of cocoa.

'You all right?' Liz says to her.

Ellie nods.

'Sorry I shouted at you.'

'Been a night for shouting,' says Ellie.

She looks up at Liz and gives her a timid peace-making smile.

'Took some guts to come down here,' Liz says to her.

Annie, on her way out, turns to Liz.

'Alan was right,' she says. 'You do understand.'

Then they're all leaving. Annie takes Mitch in her car, and

Ellie goes with Franco in the red pick-up. Liz and Alan stand in the doorway and wave them off.

Lying in bed in the dark, by Alan's side, Liz says, 'You know your beautiful aliens?'

'Yes,' says Alan.

'They have to be free or they die.'

'Yes,' says Alan.

'They're you, aren't they? They're who you want to be.'

'Are they?'

'Beautiful, unpredictable, and free to fuck whoever they want.'

'Maybe.'

'But we're not beautiful aliens, even if we want to be.'

'No.'

'We're humans. We mess up.'

61

Henry has returned home in a thoughtful frame of mind. Laura feels the change in him.

'Must've been a good lunch,' she says.

'Nothing special,' says Henry. 'Michael has an idea for a project to keep me happy.'

He blushes. The pill is in his pocket.

'Is there anything in it?' says Laura.

'There could be.'

He tells her about the martyrdom proposal, and how Muslim martyrs are promised sex in heaven, where 'the erection is eternal'.

'What about the women they have sex with?' says Laura.

'They have appetizing vaginas,' says Henry.

'Sore vaginas, more like.'

Laura has put work to one side and spent the afternoon clearing Carrie's room. She wants Henry to see it.

'She tidied it herself before she left,' she says. 'She did her best, but it was still in quite a mess.'

He follows her upstairs and into Carrie's room. It no longer feels as if Carrie's there.

'You think she's really gone?' he says.

'How can we ever know?'

'Now you've cleaned it, it feels like she's gone. Is that what you wanted?'

'I don't know,' says Laura. 'Maybe it is.'

They sit down side by side on Carrie's empty bed. Henry sees the Lichtenstein print with its speech bubble: *I'd rather sink than call Brad for help*. He remembers Carrie's hand in his, squeezing his fingers.

'You're right,' he says. 'It's no good, living at home at her age, never leaving her room. But at the same time . . .'

He stops.

'You miss her.'

'I wish she was here. I can just see her, sitting on the floor, her guitar in her lap, her sullen little face looking up to me.'

'Her sullen little face.'

Laura takes Henry's hand. She feels his fingers on her rings.

'Have I made it too tidy?' she says.

He looks around the room. Its layers of childhood are laid one on the next, like the strata of geological time.

'When does it stop being Carrie's room?' he says.

'Never. Or, at least, not until we sell the house.'

'Then another family comes, and another child makes it her room.'

'Maybe Jack and Alice will get married and come and live here. Maybe there'll be a grandchild.'

'That's how it used to be,' says Henry. 'Generation after generation in the same house.'

'That's what old people want,' says Laura. 'Everything to go on being the same. When you're young you want to get away, make your own life somewhere new.'

'Yes,' said Henry, looking at the door onto the landing.

There's an idea stirring in him, of which this is a part. It's all to do with waking in the night, and the nameless dread.

'I didn't vote,' he says.

His words seem to be disconnected, but she follows him.

'You told me. You left your ballot blank.'

'It all seemed so pointless. You think you matter. You think what you do makes a difference in the world. But it's not true. So why bother?'

But as he speaks, his voice is light. It feels more like a liberation than a loss.

'Everyone makes a difference,' says Laura. 'Here we are in Carrie's room. She wouldn't exist if it wasn't for us.'

'And now she's gone.'

'Yes.' This is why Laura has brought him up here. 'What happens next?'

That's the question. You build a life, a family, a home. You work at a job, earn money, worry over making ends meet. You drive the children to school, you suffer through their exams, you look on helpless as they fall in love and are hurt. Then they're gone, and this great edifice you've constructed, this family ark, drifts rudderless, becalmed on a windless sea.

What happens next?

'A few weeks ago,' she says, 'I came and sat in Jack's room, just like we're doing in Carrie's room now. I don't even know why I'd gone up there. But I found myself thinking, He's not coming back. Carrie's still here, but only just. They don't need us any more. It was like I was looking at an open door, the door they'd gone out through. And then I thought, It's an open door. What do you do with open doors? You *go out*. Does that make sense?'

'Yes,' says Henry.

'And when you go out, you become a new person. I can't be young again. I don't want to be young again. But I can be new.'

'Yes. I get that.'

'And the not-eating-meat thing, that's like the outer sign of being new. I've thought about it on and off for years. And now I've said to myself, It's time.'

Henry's nodding. Accepting.

'Can you cope with that?'

'Am I allowed to go on eating meat?'

'So long as you buy it and cook it.'

'Maybe bacon. And Parma ham. I do love Parma ham.'

He's got that little-boy look on his face.

'What?' he says, seeing how she's smiling at him.

'You. Wanting things.'

'Is wanting things wrong?'

'Just so long as you understand that mine's a kind of wanting too.'

I want to be part of the future, she thinks. But she doesn't say it aloud. It feels like too big a claim. And she doesn't want to frighten Henry off now he's beginning to accept that she's changing.

'Wanting's the start of everything,' he says. 'It's the prime mover. I think maybe wanting is God.'

Not hard to guess where this is going.

'You mean sex,' says Laura.

'Look what I've got.'

He takes out a paper bundle and unwraps it. There in his hand lies a little caramel-coloured pill.

'Michael Marcus gave it to me. It's like Viagra.'

'Oh, Henry! Do you really want it?'

'I think need is more the word, after last time.'

'That was just a one-off.'

'Well, I thought we might try it.'

Laura fingers the pill curiously. 'How does it work?'

'It's magic,' he says. 'At least, I hope it is.'

'Why did Michael Marcus give it to you?'

'He's been having Tantric sex,' says Henry. 'In Dorset.'

Laura covers her eyes as if by doing so she can shut out the mental image.

'I don't want to think about it,' she says.

'Anyway,' says Henry, 'if I'm going to try it, we have to have supper early. Michael Marcus says it works best on an empty stomach.'

'All right,' says Laura.

Henry feels a rush of love and tenderness for Laura. Somehow he had never expected to be able to have this conversation in this way. The matter-of-fact manner in which she takes the subject comes as an immense relief to him. The secret shame that is not a secret to her, the failure of his erection, has been hovering somewhere just out of sight ever since Wednesday night, almost a week ago now. Inevitably it's become linked in his mind with the shock of his ejection from *English Gardens*, and his failure to vote, and his collapse on the landing in front of Carrie, and reaching the top of High and Over, and beginning the long descent down the other side. But Laura, faced with his failure and the little pill on which he's forced to rely, says simply, 'How does it work?' She hears no mournful drumbeat announcing the approach of death. It's just a practical option that's worth a shot. He tells her he needs an early supper for the pill to work and she says, 'All right.'

So what's all the fuss about? Why the panic and terror?

Because I fear impotence. Of course I do. I fear it in all its forms. I have died the half-death. Power is ebbing away from me, in my body, in my work, in my society. I can no longer walk as fast and as far as when I was young. I can no longer make love as I did when I was young. Soon I'll be sixty. No longer the beginning of old age, as it once was, but undeniably the end of youth.

This was the dread that woke me in the night. No pill can bring that back.

For their early supper Laura makes a risotto with roasted squash, spinach and Parmesan. She's showered and changed out of her cleaning-up clothes and taken some care to look pretty. She's put on her favourite wraparound dress, buttercup-yellow and clingy, and is wearing her favourite silver earrings, very architectural minimalist, known to Henry as her moon-rockets.

Henry is filled with admiration.

'It's to show I'm a new person,' Laura says.

As they eat their supper Henry tells her more about the idea that fills his mind, the idea of the half-death.

'It's like we all have to die twice. The first time takes away your power, but you're still alive. So you have to learn to live the rest of your life in a new way.'

'Do you like it?' says Laura.

'It's just how it is,' says Henry.

'I mean the risotto.'

'Oh. Yes, I love it.' For a moment he smiles his gratitude, then he's back to his absorbing idea. 'The question is, can we be weaned off our addiction to power?'

'I don't really know what you mean by power,' Laura says. 'Apart from the sex bit, of course. You're not Ed Miliband or Nick Clegg.'

'Maybe I don't mean power after all.' Henry tries to think it out as he speaks. 'Maybe I mean fame and glory.'

'Do you want fame and glory?'

'I have done.'

'I don't think I do at all,' says Laura. 'I want to be taken seriously. I want to be good at what I do. I suppose I like being admired. Most of all I want to feel I'm some use. But I don't think I want fame and glory.'

Henry finds himself puzzled to say what it is he's pursued with so much energy for so long. Why has he striven for success? Why has he feared failure?

'It's all about the goals you set yourself,' he says. 'Getting a good job. Having a new car. Being your own boss. Making good money. Marrying a beautiful woman. Raising beautiful children. Winning the respect of your peers. You're always setting yourself goals, reaching ahead, doing better. So you can never rest. You're never satisfied. There's always more to achieve. Maybe not this year, but next year. Or in five years' time. Or ten.'

'So exhausting!' says Laura.

'Isn't that how it is for you?'

'I suppose so.' She thinks about it, interrogating herself.

'I mean, I suppose I'm ambitious too. But there always seems to be too much to do. I'm just trying to get to the end of the day.'

'I remember feeling like that,' says Henry.

And he does remember, suddenly and with great force, the emotions of childhood, when each day had its own colour and taste, and the school timetable created such peaks of terror and islands of calm that often by the end of the day he longed for the safety of his bed. He remembers how tomorrow felt like a brand-new day, waiting to unfold, in which old wounds could be healed, and new joys discovered. The same switchback of emotions as his adult life, but the horizon was so much nearer. He lived by the day, or by the week, not by the year.

You begin out of control, living from moment to moment. Then you exert control, first over the days, then over the weeks, then the years. So you reach ever further into the future, marching your armies ahead down the roads of time to subdue all opposition, to silence all critical voices. Then the power passes, and the armies desert you. So it's back to childhood.

'You're right,' says Henry. 'Really all we ever have to do is get to the end of the day.'

Can it be so simple? People talk of a second childhood, meaning the time of helplessness in old age, the return of being assisted when you walk, the return of nappies. It should really be called a second babyhood. There's humiliation there, and the horror of becoming a burden. But before that there's a stage that can truly be called a second childhood. The responsibilities are lifted, the pressures of work ease, and the day stretches before you, bright and free. A better childhood than the first because you're older now, and wiser, and more able to see the monsters that once so terrorized you for the self-generated illusions that they are.

So now let time pass more slowly. Let this be not the withering but the fruit. Everything before now a time of tilling and planting, tending and watering, waiting for the warm weather. Now the harvest.

Laura is interested in the workings of Henry's pill. He gets himself a glass of water and drinks it down before they go up for the night. Quite quickly he begins to feel its effects. A tingling sensation in his skin, a glow of heat in his face.

'You've gone all pink,' Laura says. 'It's not going to give you a heart attack, is it?'

'I certainly hope not.'

The signs are promising. As he prepares for bed, he can feel the tingle has reached his groin. How does it know where to go? Presumably the magic is non-specific, and covers all of his body. His flushed face is proof of that. He avoids exciting himself unduly, wanting to save the pill's virtue for the point at which it's needed.

He's in bed ahead of Laura. He turns off the main light, but leaves on one small lamp, which he fitted long ago with a ten-watt bulb for just these purposes. Its faint illumination is flattering to both of them.

She comes from the bathroom in her robe, closing the door behind her. She crosses to the cupboard and takes off her robe and hangs it on the cupboard door. Turning towards him in the soft light she's naked and beautiful. She comes to the bed-side and stands there for a moment, knowing he loves to see her. Then she gets into bed beside him.

He touches her beneath the duvet, gently stroking her naked body. He can feel his cock tingling.

'Do you think you're ready?' she whispers.

'Only one way to find out.'

She reaches down his body and feels his cock, and fumbles it. Obediently, magically, it starts to rise.

'Seems to be working,' she says.

Rising from the dead. His own private resurrection. The dread drops away.

'I love you so much,' he says.

'That's just lust.'

She strokes him, inciting lust.

'Just lust,' he says. 'Just wanting you.'

'But let's go slow, even so,' she says.

They go slow. As Laura's body wakes she becomes more vocal. They have the house to themselves, there's no one to hear. Then it's not slow any more, and she's shouting. Then it's over and they lie in each other's arms and he kisses her shoulders and neck. She lies with her head thrown far back over the pillow, her eyes closed, her body shuddering. He pulls the disarranged duvet back over them both.

Later as they slip into sleep she reaches out and takes his hand. For a few moments she holds it, and they lie still. Then she lets it go, and they sleep.

AUTHOR'S NOTE

Many of the characters in *Adventures in Modern Marriage* have appeared before in earlier books. Each of the novels stands alone, each has its own cast of characters and its own stories, but alongside those stories I have been quietly tracking the lives of some dozen characters over fifteen years.

The Secret Intensity of Everyday Life is set in May 2000; *All the Hopeful Lovers* in December 2008; *The Golden Hour* in July 2010. *Motherland*, set in the 1940s, and *Reckless*, set mostly in 1962, follow past generations of my characters. *The Lovers of Amherst* is set in 2013. And this latest novel, *Adventures in Modern Marriage*, is set in 2015.

My novels are located largely in Sussex, where I live, and some of my characters share the trappings of my life, but at the risk of stating the obvious, I write fiction, not autobiography. I absorb ideas from many different sources, and build my characters out of many different parts; and once the building blocks are in place, I bring each character to life as best I can. The only way I know how to do this is to become each character myself; which means that all of them, male and female, young and old, are to some extent fictional versions of myself.

While writing this novel I found myself questioning something I had always believed: that men and women differ in the way they experience sexual desire. I'm now open to the possibility that the apparent gender difference is in fact culturally induced. For those who wish to explore further the controversial claims made by my character Liz in her fictional newspaper article, the book that triggers her (and my) thinking is real and available: *What Do Women Want? Adventures in the Science of Female Desire*, by Daniel Bergner.

I owe thanks to Jessamy Calkin, who gave me a tour of the *Sunday Telegraph* offices, and explained their editorial processes; to Joan Winterkorn, doyenne of archive and manuscript consultants, who advised me on my character Laura's professional life back when I was writing the first novel in the sequence; to Richard Cohen, who drew my attention to lines in the Islamic hadith that were unfamiliar to me; to my agent Clare Alexander and my editor Jane Wood, whose skill and wisdom have guided and assisted me through these seven novels; and of course to my family, who have followed my writings with amused tolerance over the years. So thank you, Virginia: your love creates in me the power to love that drives everything I write. And thank you Teddy, Julia and Maria: you're all grown-up now, and more than able to tell me how much I get wrong, and yet you go on loving me.

William Nicholson
Sussex, January 2017